PUSHKIN PRESS

WILL

JEROEN OLYSLAEGERS (b.1967) is a
Flemish author, poet and playwright. *Will*
won four major prizes in the Netherlands
and Flanders and is being translated into
eight languages. He lives in Antwerp, on
the Kruikstraat, where police helped the
Nazis round up the city's Jewish residents
during the Second World War.

© Koen Broos

PRAISE FOR *WILL*

'An important and confrontational book in which the past continues
to resonate with the present'   *NRC Handelsblad* *****

'What moral boundaries would you be willing to cross? Nobody
knows… More than a meeting with history, this is a meeting with
ourselves'   *Livres Hebdo*

'A gripping panorama which moves the reader from tears to laughter, one minute turning the pages avidly, the next filled with dread'
                                                        L'Express

'A book that manages to cause this degree of disquiet is a classic'
                                              De Standaard *****

'A lyrical meditation on guilt and evil'   *De Tijd*

'A book like a slap in the face'   *De Morgen*

'A truly epic story'   *Transfuge*

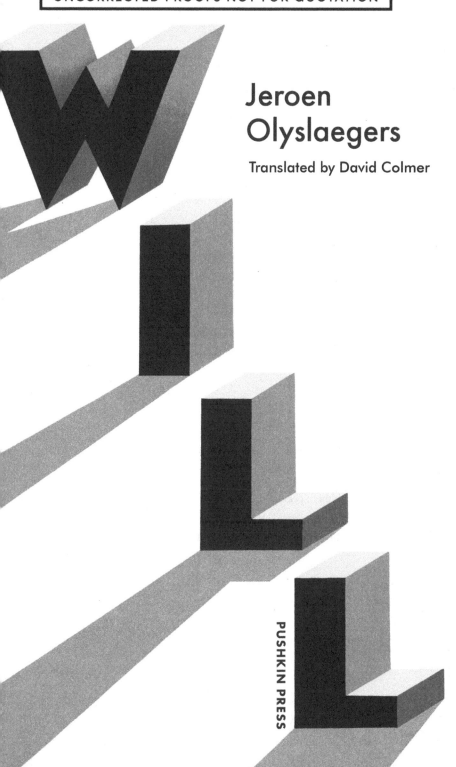

Jeroen
Olyslaegers

Translated by David Colmer

PUSHKIN PRESS

Pushkin Press
71–75 Shelton Street
London WC2H 9JQ

Original text © 2016 Jeroen Olyslaegers.
Originally published by De Bezige Bij, Amsterdam / Antwerpen
English translation © David Colmer 2019

Will was first published as *Wil* in Amsterdam, 2016

First published by Pushkin Press in 2019

1 3 5 7 9 8 6 4 2

ISBN 13: 978-1-78227-424-7

Designed and typeset by Tetragon, London
Printed and bound by CPI Group (UK) Ltd, Croydon, CRO 4YY

www.pushkinpress.com

For the Nymph &
For My Son, Quinten

A SUDDEN SNOWFALL

A SUDDEN SNOWFALL. It reminds me of the war. Not because of the cold or some other inconvenience, but because of the silence that takes hold of the city. It's coming down thick and steady now. It's night. I hear the sounds congealing into a dull nothing. And then someone like me has to go out, no matter how old he is. I know, son, everybody thinks: He's going to slip and break his hip. Soon he'll be lying in a hospital bed at St Vincent's with his legs up in the air. And that'll be the end of him, laid low at last by the kind of bug they cultivate in hospitals. It's odd how the elderly get infected by other people's fear. The fear that makes them consent to being cooped up in homes, letting themselves be fed codswallop and cold porridge, going along with oh-bugger-off bingo nights and submitting to a Moroccan assistant nurse with an arsewipe in her hand. They can keep their fear. I've never been afraid, not really, and nobody's going to teach this clapped-out old dog new tricks. Outside, the snow crunches under my boots. No, not fancy shoes, but the old-fashioned boots I've stayed true to for years, taken to the cobbler's dozens of times and greased almost weekly, walking boots that now allow me to take a step back in time. The flakes are still drifting down. Recently I saw an enlargement of one in a newspaper in the library reading room. All one-offs, those snowflakes, beautifully

9

constructed mathematical worlds landing on my cap and coat. No, I'm not going to write a poem about it. Nobody reads them any more and I've run dry. The snow transforms the city, imposing not just silence, but maybe thoughtfulness too, remembering—on me, anyway. When it's snowing I can see better. As long as the snow is falling, you know what the city really means, what it's lost and what it's trying to forget. The city gives up the illusion that the past is past.

In front of me City Park is shining white. I wait and close my eyes for a moment. The yellow light on the streets turns blue, as blue as the tinted glass in the old gas lamps. Picture a city with hardly any light. Faint blue light on the streets out of fear of the fire that can fall from the skies. Those of us lucky enough to have the use of a torch on night duty considered light a privilege that was no business of any Germans, war or no war. It was already dark enough, after all. I remember the Germans being furious about their inability to get it under control. They had to threaten insane fines and ultimately the death penalty before people started to be a little less casual with light. I've seen field gendarmes burst into spasms of rage because we were using our torches unscreened. Sabotage! And so on… and so forth. At the station our chief inspector would cock an eyebrow: 'Come on, lads… no mucking about.' No reprimand—we had to stop mucking about, that was all. Anyway, City Park bathed in faint blue light, that's where we were. But I turn right. Pacing slowly, I enter Quellin Straat. Your great-grandfather is no longer looking at shop windows. I see the city as she really is, a naked woman with a white stole draped over her shoulders, the kind of woman doctors and surgeons can't keep their paws off: a new bosom, then a different face. Magnificent buildings have been razed here, office blocks put up in their place. Did you know there was a grand hotel on the Keyser Lei corner, just near the opera house? Built by a German before the First World War. Ever learnt anything about Peter Benoît at school? Probably not, and no need as far as I'm concerned. They used to teach names and dates; nowadays they act like that was a mistake. But nobody—not then, not now—gives you the smack on the side of the head that history really is. A stream of filth, bastardry that never stops, not really. It just keeps going. Peter Benoît has become a street name. When I was at school we almost had to go down on our knees for him. 'He taught our nation to sing.' A real hero, in other words. A statue of this once-worshipped composer stood directly opposite the opera, surrounded by what people used to call Camille's lido, named after a mayor you've definitely never heard of, who I can only vaguely remember myself. So the revered artist, the man who once gave his nation singing lessons, looked out over a paddling pool that was used as a public urinal, mostly by drunks. The statue's been relocated; the so-called lido was demolished and as for that grand hotel where smart German officers drank aperitifs with their sweethearts during the Second World War... now it's the site of a concrete monster that towers over nothing much. So things were better in the old days, were they, *Bompa*? I can already hear you thinking it, and besides, if we ever get to see each other, if the family I helped create, which no longer wants anything to do with me, allow it, I am sure you will call me *opa*. After all, the word *bompa* is dying out. But of course, the old days weren't better. They were just as bad. Imagination is everything. In the beginning there wasn't the Word and definitely not God's. In the beginning there was an imagined darkness—remember that. I stop for a moment in the middle of the street. Two big black banners are hanging from a building that no longer exists. Each banner emblazoned with two lightning-bolt runes. I'm standing in front of the headquarters of the Flemish SS. Those uniforms used to drive us cops crazy. A mate got the book thrown at him for not saluting some cocky little bastard in black. He wasn't even German, though he obviously wished he'd popped out into the light of day somewhere more Teutonic. Bullyboys. So many different uniforms… they made your head spin. When to salute and when not to salute? Many's the time I had to grit my teeth. Some of those posers had absolutely no respect. For people like that I might just have well been stand-ing there in my birthday suit. At the end of the street I turn right. It must be about four in the morning. Still absolute silence, snow falling and not a soul in sight. OK, apart from a junkie who asks me for a euro. 'Get stuffed,' I say. 'Come on, grandad,' he drivels. I look deep into his red-ringed eyes as if I'm already sinking my fangs into his soul like a wormy hellhound and tell him he'd better piss off before there's nothing left of him. Did you know your great-grandfather eats blokes like that for breakfast? You don't believe me? Later you will, maybe: unfortunately. Bearings. On my right, at the end of Keyser Lei, I see the railway cathedral officially called Middenstatie, a name nobody uses. On my left, on the corner of Keyser Lei and Frankrijk Lei, is Café Atlantic, with Hotel Weber above it, headquarters of German Field Command. The men in field grey swarmed around it, triumphant at first, dragging themselves from one fancy dinner to the next, where they would invariably be entertained with all due respect, their boss for instance bending over a folder full of old ink drawings of our city, offered to him as a gift by our mayor, who was blinking like an owl on tranquillizers... All this trouble so that they could later, after just a few years, be reduced to a parody of their own triumph, knowing very well that by then their so-called thousand-year Reich was already in injury time. Now I turn right, towards the station and, a dozen paces later, right again, into Vesting Straat. It's cold. I'm twenty or thereabouts. Someone behind me calls out 'Wilfried!' That's not my real name, but more about that later. The person behind me—Metdepenningen, Lode by name—catches up and slaps me on the shoulder. Does that name ring any bells? It may very well. But I'm not going to lay all my cards on the table at once. Read on and all will be revealed. 'I'm freezing my balls off.' Lode slips, almost twisting his ankle—I manage to grab him by the elbow—and swears. We've just finished training together. Three months of listening to people talk bollocks at us and then we were probationary constables. What it came down to was that we had to keep our uniforms clean and always obey anyone who had an extra stripe. All through those three months I watched Lode sucking furiously on his pencil and staring intently at the blackboard. Whenever the instructor asked a question he put up his hand. A show-off, definitely, and handsome to boot. Pitch-black hair, roguish smile, son of a butcher who had a shop the other side of Astrid Plein. He was the one who got our friendship rolling. The kind of bloke who declares after just a week that you're mates for life. 'You teach me something new every day...' I can still hear him saying it. Just when we're about to

13

go up the two steps to the station, two field gendarmes come out the door. They look at us and one of them roars at us to follow them: '*Sofort mitkommen!*' Some clichés just happen to be true. All Germans in uniform talked like that. So we went with them, immediately, because we already knew we didn't have a choice. Normally we had to check in to get our orders, but when one of those field arseholes roared, you followed. We carry on south to Pelikaan Straat, Lode and me tagging along behind the two uniformed supermen in complete silence like a couple of schoolboys being punished for something. The Germans have only been here six or seven months and it's like the whole place has been theirs for years. The city lay down for them and spread her legs wide. Everything is organized. Pedestrians going from the railway station to the Meir have to walk on the right-hand pavement, with people headed the other way on the opposite side, and woe betide you if go against the flow by accident. If someone had predicted something like that in the years before the war, everyone would have been rolling on the floor, spluttering out beer froth while they roared with laughter. But one squeak from the master race and everyone's following orders. And what's more: they like it. Discipline at last. We cross the road and go under the railway viaduct to the Kievit district. Two streets further we stop in front of a house with a flaking facade. One of the field gendarmes shakes the powdery snow off his shoulders and pounds on the door. The other one looks at us with an expression that says 'watch and learn'. But nothing happens. The knocking only seems to have made the house quieter. He hammers on the door again with his fist. Now we hear some noise inside. Someone comes downstairs wailing in a language I don't understand. The door creaks open. Through the chink we see a sinister face with big eyes. He immediately gets a whack on the head with the front door as the two Germans shove it all the way open. 'Chaim Lizke?' one of them yells. We hear some mumbling. They go straight in, gesturing for us to wait outside, and shut the door behind them. 'Another work dodger, I suppose,' I whisper. Lode doesn't say a word. He stamps his feet against the cold. Tough luck for him that he can't afford the sturdy boots I'm wearing. You have to know that in those days the provision of uniforms was a complete shambles. Those who had enough money for textile coupons were better dressed than the rest. That was another thing that drove the Germans crazy. A couple of years later we all had to buy new uniforms they'd designed for us. But that rule only made things worse. By then only a few inspectors had the means to get one. Everybody tried to wear something that looked good from a distance if nothing else, hoping to avoid a bollocking from somebody or other. Meanwhile there's a racket inside the house. People shouting and crying. We hear children screeching. A cupboard falls over. Somebody comes crashing down the stairs. More screeching. But the orders bellowed in German are far louder than anything else. The door swings open again and there they are: the Lizke family. Five half-dressed children aged four to twelve, a weeping woman with a cloth draped skew-whiff over her hair and the father of the house keeping his eyes on the ground while blood drips from his swelling ear. 'The pride of Israel,' Meanbeard would have sneered. He's someone you'll encounter later in the story. I'll tell it like it was: I don't have a clue what those people had been cooking up for themselves, but the consequences were far from salubrious. They were rank.

To be fair, I have to add, I could also feel pretty woozy sometimes when I got too close to Lode. That lad could stink to high heaven of blood and guts. I'm sensitive to smells, always have been. My father used to say I have the olfactory capacity of a pregnant female. Hilarious, of course, but I felt like smashing his head in every time he casually let it slip, preferably at a party with lots of drunk people around.

One of the field gendarmes waves us over and points a gloved finger at a sheet of paper, using it to underline an address in Van Diepenbeek Straat. That's where we have to go, and apparently they don't know how to get there. Lode avoids my gaze as if he's not even here. It's not too far from my place. Follow the railway, then cross back under on Van de Nest Lei? I give the Germans a nod. The address is not in our division; it's in the seventh, but I'm not crazy enough to tell them that. And off we go. Us in front with one of the Germans beside us, behind us the foreigners with the other field arsehole. The woman won't stop crying. Her husband whispers quietly, trying to keep her spirits up. In Polish, I think, but it could be Hebrew or God knows what. The field gendarme hisses something and we hear him give the man a whack. Right away the children start sobbing again. I would have gone about it differently. Lode too, I suspect, but who are we? Tourist guides in the dead of night. It's got slippery. The snow has lost its crunch, turning the streets into a skating rink. The Germans are trying to force a pace that a family with small children can't match.

One after the other goes arse over. Another stop, more bawling, more blows, even more crying. Lode still hasn't said a word. I see his face tensing. Looking back on it, I have to think of the seaside. At that stage I'd never been there, but when I went later and was lying on the beach nibbling a waffle and pretending it was worth all the bother, I saw a large family in full retreat with their bags and chairs and parasols and all their children with faces as red as tomatoes and completely over-excited. The father exploded: he dragged one of the youngest roughly over the sand while carrying one of his daughters in his other arm, and his mortified wife had to undergo the furious glares of the bystanders while pulling a child along with each hand too. I swear I saw it snowing then too in the scorching heat. And I can assure you just as firmly that I also heard someone bellowing in German. '*Nicht* far *jetzt*,' I told one of the field gendarmes. Broken German, I know, but by now I'm so sick of the ridiculous situation I've resorted to their language for the very first time, if only to temper the rising fury a little, because that's not going to get us anywhere. It's hardly going to scare the Jews into suddenly skating along like lunatics. It's true, too: it's not far now. We just turned into Van Diepenbeek Straat. 'This lady and her children are work-shy too, are they?' Lode whispers, his voice trembling. 'Fuck this bullshit. Is this any way to behave?' I don't say a word. What am I supposed to say? He hasn't told me anything that's not already obvious. But we're a part of it, we're walking along, we're being obedient and respectable and accompanying the stinking gang to an address on a scrap of paper. The moon comes out and the ice on the streets starts gleaming like silverwork. And then it happens. One of the children, a boy of about twelve, lets go of his father's hand and shoots off ahead, rushing past us. I don't know why. We hear the father yell. For a moment or two the field gendarme in front with us doesn't do anything. He's as surprised as we are by the little fellow racing over the ice with his skinny legs wobbling like a new-born foal's. It only takes about five seconds until he slips over again. Before he can get back up onto his feet the field gendarme has caught up to him and given that little boy a kick up the arse… unbelievable. We see him literally sliding over the ice like a sled until he slams headfirst into a lamp post and lies there motionless. The Germans crack up and it would be a funny sight if not for the mother shrieking as if somebody's twisting a jagged-edged knife into her guts. She collapses on the spot. Her crying husband puts his hands together and raises them up, as if the Almighty might descend on his request to re-establish order with his flaming sword, or at least rise from his slumber to see what's going on. '*Aufstehen!*' the Germans shout, at both the mother and the boy a little further along. The lead German starts to stride towards him, but Lode beats him to it. It's like he's wearing skates, he's that fast. He reaches the little fellow, goes down on his knees and curls his whole body around him like a cocoon, like a shell of muscle. He doesn't let him go, not even when prodded by the still-smiling gendarme, who now says, '*Schon gut*,' a little more quietly. The German pokes him again, and then kicks at Lode's backside almost playfully. Lode roars, 'Fuck off, you bastard!' From his voice I can hear that he too is now crying. I see part of his red cheek, his handsome, brilliantined hair falling in black arrows over the boy's face, his white helmet a little further along, lying upside down in the snow like a gaping thunder pot. The

German loses his sense of humour, swears and reaches for his rubber truncheon. Before I've even realized it, my own hand has shot forward and clamped the field gendarme's wrist in a vice-like grip. We look at each other, me and the German. What saved me, son, was the momentary astonishment on that field arsehole's face. He can't believe this is happening in this ridiculous country they have occupied almost effortlessly. For a few seconds he can't quite process it: in *this* city they've plonked their fat arses down on so easily. A stupid toerag like me in my ridiculous uniform grabbing him by the wrist and staring him straight in his arrogant mug is a scene that feels like it's taking place on another planet. Anyway, I let go and he doesn't do a thing. He keeps staring while his mate jerks the mother up onto her feet while keeping the children at bay. The father too is watching Lode and me, seeing how I pick the helmet up out of the snow, put my hand on Lode's shoulder and gently help him up with the boy in his arms. He watches while I pat the snow off Lode's back and sees Lode, still crying, wipe the blood from his son's forehead and use his thumb and index finger to purse the boy's half-open lips, as if he's fished him out of the water and is about to save him by performing mouth-to-mouth resuscitation. Then the boy half opens his eyes and Lode sighs deeply while hugging that skinny body closer to his own. He doesn't want his helmet. Without saying a word or giving us a second glance, he walks on with the boy in his arms and his head held high and we follow him in silence, the Germans too, like after a family row that has suddenly cleared the drunken father's boisterous head, struck him dumb and left him to quietly appraise the havoc he's created. The two policemen on watch at the entrance to the old army bed depot, final destination of this wild walk, don't speak either. They haven't seen any of it, though they might have heard the shouting. They stand there pale and rigid at the sight of a helmetless Lode with a child in his arms, like an embodiment of the now probably almost forgotten Hollywood hero Errol Flynn, even forgetting to salute the Germans. Before being dragged inside with his family, the father carefully takes his son out of Lode's arms, looks in my friend's eyes and mutters something. And then they're gone, swallowed up by the hollow darkness inside the building as if they'd never existed. We stay outside, Lode and I. It would be wisest for us to make ourselves scarce, but my mate doesn't feel like it yet. He swallows, tidies his hair, takes his helmet back, and then calmly asks the sentries if they have any cigarettes on them. We smoke while the snow makes a half-hearted attempt to start falling again. One of the sentries, a cop in his thirties with a walrus moustache who's known to everyone as Gus Skew because his eyes start turning in all directions once he's had five stouts, says that the whole pack of them, everyone they've got locked up inside, is going on the train to Limburg tomorrow, Saint-Trond to be precise. Nobody asks what they're going to do with them there. 'And I have to go on the train with them,' Gus Skew adds. 'Fun and games. Anyway, there's a bonus in it, so I'm not complaining.' Lode sucks the smoke deep into his lungs and asks how much. 'Forty-five francs,' Gus replies. 'Not bad,' says Lode, flicking his butt into the snow.

The chief looks at us from behind his desk and sighs. He pulls out the incident log, a thick book with blue horizontal lines and a big red line down one side, and dips his pen in the ink.

Together with him, I listen while Lode tells the story, his rage flaring as he progresses, which makes me, in turn, more and more nervous. Finally the chief lays down his pen, takes off his goggles and gives me a weary look.

'Do you agree with what your chum here has to say?'

I tell him it's true that the Germans never once said what the Lizke family was accused of.

'Your mate here says they were unlawfully accused of something. That's a totally different thing. Did those men show you any documents?'

'Just a piece of paper with the address of that bed store on it.'

Lode slaps the wooden desktop. 'It's not right, chief! Not one of those children was over fifteen. A woman and a bunch of kids? And how are we supposed to know if the father really was a work dodger? Has everyone gone mad?'

A fiasco. But what do you expect? Most people run around like headless chickens. You need to know that I had to convince Lode to make a report in the first place. It took a lot of effort on my part on the way back. He kept saying that we shouldn't start shit-stirring. It was mainly his disgust speaking. But he had it wrong. That was exactly what we needed to do. The reasoning was pretty obvious. We could assume that those two field arseholes would go and make a report of their own once they got back to Field Command. That meant there was a reasonable chance we'd be called to account. Those fellows were thorough and may very well have taken note of our numbers. Not having given our version of the facts beforehand would put us in an even worse position. There was only one important thing that we—and this is how I emphasized it to

21

Lode——needed to be totally clear about. I had held that field gendarme back because I was worried he was going to attack my fellow officer. That was all that mattered. The rest of it had nothing to do with us. We had to cover ourselves. In the end Lode said I was right. But I had misjudged him and, most of all, I should have spoken first. Instead of concentrating on that one fact while dictating his report, his rage began to play up and he couldn't resist making it a complaint, emphasizing the great injustice he thought he'd witnessed… And that wasn't all. There was something else, something I only understood later. If Lode had told me that one thing then, I wouldn't have believed him, not even if he'd crossed his heart and hoped to die. Lode knew that foreigner. He knew the Jew Chaim Lizke, who we had helped put on a transport along with his family.

'You do understand, Metdepenningen, that this is going to Field Command?'

'It goes to the mayor too, doesn't it?'

The chief inspector scratches the side of his head and puts his glasses back on.

'So, boy, are you trying to teach me how to do my job? How long have you rookies been here anyway? Four or five weeks? What's this got to do with the mayor?'

The chief's patience is exhausted and Lode has finally realized it. He hesitates, uncertain.

I just described him as a Hollywood hero and I'm not taking any of that back. He was impressive and single-minded, radiating a strength people seldom see and normally associate, perhaps justifiably, with long-forgotten heroes or the terrifying beauty of gods. But more than anything else, people are pitiful, they're not consistent and they seldom face facts. Nobody stays a hero a whole life long.

'Well? Cat got your tongue?'

I hear Lode swallow.

'It is a case of maintaining public order and then it falls under the, um...'

With his thumb and index finger almost touching, the chief says, 'You are this far away from getting night duty for the rest of the winter. Is that what you want?'

He looks at Lode first and then at me, the reasonable one. 'The word "unlawful" is not going in it. Now get out of my sight.'

When we get back outside Lode is as good as convinced that the chief is a 'real one', a mole in other words, who was already conniving with his fellow fascists before the war, part of a secret society dedicated to undermining city and state, or rather bending them, with or without violence, to the whims of the occupier. The way he tells it, early on that January morning in 1941, makes me picture a huddle of masked men swearing eternal loyalty to each other and their new Fatherland by flickering torchlight. By this time I already know treachery exists; I don't need kitsch images bubbling up inside me. But they're something I have never been able to resist.

I must have been about seven. My father told me that on my mother's side the family once lived in a small castle. That night I had a dream: me in the middle of that castle, with my first sensation the horribly cold marble floor under my bare feet. My mother is standing at the top of a high staircase, beckoning. An enormous door swings open. I follow her, but she keeps slipping ahead. Door after door opens, all lavishly ornamented with figures carved into the wood: angels swarming over each other, eagles pecking at each other's bodies, writhing snakes. The last door opens. My treacherous mother has disappeared. I see a countess clawing at her neck, trying to dig out something rotten. She is followed by a maid in a white bonnet spewing blood in the privy. I see a count as a knight, holding his sword high in the throne room and with churning madness in his mouth. A greybeard, dressed in rags, sticks an admonitory finger in the air while a dog licks his unshod toes. A carelessly discarded banner lies at the foot of the stairs, stinking of mould. Outside the fish in the evaporating pond gulp for air, baking in the sun. Around that stagnant pool: the mutilated bodies of men, women and children with millions of green blowflies swarming around them, crawling in and out of their wounds, laying eggs. And yes, men with torches, them too. In the morning I woke up with the flu.

'We can't trust anyone.'

'Who says you can trust me?'

Visibly shocked, Lode looks at me, searching my face for mockery or sarcasm, then decides to burst out laughing anyway.

'Will, come on! Pull the other one!'

'No, I'm serious. Who says there even is a "we"? Who says you can trust anyone without knowing?'

'But you, I can!' Lode cries, giving me a sharp poke in the ribs. 'I can trust you.'

*

Me? That's questionable, son, and I mean it. Not that somebody like me would have been capable of betraying Lode
for any reason at all. He would have risked charges, possibly
deportation and then death. That sounds a bit exaggerated,
but it's anything but. Two years after that poke Lode gave me,
when the Germans had really started to shit themselves, they
dragged people off to concentration camps for a lot less. In any
case, does someone deserve to be trusted, even if he wouldn't
do anything to harm or betray his mate? There's an old French
police film from the seventies where Alain Delon's character
says that when it comes to cops, there's only one correct way to
approach them, and that's with a combination of ambiguity and
contempt. The reason I had to laugh when I heard him make
that cool pronouncement was that Delon was playing a cop
himself in that film. Policeman's a strange profession anyway.
I'll tell you later how your great-grandfather stumbled into it.
Or why not now? Get it over with. I accepted the job that had
been arranged for me as a way of escaping the forced labour
imposed by the Germans. Do you already feel that 'ambiguity'
turning in your stomach? Youngster becomes a cop to avoid
being carted off to Germany as a worker and, as a cop, helps
to pick up people who want to escape that same forced labour.
But of course with the Lizke family and their kind it wasn't
about work. Which is not to say that the Germans themselves
knew what they were supposed to do with those people in the
winter of '40–'41. They had to get rid of them, that was all.
Worse still, back then there were plenty of people in town who
were pissed off that there were still Jews walking around at
all. It wasn't going fast enough for them. It's one or the other,
they said, you can't have it both ways. If these people are so

dangerous and reprehensible, why is the city still lousy with them? How is it possible that the master race still tolerates this enemy of the people on the streets? Are they really going to wait until this riff-raff have been terrified into adjusting to our way of life? They could wait a long time. Never gonna happen. A leech can only do one thing—it doesn't adjust. The Germans had been here since May. They'd conquered a whole country in under a fortnight as if it were nothing. Weren't they ashamed of themselves for not finishing the job? And then, of course, the rumour went round that it came down to the sparklers, that the Jews were being allowed to stay to safeguard the city's pride and prosperity: the diamond trade. They're all the same, people said; even the Germans have succumbed to filthy lucre. Only a month earlier, according to a friend of my father's who worked at the town hall, the Jews had come in to register as Jewish around the back of the town hall in Gildekamer Straat. There was an endless stream of people. Everyone at the office had to work overtime. My father's friend said they were queued up out into the rain under big black umbrellas. They'd been 'summoned' to present themselves with their identity cards, a bureaucratic way of saying they'd better obey. 'You have no idea, the things I saw there… It beggared belief. The way those fellows came in and all the documents they had with them. Don't get me started. Poles, Germans… Family here, family there, and all those names. Some of them had been living here for years, but they still couldn't speak a word of Dutch or even French. But the thing is, it wasn't all beards and black overcoats. Sometimes women came in… real pin-ups. You'd fall over backwards if you saw them… Who'd have thought the tribe of Abraham included such magnificent specimens?' My father's friend held his glass out for a refill. Only a couple of weeks before the mass registration cafés and restaurants had been forced to post a notice on the door if the business was in Jewish hands. But all those measures weren't enough for the old bags and drivelling fools, the bellyachers and troublemakers. And suddenly they were getting what they wanted. Loads of Jews were being put on trains to the orchard town of Saint-Trond, which they threw into a complete uproar. People moaned and whined. 'Why do we have to take care of the foreigners? Do you know how much it costs? And what are they going to do here? Help pick the apples? It's the bloody season for it!' After a few months the Germans let the lot of them quietly return to the city. That's completely forgotten now because two years after that debacle they did know what to do with them and shipped them off much further east to places where the chimneys smoked and corpse after corpse fed the fires day and night. And no, we didn't know those details at the time. But that the Jews and others were being dispatched to places where they would be given an opportunity to earn a place in the Reich by the sweat of their brows, no, that was something none of us believed. Only gutless wonders claimed otherwise after the war, and some of them kept broadcasting their craven slave morality by weighing one thing up against the other, what they'd seen and what they hadn't seen, with an emphasis on that 'hadn't', with their sudden myopia accepted by others for the simple reason that nobody, from high to low, from the permanent secretary to the provincial governor, from the mayor to a rookie in uniform like me, was free of blame. Difficult times—you'll still hear people saying that today and also that you have to see everything in context. I'm with

Alain Delon—I say his view of cops applies to everyone: they were times of ambiguity and contempt, and in that they're no different from any other times. In other words, they never ended, they're still haunting us now.

A few years before you were born I had already considered writing down my experiences. I'll tell you how that came about. It's 1993. I'm sitting in my study, which looks out over City Park, and sorting out my papers. Not really. I'm actually just pretending to sort them out. In the next room your great-grand-mother is lying on our bedspread, crying. I'm finding it an enormous strain. Powerlessness is exhausting. It cuts someone like me off from everything. Of course, I know why she's crying. I just don't want to feel it. I don't want to think about it. And more than anything else, her tears make this the last place in the world I want to be. Anyway, it's almost noon. There's no food in the house. I'm hungry and my wife is definitely not planning on doing anything about it, even if I had the gall to ask her. I feel like some potted meat, duck rillettes to be precise, and I know a good butcher's in Carnot Straat. The main thing is to get away from here, because I can't bear another second of her wailing. The city has let itself be crowned European Capital of Culture and posters everywhere are celebrating the fact. If anyone had asked my opinion regarding which image to use, I would have pleaded the case for *Mad Meg*. It's a miracle you can see this extraordinary painting by Breughel the Elder here in a small room in a small gallery. That alone shows who we are in this city and the painting itself is just as revealing: naked terror in plain sight, plunder at the mouth of hell. Having it right in front of your face doesn't make a revelation any less a revelation. Mad Meg rages and rants through an insane landscape full of war and memories, rendered in bright reds, blacks and browns. Eyes wide to see everything and nothing. Has she caused this horror or is she just caught up in the general bastardry and going along with it? You should go to that art gallery one sunny Saturday and take it all in. True, you can see it on the Internet and kids of your generation always find more than they search for. Go and see the painting itself and then look up how this revelation came to be hanging here. Maybe then, with your own brainpower alone, you'll work out why it says so much about this city. But fine, back to 1993, when a poster with a photo of Laurel and Hardy as jailbirds was thought enough to herald a year of culture. They look crestfallen, as only they can. It's obvious that they've just tried to dig a tunnel only to end up back in their own cell. I look at them and recognize myself. Blazoned above their daft faces is the question 'Can art save the world?' Get stuffed, I think. I want toast with duck rillettes. But at the end of Quellin Straat I don't turn right towards Carnot Straat. I'm suddenly thirstier than I am hungry and keep going to the Geuzen Gardens, the square that only gets called that by the city's most elderly residents, where there used to be four public gardens, each with a handsome statue of a renowned painter or notorious mayor in the middle and surrounded by trees that once shaded infatuated couples, who sat under them to hold hands. Now it's always full of choking buses waiting to get a mass of day-trippers back home as fast as possible. There on the corner, on one side of the opera, is a large café with pillars that flaunt its faded elegance, a place I sometimes go to meet my old friends. It's around 11 a.m.

I've hardly set foot in the place before somebody's calling, 'Look what the cat's dragged in.' A few old mates of mine are sitting in the middle of the dining room playing cards. I'm glad to see them, glad that I won't have to sit at a table by myself like some kind of sad pot plant while I drink and reduce beer mats to little molehills of torn cardboard out of sheer boredom. Richard—built like a brick shithouse and a pal of mine, who, little over a year later, would be discharged from hospital with a plastic bag on the outside of his body instead of a stomach, and then carry it round with him like a walking skeleton for another six months before taking it with him into his grave—beckoned. Another one of the card players is called Leo. Since finding out that I'm a poet, the twerp has been addressing me as 'Maestro', half surly and half serious. He's actually only known for a year or two, after I've been publishing for forty bloody years, but his attitude is typical of this city, as typical as it gets. I only vaguely know the other two. I sit down at their table and order a beer. They're playing whist, a game I've never really understood. I sip my beer and look around. 'Diamonds trumps!' Richard shouts and winks at me while wiping the froth out of the tash that has won him honorary membership of the local Moustache Club, something he prides himself on. At that moment I'm already over seventy, but the salutary proximity of these card players reduces me to a child. It doesn't last long. Between tricks Richard asks if I've seen Lode. He might just as well have given me a kick in the balls. 'No,' I say, looking away. In that instant I notice that a man at a table on the other side of the room is meeting my gaze through his thick glasses, completely unembarrassed. Balding and badly shaved, he's looking at me as if I'm an exotic rat in the nocturnal house at the zoo. I think I recognize him, but that's impossible. The last time I saw him I was a cop of about twenty-two and he—and this makes my hair stand on end—*just like now*, was in his mid-forties. I'm sitting in one of the corridors of the SS Intelligence headquarters—at the time they were still housed in an enormous mansion on Della Faille Laan—waiting for some document I have to pass on to my inspector. It's unusual because we don't have much to do with the Gestapo. They run a regime within the regime. Still, around this time they have started to interfere more and more with ordinary policing. Field arseholes aren't easy, but these plain-clothesmen in leather coats are something else, one step up in the theatre of gross violence, where we have front-row seats and will later claim to have seen almost nothing. An office door is ajar. I see Four-Eyes standing there in a black uniform, his cap slanted on a bronze bust on his oak desk. I see him and I hear him, although I turn my head away now and then, just as I also turn away from him here in this café. He's shouting and hurling papers at a woman, a Jew or a Jew's wife. Yes, that's it: she's married to a refugee from Austria. I see her regularly at the baker's in Jacob Jacobs Straat, where she buys cheese cakes and I sometimes queue up for my father because he's so crazy about *rugelachs*. I recognize her profile immediately. She looks away from his black-uniformed spitting and yelling. He screams that she's arranged it all very nicely, that every Jew out there knows somebody who'll lend a hand in an emergency, and here, here are your papers, you lackey to a Christ-killer, here are the papers, and now your bloke can carry on profiteering, he won't be put on a train to a work camp, relax, shouts Four-Eyes, rest assured… She stands

31

straight and proud, even thanking him while picking the coveted papers up off the floor. She doesn't look at me on her way out, but he does. Four-Eyes stares straight at me. Just like now, in 1993. He hasn't changed a bit. Not as well groomed, perhaps, but the expression behind those convex glasses is exactly the same. He stares at me through a rip in the curtain of time, then folds a piece of card and uses it to push bits of food caught between his teeth back onto his tongue before swallowing them. 'Look at me here,' he says soundlessly, 'and know that I recognize you, and that you were once witness to an incident that almost cost me my head, or rather saved it, because in the end the bitch I treated with such disdain was willing to testify on my behalf when I was locked up with my comrades in the Harmonie. I had saved her husband, after all. Against my wishes, but still, I saved him, and in the end that saved me too.'

While Leo shouts that Richard is a first-class cheat because he keeps on winning and the others boisterously back him up, Four-Eyes stands, buttons his coat and nods his fucking head at me before leaving.

Richard, who's sick of all the malarkey about his dumb luck, looks over to the bar and calls out, 'What's today's special?'

According to the waiter, who knows his customers, it's something light and easily digestible. I raise a hand, order a Duvel to go with it, and hope for the best yet again. Since retiring, I've had enough of excessive dinners. My stomach can't cope and I go for the lighter things on the menu, but I keep getting it wrong and ending up with indigestion from a chicken salad that some twerp in a chef's hat has drenched in *balsamico* or some other foreign vinegar. And bam, I've fallen for it again.

A salmon lasagne. Unbelievable! Surely this is the last thing you'd want to eat between twelve and two? So there I am… burping in the toilet with visions of Four-Eyes every time the strong beer and the so-called light salmon lasagne repeat on me. When I get back from the gents there's another Duvel on the table. I drink it and then I drink another. With my head spinning and an unsteady hand, I finally say goodbye to my friends, explaining that I still have to go to the butcher's. 'The missus wants duck rillettes.'

At home your great-grandmother is still lying on the bedspread with that old, clapped-out body of hers, and still crying. It's deteriorated into something that's closer to a soft whimpering and to my not entirely sober ears it sounds almost melodious. In the old days she used to sing along to the operetta music pealing through our modest flat. She was the daughter of a peculiar butcher who had accepted me fairly quickly as a future son-in-law, but could no longer bring himself to trust me once we were actually married. Your great-grandmother had always wanted to be a nightingale of the stage, deploying her lungs in the service of Franz Lehar's 'Meine Lippen sie küssen so heiß' or giving a rendition of something risqué by Offenbach with lots of feathers. But her father had never allowed it. 'You can make a whore of her yet,' he snapped at me just a few years after our marriage when the subject came up again over Christmas dinner, where he was tucking into the turkey rissoles daughter-dear had prepared with love, the very first since the wartime shortages. But it turned out to be too late. She already had her arms up to the elbows in suds washing our son's nappies and shook her head the next day when I suggested she could still go to the conservatory. 'How would you cope?' she'd asked and shrugged before I could answer.

I knock on the bedroom door. She's finally let our cat out of the room and now the creature refuses to budge. I push her out of the way and, holding a plate of toast on which I have painstakingly spread duck rillettes, address the closed door. 'Come on, you have to eat something.' The sobbing stops for a moment.

She says, 'Leave me alone. You have no heart, never have.' She sounds like someone has forced a wad of fabric into her mouth.

I demand she open the door.

No answer.

'It can't go on like this.'

No answer. I hear her sucking in breath for a new round of tears. The cat yowls around my feet, then hooks her claws into my trousers, already angling for the delicatessen on the plate. The all-too-seldom-celebrated poet and once-capable cop just stands there.

'I've got toast with duck rillettes. From the butcher's on Carnot Straat.'

'Give it to that filthy cat!' she shrieks. I clench my fist.

'I will do if you don't open this door!' No answer.

A marriage, dear boy, is an exercise in humiliation till death do us part. What people call 'living together' is a many-headed monster. If I strung those moments together, it would look like a cannibal's trophy. The Hindus understand that too. You should look up their depictions of the goddess Kali some time.

She pokes out her red tongue and her blue neck is hung with hollow-eyed skulls that represent the humiliating moments both husband and wife know are best kept private. The only thing that keeps people going is the thought that this union has an unmistakeable purpose: everyone thinks you are part of it. I secretly hated your great-grandmother with a passion, but now I miss her like a typical loner whose life has crumbled away.

'Here, kitty,' I say. 'Mother's not hungry.'

The cat's going berserk. She yowls as if she's going to drop a litter any moment and follows me into the kitchen. Oh, by the way, are you a cat lover? If so, it might be better to skip the next bit. I scrape the meat off the toast and dump it on her saucer. She eats it with relish. I ask if it's tasty. With a sigh, I plonk myself down. The supermarket vouchers my wife has clipped out of the newspaper are on the table. Ammonia: two for the price of one. Spare ribs on special. Free suntan lotion with the purchase of a deckchair. The washing-up on the worktop is from the day before yesterday. Unheard of. A smell of burnt bacon in the kitchen we haven't renovated since the sixties, despite your grandfather's complaints. 'This is so out of date… How can Mum get anything done in here?' Nothing doing, money's money and what works works. The cat has hardly finished her saucer full of the most succulent meat you can buy before she's started begging and butting my leg again. More, more, more. It's never enough. Don't, she's had enough. And yes, she's sinking her claws into my trousers again. Meow, meow. Then suddenly she's sitting on her arse and scratching furiously under her chin. They're back again: fleas. I reach for my ankle where a stubborn fleabite kept me awake just last week. My wife has resumed her blubbering. Soon she'll have cried her throat raw. I close the door. The cat won't stop scratching. I take a bucket out from under the sink and fill it with tepid water. I take an unopened jar of full-cream yogurt and slop two big spoonfuls into a small bowl. 'Here,' I say, 'you bloody fleabag.'

The cat can't believe her luck and throws herself on the yogurt. The bucket is full. I push the spout out of the way, open the bottom drawer of the cupboard where I keep the gardening tools and pull out my gloves. They've hardly been used. Gardening is not for me and since the time she put her back out, it hasn't appealed to your great-grandmother either. Did you ever meet her? No, you can't have. Anyway, I pull on the gloves and bend over the cat, who doesn't look up, of course, lapping and slurping as she is. If she could scratch herself while scoffing food, she would. Gripped by the scruff of the neck, she's scarcely able to move. She growls, claws the air, then suddenly stiffens with her pupils wide. In a single movement I've plunged her deep into the bucket of lukewarm water. She thrashes like mad. Both hands push her deeper. The water goes in all directions. I press her down against the bottom as best I can and wait. Air bubbles rise and burst. I feel my old strength, no longer garnished with rage perhaps, but still. And then it's like the cat swells up. Immediately afterwards she shoots up out of the water like a rocket, hissing and spluttering like crazy. All my squeezing in vain. Sopping wet, hair on end, she hurls herself against the closed kitchen door like a thing possessed, letting out a growl that no longer sounds like a cat's. Thump! And again. And bang! Once more. I stare at my wet work gloves.

36

I hear her calling from the bedroom, 'What is all that?'

Not a sign of sobbing in her voice. My hand on the doorknob. The cat takes a swipe at my ankle, her claw going through my sock. I make a failed attempt to boot her through the room, then finally open the door. The cat shoots under a wardrobe in the hall, still growling and spitting. An avenging demon has been born. 'Proud of ourselves, are we?' I hear her meowing viciously, 'Very proud.'

That same evening I started writing. The heartburn wasn't going away and I couldn't get over Four-Eyes and how he'd kept staring at me. I never finished the manuscript and you can tell from the opening sentences how I was feeling at the time:

> Listen to me. I am a legion of voices, most of which you detest, few of which I cherish. I am still breathing—of necessity—but all of you, if you knew this story, would begrudge me every breath I take. And that's something I understand, because really knowing someone in the long term is not in your nature and I—unfortunately—am nothing but long-term. It has turned me into an avenging angel, anchored in the wrong, cowardly era. For me it's truth that counts, for you the opposite: living day to day.

Can you sense my arrogant rage? It's strange for someone like me, who was already at a ripe old age back then, to get the chance to reread something like this years later and recognize how silly it is. Also important: at that stage I still considered myself a great yet misunderstood poet. I felt that what you could call devils, if you like, had grabbed me by the hair and were dragging me back into history after all those years to show me what I now consider the truth: it never ends. It's also a fact that back then I felt too superior to even imagine that there wouldn't be any readers for a book like that or realize that I wouldn't have been able to bring it to a satisfactory conclusion anyway. I had to wait more than twenty years to realize finally that my story is only suitable for one person, and that's you, my great-grandson. Something else—and I know how grotesque this is, as if an aged prostitute is running through her old tricks one last time in the hope of outwitting her wrinkles, but I have to be honest with you and own up to it. I wasn't planning on publishing that book under the name Wilfried Wils. I feel what little shame I have left rising, but I won't back out now. I was going to publish the book under the name Angelo, my secret name, which now, unfortunately, in contrast to the old days, when I often used it as a nom de plume, suits these worn-out old bones like lipstick on a pig.

It was in a wrought-iron bed, my mother had told me, a bed once made by my grandfather, a child's bed made to pass the time, that I fell ill. I was wasting away. I was five and hope was fading with every hour that let itself be mustered into days that became weeks and finally months. But not a tear ran down my father's cheeks. He had always known that his son, his only child, would survive him. My mother, less self-assured, convinced that she was and would remain a victim from the cradle to the grave, was already picturing herself walking beside a tiny coffin with a permanently smoking crater in her chest where her heart had been. The doctor—'Geerschouwers by name,' my mother said emphatically, as if a name

38

added even more gravity to this inauspicious story, and by the way, 'long dead, son, stumbled in the street and broke his neck just like that'—well, the doctor had said that the trouble was inside my head. Meningitis. Whereupon years later my father still added 'but the man-ain't-rightus', as if that daft claim possessed a magic to make people laugh the story off. Meningitis. And it was no laughing matter. It was 1925 and I had one foot in the grave. I can't remember it at all myself, neither the illness nor the period that preceded it. The first thing I do remember, after four months in coma, is looking up at a strange man and a strange woman, and the woman being unable to stop crying because I'd opened my eyes. The man shouted, 'Wilfried, Wilfried, you're alive! You're cured!' but I didn't have the faintest who this Wilfried could be. If my head hadn't hurt so much I would have turned around to see if somebody behind me was answering to that name with a smile. They called Dr Geerschouwers, afraid that my illness had robbed me of my senses, and he explained that things like this did happen. And so this physician introduced me to my father, my mother and myself. 'Your name is Wilfried, Will-Freed.' They had to teach me everything all over again. I had to take them at their word. Believe that this funny man was my father and this bleating sheep my mum. I was five. I repeat: it was 1925. And after a while I worked out that it was better to act like I believed everything they told me. But it took more than a year before I automatically looked up at the sound of my twice-given name. Recognizing my mother and father and addressing them as such was easy, but the name Wilfried always chafed at a spot in my head where there already was a name, maybe one I had chosen myself or one that had been

39

whispered to me during my 'man-ain't-rightus' period. Later, during catechism, I began to suspect that an angel had given me my true name: Angelo. That's what I'm really called. Deep inside I'm Angelo. Maybe this Angelo was really a demon sent to deceive me, but in that respect, he differed little from the two I was forced to call my parents from the age of five, who also forced me to act like I was called Wilfried. No. No. No. Wilfried doesn't have a story. Angelo does.

I'm more or less halfway through the *moyenne*, which is now called secondary school but also translates as average. I am a very average student and the time has come for everyone to see that as an insurmountable problem. My French is useless according to Cyriel Goetschalckx, a teacher who reprimands me with 'Willlllfrit' before I've lisped a French sentence to complete ruin. A failing memory makes you jump shame-lessly from one thing to the next. It's all one big movie show and you project your own reminiscences at will. That's why I can effortlessly convince myself that I sensed how the system works right from the start of the so-called *moyenne*. Factory and machinery. Cogs that turn. The screw that goes through the teachers' skulls drills deep into the students' heads. They sell it as knowledge, but you, my beloved boy, have surely worked out by now that it comes down to acceptance more than any-thing else. You're seventeen now, aren't you? I suspect so, but I'm not sure. The things everyone believes have to be drilled into tender souls as truths. So there I am sitting at my school desk at the Royal Atheneum, like you now, and that's why I'm telling you this. Maybe you can identify with it. I'm surprised that my fellow students, who act so free in the schoolyard, have no difficulty at all in accepting this so-called learning process. For most of them it goes in automatically and those who can't keep up are shipped off to trades. There is a blonde boy in my class called Karel who is regularly ridiculed by the teachers because of his parents' political inclinations. The history teacher in particular can't resist: 'Next week we're going to talk about Germany again, Karel. That will make you happy, won't it?' Usually a few idiots laugh along in an attempt to suck up to the teacher. Karel himself remains imperturbable, which I find fascinating. He's not top of the class, but still gets decent marks. He's invariably obedient and eager to learn. Never once does he show any signs of feeling humiliated, not even when others laugh in his face because he's given the correct answer to yet another question. He'll pop up again later in the story. Anyway, as for myself, I can cope with the material, but I regularly freeze up when I have to reproduce it. I stutter and stammer and of course I get teased for that too. It's turned into a massive scandal. The last few years I've lagged behind and eventually had to repeat a year. I blame it on the declining power of Angelo, the master hypnotist with the inaccessibly poetic heart of a child. Those first years he kept me above the fray and it's maddening to not know why he's failing me now, why he can no longer impose his will on others. Could it be that this being inside of me is no longer willing to play the game? That he, even more than Wilfried, understands that the appreciation of others is worthless? The one who calls himself my father reaches for his belt at the sight of my monthly misery, furiously annotated by my teachers: 'A D for French grammar! An F for folklore! Algebra… it's a bloody farce!' He ignores the A-plus for sport. In contrast to the rest, I have no difficulty accepting gymnastics or the gymnastics teacher, who, with a beard like a biblical hero, rules over sweat, the limits of the body and the fear of failure. But that serves a higher purpose, a purpose I keep hidden from everyone else. The body that others always see as awkward is not mine. There is another body inside it, an angel's body, that needs to be strengthened by training. But that A-plus has no value to my father. French, that's what matters. A mastery of French would make it possible for me to rise higher and higher on the mechanical wings of acceptance so that I could finally touch down again as a civil servant in the employ of the universally reviled state, made for life, permanently appointed. My father's belt is figurative, by the way. He never thrashed me, and anyway, a seventeen-year-old is no toddler. As a result his rage immediately collapses into melancholy. He tells me these are difficult times. It won't be long before it's war again. The taxi company where he works as a bookkeeper is on the verge of bankruptcy. The bills are piling up. My mother's wealthy family have said they can't keep lending a hand, enough is enough. And to make his suffering complete he has a son no sensible person could be proud of. 'You've had it too easy.' I can take his anger, but this sighing and groaning, the defeat he accepts without putting up any kind of fight, it's too much. It makes me suspicious. An outsider would have thought my mother unaffected by her husband's harping, but I see the red patches on her face, the annoyance. She's standing at the kitchen door, drying her hands on a tea towel. Her wig looks a little crooked. A year ago a dermatologist recommended she wear her hair short so that the black ointment he's prescribed, which smells of paraffin oil, can more easily be absorbed by her scalp. She has confided in me that she's suffering from eczema, but also said it is gradually getting better. She says I needn't be afraid, she's still the same person. But the wig stays on her head and is seldom straight because the itch keeps tormenting her, which drives her husband to disgust and despair. When she insists that I immediately drink a glass of warm milk it finally knocks the legs out from under my father's sad tirade. Everything seems to have been said. For a whole week nothing happens. But just when I'm hoping that my so-called father has convinced himself that he no longer has a son, that he's given up on me as a lost cause, he informs me that he's found someone to help me. He's called Felix Verschaffel and he lives around the corner. Sometimes things just fall into place.

On a Sunday morning at ten o'clock I'm standing at the door of a closed shop on Plantin en Moretus Lei with cold knees and my French books under one arm. The door opens and a smart woman in her sixties purses her cherry-red lips and asks if I'm the Wils boy. Inside there is a smell of fine leather. I have to take off my shoes. Everything is excruciatingly tidy. Somewhere deep in the house I hear the screech of a parrot (Gaspar, as I learn later, a creature best given a wide berth). 'Just go upstairs, child, my son is expecting you.' The stairs creak. An open door at the top reveals a study with books arrayed behind green glass. Tobacco smoke as thick as fog over a marsh. I give a little knock. 'Knock, knock,' I hear immediately, '*ça doit être le petit seigneur Wilfried, n'est-ce pas? Mais entrez, bonhomme, entrez.*' Around the corner, stretched out on a threadbare chaise longue, Felix Verschaffel is chewing on a pipe. He asks me to hand him my textbooks and indicates a chair. He is wearing a brown three-piece suit; his bulging eyes betray a temper and his meticulously trimmed goatee makes his face look even meaner. He turns page after page, sometimes sighing, sometimes chortling. 'What's your teacher's name?' he finally asks without looking at me. 'What? Goetschalckx? One of the Paarden Markt Goetschalckxes, I suppose. Not Cyriel? I thought so. The whole family's two-faced. His brother's called Robert. A lawyer... of course. Only two things need to be well greased, you know... Well? Spit it out, Master Wilfried! What needs to be well greased? Cartwheels and lawyers, *jeune homme*. Remember that. Anyway. We are going to converse with each other in French as much as possible, is that understood? Which is to say, I speak and you listen. This here...' He tosses my books onto a side table stacked with newspapers. 'This is not French. It is not alive. If you want to master a language, you have to leap feet first into *le fleuve culturel*. You have to get drenched head to toe in love for the suppleness of this highly civilized language. Our heartfelt love for our mother tongue does not prevent us from keeping a *maîtresse*. You should see your face right now. You don't get that last bit, do you? I see you thinking: Does he mean "mattress"? And yes, sometimes that too. A *maîtresse* can be a mattress...' Meanbeard smirks and knocks his pipe out into the overfilled ashtray. 'But those are vulgarities and we're not going to get into that now.' He reaches behind him for a book, while using his other hand to pour a purplish liqueur into the smallest glass I have ever seen. Without trembling, he fills it to the brim. Just as I too, after spending several Sundays with Meanbeard, will be filled to the crown with intoxicating poison. Without looking at me, he says, 'We will begin with *Les chants de Maldoror*, written by Isidore Ducasse, better known as the Comte de Lautréamont...'

Look that up on your computer, son. Or better still, let me write down the beginning of that book for you. In translation at least, because I suspect that the apple never falls far from the tree and, for now at least, your French is probably as execrable as mine was then.

> May heaven grant that the reader, emboldened and momentarily as fierce as what he is reading, not lose his way, but find a wild, untrodden path through the desolate morass of these dark, poisonous pages...

It hits me like a slap in the face. Angelo feels the earth move and both he and I know that my balls are trembling too. It's 1937.

Weeks later I again walk the now-familiar route from Kruik Straat, where I live with my parents in a somewhat rundown house, to Plantin en Moretus Lei and my miracle worker's study.

'How are your marks, *jeune homme*?'

'Better.'

Meanbeard's bulging eyes are like two black mirrors. Not everything disappears into them, but enough. 'You can't fool me. Definitely not with *un coeur encore assez simple* like yours.' A stab in my apparently still-too-simple heart. I thought I was already depraved, but apparently more patience is required.

'I have my report here if you'd like to see it.'

'Bravo. Now I believe you.'

My stuttering is over. Gone from one day to the next. Thinking back on those days I see myself as a rambler, lost and treading on the spot. Meanbeard lifted up the overhanging branches and revealed a path. That was all it took. I could walk on.

He tells me he saw my father last Saturday. I saw Father leaving that day. He refused to say where he was going, only that he would be late home. It turns out he was in some village in the Campine, together with my temporary tutor and many others beside.

'We were in the Royal.'

'Knocking them back…'

He chuckles. 'Definitely. And we had a good laugh too. It was a special evening I organized with some friends, right in the devil's heartland. I thought it was a shame he hadn't brought you along and I told him as much.'

'Now I think it was a shame too.'

'That whole village is full of beautiful houses. English style, more or less. Did you know there's a synagogue there? In the middle of the Campine… The place is lousy with Israelites. We had an entertainer come. The terrace was packed. You should have heard the things he came up with. He came on stage with a big fake nose, just like one of those people. We almost pissed ourselves right then and there. Humour is a weapon, my friend. All those Shlomos and Isaacs and whatever-elses heard our laughter echoing all the way into those big fancy shacks of theirs.'

Meanbeard slaps his right leg hard, braying with laughter. He even has to pull out a hankie because of the tears in his eyes. 'Eventually I couldn't take it any more. Neither could your father. Afterwards I told him, "Jozef, it has to come from the bottom up. That's what this evening's taught us. You see the kind of people we can mobilize." He couldn't have agreed more.'

'He didn't say a word to me about it.'

'Anyway, it got late and we had to catch the last train. So a whole crowd of us are hiking it to the station when suddenly I spot something on the ground. Just like a train ticket. I pick it up and... Wait, I'll show you.'

Meanbeard hops up off his chaise longue, reaches for a piece of paper and hands it to me. From a distance it really does look like a train ticket, except it's printed on a different kind of paper. In messy letters it says, 'All Hitler lackeys to Berlin in fourth-class cattle-trucks!'

He stares at me, waiting for me to catch on.

His voice goes down an octave. 'The whole platform was covered with the things. Can you believe it? In our own country? Those bastards had them printed just for our night out because they, of course, are not short of money. Read it again. "All Hitler lackeys to Berlin in fourth-class cattle-trucks!" Enough said, eh? That's what they want to do with us. That's what all the Freemasons, Bolsheviks and hook-nosed sons of Judah would like to see happen. Do they ever mention freedom of speech at that school of yours? Well, around here it's dead.'

He presses hard on the piece of paper in my hand with his index finger. 'It won't be us. You'll see. Not us.'

Who are the people around us? And most importantly, what role will they play in our lives? I can imagine that's a question you haven't yet asked yourself. At your age friends grow on

47

trees. They're there. That's all. At least, I hope so. I hope you celebrate life with your friends, even if you don't realize that's what you're doing. But my circle of friends has been seriously depleted, almost all dead and buried, and my family, as you know all too well, sees me as a curse. Sometimes I feel like the whole world is shouting at Wilfried Wils that there is no place for him any more, that I should just die. But I admit that those feelings mostly rise after I've been at the Calvados. No old folks' home for me, you know that too. But before you start thinking I've been abandoned to my fate, let me reassure you. Your sire twice removed has a nurse at his disposal. 'Homecare' they call it, and she herself is called Nicole, a strapping lass in her fifties. No, I don't need her to wipe my arse or help me into the tub. The woman's a good cook, she does the weekly shop, and if I don't snap at her the moment she comes in, she's liable to start singing in the kitchen. That might lead to me slamming the door of my study or shouting 'Give us a break!' because an old bastard like me is expected to be bitter and bad-tempered, and it's best to live up to that expectation. But last week, when there was still no sign of snow, and rain was lashing the windows, I heard her singing and for the first time I wasn't annoyed. In a soothing voice that wasn't sad at all, she sang Charles Aznavour's 'La bohème'. That name doesn't mean a thing to you, does it? Don't look it up, it's old tosh you wouldn't like anyway. The song is supposedly about Aznavour himself when he was flat broke in Paris but oh-so-happy. He sings about him and his mates being young and crazy together. On the telly Yvette and I had acquired not that long before, we saw him singing the song with one clenched fist and a white hankie in the other hand. Anyway, hearing that song I asked myself for the first time what Nicole was going to mean to me besides being someone who throws the clothes in the machine and does the washing-up and plonks a cup of herbal tea down in front my nose every morning. That question thrilled me, son. Because there's a fair chance she's going to be the last person to play an unexpected role in my life. I have long since figured out all the other people who have crossed my path, placing them on the chessboard one after the other over the last few years, like a former chess maniac setting up the pieces to relive the games that once meant so much to him. His playing days are over, only the memories are left, by which I'm trying to say that my life is no longer that complicated. But her singing about those artistic Bohemians made me realize that there is still a game in play after all, albeit a much simpler one. Something with dice, maybe, and two counters on a snakes-and-ladders board. That's enough for me. When you're playing a game, time's claws aren't in you quite so deep.

That Aznavour record came out in the mid-sixties. I was 'on tram four', as we used to say here—in my forties. The first time I hear the song I'm not with Yvette, but playing chess with Lode. We're in the Terminus, as we often are, on Statie Straat, close to Koningin Astrid Plein. They have a jukebox. One person after the other drops a coin into it to listen to 'La bohème'. Everyone knows it inside-out and there's always somebody who'll stand up and bellow: '*Je vous parle d'un temps que les moins de vingt ans ne peuvent pas connaître!*' Whereupon everyone, either drunk already or well on their way, joins in with, '*Ca voulait dire on est heureux… La bohème, la bohème. Nous ne mangions qu'un jour sur deux…*' I know I just described it as 'old tosh', but that song does something to blokes like us. In that instant it makes us maudlin and raucous and we both laugh at the gusto with which the other is belting it out. At that moment there is already an irreparable breach between us, something men don't talk about, something to do with resentment. Lode is still handsome, though you can already see signs of occasional bingeing. But that applies equally to me, like the bulk of our fellow officers. We're still in what they call our bloom though. He's working for immigration, I'm in vice. Behind his back they call Lode 'the Bull'; my nickname is 'the Velvet Monkey'. But that's irrelevant. We play chess once a week because we're brothers-in-law and we fight our battles out on the board. He and I are bound together and neither of us can take it any more. We're like two Belgian shepherds chained permanently to a shed, with an owner who never takes them out for a walk. But we don't howl at the moon; we play chess and have a beer. That's enough. No, we pretend, we accept the game.

Almost thirty years later. Lode asks how things are at home and I shrug. I'm more interested in the bishop he's slid forward to attack my queen together with the rook he positioned beforehand, something I can't do anything about. I'll have to give her up and that makes me particularly bad-tempered. This is still our weekly ritual and I am always too cowardly to think up an excuse to wriggle out of it.

'How is she now? You never tell me anything.'

'She spends all day lying on the bed blubbering.'

I take his bishop with my knight and he sighs while taking my queen with his rook, which—infuriatingly—will have to go unpunished.

'Didn't you see that?' he asks.

'Piss off. Of course I saw it. I just couldn't do anything about it. Anyway, I'm not sure you realize this, but chess is a game in which the purpose is to checkmate the opponent's king.' My voice sounds too irritable of course, too childish. It's not enough to have him humiliate me—I have to draw attention to it as well.

'Will, your granddaughter's missing. It's making me feel sick too. I understand Yvette being a wreck. But you…'

'I'm working on it, Lode. Don't worry. I'm working on it.'

'On what?'

'She's twenty-one. You know what she's like. She's always doing crazy stuff. Soon we'll get a call to say she's off somewhere or has taken some drugs or is with some bloke in the Ardennes. What the fuck do you want me to say?'

'She's one of a kind. But you still get on well with her.'

'You do too, don't you?'

Lode lights a cigarette and looks at me. 'What do you mean by that?'

'She's crazy about old grandads like us. I've heard she's been to see you a few times.'

'That was to do with her course. I helped her a bit. Hey… what's up with you all of a sudden?'

While writing this down, son, this conversation about your aunt from so many years ago, I hear that Armenian again, with his wistful song. Bohemians, Bohemians, we were young, we were mad.

And then I immediately see Lode humming along too, his hand elegantly teasing out the beat over the chessboard like an effeminate choirmaster's while he thinks about how to twist the knife further with his rook or knight. He always plays defensively, waiting for me to launch a furious attack on his position. It's not serious chess but, like I said, that's not what it's about between the two of us.

I raise a hand to order another round.

Not taking his eyes off the board, he says, 'It's on me. It's my birthday after all.'

'Oh, bugger,' I mumble. 'Completely forgot.'

He looks at me. His bright-blue eyes are sinking in an advancing forest of wrinkles. But now I no longer see cruel mockery in his gaze.

'Do you remember?' he asks.

It's Wednesday, 19th February, 1941.

Lode says, 'Ah, you made it! What a downpour. Come in, quick!' while opening the door wide. He leads me up the stairs to the family home above his parents' butcher's shop on De Coninck Plein. Yesterday he told me there was a party at his place and asked if I felt like coming. We've known each other for about six months now, with our paths crossing almost every day at the station and going for a beer together now and then, but the invitation still came as a surprise. We both still live with our parents, but inviting him to mine doesn't bear thinking about. My father's been withdrawn for quite some time because he's lost his job, and Mum, with her wig and that possessive anxiousness of hers… I wouldn't inflict it on anyone. That was why I wavered for a moment before accepting the invitation, worried it might oblige me to invite him round to ours as well sometime. But meat has grown scarce and a party at a butcher's is not a thing to turn down, come what may.

His mother is at the top of the stairs. She's the kind of woman who immediately makes you feel at ease, motherhood personified with fleshy arms and a laugh that is always about to come bubbling up, a laugh that will set her flesh to quivering.

She says, 'Ooh, is it raining again? Get that coat off.'

I give her my mac and quickly run my fingers through my sopping-wet hair. The living room is dark, but pleasant. Outside it's still light, but they've already drawn the heavy curtains. In the left-hand corner an armchair is turned to face the windows. Cigar smoke curls up above it and I hear the rustling of a newspaper. To my right, sliding glass doors with yellow light shining through the matt bubble glass divide the room in two. From the adjoining kitchen come the very promising smells of a feast in the making.

'We've got wine,' Lode winks, triumphantly displaying a corkscrew.

'Yvette!' his mother blares from the kitchen. 'Set the table! Lode's friend is here.'

I hear some bumping and the sliding doors open.

'This is my sister. Wilfried, our Yvette.'

She has her brother's black hair and the same blue eyes. Her lips are painted red and she is wearing a dress that would be more appropriate in summer: cream with a pattern of black and purple stripes and puff sleeves that extend halfway down her upper arms. A black patent-leather belt low on her waist. She is thin, or rather, wiry—a swimmer's body. Meet your future great-grandmother, son, in the glory of her heyday…

I hold out a hand. 'Good evening, Yvette.'

She grins at me and says, 'Oh? Where's your present?'

'What… Is there something I don't know?'

'Really, Lode!' She takes a playful swing at her brother's arm while he's trying to open the bottle of wine. 'Didn't you tell him?'

Lode puts the bottle down and gives her a little poke in reply. 'My mate's only just stepped through the door and you're at it already. What kind of manners is that?' He tries to pull her closer to tickle her.

Fighting him off, she screams at me, 'It's his birthday, smarty! His twenty-first. A grown-up at last. At least, he thinks he is. Stop it. Let me go!'

I've broken out in a cold sweat. His birthday and I'm standing there empty-handed.

Brother and sister keep teasing each other, ignoring me. I watch them and don't know what to do with myself.

Finally a thunderous curse rises from the armchair facing the curtains.

'Can you two cut it out?'

'Our dad,' Lode whispers, raising a finger to his lips.

I step over to the armchair. 'Good evening, Mr Metdepenningen…'

A man with cauliflower ears, a moustache over his cracked lips and very little hair on the top of his head accepts my hand and holds it tight. 'Wils, I believe?'

'Wilfried Wils. Good evening.'

'Not the Wilses from the barber's shop on Rotterdam Straat?'

'Come on, Dad,' Lode exclaims. 'You'd have seen him before. That's just here across the square.'

'No, Mr Metdepenningen,' I say, 'not the barber's.'

'Thank God for that…' the butcher growls. He looks a little reassured and releases my hand. 'Good. We're having beef olives. Yvette, will you put those plates on the table at long last?! Lode, give that guest of yours a glass of wine.'

I have to tell you, son, that at that moment I myself had little interest in the carnal love that dominates personal relationships. To me, it seemed like a contract you close, nothing else. I couldn't yet picture myself lying in bed fiddling with someone else. I fiddled with myself shamelessly and that was enough. It never even occurred to me to fantasize about a woman obeying my every command while I was at it. And no, I didn't need to think of a bloke's body either to ejaculate while standing at the window of my stuffy little room. Because isn't that the first thing you thought of while reading these lines? No, I thought about other things I have no desire to tell you about. And before you go off on another tangent and start thinking we were all cowed by the cross and suffering under rules and commandments, I have to call a halt to your imagination again. My parents were no knee-benders, especially not my father. He felt nothing but contempt for all those churchgoing pallbearers who slept with their hands over the sheets and saw the soutaned priest at the altar as their merciless guide to the zoology of lust. He was a freethinker, but kept it private because of a stubborn conviction that it was nobody's business but his own. In retrospect he was a hunter, through and through. He could spend days only letting out the occasional grunt, but when the conversation turned to women he couldn't hold his tongue. I can still hear him saying it, between the soup and the potatoes and with my mother sitting right there at the table: 'The first thing you should do as a young fellow at a dance is look around calmly. Don't go straight to the bar for a beer. But don't drag the first girl you bump into out onto the dance floor either. Before you know it you'll have to spend the whole evening with someone you have to be polite to but don't really fancy. No, Wilfried, have a good look first, always have a good look around. Where are the opportunities? Who has good posture, because a woman who doesn't sit nice and straight… Your Aunty Emma now, does she sit nice and straight? Where do you think those stomach problems come from? I'm not saying a word, don't get me wrong. But posture is one thing. Another's—' This was where my mother interrupted him. 'Jozef, is this necessary?' My father held his breath and finally added: 'The other thing is inclination. You can develop a sense for that. You can sniff it out.'

It's a memory I enjoy. It was actually the only time I didn't view him as a sinister accomplice to a conspiracy whose sole purpose was to turn my life into a prison. Do you feel trapped too? If you do, it's a sign you've got a head on your shoulders.

Yvette studies me while a stack of beef olives in gravy gleam on a dish on the table. If we're talking about the hunt, it's me who's her prey at that moment, something my father would have undoubtedly seen as an inversion of the proper order. An amused Lode has seen through his sister immediately. Their mother keeps dishing up the food and their father leads the discussion. As heavily built as he is, his conversational techniques turn out to be finely honed, as sharp as the knives he uses to bone beef in the back of his shop. The word 'bookkeeper' makes him mistrustful. Once that subject's been dealt with, he tells us about a procession he saw a few Sundays ago: all local boys dressed in black uniforms and marching behind a banner with crowds on either side. Lode wants to butt in, but his father lets him know with a glance that his opinion is not required. Then he moves on to the king, who has stayed in the country, and the government, which doesn't seem at all keen to come back after fleeing to London. I say I don't really know much about politics. With his mouth slowly chewing a beef olive, he joins his daughter in studying my expression. It becomes clear that he wants to know where I stand, whether or not I'm pro-German. But he's so cautious about it that I, in turn, try to find out where he stands first. Do you know the joke about two hedgehogs making love? Bit by bit and very carefully. A corny joke, I know. Meanwhile I'm eating my meat just as carefully, like a nun in a white habit, because I suspect that the slightest spillage will make all-seeing Yvette burst out laughing. I feel a clamminess growing in my armpits when I see that I've accidentally nudged a pea off my plate. And that father of theirs just keeps on going. Whether I've read this in the newspaper and what I think about that and if we have a radio at home. Concerning the last one, I say that my father likes to listen to Beethoven. Blithering nonsense of course, but inside of me Angelo considers it fitting, imagining himself with a father who pulls on a pair of waders to go fishing in the cultural river, as Meanbeard would have it.

'Beethoven...' says Mr Metdepenningen thoughtfully.

'The composer...' Lode adds.

He catches a glare from his father that makes him go quiet again.

'Music makes us more human,' I say quickly as Yvette smothers her laughter in a napkin.

'Most people adjust to circumstances…' the butcher concludes slyly.

Lode has already forgotten his temporary silencing. '*Kanonenfleisch!*' he says. 'That's all we are. Cannon fodder! *Wir sind Kanonenfleisch!*'

I can see what he's referring to in his eyes. At least, I think I can. Since that cold winter's night, when we led the Lizke family to Van Diepenbeek Straat, we haven't said another word about it. Our going through it together was coincidence, a consequence of the field gendarmes grabbing us both at the same time. Normally they don't send two probationary constables out on patrol together. That means I don't know what he's been through since and he knows just as little about me. In the meantime a few other things have happened. Sometime in January, for instance, I had to accompany a few 'racial itinerants' with an older constable. That's the official term for Gypsies—what we call Bohemians—and they'd been daft enough to register for a temporary residence permit at the office for foreign nationals on Steenhouwers Vest. The staff couldn't believe it. The police there on the phone to us, us on the phone to the Germans (our inspector, at least), and next thing we know, we're off to Van Diepenbeek Straat. We managed it without too many incidents. Those Bohemians were oblivious to just about everything, my partner laughed. If you asked him, he said, they were just pissed, and it's possible. What I'm trying to say is it's almost routine now. Everyone keeps mum. Hardly anyone ever complains about anything; most people just keep their heads down. After all, you never know where other people stand. I hear on the street that some divisions always roster the pro-German cops together. I have no idea if that's really true; it's definitely not the case at our station. Of course, the few who are pro-German let their sympathies show; the rest shut up, as if there's an agreement to not make things too difficult for each other. Not forgetting the constant menace, the threat of betrayal. You soon find out that even the friendliest of people can get you into trouble if you've let something slip, and Lode knows that too because he's far from stupid. But what becomes clear at that table is just how much that whole Lizke affair is still churning around inside his head.

Yvette asks if we shouldn't raise a toast. She's already holding up her glass. Their father wipes his mouth as a sign of consent. We clink glasses and wish Lode good health.

'And a good girlfriend!' cries the birthday boy.

'Steady on,' says the butcher.

Yvette looks at me and points discreetly at her chin. A splash of gravy on mine. I turn red.

Back home there's no Beethoven ringing through the living room. My emasculated father is just sitting there. My job is all that's keeping the household afloat and my first steps towards a new life, no matter how far away it might seem, fill him with deep envy. What's more we have a visitor. Aunty Emma, the woman who, according to my father, can't sit straight and therefore suffers stomach problems, has dropped by. She's drinking a glass of liqueur with my mother, her sister. What Mother lacks, Aunty Emma has in abundance: charm and vivaciousness.

'Oh, Wilfried,' she calls out, 'people would pay good money just to look at you! Didn't you have to work today? I'm dying for a chance to admire you in uniform!'

I've already told you that my mother comes from a posh family and that she and her sister represent the tail end of this fortunate lineage. Mother married beneath her station (by no coincidence, this mainly annoys her husband), and in the twenties Aunty Emma got a little carried away with a divorced banker, which cost her a place in her parents' good books. We don't see that much of her, even though she lives nearby. Our house is in Kruik Straat, which leads to Boey Straat, which leads in turn to a crossroads called Van den Nest Lei, where she lives in with a wealthy family. 'Jews,' my father confided in me. 'She's there at their beck and call day in, day out.' She's a maid, in other words, which apparently doesn't dim her joie de vivre, on the contrary. She is more than happy to wear Madame's hand-me-downs and they always look good on her.

I ask her how her stomach's holding up. She touches her belly and looks at me in surprise. My father feigns ignorance.

'Darling, I have a cast-iron stomach! You wouldn't believe all the things I have to make for my people and I always eat it up bravely myself too.'

'It's getting late,' Father says.

Aunty Emma turns to my mother. 'I haven't even had time to tell you why I'm here.'

'Come on,' Mother says with sparkling eyes, 'quickly.'

Aunty Emma takes a sip of her liqueur, which adds gravity to her voice. 'With all the bad luck I've had in life, I think it's only appropriate to let my family know when things are going well for once.'

'You've won the lottery,' my father jokes eagerly, his curiosity aroused now too.

'Much better than that...' announces Aunty Emma. 'I have a new beau.'

'No!' Mother exclaims in disbelief.

'And not just anyone. He's called Gregor and he's an officer in the SS.'

'Do I hear *Kanonen*?' I whisper. Nobody pays any attention.

'Emmy...' my mother says quietly, 'shouldn't you be careful with that? Next thing you'll lose your job.'

People say that men think about sex every however-many minutes. It's possible. Presumably you'd agree. You're a growing boy and a female glancing in your direction is probably enough to set you off. Sometimes it feels like we're trying to convince ourselves that we still have a raging beast inside of us, a beast that wants to mate, but maybe that's only camouflaging a deep despair. There are other drives, after all, at least as strong or gradually growing stronger, and I don't know how thoroughly they've been investigated. The longing for normality, for instance. When you live through a war, everything changes; the city puts on a new mask. It's the shock of the new. When someone's been having it off and is about to become a father or mother, everyone warns them: watch out, everything's going to be different from now on. Having kids is the most normal thing in the world until you've got them and find yourself looking at a creature in a cradle and everyone expects you to change everything to accommodate it. Everyone acts like it's the most normal thing in the world, but it doesn't feel like it. Everyone gathered round the cradle bleats that you should be happy to have a healthy child and that's all there is to it. When a city is occupied by new masters, new customs, you get the same thing. After the shock, most people can't wait to act like it's normal. Life goes on, you have to adjust, as Lode's father told me. Just keep doing what you're doing and the rest will work itself out. The flags in the city, all those uniforms and the bars full of soldiers. All normal. The craving for the ordinary is so strong you can almost smell it and then human adaptability comes into play. In the cinemas you don't see Hollywood movies any more, but that doesn't matter, because the German films are just as enjoyable. They have laughter, men chasing women and getting romantic, murders that urgently need solving, and now and then the beautiful Zarah Leander sings a song that has all the women reaching for their hankies. I've always loved the cinema. I'm sitting in the Scala in Anneessens Straat. The film is being introduced by a fellow from the People's Defence, an organization that counts Meanbeard as one of its members. His speech is moronic. He talks to us as if we're little brats who don't know a thing. We have to face reality. The Israelites are poison. Come off it, everyone's poison, is what I think at that moment. How can this fellow with his grand gestures and swollen voice not see that? What's poisonous is the craving for normality, the hypocrisy it brings and every-one's slave morality. But this film has come with an express recommendation from Meanbeard so I stay put. It's a period drama with wigs and beautiful expensive sets. A bigwig with a pencil moustache and a beer gut gets crowned duke. But he needs money, a lot of money, to lead the lifestyle that goes with being a bigwig and a duke. He gets that money from an Israelite with cupboards full of gold and jewels. The Israelite shaves off his beard and ringlets and puts on a wig so they'll let him into the city where they actually despise Israelites. I find the charming fiendishness of the actor who plays the Israelite amusing. He becomes the bigwig's adviser, then takes over and bleeds the city dry with extra duties and taxes. He has his adversaries tortured and hung, and blackmails and rapes women who refuse to bend to his desires, but the people rise up against him. In the end he's defeated, the bigwig has a heart attack and the liberated people declare that everyone must take this as a warning. Curtains. Applause and a little bit of booing. Jews out! Everyone off home, acting normal.

'And? How was the film?'

Meanbeard accepts the copy of Rimbaud's poems I borrowed from him and urges me to sit down. Gaspar the parrot is not in a good mood. I can hear him screeching all the way upstairs.

'He's got colic,' says Meanbeard.

'I enjoyed the film,' I say.

'Big audience? How did they react?'

'There was some shouting.'

'I know you have an inner self who is keen to match deeds to words. Shouting is not enough, I agree. But what matters is planting seeds that will soon grow to maturity. Have I made myself clear?'

I nod out of habit.

'What did you think of our friend Rimbaud?'

'Masterful.' That wasn't a lie. You have to read that sometime, son, if only in translation. Those poems will make your head spin. The power. The ruthless power of them.

Meanbeard is clearly delighted by my enthusiasm.

'I am pleased, very pleased. Giving someone like you a taste of a different world is gratifying, even if your schooldays are over—temporarily, I hope. Did you know, by the way, that I also knew your father's father? Had I told you that? I can still see him sitting in the Old Dutch, rubbing his moustache and watching the billiards. Not cultured at all, if you don't mind my saying so. But consider the leaps your paternal line has made. Never forget your origins. Your grandfather a peasant, your father a bookkeeper and look at you now, a true intellectual, for whom French holds almost no secrets. Realize that you represent modernity. That's the odd thing about progress: it's internalized through the bloodline. We're not serfs any more, understand? There is a slumbering...'—Meanbeard rubs his thumb over his index finger, searching for the right arrow to shoot at the bull's eye of my heart—'...poetry in edification. Think of Rimbaud, whom you admire as deeply as I do. His father? An infantry captain who didn't give a tinker's about his offspring. Mother? A farmer's daughter. He called her *La Mother*. Priceless, don't you think? And then a young man like that ascends to the very top by willpower alone. His talent cuts through all that hereditary ballast like a razor. "*Arrière ces superstitions, ces anciens corps, ces ménages et ces âges. C'est cette époque-ci qui a sombré!*" What is Rimbaud saying in these lines? That all that feeble blather is outdated, that the era in which he lives has swept it all away. We too live in an era like that, Wilfried. An age of acceleration, of radical choices. You feel it, don't you? This is no esoteric waffle: you smell it, a sensitive lad like you breathes it in with every gulp of air.'

Gaspar lets out another piercing screech. 'Now I've had it!'
I hear Meanbeard's mother shouting in a voice that is anything
but refined. Silence. Maybe she's hung a cloth over the cage.

'Are you doing anything on Easter Monday?'

'No,' I say, 'I've got the day off.'

'Come to the Rex on Keyser Lei. Ten o'clock. I'll get the
tickets.'

14th April, 1941. For the time being the longing for spring
remains unanswered and that makes some people gruff. In
warm weather a city seems less occupied. It's the morning of
Easter Monday and hardly anyone is out on the street, just
a group of people in front of the cinema with Meanbeard
among them, decked out in his very best clothes and apparently
impervious to the cold. His bulging eyes grow even bigger
when he sees me approaching.

'Wilfried! Glad you could make it. I'm going to introduce
you to someone. Mr Verschueren? This is Wilfried Wils, the
young fellow I was telling you about earlier.'

'Pleased to meet you,' says Verschueren, who turns out to
be a lawyer. 'Call me Omer.' He has short arms, a massive
gut and a bald head. The deep voice issuing from his mouth
seems to arise from the very bottom of that dense body as
if echoing up out of a crypt. His fingernails gleam and he
smells vaguely of jasmine. The people around him all seem
to look up to him. The group turns into a crowd. Hardly any
women; the majority are men with determined expressions,
though some have clearly been celebrating Easter to excess.
Many are well dressed, à la town-hall middle management or
the better class of Sunday-suit merchant. But I also recognize

a few I've arrested. One, for example, smashed up a bar close to Carnot Straat because he thought a whore had laughed at him. It took three of us to get him off her. Now he's looking skittishly in my direction. A big change from the mouthful of cheek he gave me a month ago, when he insisted he knew people and wasn't going to leave it at that. My fellow officers didn't lift a finger to stop me when I pounded my fist into his face until he let go of the woman beneath him and started whimpering. Despite her loud protestations we had her carted off to hospital straight away; with him we waited a little longer. The stitches above his eye are already out, I see. I should have hit him a bit harder. I had definitely expected a reprimand, maybe even worse, but the others backed me up at the station and that was that. 'You're a little too excitable,' my older colleague Jean told me. 'You should save your energy with scum like that. He was already down on the floor with his arse in the air. In a situation like that a boot in the balls is more than enough.' From him, I accept that. The man is a bruiser with tactical insight. I'll tell you more about him later.

'My friend here tells me you're a literary man…' Omer peers at me through his puffy eyes and quickly rubs his thumb over his fingertips as if to make clear that a predilection for literature is always accompanied by a hunger for money. But he means something else. He's referring to sensitivity, a sense of subtlety, being a man of the world. 'I'm a great reader myself too. Greek tragedies—I read them in the original.'

'Impressive, Mr Verschueren. That's well beyond me.'

'You're still young, so you never know. And it's Omer. Don't make me say it a third time.'

*

Afterwards everyone will say the cinema was full. That's not entirely true. Two-thirds of the seats are occupied. The atmosphere is strangely distracted. Years later I will be invited to the premiere of a local cinematic production and notice a similar mood—expectation that is not really related to the film but has more to do with what will follow: a magnificent reception with plenty to drink. And here, too, as with that other film, there will be an introduction, this time given by a lawyer, who, as Meanbeard whispers in my ear, 'used to earn a lot off the Israelites, before the scales fell from his eyes too'. As you know, he doesn't think all too highly of lawyers (they need to be well greased, like cartwheels), and I am surprised that he apparently counts some as friends.

On the leaflet distributed beforehand, People's Defence introduces itself as 'a popular movement', which makes me picture a crowd applauding a steaming turd. The speech is dismal. The man thinks he's in a courtroom full of paid-off judges. It's all wheedling variations on 'We all know that…' and 'We too feel sullied by…' There are occasional growls of assent as well as a somewhat impatient 'Hear, hear!'

The film is pitiful. It makes the period drama look like a sophisticated masterpiece. This so-called documentary shows how under the surface every Israelite, no matter how Western their clothing, is a rat, a parasite that latches on to all that is beautiful and pure, which, of course, includes all those present in the cinema. 'Sickening!' someone shouts, and he's not talking about the quality of the film—he means the things that are being palmed off as truths and making his stomach churn with indignation.

Meanbeard has read my expression in the semi-darkness and spontaneously whispers that it *is* rather crude, though based on fact, because this is real footage from the Warsaw ghetto, and I shouldn't start thinking the whole thing has been staged.

'It's really like that there,' he concludes, before somebody behind us hisses for silence.

With the credits still rolling, someone starts shouting that he's 'fed up with it'.

Another joins in and bellows, 'Jews out!'

'The bastards, the dirty bastards!'

'It's gone on too long!'

I start to stand up, but Meanbeard grabs me by the wrist and tells me with a wink that I might not need to see the rest, given my position. Without giving me a chance to reply he hops up out of his own seat and into the aisle. Together with him the whole audience has risen in an uproar. People throng to the exit as if they've been putting up with the lice and fleas for too long and can't wait to rush home for a soothing bath.

Outside, a gathering mob is openly wielding sticks and iron bars. For a moment I think we're their target and I'm going to be stuck in the middle of a bloody riot on Keyser Lei with no other cops to lend a hand. After all, on Easter Monday almost the entire police force is on leave. On days like this there are never more than two or three patrols doing their rounds in each division. The armed gang at the exit greets us with a mighty 'Jews out!' They've obviously been waiting for us to join them. I see the uniforms of the Flemish SS here and there and start getting jittery. I feel naked standing here as an ordinary civilian, an anonymous cop on his much-needed day off. The mob forms a raucous procession and turns into Pelikaan Straat. Some of the cinemagoers walk away, but most join the demonstration. Even before reaching the corner myself, I hear a shop window shattering. Meanbeard is nowhere in sight, probably at the very front, surrounded by his lawyer friends. In Pelikaan Straat I see bricks flying. One shop after the other takes a battering. People on the upper floors look down from behind curtains. A furious shopkeeper rushes out, but only just escapes the clubs that threaten to rain down on him. He quickly slams his front door behind him. I distance myself a little, then sprint unnoticed down Vesting Straat. The station is dozing in a siesta silence like a Mexican cantina on a scorching-hot day. Nobody in sight. I shout and bang on the wooden desk.

'Red alert, lads, red alert!'

The chief finally shows his face. 'Wils, don't you have the day off?'

My story has him reaching for the telephone. Before speaking into the receiver he gives me a quizzical look. 'Which direction are they going?'

'What do you think?' I shout.

I run out, following the distant racket to the Jewish quarter.

You may be asking yourself, dear boy, why I followed them. I couldn't stop them. Out of uniform I didn't stand the slightest chance, and my presence as an ordinary citizen could count against me later. In all honesty I have to admit I was probably being dragged along by the excitement of it, nothing else. Does that make me an unthinking follower and, therefore, a dirty bastard? You can answer that question for yourself and if I am a bastard in your eyes, maybe you should skip this bit. Because, yes, of course, it's true: there's a bastard inside every follower. But I think you'll keep reading, whatever you think of me, because nobody, not even you, is consistent, only lunatics in a loony bin are consistent, locked up in their own heads, fanatically clawing at their version of reality, which nobody understands but them. But let's not talk about that, not yet anyway. Now we're heading for the synagogue on the corner of Van den Nest Lei and Oosten Straat, in retrospect the mob's obvious target.

I catch up to the racket near the corner of Baron Joostens Straat, where someone or something I can't see is causing a hold-up at the front. There is glass everywhere. A Jew is lying on the street, groaning and bleeding, almost engulfed by the furious crowd. Someone drags him back into a house by the collar of his coat. The street noise sounds hollow, echoing off walls, making me think of fairground revelry that has got completely out of hand. At the front of the demonstration I see sticks raised in the air and then policemen beating a retreat, jeered by everyone. They probably tried to stop the mob, but with only two of them that was hopeless. Running away in the direction of the railway viaduct over Plantin en Moretus Lei, one of them blows his whistle. The shrill blast has the demonstrators cracking up, like a gang of guttersnipes seeing their fathers humiliated. Immediately afterwards the stained glass of the great synagogue is shattered. I see Omer, the lawyer with the deep voice, pull a fence over before joining others in furiously kicking at the front door, while the rest cheer them on. The wood cracks and they're inside. Applause. Frightened wailing is heard from inside and then it's like the building itself vomits out a family that was apparently living in the caretaker's apartment. A woman, two children and a man are kicked down the steps and run for their lives, unable to completely avoid the sticks raining down on them. They're lucky that, apart from a couple of hotheads, nobody wants to pursue them too stubbornly. I see them following the railway towards Grote Hond Straat, where the seventh division has a station. Then the building starts coughing up things instead of people: chairs, books, rolls of paper. The rioters trying to force their way into the synagogue shrink back a little until there's a lull in the hurling. Omer comes out gripping a long iron rod he uses to smash the windows that haven't been shattered yet. People grab the prayer books and Torah rolls and rip them to shreds. Smoke starts wafting out of the synagogue. More applause and whistling. Everything is being filmed. I see a camera crew standing to one side. Germans, presumably. It's all been arranged in advance. It's all a performance, as serious as an Easter procession, but with slogans and shattered glass instead of candles and hymns. Look, says Angelo, this is your epoch. Look at what you've let yourself be led to, the event where you can still do more than just be a witness. Participation is only one stone away. I see a grotesquely fat woman kick one of the books over the ground, follow it, kick it again, shouting all the while that she doesn't want to dirty her hands on it. She reaps a few chuckles of appreciation. The rest of the fences around the synagogue are down now too, bent like reeds by what's known as the will of the people. More black smoke billows out of the smashed windows. I'm standing in the doorway of one of the houses on Van den Nest Lei, somewhat sheltered. A well-groomed man in a three-piece

71

pinstriped suit asks me for a light, calmly, as if what's going on is no big deal, and I provide it, as if we two are standing together at a summer festival with a few innocent traditional games as entertainment. He cups his hands around the flame, lights his cigarette, nods his thanks and whispers, 'It's taken long enough. They were warned. Now they're getting their just deserts.' Without waiting for my reaction, he strolls off to the debris that has accumulated around the building, uses one hand to pick up a chair that has not yet been completely destroyed and smashes it down on the cobbles before striding away from the chaos. Meanwhile Omer has wrecked every last window. He balances the iron rod on one shoulder, looking around for more work, sees me standing in the doorway and winks, as if disassociating himself from the violence he has helped cause. I look away, pretending I haven't noticed. The fire brigade siren comes closer. That doesn't make any kind of impression on those present. There are still no police in sight. I watch as Omer kicks a Jewish woman in the stomach. She is down on the ground with her arms wrapped around the bars of the bent fence and doesn't make a sound. She is lying there like a stuffed doll. He kicks her again, then looks around as if he has done something daring and liberating and is waiting for applause. But I am the only one who has seen what he just did and he's not looking in my direction. I am the only one who is picturing Omer's head in a puddle of blood. The fire brigade arrives; the firemen leap out and rush to attach the rubber hose to the fire engine. They are abused as the lowest of the low. Someone throws a stone at one of them. It glances off his helmet. Without a moment's hesitation, the fireman storms over to the stone thrower and floors him with one mighty blow. Police whistles sound. They now come running from all directions to form a cordon around the firemen. The party's over. I slip off—my house is just a hundred metres away in Kruik Straat. Windows have been broken in my street too; I can hear people crying and there are still a few rowdy youths wandering around with sticks. One of them is squinting at our front door, probably to see if there's a name over the bell that could be Jewish. I grab him by the scruff of the neck and bash his head against the front door. 'Not here...' I say. The boy collapses in a crooked heap on our doorstep, his hands over his face, whimpering. I grab him by the throat with an iron grip and lift him up against the front door. His nose is buggered and blood is gushing out of it. I squeeze harder. I swear I notice my heartbeat slowing down. I swear equally solemnly that I feel like going further and I know I'm capable of it, no problem at all. His companions are keeping their distance, too scared to do anything, mouths gaping. 'Please,' the boy jabbers, 'please.' Bubbles of blood and spit on his lips. 'Please, who?' I ask. 'Please, sir...' I let go.

Upstairs those who call themselves my parents look at me with frightened eyes.

'I thought they'd already got inside,' my mother quakes.

My father scratches his ear and says, 'You've got blood on your suit.'

Afterwards the rabbi lodges a complaint. This destruction of property cannot go unpunished. He argues that the city has to reimburse the costs. The court accepts his reasoning and holds the city council liable. But the Germans are implacable. Compensation is out of the question. What the city does do—saddling us with the task—is station a permanent guard at every synagogue for the duration. Anything that is threatened and could cost the city money if destroyed must be protected. This seems normal enough to everyone; it's the law.

My nurse says I'm gloomy and there's no reason for it. She gives me a cup of herbal tea and a biscuit, then goes over to my bookcase and I see her searching. Finally she pulls out a massive volume and hands it to me.

'Here,' she says, 'this always cheers you up.'

I recognize the book and can't help but smile.

'See? I knew it.'

She gives my shoulder a gentle squeeze, then disappears back into the kitchen. I hear her singing and, thank God, not 'La bohème'. Lying on my lap is a weighty tome titled *Overview of Dutch and Flemish Literature*. I take the book out of the box and look up my name. Wilfried Wils, there I am, pen name: Angelo. And this is there too: 'One reads the work of Wilfried Wils, better known under the name Angelo, with some degree of bemusement, yet also pleasure.' That sounds as if my poetry needs to be tasted like an exotic dish, doesn't it? *With some degree of bemusement, yet also pleasure.* How did they come up with that? Or rather, how did 'one' come up with it, because that 'one' in the entry gives it that little cachet of additional authority, as if nobody else can now do anything but read my poetry 'with some degree of bemusement, yet also pleasure'. An anonymous god who tolerates no dissent is speaking here. My fire is given equal praise: 'Wilfried Wils has an idiosyncratic quality, a certain recalcitrance, which manages to unite post-war existentialism with dark romanticism in the

74

most authentic sense of the word, arousing the suspicion that he has found a deep well not only for his poetry but for his private life as well.'

So, for once it's not just me blowing my own trumpet. Nicole is a she-devil with a perfect understanding of how I fit together. That is to say, she deploys what she knows about me perfectly. Yes, I am proud, always have been. But that's not all, and with a little extra explanation you might be able to imagine what that brief entry means to me. The world of literature and poetry is, after all, a closed one. It's not easy to penetrate, definitely not when you're a cop, and especially when you don't know any other poets. It's a world of one good turn deserves another, praise and be praised, with all the clannishness of a crew of dockworkers or, if you like, a squad of policemen. I never showed this entry to Lode, though I often felt like it. When he heard from his sister that I wrote poetry, he began to see me in a different light. Poetry was clearly something he associated with weakness. Had he misjudged me? Could he really trust me? I had one face for some people and another for others.

After the war I peddled my poems to the little magazines. There were quite a few of them at the time, printed on cheap paper, but they almost all proclaimed the same thing: after five years of misery the world had to start over again, as if it had been given a second chance. For me it was the other way round. It never stops, nothing ever stops. It all keeps going and it never goes away, no matter how much everyone wants to draw lines in the sand that say 'this far and no further'. If time exists at all it is a rapidly spinning spiral to nowhere, not a line from A to B. It always makes me think of a malfunctioning toilet where you press the flush and see the water swirling and gurgling all the way up to the rim, where it comes to a halt just before it overflows. Get an earful of me, the philosophical fuck-you-too poet! Anyway, I didn't quite realize all of that at that stage. I wanted my truth in verse on paper, but first I had to convince the people who produced those magazines that a copper could write poems too. Of course, I could have saved myself a lot of trouble by not telling them I was in the police in the first place, but Angelo, who was obliged to go through life as Wilfried Wils, thought my uniform would make me irresistible to the pack of schoolteachers, newspaper hacks and inspired idlers who accounted for most of the poetry written in this country at that stage. And when I finally managed to convince them to read my poems, they considered them far too sombre, gloomy even, and therefore unsuited to this new age in which nihilistic filth would be consigned to the past forever. One of those newly purged souls who rejected me—his name was Achiel Punt and he died long ago from complications after bowel surgery—hadn't expected me to visit him at his downstairs flat on Paarden Markt, and yes: on duty and therefore in uniform.

Completely bewildered he looks me up and down one beautiful spring morning in the year of peace 1946. In his letter addressed to me he felt like he was really something, but now I'm standing before him as large as life, he treats me to a nervous joke about not feeling entirely safe knowing there's a policeman walking round town who spends his free time jotting down such morbid thoughts. Admittedly that *is* gratifying. So much so that I accept Achiel's nervous, hypocritical promise to pass my poems on to the editors for their appraisal. As a parting shot I caution him for the rubbish bin he's put out too early.

Writing is strange, son. While telling you about Achiel Punt, I see Café Vondel before me, four doors up from where Punt was living in 1946. I remember it staying closed for a while after the war because the resistance had smashed the windows and furnishings during their hunt for collaborators. And that takes me straight to a vision of that same café during its glory days in the middle of a stylish neighbourhood and makes me realize there's something I've forgotten to tell you. Maybe it's not that important. Judge for yourself.

It's late August 1940. The city has been occupied for almost four months. I'm twenty and have finally completed my last year of school, but that doesn't raise my father's spirits. He's lost his job in the meantime and is wallowing in misery. Meanbeard, on the other hand, thinks my diploma needs celebrating because fair's fair, it's his victory too. He lets me know a week beforehand that he's sorry we've lost touch with each other. If nothing else, I've earned a drink in one of his favourite bars on Paarden Markt. I don't exclude the possibility that my father has put him up to it, that he's sick to death of me lying in bed surrounded by books, waiting for nothing. At that moment I feel trapped. My mother's family has cut us off and, with an unemployed father, further studies seem completely out of the question. One look at him tells me enough. He won't find a job until it's presented to him on a silver platter. His weak spot, a lack of initiative, has been hidden for years by the money he's brought in. Now he's stripped naked and as weak as an infant. But I'm just as much a lamb that could be led to slaughter at any moment. The one thing I definitely don't want is to be carted off to Germany, a fate that is already menacing everyone who is young and unemployed. Some of my mates see it more as a lucky break, an opportunity to kiss the parental home goodbye. Independence ahoy! I'll have to find a job here instead, and despite the uncertainty of that prospect it fills me with budding joy, like a promise I whisper to myself. If I become this family's breadwinner... vengeance will be mine. Revenge for the life these two have been mapping out for me for years without worrying about what I might want myself, without even asking what my plans might be. Having to bear the burden of your parents' mediocre ambitions is idiotic, a joke, all things considered, but if you don't have anyone to discuss it with, there's no liberating guffaw after the punchline.

And now Meanbeard and I are sitting in the Vondel.

'Well?' he asks, putting down his glass. 'You're off in the clouds. You've hardly touched your beer.'

'Sorry. You're right.'

'How are things at home?'

I shrug. 'No work, no money, and it's war.'

Meanbeard laughs. 'The war is over. France has fallen. Bombs are raining down on the Brits. Germany is triumphant. And your father has connections. Things will be better soon.'

'I think I'll have to find something myself.'

'You? And what about your studies?'

Do you hear the pad of his velvet paws? But I don't say a word. I drink.

'So you want something else...'

'I don't know what I want.'

'Oh, yes you do,' Meanbeard whispers. 'You know what you want. I recognize myself in you. That's why we get along so well. What do I live off? People will tell you I'm a sports journalist, that I scrape a living together from the odd newspaper article here and there and, let's be honest, that's something most of them look down on. What did *I* do? I studied law for a couple of years and that turned out to be a mistake. Then languages… Never graduated. And yet I can tell you that I am rarely short of money. From the beginning I was able to assure myself of sufficient income. It comes of its own accord and I don't think that will ever change. Even as a student, I had money. But it doesn't actually interest me. They're all opportunities and a man like me enjoys them without paying a price. Do you get my drift? It's here, in your head, that things have to roll. Money is a means, that's all. And there are enough people around here willing to provide it.'

'That's another way of seeing it,' I say finally.

'We live in a country where people would rather you knew what kind of knickers their wife wears than found out exactly how much they earn. Ask directly and everyone starts to moan and sigh. I'm an idealist—you know that—always have been, and I count myself lucky that I am able to see my vision of the world becoming reality. It's actually never really surprised me that that vision has made me money, as if I get paid for the simple fact of having ideals. How incredible is that? Incredible enough in incredible times.'

'I don't know what exactly you're trying to say.'

'No? I've already said too much.'

*

Do you read comics, son? I know it's a silly question to ask a seventeen-year-old, but it suddenly occurred to me. Your grandfather was mad about *Suske and Wiske*. Do people still read that? I remember one book that ended with the heroes being catapulted back to the present by Old Father Time. Decked out with a long white beard and a scythe, he opens up an enormous book and lays them on the page with their year written on it. 'Ka-boom!' your grandfather always said whenever I got to that bit when I was reading it to him. Although there wasn't a picture of it happening, as a little boy he was convinced that Father Time was going to slam that book shut. He must have been about five at the time, though I'm not sure of it. And now it makes my head spin to be describing your grandfather as a child who's only just outgrown his nappies. His being dead makes it even worse. In that album, which came out a few years after the war, there's an enormous dragon called 'To-tal-krieg'. And the dragon Total War devours pieces of gold, taxes the citizens have to put out on the street in slop pails (the story is set in the Dark Ages). I have no idea if Willy Vandersteen, the author, did that as an anti-war statement. I think his main concern was those taxes, the money everyone in this country is so obsessed with. We consider ourselves permanently occupied, a land of serfs, who rarely lay claim to knighthood. Start off about your wallet and everyone pricks up their ears. Meanbeard was right about that. In this country there is a constant omnipresent sense of being a martyr to the state, as if it's constantly got its fingers in your pocket.

'If the people in this bar found out about all the things that have been going on here right under their noses… Do you think we've been twiddling our thumbs these last few years? You think we didn't know what was coming? Men like me know when the time is ripe to make ourselves useful for the ideal we believe in. I got paid two thousand francs a month for almost four years. It was simple. I kept my ears open in the right places and collected information about the harbour. And this is where I always arranged to meet him.'

'Who?'

'*Mein Freund Gregor*... a real carrot-top. German, of course. I have a feeling you're going to meet him too one day.'

'They can lock you up for that.'

'Not any more, they can't. Another beer?'

Before he's stood up, a woman joins us at our table.

'So, fungus face? Forgotten me, have you?'

Into the underworld: over to the other side of Paarden Markt, then down a narrow, diagonal street onto Falcon Rui to get to Falcon Plein, Ververs Rui, Schipper Straat and then further north, across Brouwers Vliet to Spanjaard Straat and the quays of Bonaparte Dock. Not very salubrious. We go from clip joint to seedy bar: Meanbeard, your great-grandfather and a lady called Jenny who sometimes needs assistance on the cobblestones because of her heels and the amount of booze in the fading glory of her body. Her scent lingers. Meanbeard is greeted with enthusiasm in every dive. For me, at that time, it's still an unfamiliar part of town, definitely at dusk, but Angelo, who has burrowed deep inside me, is in his element. Everyone here zigzags from hole to hole, giving him ample opportunity to plumb the depths of their bullshit. Everybody takes while they're being taken in this bottomless crater. It's the first time I've seen this many soldiers and sailors in one place. The men from the Kriegsmarine are the most boisterous. In the distance in the daytime they look like little boys in monkey suits, with blue stripes around their white collars and comical hats on their heads. From far away you expect acrobatics: you can already picture them playing the fool in the ship's ropes, hanging off gun barrels, tossing caps. But up close in a crowded bar they stick together, hardly able to stand while they try to squeeze women's breasts or bums. Here the white of their uniforms takes on a rancid edge and you can smell their sweat. They're on a bender, knocking glasses over before they've drained them completely and looking for trouble. The city is theirs.

'Our Jenny's in a bad mood,' says Meanbeard.

The three of us are sitting wedged in together at a very cramped table. Now and then one of us gets splashed with beer or has to lean out of the way to dodge an elbow.

'Leave me be…' Jenny mumbles while trying to light a cigarette. For all I know she's over forty; for all I know she's younger than me. Her lipstick shines deep blue in the bar's green light. Her blonde hair looks yellow. There are crumbs stuck to her lashes. 'Just leave me be…'

'Tell my young friend here why you are in such a bad mood.'

She waggles her index finger. 'Don't, sweetie. It's nothing to do with this lad.' She's almost begging.

'From now on she has to get a medical check-up twice a week.' The beer has tinged his voice with a casual cruelty. Jenny slaps the table hard, making the glasses jump, but immediately afterwards her strength fades again. She plays with the ruby-coloured ring on one of her fingers.

'Ooph,' I say, 'not cancer, I hope.'

Brief silence. Jenny and Meanbeard look at me, then burst out laughing.

Jenny bends forward and he slaps his knee.

'Priceless!' Then he reaches for her handbag. 'Wait, I'll show you!'

Jenny immediately fights back like a lioness. 'Let go of that!'

Meanbeard parries her effortlessly and, laughing, continues his search.

'You bastard,' Jenny roars. She gets hold of one of the loops of her bag and tugs it, sending the entire contents spilling out over the floor. Little bottles, compacts, screwed-up handkerchiefs, cards and a purse. She feels under the table like a blind woman, but again he outwits her. Triumphantly he holds up a book.

'You have to see this,' he winks. Under the table, Jenny gathers up her things, digging her nails into my knee for support. She doesn't realize that Meanbeard has found what he was looking for. In a haze of booze and lust, some of the sailors stare at her bum in the tight green skirt, her fishnet stockings and her cheap patent-leather shoes, her defencelessness.

On the book it says 'Health Pass', followed by 'Department of Vice'. Inside there are stamps with 'St Elisabeth's' written alongside each in fountain pen. Jenny emerges from under the table, snatches the book out of his hand and disappears in the direction of the ladies with all the dignity she can muster.

'Nothing's clean enough for the Germans. All prostitutes have to register for a medical check-up. So now you know, my friend. If you feel your blood racing, always ask to see their little book first. You don't want to pick up one of those diseases. Remember now.'

'Yes, sure,' I say, looking away.

Jenny comes back. Her make-up has run a little, but she really does seem to have perked up. She pushes a sailor who tries to grab her out of the way without even looking at him and stops at our table.

'Listen, you bastard…'

He looks up, smiling. 'It was just for a laugh…'

'Really?'

'I was just playing the fool.' All at once Meanbeard doesn't seem quite as drunk. It's like the racket is dying down, the glasses no longer clinking, no more slurred orders at the bar. He reaches for her hand. 'You know that, don't you?'

She bats him away. 'Get your paws off of me. I've had it with you.'

Resolutely she shoves her way out through the tightly packed sailors.

'Jenny?'

She doesn't look back. He raises himself up off his chair, sticks a hand in the air.

'Jenny!'

The door closes behind her. Almost despairing, he sits down again.

'She'll come back,' he coughs.

I see moisture gleaming on his big, bulging eyes.

Meanbeard tries to order a round of what we call 'headbutts': jenever shots with beer chasers. I refuse politely. I've already seen what jenever can do to you. My father is what you call 'a mean drunk'. I also know that I still have to get home. It's almost ten o'clock and soon the curfew will be in place for everyone who doesn't have a special exemption.

It takes quite some effort to convince Meanbeard to come with me.

'*Ich habe eine shpezial* exemption!' he crows, visibly pleased with his German.

'*Ich nicht,*' I say.

Laughter with melancholy quick on its heels. I recognize that too: jenever.

'I don't open my book for just anyone, Wilfried!'

'No.'

'I'm no book tart.'

'Far from it.'

'Our Jenny,' he said mournfully, 'where's she got to? Where is that book tart?'

'Come on, we're going home.'

'Piss off. Suck my book!'

With the help of a few sailors, who are just as drunk as he is, I get Meanbeard up onto his feet. Together we lurch along The Boulevard. He holds his face pressed against my lapel and lets his tears and snot flow free. Now and then he yelps something incomprehensible, finger in the air. Somewhere halfway up Keyser Lei, where he's not the only drunk trying to make it back home, he pulls himself more or less together. He runs his hands over his slicked-back hair, straightens his dicky, and no longer needs my help to walk.

'You're a fine fellow. You are… someone a chap can count on, you know that? Someone you can count on.'

At long last we've followed the railway viaduct, walked through the Kievits quarter and made it onto Plantin en Moretus Lei. At his front door he puts both hands on my shoulders.

'I'll arrange something,' he says, suddenly firm. 'I'll arrange a job for you. Police. Get it? I'll get you in. Me and my contacts, me!'

He searches for his keys. I help him get his door open. He falls straight through it into the hall and before I've stepped in after him, he's kicked the door shut behind him with an almighty bang.

I turn to go and hear his mother bellowing, 'You lush!'

The demon alcohol suddenly rushes to my head too.

Everything starts to spin and I throw up all over my shoes.

Stroll with us, son. It's a Sunday afternoon, 22nd June 1941, according to the neat handwriting on the back of the photo I'm holding. Your future great-grandmother is walking down Keyser Lei between her brother Lode and me. She has hooked her arms through ours. We are a harmonious trio. It's beautiful weather, not a cloud in the sky. Hook your arm into mine and we'll be a quartet of delight. Do you see how the city's residents are smiling and nodding to each other? Beautiful weather makes you forget everything. People even accept the totally insane food prices. On the black market you now pay six times as much for things you could buy in ordinary shops two years ago: butter, milk, eggs, meat. Last week my fellow officers and I picked up another black-marketeer. Without so much as a word, we took care of it the way we've been doing it since the winter: sharing the spoils between us and letting the offender go. What we used to see as the law has been replaced by unspoken agreements, rackets, with calculated risk on both sides. Everyone estimates what they can get out of it, weighing the pros and cons. Those who consider it dishonourable lose out. Those who pooh-pooh it learn better. You understand that it's not without risk. The Germans want strict punishments and we too would be shown no mercy. The days follow one after the other and at the end of each day your future great-grandfather nods to himself in the mirror, that's all. It's every man for himself. We're plundering at the gates of hell; these are dramatic times and we act like everything's normal. And meanwhile, everyone wants to dance, dance, dance. Under the Farmers' Tower, at the end of the Meir, is a jazz club you can hardly squeeze into on a Saturday night. Before the war they played swing there and they still do, even if the lyrics are sometimes in German and band leader Stan Brenders announces a song like Duke Ellington's 'Mood Indigo' in Dutch as 'In een Purperen Stemming' to outsmart the Reich Chamber of Culture, the still fairly naive censorship body. Nobody minds as long as they get to dance. Today there's a particularly cheerful atmosphere in the air, it's all 'Seize the day' and 'Let's have another round'. This morning on Radio Brussels, in what we call 'the spoken newspaper', there was a bombastic announcement that the Germans had invaded Russia. 'Finally,' my father said. 'Or did you think the Germans were going to stay friends with those Eastern barbarians? See? What did I tell you? Men like Hitler don't rest on their laurels. He's going to show his strength again! And it won't take long. The Russians are already running head over heels. They're going to hightail it all the way to Vladivostok!' Yes, he's happy, because he's finally got a new job, working as a pen-pusher at the town hall. His pal there moved heaven and earth to get him there. The only thing my father had to do was establish that he was sufficiently Flemish, which meant: join the movement. According to him it was almost too late. We'd been teetering on the edge of the precipice. 'If we'd had to keep living off the pittance you get from the police…' All's well that ends well, he says. He's got money again, along with self-respect and Flemish credentials as a cover for running after the secretaries, and Mother's relieved to be rid of his moaning. As for Hitler: there's not a stronger person in the world. As far as my father's concerned, he rocks us in his arms like a giant. My father is definitely not the only one enjoying the sensational offensive against the godless Bolsheviks. Do you hear the thrum on Keyser Lei? Everyone's talking about it. But do you know how I feel? Classy. Because I have three tickets for a matinee at Café Atlantic. A singer they're already calling 'our Zarah Leander' is performing there. Yvette's arm in mine makes me realize that things are starting to pick up. I'm not going to tell you I've come to know love. It's more that I'm starting to understand it better. Your future great-grandmother is a good-looking woman: men's heads turn and women assess her taste in clothing—simple and elegant. I think she enjoys confusing people by walking arm in arm with both of us. Which one is her boyfriend? The fellow who vaguely resembles Errol Flynn and has worked so much pomade into his hair that Yvette is teasingly calling him 'glue head'? Or is it the other one, me that is, with the dark carbuncle eyes, strutting in a second-hand suit, off-white, which makes my father think of waffle peddlers on a beach on the Côte d'Azur? In other words, son, it's game on and

I'm one of the players, without anything being spoken, as if I simply belong.

Do you hear that? We're inside. It's busy. Sit down next to us. There's a spare chair at the table. Have I already told you what Yvette's wearing? A black skirt cut just above the knee and a blouse with orange flowers sewn onto it. She's put up her hair again, with auburn clips. Her mouth? Painted reddish brown, as usual. Of course, she's very happy. I've already told you how much she loves singing. Waiters are walking around everywhere with their noses in the air and white cloths over their right arms. We are the last to be served. It's all German officers at the tables behind and in front of ours. Their girlfriends are in high spirits, drinking wine or crème de menthe. They speak a little German and giggle amongst themselves. The accordionist sits down. The pianist gives the audience a nod, then cracks his knuckles. Here comes the tenor José Corazon. He's actually called Jos Malfait, the son of a famous opera singer who was a local lad but celebrated triumphs in Milan, Paris and New York. After his father's death, 'José' attempted to pick up the baton. Before the invasion, during the civil war in Spain, he was briefly known for his song 'Spanish Refugees'. At the time, everyone was singing along to his voice, which could suddenly shoot up as if somebody had grabbed him by the balls mid-song: 'I wander down abandoned roads / A hell on earth, where I sing in misery / Life knows no mercy, I am all alone / Take pity on me, a Spanish refugee.' And yes, he's given up singing that particular song now that the audience is packed with officers who made such an exemplary contribution to that same civil war, taking the opportunity to test their planes so that just a few years later they could sweep over our country too with their bellies full of bombs. But the Spanish style is still his trademark. With his dyed, slicked-back hair, a little kohl around his eyes and a grin full of white teeth, he sings of bullfighters, Señoritas and the sound of guitars echoing through the empty streets of Seville. Even if he now sings in German.

'I should have brought my fan,' Yvette whispers cheerfully.

'A torero like that,' her brother joins in. 'Just your thing.'

'He's wearing make-up—that's definitely not my thing.'

She favours me with a glance as she says that.

'All the artistes do it…' I say.

Watch now that almost everyone has started swaying to the music. José sings about the kiss of a Gypsy girl who has stolen his heart. In front of him one woman after another is being led out onto the dance floor.

'I'm getting sick of this,' Lode growls. Fruitlessly, he snaps his fingers at the waiters hurrying past. 'Just a beer, that's all I want.'

Suddenly someone in a Waffen-SS uniform is standing at our table.

'May I invite the young lady to join me on the dance floor?'

We look up. It's no German. He's one of us, but clicking his heels and with his hair shaved up high on the sides, he seems almost like the real thing, as if his body and mind were steeled in Prussia and this city is only useful as a place to relieve himself. I recognize him. It's flipping Karel, the blonde boy who used to be in my class at school. I already told you about him being such an exemplary pupil and the teachers not being able to stand him because his parents were pro-German. I don't have the foggiest if he recognizes me. He doesn't bat an eyelid if he does.

'The young lady's taken,' Lode snaps. 'Get lost.'

'I'd rather hear it from the lady herself,' says Karel, the ersatz Prussian, calmly.

'Forget to clean your ears this morning?'

'It's all right, Lode.'

'Ah, the charming young lady can produce sound.'

'If you're not careful there'll only be one sound coming out of your throat.'

Lode gets up. He's standing nose to nose with Karel.

Yvette tugs on his wrist. 'Stop it.'

'You have your papers on you, I hope.'

Lode shakes his head in disbelief, looks at me and says, 'This feller's asking me for my papers. Can you believe it?' Lode pulls out his badge and holds it in the SS man's face. 'What do you think of this?'

Behind our table the officers' girlfriends are complaining about not being able to see any more.

'Sit down!' one of them hisses.

Imagine you really are sitting at our table, as I've described it. You're sitting with us in the lion's den, surrounded by Germans and people who want to be German, and sooner rather than later. Would you stop Yvette from dancing with a member of the SS? I can already see you shaking your head. What difference does it make now? you think. Wasn't everyone convinced by then that the Germans had already won and you were better off going along with it? Definitely, but all the same there were some people who didn't entirely trust it, who thought it madness to assume that the facts as they were at that moment would remain the facts and that the whole thing couldn't flip completely in no time at all, with black becoming white again and vice versa. I'm not saying everyone felt like that, far from it. There were some who kept waiting, weighing things up and watching, without ever taking a position one way or the other. Still sitting on the fence, as if they were back in the thirties, before the war had even started. Some of them, the ones who didn't stop thinking, felt like they'd ended up in a lottery with all they have and hold, where every twist of fate could have dire consequences, maybe not right away, but later, definitely. Stand out from the crowd and who knows, maybe you'll pay the price after the war. In that world some bastard might later, when the fortunes of war have taken a definitive turn, suddenly remember that a beautiful woman by the name of Yvette dared to cut the rug with an ersatz Prussian. Maybe that was why Lode jumped down Karel's throat like that, which in the moment itself was far from cautious (and something I tried to warn him against). And as it turned out it was more trouble than it was worth, because naturally it was your future great-grandmother who overruled her brother, and the friend she had an eye on, by making her own decision, if only to put an end to all their nonsense.

Yvette grabs Karel by the hand and whispers, 'Come on.'

Before Lode can say a word they've headed off to the dance floor, hand in hand.

'Fool,' I say.

'Me, a fool? That's rich. What about you, Will? You're just letting it happen. When that bloke goes for a leak later, he'll bump into me. And then he'll be bleating for Mama.'

'And what will that solve?'

'It makes me want to puke. Friday for instance... unbeliev-able. I'm on patrol with André. A lady comes up to us beside herself with fright. Two blokes at the station. Not even in uniform. They're asking everyone who comes out of the station for their papers to see if they're Jewish. Can you believe it? We go there and ask *them* for *their* papers. No, they don't have them on them. And they give us a look as if that's completely normal and we're fools for asking. "Sicherheitsdienst," says one of them, "that's who we're working for. Official orders. Stay out of it." But the thing is, they weren't even German!'

'Not so loud.'

Lode looks around and carries on in a whisper. 'André tells them that they can't just go around behaving like that. You know what one of them said?'

'You're getting too wound up, Lode, you have to be careful of that.'

'Kiss my arse.'

But he still casts a quick glance around, before continuing angrily, 'One of those bastards looks us over and asks calm as you please if we're really in the police force. Don't you get it? If we take that, we've all moved into the madhouse to stay, fancy dress every day with us as the resident clowns. Wanting to know if our uniforms were real... Anyway, we took 'em in. Big fuss at the station, of course.'

'*Meine Damen und Herren*, ladies and gentlemen, *liebes Publikum*, it is my pleasure to introduce to you a young lady who will take to the stage of Café Atlantic to entertain you with the wonderful songs of Zarah Leander. Give her a big round of applause... La... Esterella!'

People clap. Some even whistle.

A young, fairly large and rather shy woman emerges. Her warm lips mumble thanks. She looks at the pianist, then launches into a nostalgic Gypsy song to more loud applause. Yvette and Karel dance again, while she keeps looking at the singer. '*Sie singt wie eine Kanone,*' I hear a German officer behind us laughing.

Yvette and Karel return as La Esterella is starting her third song. He nods as if there hasn't been so much as an angry word between us and doesn't hesitate to accept the chair Yvette offers him. Lode clenches his fists, but his sister glares at him so hard he has no choice but to bite back his anger.

'So, Wilfried, are you in the force too?'

'Probationary constable,' I nod. Now, all of a sudden, Karel does know who I am and, more than that, is acting like we're old friends. He tells Yvette we went to school together.

'You didn't make things easy for them, did you, Wilfried? You never wanted to buckle under. That's how I remember it.'

He snaps his fingers and a waiter appears immediately.

'Beer?'

Lode doesn't say a word. I give another nod.

'A sweet wine for me,' Yvette laughs.

'If you'll dance with me again later...' Karel wheedles.

'We'll see.'

'It has to be today. Next week I might not be here any more.'

Then he tells us about his imminent 'rendezvous with history' as if it will make us swoon before him.

94

'Sounds like a hot little missy,' Lode sneers.

'Fighting the Russians,' Karel laughs. 'Can't get much hotter than that.'

'It's only just started over there…' Yvette takes a mouthful of wine.

'I signed up today straight away, even though it was still too early, so they said. I just want to be part of it. I hope they accept me soon, otherwise it will all be over without me ever drawing a bead on a Russian. I wasn't the only one. Lots of my friends are going too. I'm glad. We have to let Germany know she's not alone in this great struggle. It's part of the rebirth of our nation.'

Karel drains his glass and stands up. 'Excuse me. I just have to pop out the back.' He nods, looks around for a moment, then heads off in the direction of the toilets.

Lode runs his fingers through his hair and says, 'OK.' He goes to get up, but I stop him.

'What's wrong with you?'

'Don't—' I say.

'Don't what?' interjects Yvette.

'Your brother wants to knock your new dance partner's teeth down his throat in the gents.'

'You should be ashamed of yourself, Lode!'

'Let go of my sleeve, Will.'

'Don't do it, Lode.'

Lode looks at me and Yvette, gulps down his beer and says, 'Do whatever you like if that's how it is. I'm off. If you enjoy laughing along with that windbag like a spineless imbecile it's up to you. It makes me feel sick to my stomach.'

And he's gone.

'He's had too much to drink,' Yvette apologizes.

'Nowhere near.'

'No, you're right. It's just his character. You're different, aren't you? You're… how can I put it?… more realistic.' She looks at me and smiles.

'I wouldn't know what that's supposed to mean.'

'Have you got a light for me?'

I flick my lighter open and hold the flame up to her cigarette. For a moment her hand touches mine and that's no coincidence because the touch is accompanied by a deep look.

More realistic… It feels like a slap in the face. Inside of me Angelo swears contemptuously.

She asks if she's said something wrong.

'What I mean is you come across as a survivor.'

'Lode's a survivor too. We all are. Until we aren't, of course.' I laugh a little nervously.

'No, you're different. I know that much. You're not like any of us. You see through everyone. And there's something hard inside you.'

'Goodness.'

'That's something, isn't it, me seeing that.'

'It really is.'

'Are you making fun of me now? Am I wrong?'

I look her straight in the eye and for the first time in my life I let someone else see Angelo.

Now I'm wondering if that really did happen then. But it's not that important. Was it a reflex because she already had me under her spell, or did I do it to put her under my spell? Do you show your vulnerable side to girls? You might think

96

you do, but I'm sceptical. You're too young for it, if you ask me. There's no need for it either, it's not a prerequisite for a healthy life. It's not even necessarily good for the soul, no matter what they try to tell you on that score. It's exciting, true, but then you have to accept the kind of circumstances people describe as 'romantic'. That's why I remember showing her Angelo in that particular place, Café Atlantic. The circumstances couldn't have been better. Her dancing with the ersatz Prussian first, the latter's toilet break, Lode's fury and what she said to me. Don't forget the Gypsy-obsessed singer, the piano and accordion music, and me feeling classy about having acquired tickets for that matinee. In retrospect, a fellow can say it happened in such and such a way and pat himself on the back for having wanted it like that, but someone like me would do better to humbly admit that it was just as likely Angelo who decided to reveal himself and bent things to his will.

The look in my eyes makes her blink for a second in confusion. I tell her not to worry.

Karel is back at the table, rubbing his hands.

'Another dance?'

'Later perhaps,' Yvette says. 'Wilfried just asked me.'

And that's it as far as Karel is concerned. Never in a hundred years could I have predicted the transformation of goody-goody Karel into a self-assured member of the master race. If the Germans had never set foot in this country, he would have long since followed in the footsteps of his father the notary, bending over deeds of title and other documents. Instead he went off to the Eastern Front and came back a year later with a piece of shrapnel in his skull. He let them patch him up a little, then hurried back to his white hell. Immediately after the war I heard that he had been sentenced *in absentia* to death for high treason. But then he popped up again six months later, just when the first unsteady skeletons were returning from the camps and everyone was getting furious all over again, or at least pretending they were. They arrested him at Liège railway station, somewhat thinner, and definitely dishevelled, I assume, thanks to the Russian steppes and the horde of subhumans out for his blood, who had chased him and his SS buddies all the way from Ukraine right up the arse of his beloved Germany. His father set a bunch of lawyers to work: death was commuted to life, and in the end life was reduced to some thirty months after a couple of rounds of pardons. After that, clean and tidy Karel led the life of an accountant. His clientele was made up for the most part of former brothers-in-arms who he, as part of our never-ending national rebirth, was delighted to assist in scamming the state that had once tried to extinguish the eternal flame of their heroic courage. He died three decades later and left a bunch of sons behind, accountants to a man. Men like Karel never stop saying that they were the true idealists. Death to the Bolsheviks! There there, it's OK, you idealist, you... They want you to forget the insignificant fact that before the war their lives were mapped out from the cradle to the grave. Escape was once nothing but an impossible dream, a task for a demigod like Hercules and not a shorn sheep called Karel. suddenly it was war, and life became a game again a trap. Hidden under the white camouflage of idealism was boredom, a life sentence that didn't even require a post-war court case.

After the music your future great-grandmother suggests a little walk in City Park.

The sun is still doing its best. We saunter. Pigeons take wing, blackbirds are singing. A lot of people are out enjoying the weather. All in their Sunday best, of course. It's their park or, rather, the park is there for every citizen who has a right to a free day and wants to show, with wife and sprogs, that he is master of his own destiny and life is smiling on him. She's taken my hand. It feels cautious and I allow it. My heartbeat does shoot up a little, true.

'Don't you mind us being almost the same height?'

'No,' I say, slightly thrown.

'Most men prefer being a little taller.'

She's making me nervous. Next thing you know she'll be talking about where we're going to live and how many children would I like to have. Slowly we climb the hill because she wants to cross the bridge over the pond.

'What for?'

'No reason. It's beautiful up there.'

She hugs herself while leaning forward. 'Look,' she says, pointing at our reflection in the calm water. 'There we are.'

'Made for each other,' I hear myself say to my own, instantaneous horror. Yes, laugh at my naivety. Just when it seems necessary to weigh every word, people are doomed to use phrases they haven't got a clue about, that have already been used all too often.

She smiles and says, 'What would you know about it?'

An uncomfortable heat rises from my arse up. I'm not good at this game. I'm an oaf. I hear Angelo sighing inside of me. Does it have to be this sentimental? Why not a poem? In the post next week? A poem full of words I've chosen myself can be warm, controlled and supple, but still have scope for some concealed darkness, sensual suggestions of things only soul-mates can understand, a secret language evoking an abyss. We wander off the iron suspension bridge and head to the right, still strolling, drawing out the time.

'Are you happy, Wilfried?'

She doesn't even look at me while asking. It's not a particularly unusual question, but it's something I've never thought about. It's not even a word I have ever used in relation to myself—it would never have occurred to me. Now that she's asked me, I suddenly know why. It's a trap. It calls out for other words, for a future, for a life like everyone else's, a single path you will have to stick to forever.

'Should I not have asked?'

'I'm thinking about it.'

'If it takes that long, I already know the answer,' she says, thoroughly piqued. She hasn't let go of my hand just yet, but that probably won't take long. We reach the monument for the fallen with the king as a knight on horseback looking heroic on a plinth while heroes lie below him and someone holds up a flag. It used to be somewhere else, as if heroism can never settle down. I was ten when the king himself came to unveil it. Afterwards my father said: 'The bastard, the bloody bastard... All the things he promised us, and he gave us nothing.' When I cried in indignation that the king was a hero and his wife a saint, he gave me a whack over the back of the head and sent me to bed without any tea. 'Your father doesn't like to be interrupted,' my mother told me the next morning.

'Oh, you poor boy...' Yvette laughs. My deceitful story has done the job. Angelo breaks into a teasing refrain inside of me: 'He does it now, he did it then, he's conned them all again...'

'Come on,' she says, 'I want to sit down somewhere. Preferably in the sun.'

We leave heroism behind and move deeper into the park.

'There, a bit further along,' she points, 'near the sandpit. I like watching children play.'

People nod as they pass. We look like we're engaged.

I brush some sand off the bench. She waits patiently, then settles down.

There are a few foreigners present, their children yelling and horsing about.

'Busy, here. Nice, isn't it?'

'No surprise with weather like this.'

'Can you believe that?' says an old man who's seen us looking at the children. He leans on his walking stick and hopes we've understood, that we too see the decline, the defilement.

Yvette doesn't answer, which says enough.

'Stupid old git,' I whisper.

'You mustn't say that, Wilfried.' But she's smiling.

Anyway, it's only a question of time, dear boy, before the old grouch has it his way. By the end of that summer Jews aren't allowed in parks or swimming pools anywhere. Even before the war there were conflicts about it. People kept complaining about the Jew-loving mayor we had at that time, who didn't do a thing to stop our parks from being overrun. How could he, they cried, how could he simply decide to shelter all that foreign scum in our city? Were we still living in a democracy or were we on sale to the highest bidder? Because twinkling behind everything in this city are the sparklers, the diamonds, and every new cleaver, cutter and polisher was another foreign degenerate to drag our city down, usually arriving as a refugee from a country that no longer tolerated their double-dealing. Decades later a famous cartoonist—no, not the one who did the book about the dragon—offered the city a statue of his best-known character, completely free of charge. But when he heard that the aldermen had decided to put it next to the City Park sandpit he was furious. According to him there were still too many Jews in that park. Ghosts never stop haunting you. Later he claimed to have been misquoted, if I'm not mistaken, saying it was the drugs and illicit sex that went on there that bothered him, but that was a feeble excuse because those sorts of things have always gone on and always will, especially sex. But more about that later; now I have to get back to your future great-grandmother and me for the moment of truth. Just as an aside, I hope you don't find this annoying. I draw strength from the thought that even a modern lad like you will want to know what things were like in the old days. Dead sexy, actually, if I can be coarse about it and express myself in a somewhat pathetic contemporary style for the benefit of your impatient generation.

Anyway, what does she say as the old man disappears out of sight?

'Come here, you.'
   'I am here.'
   'A bit closer.'

I slide over to her. Boom, boom, goes my heart.

'I'm going to write a poem about you,' I hear myself saying.

Angelo doesn't say anything. I think he's trying not to laugh.

'That's very sweet of you. Is that one of your talents?'

'A doddle,' I whisper.

Her lace glove brushes my cheek. Her face is now very close to mine.

'Come on...'

And then her slightly flaccid lips press against mine. I gulp down my spit, and break off quickly.

'Again...' she says.

This time I feel a hesitant lick of her tongue. I hear a gentle growl too, that makes way for a deep sigh, because my tongue has found hers for a moment. French kissing in public, that's looked down upon, but Yvette couldn't care less.

'You're cautious...' she whispers.

Then I take her face in my hands and kiss her again, hardly able to control the galloping horses in my heart, my tongue suddenly writhing around hers. A kiss that knits our fates together. All at once I spot a ladybird traipsing over her collar. That's good luck, I hear my mother saying. Inside me it's all Angelo and he's showing me dead bodies.

A mother comes over to us. 'Hey, come on, not in front of the children.' But her voice sounds gentle. 'It's beautiful, isn't it, love?'

'Look at him nod...' Yvette laughs.

I'm nodding like an illegal alien who's just been stopped on the street. I form a smile and hope for a little benevolence. I am not yet a man, but I'm not a boy either. I'm a character on a postcard, the punchline of an affectionate joke.

'You're a handsome couple,' the woman winks, 'but tone it down a little.'

I gulp for breath. Angelo shows me women's nipples and mouths closing over each other. He shows me Yvette writhing underneath me or riding me like a goddess with her eyes half closed, groaning at every thrust, every shiver. I try to dispel it all with the thought that I'm, how should I put it, *in*… accepted by another person, bound by what must now come.

Oof, just like that it's snowing again. 'Be careful on your bike,' I tell Nicole, my nurse, glad she's finally going and I'll have the place to myself again. This morning she bought me a massive piece of bread pudding. 'Don't eat too much of it or you'll get heartburn again.' But a heart *should* burn, shouldn't it? I take a big bite while gazing out longingly at the quiet that will soon return. I've spent a long time pondering that kiss I described for you. I shouldn't have done that, because now your great-grandmother is much too young for me again, and too alive as well. That wasn't the intention, which is to say, it's something I hadn't expected. The wall between my late wife and me went up years before she died. Do you know that poem by the joker who used to call himself Willem Elsschot? No, probably not. It's called 'The Marriage' and it starts like this: 'When he observed the way the creeping mists of time had dulled the sparkle in his wife's blue eyes…' People think it's magnificently bitter and cynical, but of course like all cynics the author was really hopelessly sentimental. He didn't have a clue what he was writing, whimpering in a corner about his wife's weathered mug. You'll probably accuse me of cynicism too; maybe you even see it in yourself, because you and other members of your generation are cynical without ever having experienced anything. It's a pose that never grows old. Give it a little scrape with a sharpish knife, like scaling a fish, and what's lying there? Bare-skinned passion. Without knowing it, we all reflect the things that surround us and everyone thinks that's what makes them special and different from the rest. I see your great-grandmother dancing naked in the living room and she calls out to me to put the stylus back on the record because it's such a beautiful song and she likes me to see her dancing like this and know that she's happy, especially now, just after we've hurled all kinds of recriminations at each other. When exactly was that? I've forgotten. And that image of my dancing wife in the altogether makes me realize in turn that, no matter how much it annoys me, I mustn't keep anything from you, not even things that happened between us as man and woman. It is still much too common for people to skirt around all those things as if they don't have anything to do with what matters, what's really serious, but all at once I'm struck by the conviction that that's complete tommyrot, as we used to say, nonsense, and that the flesh mustn't be avoided, and I have to stop feeling unsolicited embarrassment or worse on your behalf: all those memories of her body I summoned up to treat myself to a little melancholy, like an ex-smoker suddenly getting nostalgic about the days he spent rotting his lungs away one drag at a time.

My faithful boots back on and we're off. Instead of just crossing the road, I prefer to take a circuitous approach to City Park's green triangle, now covered with white, stalking it like a puma with worn hips. I start by shuffling patiently and cautiously to the end of the street, where Quinten Matsijs Lei begins and where there is now a large police station. In my day, the police were not yet housed in this imposing building with its facade full of Freemasonry symbols. The police cars and vans in front of it are covered with snow. I cross over and go round the corner. Standing on the edge of City Park is a statue of a 'socialist leader' they plumped down there sometime in the late eighties. I see it and burst out laughing for the first time in ages. The snow has given the sculpted leader a dunce cap. The sculptor provided the smirk on his face. He stands there eternally relaxed. His right hand is resting casually in the pocket of his waistcoat and his raised left hand (he is a socialist after all) is pointing ahead. If you follow the direction of that finger it seems to be aimed mockingly at the church on Loos Plaats, which has now been taken over by Orthodox Russians. You can almost hear him thinking: 'Just look at that, look at the faithful thronging together in that building to pray to God and whatever. It's so primitive.' At the same time he seems to be trying to distract attention from what's going on behind his back, as if what happens in City Park doesn't count. Yes, that's how I read him: 'Follow my socialist-leader finger and, whatever you do, don't look at the park.' I told you about the cartoonist who thought it was Sodom and Gomorrah, didn't I? He seemed to be suggesting that it used to be different, that in the old days, homosexuals didn't go there to grope each other in the moonlight or that the park never used to accommodate other forms of carnality. Total bullshit, of course. I can tell you this: during the war a lot of policemen avoided that park like the plague once it got dark. People were having it off there all the time, both men and women and blokes together.

Was it the autumn of 1941? I'm not entirely sure. I'm standing on the edge of City Park with my older partner, Jean. In earlier days he might have been a Viking, the kind who leaps out of his longship feet first into the swash to plunder a port at a hundred miles an hour, ravaging women, setting houses on fire, then sailing further up the Loire deep into the heart of ninth-century Franconia. There's no point trying to calm someone like that down. You trudge along behind and hope the damage won't end up being too disastrous. His wife runs a bar on the Waag that doesn't have a single respectable customer and that's thanks to Jean's reputation. The place is full of riff-raff: gangsters, pimps and seriously disturbed womanizers with political connections. Jean knows them all by name. They hardly make a profit. 'Zulma, give us another round!' is one of his favourite exclamations. But anyone who runs his tab up too much and then lets it slide for weeks on end is dicing with danger because Jean is just as likely to pull out his truncheon and beat the miscreant within an inch of his life. He's had a few opportunities of promotion and has always turned them down. Since then his superiors, too, have treated him with some degree of caution. Or is it because he knows so many people around town, a lot of people, and doesn't use those connections openly, so you never know for sure? He's told me straight out he's in the lodge, an organization of freethinkers the Germans dissolved some time ago. If anyone with bad intentions had found out, he'd have been picked up long ago. But he trusts me. At this stage everyone still seems to trust me.

I say, 'Jean, just go by yourself.' It's about 10 p.m. and Jean is bored. There's not enough happening. The streets are quiet and we have at least four hours to go.

'Don't be so gutless. We'll just walk through the park, that's all. Are we in charge here or not?'

I'm better off not answering that question.

'We're just going to have a look to see who's skulking around in here with his pants down around his ankles. And you're coming with me.'

We walk over the iron suspension bridge. Nothing to see. But further along in the bushes, as expected, we hear the drunken laughter of German men, coupled with giggling in our own language.

'See, told you so...' Jean whispers.

'Come on, this is ridiculous.'

'Public indecency ridiculous? I don't think so.'

Jean creeps over to the bushes the noise is coming from and says loudly and clearly, '*Polizei! Papiere, bitte!*'

Two stupefied Luftwaffe officers push the shrubbery aside. They have two women with them, clearly locals, completely sloshed and with their tits out.

'Have you no shame?' one of them slurs.

'You, too, ma'am. Papers, please!'

One of the officers recovers from his astonishment and dismisses us with a haughty little wave, '*Verschwinden Sie!*' He raises a bottle to his mouth and burps. His cock is still half erect and peeking out from under his shirt. I try to hold back my laughter.

'*Verschwinden, los!*'

Jean remains imperturbable.

'*Papiere, bitte.*'

'*Arschloch!*' spits the other officer.

He bends and pulls his pistol out of its holster in a single movement. The women laugh, leaning on each other for support. They see me looking at them and one calls out, 'Fancy a bit too, do you?' She rubs her nipples and grunts like a pig.

'*Ich scheiße auf die belgische Polizei!*'

The officer points the pistol at us. We ourselves do not have firearms, only truncheons.

But Jean just looks at the weapon as if someone is offering him some grimy candy floss.

'*Ich frage noch einmal…*'

'*Wie dumm bist du?*'

How he comes up with it I don't know, but Jean proves he's not dumb at all by very calmly and very menacingly saying all kinds of things in German, from which I pick up regular mention of 'Field Command' combined with several other terms. I can't follow most of it, but in the end the man with the pistol lowers his arm. The other fellow pulls his trousers back up. And the women, too, who probably understood just as little, fall silent and get dressed. The men hand over their papers, and so do the women. I write down their names and ranks.

'*Können wir das nicht einfach vergessen?*'

Jean shrugs. Maybe he could forget it. One of the officers takes him aside. I can't make out the conversation, but I see Jean nodding patiently. Finally, I see the officer fish something up out of his inside pocket, which Jean secrets away.

'Friends for life,' he laughs cheerfully. One of the women blows us a kiss.

Sing, oh Muse, of resentment. I smile while writing this, son, because how ridiculous is it that all of our literature arose from this opening sentence from Homer's *Iliad*, without our really understanding it after more than 2,800 years? We remember a procession of heroes, take it for granted that there was great valour on those Trojan battlefields and have a vague knowledge of a ten-year war. Before we can appreciate the value of literature, our minds turn to kitsch: it happens automatically. But that doesn't detract from all of our literature being born in a tent where a hero by the name of Achilles was sulking because he, the greatest of them all, had missed out on a pretty girl he'd seen as his prize. He'd had to relinquish that honour to his tactless boss, Agamemnon, who grabbed everything for himself regardless of who he was dealing with. It starts with resentment, Achilles sulking about a great injustice that's been inflicted on him and isn't recognized as devastating by anyone else. Worse still: nobody even knows about his resentment because he keeps it to himself. The pettiness of it all should be beating us about the head. Something is wrong here. This isn't an account of yet another battlefield, this is not just a paean to a hero. That first line holds up a mirror. More than that: maybe Homer is giving us a warning right from the word go. Watch out for resentment, watch out for the pettiness that is inside all of us. No, everybody would rather know about that ridiculous wooden horse the Greeks used to outsmart the Trojans—a scene you won't, by the way, find in the *Iliad*. Everyone prefers to forget about the resentment, the whining banality that won't go away and tugs on your trouser leg like a bothersome child. And yet the resentment everyone feels is much mightier, much more powerful than pride, much more tragic too for the very reason that nobody likes to admit to it and everyone continues to hypocritically deny it even when the facts are out in the open and plain to see; resentment is the only thing that can consume the soul of a person, city or nation and the hypocrisy that comes with it is what's worst of all. Resentment? Nobody can shake it off. Far too many warnings have been ignored, too much blindness has been permitted, too much viciousness has been tolerated for it to ever be wiped out for good. Hypocrisy has a different flavour in each country, accompanied by a different crime of omission, sneaking in an ambiguity peculiar to each mother tongue. And afterwards—in those cases where an afterwards exists—everyone keeps silent about it in their own highly specific, culturally and regionally determined way. So tell me more, Muse, about resentment and how it seethed in this city and still does. And tell me about how money sometimes soothes it, Angelo adds.

In my wartime diary I wrote poems, scribbled down a few revenge fantasies, kept note of my weight-lifting and other physical exercises, and jotted down jokes I then learnt off by heart to amuse my fellow policemen. Sometimes, but not that often, I find something that refers to the war itself. Towards the end of October 1941 it suddenly says 'White Brigade' followed by a question mark. I vaguely remember that it was around then that I first encountered the term. It was the name of a resistance movement that was supposed to be active in our city and elsewhere at the time. In my album there's a clipping of an article from *Nation and State*, a paper my father sometimes read. I'll copy it out for you here: 'Against the "White Brigade" we deploy our manly comrades of the Black Brigade. Every day new recruits rush to join our militia. If the blood of one of our comrades should stain the cobbles, woe betide those responsible, high or low.' Beware resentment.

Anonymous letters come pouring in. The words 'White Brigade' have scarcely reached the ears of the public before the denunciations begin. 'The above-mentioned X, my in-laws' next-door neighbour, is definitely a member of the White Brigade. He is constantly being visited by disreputable characters. What's more, he is secretly breeding rabbits that he clearly sells on the black market. Those animals stink to high heaven! Please take measures. A copy of this letter has also been forwarded to Field Command. Yours faithfully, in all discretion…'

Some of the accusations we have to take seriously, others our inspector ignores, waiting for the Germans to take the initiative or, more specifically, the Secret Field Police, who have the task of suppressing all sabotage, resistance or other forms of dissent. The prison in Begijnen Straat is already full to overflowing. Far too many people are being picked up for far too many trifles. A lot of cops laugh their heads off when talk turns to Begijnen Straat.

'It's one big knocking shop, mate, incredible. It used to be bad, but it's only got worse.' I'm finished for the day and want to go home, but Jean still has things he wants to talk about. 'A mate of mine works there. It's a complete den of iniquity, Wilfried, it beggars description. And everyone keeps thinking the Germans are so proper. My arse! I hear stories about Germans who take bribes from prisoners for a so-called dentist's appointment so they can go see their wives. Under supervision, mind! There are so many people coming and going, it's like a railway station. Pay enough and you can go in there as a visitor without a pass or anything. No problem. Meanwhile they're jammed into those cells and every now and then one of them cops a beating from those same German guards because he hasn't slipped them enough pocket money and it just keeps on like that. *Zu Befehl?* I don't think so. Those blokes follow orders when it suits them, otherwise they wipe their boots on 'em.'

Money talks. Jean knows all about that. He reads my expression and treats me to a shameless grin.

That very night, behind the zoo, we catch two cheeky little buggers daubing V-signs and 'England forever' on the Provincie Straat pavement.

'Defacing a public thoroughfare!' Jean says, grabbing one of the scamps by the collar.

The other one howls, 'We had to. Our dad made us!' He twists his fists in a plea for mercy. Oh, poor us!

'Nice. Betraying your own father just like that.'

Jean gives the boy a whack around the earhole.

They're shivering. The people are restless, as they say. It's another cold winter, food is scarce and hardly anyone can afford to heat their flats properly. The occupier has issued warnings: listening to foreign radio is prohibited. But behind their curtains many people still delude themselves they're safe.

Yesterday there was a demonstration for more bread, led by housewives. It didn't last long, of course. But still…

Jean straightens his belt and looks at me, 'What are we going to do with these fellers?'

'We should really take them to Begijnen Straat…' I reply, playing the role Jean expects.

'I think so too.'

'Our dad will be furious, officer!' The little chap is getting more and more agitated. His brother, who Jean still has by the collar, stays icy calm.

'Seeing as he encouraged you two to do this, maybe we should go drop in on your father too.'

The icy one looks at Jean and says, 'We're patriots. You?'

Jean gives the back of the boy's neck a good squeeze. 'Vandals, more like it.'

'Ignore my brother! He's not all there. He was born like that!'

'Really?'

'Let us go… We'll never do it again.'

The icy one shrugs. 'Do what you like. We'll track you down after the war.'

'Unbelievable…' Jean gives the boy a good shaking.

The other brother raises his hands in despair. 'Stop… Don't…'

I ask him where he lives.

'Tol Straat,' he quakes.

'That's on the other bloody side of town. Piss off. Go play silly buggers in your own neighbourhood!' Jean gives both boys a shove, followed by a kick up the bum for the calm one.

'Blackshirts!' the boy shouts as they both start to run.

Jean watches them disappear. 'It makes your head spin, doesn't it? And it's going to get worse, a lot worse. Brace yourself...'

Five weeks later it got worse.

'What?' Jean asks the chief. 'Could you say that again, please? I didn't quite get it.'

'Get your ears cleaned, Jean. I've told you. It's about what not to do. The Germans have given some individuals—that's what it says here: some individuals—permission to paint pro-German slogans on walls and streets this evening and all weekend. Under no circumstances are we to intervene.'

'Are we allowed to help, then? I mean, who knows if these blokes can even spell—'

'Jean, I'm sick to death of you.'

'That makes two of us, chief. That makes two of us.'

We leave the station. Another night patrol.

'Where were they going to make a mess of our streets again?'

'Along The Boulevard. Around the opera house, the National Bank, the courthouse...'

'Let's take the National Bank.'

'That's not our district any more, Jean.'

'Don't be daft. The whole city's my district.'

We follow The Boulevard south through the freezing cold.

'Real sausages. My cousin brought them with her from the Campine. We've got farmers in the family.'

'It's been a long time...' I say.

'I don't offer them to everyone.'

'I know, I know.' I'm on my guard. If I accept them, will it cost me? But real sausages… What difference does it make?

'I'll bring them tomorrow.'

'Thanks a lot.'

Jean stops and looks at me. 'No strings attached, huh? It's because we're partners.'

'I don't have anything to offer you anyway.'

Jean lays a hand on my shoulder and laughs. 'As if I didn't know that…'

A little further along in the semi-darkness we see three men bending over the pavement opposite the overloaded cream cake we call the National Bank. One of them is squatting down with a paintbrush in one hand. A tin of paint by his side. As if in a silent film, Jean opens his eyes wide and holds his index finger up to his lips.

He whispers, 'Let's get at 'em…'

We approach silently. The men don't look up. In big clumsy letters they've daubed 'Germany victori…'

Suddenly Jean roars, 'Is that what you call beautiful letters in the city of Rubens, Jordaens and Van Dyck! The city where typography was born?! The city where Desiderius Erasmus once lived, where he probably committed his most beautiful thoughts to the page? You should be ashamed!'

The painter falls on his arse. One of the others knocks the tin over in pure fright. The third clutches his heart. They're no spring chickens. I estimate two of them as mid-thirties. The third is in his late fifties.

'Shit,' the painter hisses as he recovers a little. 'These trousers are fucked. Thanks a lot!'

Jean picks up the half-empty tin and wastes no time in pouring the rest over the man's hat and coat. Drenched with it now, he roars, 'You bastard!'

Casually Jean brings the tin down on his head.

'We've got a permit…' one of the others bleats.

'There's no call for this,' groans the other.

Jean kicks the painter in the ribs. He's wearing a thick coat but I still hear something crack. The word 'Germany' has been reduced to a smudge after a capital G.

'I'm going to lodge a complaint!' the painter screams, protecting his ribs while trying to scramble up onto his feet.

'Wilfried! Note this gentleman's complaint!'

Shaking my head, I reach for my notebook.

'I!… Name!' Jean roars at the man, before purring, 'What's your name, sir?'

'Verschueren, Jozef…' the painter snaps.

'Verschueren, Jozef! Of…' He gives the man another boot. 'Your address?'

The two others reach out impotently to their buddy, but are too scared to come within range of me or Jean.

'Of… Come on, what else?'

'Twenty-three Maarschalk Gérard Straat.'

'Profession?'

'It's all right… I withdraw my complaint.'

Jean kicks the man's paint-splashed hat off his skull and pulls him up onto his feet by his hair.

'Profession?'

'Oh, fucking hell… Civil servant at the Chamber of Commerce. Let go of me.'

'What if we just…' says one of the others—not the one with

the red, flushed face, but his friend with wet, almost purple lips, who blows bubbles of spit when he talks. 'What if we just act like none of this happened and all go our own way?'

'And then…' exclaims Jean, not loosening his grip on the painter's hair, 'they found the magic key and they all lived happily ever after! Is that what you had in mind, sir? And by the way, what's your name, if I may be so bold?'

'Verstrepen, Kamiel,' the man bubbles.

'Also a civil servant, like your good friend here?'

'Section head at the city's department of finance,' he says, suddenly sounding assured, as if realizing that the way he makes his living might make a difference.

'And you?' Jean nods in the direction of the skinny fool who knocked over the tin of paint. He looks a bit like the rich Jews you see on posters.

'I have a paint shop in Lange Lozana Straat. That is, I used to. I'm retired.'

Jean looks at the paint tin and says, 'Hilarious! It could hardly be better, could it, Wilfried?'

'I'm splitting my sides…' I say quietly.

'And how are we going to resolve this, gentlemen?'

'We'd like to go home,' says one of them, while another nods like a schoolboy who recognizes the correct answer even though he could never have come up with it himself.

'Go home like good boys, because the missus is frying up some fish for you… Do you think that's a good idea, Wilfried?' Jean winks at me.

I tell him it's an idea like any other.

Jean promptly lets go of the painter's hair.

*

On Sunday I generally shut myself in my room and read Verlaine. '*Aujourd'hui, l'Action et le Rêve ont brisé / Le pacte primitif par les siècles usé, / Et plusieurs ont trouvé funeste ce divorce / De l'Harmonie immense et bleue et de la Force.*' I'm not going to translate it for you, son, because I don't want to embarrass either of us with my inability to capture something that needs, above all, to be felt. According to the poet these lines were written under the sign of Saturn, the dark Roman god whose festivals were once celebrated during the months of winter, and I was just writing them down in my diary when there was a knock on the door.

My mother was standing there.

'Sorry to disturb,' she says quietly. 'I just forgot there was a letter for you on Friday.'

She lays the envelope on the bedside cabinet, tells me tea is almost ready and disappears. I recognize the handwriting.

Dearest, how I long for your touch! Time has become a horror to me, a harsh taskmaster who scolds me when I think of you and curse the hours and days that separate us. It is you who have set me ablaze, so you won't hold my complaints against me, I hope. If only I could feel your fingers on my throat and your lips on mine right now! Sweetness, what we have together is so beautiful, I can't find words to describe it. You make me sing, do you know that? I can already see you laughing as you read this, or maybe you're thinking, 'Oh, the silly cow.' But I can't help it. I am yours completely! Let me know when we can meet again and when you're on duty. Lode says he doesn't see you much either, but adds that that's normal. Please write to me, even though we don't live that far apart. I want to be able to cherish your written words when I am alone in my room in the evening. Big, juicy kisses from your... Yvette.

How can I tell your future great-grandmother that letters like this make me feel a bit queasy? On the page, this quick-witted woman who is so worldly and fearless turns into a doll made of pink icing sugar. As if she feels obliged to adapt to what a love letter is meant to be and doesn't realize how much she betrays in the process. I put the letter with the others and go downstairs for the frugal meal my mother serves up as if it's another feast. My father says, 'Nice soup, but it needs to ripen a little. Save some for tomorrow.'

'Ah, my young friend, a wise man once told me that it's better to believe you chose your parents than the other way round. It is better to assume that the soul itself decided to reincarnate here, surrounded by these very people. That way everyone has made his own fate and only has to answer to himself.'

'Do you really believe that old tosh?'

Meanbeard nods triumphantly. 'What you call old tosh comes from the Orient, where our race arose many thousands of years ago. Don't let yourself be distracted by the treacherous teachings of Christianity or by overestimating the importance of rationality, which is just as bad. Your glass is empty. Would you like another liqueur?'

Without waiting for an answer, he tops me up.

'I'm glad I can come by every now and then to blow off steam.'

'You're always welcome here, as you know. But the things you say about your parents… There's nothing terrible about any of that, surely? And those letters from your girl… She actually seems very charming to me. Don't take it to heart so much. What shines through all of this is your poetic sensibility and that's what matters. You mustn't forget that.'

He raises his glass and we toast what he calls the 'new era' and the role I will play in it. Below us the parrot is making a hellish racket yet again. For the first time I hear his mother swear loudly. As if stung by a wasp, Meanbeard jumps up, throws open the door of his study and roars, 'Don't you bloody dare touch Gaspar or I'll tan your hide! Do you hear me? Or do I need to come downstairs?'

'No, no, it's fine,' is the quick and fearful reply from the depths.

Sighing, Meanbeard closes the door.

'She is going mad and getting cruel, *mon ami.* She really is, and between you and me, sometimes she needs to be disciplined. But what can I do? *C'est la vie.*'

I don't say anything else and leave the rest of the liqueur untouched.

From Monday I'm on afternoons. I check in at the desk at Vesting Straat. There is a strange tension in the station. At first the chief inspector hardly looks at me. Then he says that Gaston, a much older colleague, will be going on patrol with me.

'Why's that? Is Jean sick?'

A couple of the others look up.

After a long silence in which everyone stares at me, the chief says that the Sicherheitsdienst picked Jean up yesterday.

'What for?'

'I should ask you that, Wils. Did something happen last Saturday, perhaps? Neither of you reported anything unusual.'

'Nothing I know of.'

The chief looks over his shoulder at the rest of them and asks if everyone's heard me clearly. The temperature sinks to way below freezing. Someone spits on the floor.

'Are you sure? Wasn't there something to do with paint that night? Something at the National bloody Bank.'

'Oh, that,' I say quietly.

'Hop it, lad. I'm sick of the sight of you right now.'

They beat Jean half to death. At least that's what people said, usually adding, three of them at once, because you don't beat someone like Jean half to death easily or on your own. Apparently he was only locked up in Begijnen Straat for a little while. After that nobody heard anything else about him. After the war he showed up again, which was something nobody had expected. He came back as one of those walking skeletons. Neuengamme. That was where he'd been. A concentration camp. I heard that he never really recovered. He didn't want to be a cop any more and sent back the medal they offered him. No longer a Viking, but a ghost who spent the rest of his days sitting at a table in his wife's bar, close to the stove. An old man of just over forty and—according to the stories—an object of ridicule once the war had finally been banished from everyone's memories, something that hardly took any time at all, of course, much too little.

*

Have you ever had the feeling of suddenly being cut off from all kinds of things at once? Jean being carted off was one of those moments for me. I read my wartime diary and can picture it immediately. It's clear that, at the time, no matter how superior I acted with my high-flown poetic fantasies, I had still drawn confidence from belonging somewhere. After Jean, that was over. Without a word of explanation, the other policemen avoided me. All support was withdrawn and I had to manage on my own. At the same time I felt observed and under suspicion. Conversations died when I stepped into the station. The chief watched me mistrustfully from behind his logbook while I gave my report at the end of each shift, as if every word was a trap, as if some malicious force had me in its power. 'Are you sure, Wils? That's how it has to be phrased, is it?' I gave up going to bars with the other policemen. There was no point any more. Lode was all I had left. But he didn't say a word about what the others thought of me and I didn't insist. And many years later Lode would betray me too.

'Checkmate.'

'No, it's not. I can take that knight with my bishop.'

'I should have said, double checkmate. Take the knight, you'll still be checkmated by the rook.'

'Does that even exist, double checkmate?'

Lode shrugs. 'Whatever it is, you can't do anything about it.'

We're in Café Terminus, back in that horrible year of 1993, the year of the wet bedspread with my wife lying on it.

Lode and I look at the board. Neither of us makes a move to put the pieces back in place.

'Oh, mate,' Lode says finally.

'I know…'

'Where did they find her?'

'In one of those old bunkers near the park on Della Faille Laan.'

My granddaughter, the rebellious apple of my eye, is dead. Two days ago we found out it was suicide. I don't know what your father's told you about the aunt you never knew. Who knows, maybe he's even told you something about that suicide note of hers. I have to tell you my truth about that, but not now. I don't feel like it.

'You're so restless…'

She runs her fingers through my hair and gives one of my earlobes a little tug.

'You make me restless.'

'I can tell,' she says, sounding a little sad again.

I say I don't know what's got into me.

In reality it's quite simple. I'd rather be draped over a chaise longue, acting like I'm suffering from some kind of poetic consumption that wracks my lungs and limbs, but sets my soul on fire. The problem is I can't see myself lying there like that. I'm not consumptive and I'm not a seer. It's that longing, the ache to be something I'm not, that's weighing on me. All I want is to stare hollow-eyed at the horizon, at the birth of a fantastic vision that only I will be able to capture in verse that will leave the world staggered. I want to be praised and hated, with enough people at my feet and the rest frothing at the mouth to curse me. I need to be offered prizes, not out of love and admiration, but because of the fear of misjudging me. Prizes which I, of course, would arrogantly refuse, hurling accusations of the most dubious double-dealing into the faces of the jury members. I want to shine in people's imaginations like a creature of fable that is beyond the reach of mere mortals, a being with goat's legs and dark gentle eyes you mate with at risk of eternal madness. Piss off all of you, I want to be a poet, a lyrical genius, a monster whose satin lips adorn a mouth that spouts verse. I want to spin the wheel of fate, giving it an almighty tug, a gambler who risks everything on everything. All or nothing!

But I'm almost twenty-two and sitting here on a sofa above a butcher's shop with just one person to worship me, who seems to have completely suppressed all thoughts of the darkness she once saw in me. I sit here as an off-duty cop who, since this business with Jean, is considered completely untrustworthy by Lode and everyone else at the station. Another one of those things: off and on duty. That's how we all refer to our time. As if they're the ones who turn us on and off... Even when I'm off duty, it's on their say-so; my time is not my own. Do you see how work takes you over? An off-duty cop. Someone who sees himself that way doesn't even realize how much he's been enslaved. I am imprisoned here, that's what it is, locked in concrete from my ankles to my crotch, with a life that's still ahead of me but already seems to have been chewed over from beginning to end by toothless ancestors. So I'm just like the others, like everyone. And that takes time to process, that makes a person—Yvette, your beautiful future great-grandmother, is right—a tad restless.

'Your tea's getting cold. And I made it for you with so much love.'

'Whoops,' I say and take a sip.

We are alone, inasmuch as two young people could be alone in a parental home in those days. Her parents are downstairs cleaning up the butcher's shop and Lode is on duty. We, of course, are in the living room. I would be refused entry into her home for all eternity if I ever got caught in her bedroom.

'Come on,' she says, 'that's enough gloom and doom. You've hardly given me a second glance all day.'

Without a word I undo a button of her tightly fitted, mauve satin blouse.

'Ah, down to business, is it?'

But her voice doesn't sound reproachful and her hand doesn't push away mine.

I undo another button, then look into her eyes.

She asks if I'm proud of myself now.

A bit of her flesh-coloured bra is showing.

'Are you too scared to go any further?'

Her tone of voice makes my blood race. Like a cartoon hero who is suddenly surrounded by an enormous gang of bandits and doesn't want to let on how terrified he is, I hardly dare swallow, scared that it will echo through the whole house.

I undo another button and try to do it as smoothly as possible, as if it's routine. Trembling fingers start on the last button, which needs to be forced through the buttonhole. The blouse falls open, revealing the shape of her breasts, covered in flesh-coloured lace. She's still gazing at me, the look in her eye betraying curiosity. My heart is pounding. Hers seems unaffected. She hooks a thumb under a strap and pulls it down over her round shoulder. She slides away the other strap too. Then with one hand she raises her left breast up out of all that lacy fabric. For the first time I am staring at one of her nipples. She offers it to me, slowly pulling my head down with her other hand.

'Here. This is for you,' she whispers, and only now do I hear her own excitement. 'Here. Spoil me. It's all yours.'

Her own words make her nipple swell.

I press a kiss on it and smell her skin. She smells of things that until now have only existed in my imagination. Things from an unknown south, the south of the sun, the south of naked bodies, undiscovered still, but already filling my secret thoughts.

My kiss is a little too cautious for her taste.

'Again.'

I close my mouth over the nipple and suck.

'Yes,' she says, 'that's it.'

My trousers tighten. I try to breathe calmly. I run my tongue over her nipple, exploring its softness and its hardness at once, the lust that's shaping it.

'There's two of them, remember...'

This doomed poet is reduced to forced labour in the fields of love.

She calmly strokes my hair while my tongue looks after her other nipple. It feels like she is lost in thought, as if her head were turned away to look out through the window into the endless distance, consumed by a dream. But am I that dream? Who says it's not some film star? When I reach higher to press a kiss on her lips, her eyes welcome mine. Gently she pushes me off the sofa and forces me to kneel. She hikes up her skirt and spreads her legs, welcoming there too. My mouth goes from nipple to nipple while I press myself closer against her. As I lick, I surreptitiously look up at her and see her head tilted back. I feel a trembling pass through her. She wraps her legs around me. The shoes she is still wearing press against my back and I hound myself with questions: now? Already? Here like this, without so much as a word? I lick her throat and want to breathe in her scent there too, but she pushes my head back down to her nipples. Again I feel that her attention is drifting as I suck, that she is letting me have my way, allowing me to do as I please with something that in her heart is reserved for someone else, someone unattainable. A short groan makes that suspicion ebb away again. But my thumb on her inner thigh, on the thin strip of naked skin I find there, meets with a reprimand, if friendly and patient. Only her breasts and mouth are available; the rest must remain a promise. As excited as I am, for all that my head is spinning, and despite the painful, straining desire in my trousers, I can accept it. More than that: maybe it comes as a relief that I still have to limit myself to those areolae, now wet and warm, still half imprisoned in her brassiere, and those hard, deep-red nipples that are begging to be bitten, not hard, but hard enough for us to imagine ourselves as animals that don't know where lust ends and hunger begins.

Then she takes a sudden sharp breath and says, 'Oops.'

I hear Lode's voice behind me.

'Come on, you two…' he sighs.

21st March 1942. According to my diary this is the day I see my first dead body. Early on a Saturday morning Gaston and I are at the end of Ommeganck Straat. We're not making a fuss about it. That's Gaston's favourite expression, which he applies to virtually everything that can happen during a day's work. He also said it when they informed him that from now on he would be walking the beat with me. Early this morning, before we'd started our round, he came back from the toilets with the announcement that he'd just pissed blood. But that too was nothing to make a fuss about. My hesitant expression of concern didn't throw him. He'd been expecting it, he told me calmly. It was no surprise. 'They work us to death. One more year of this misery and I can retire. Let's not make a fuss about it, Wilfried. Someone like me making it past fifty is incredible enough as it is. The missus is always telling me I'm grinding myself down. Know what I say? "What about you?" I say. If I kicked up a fuss about things like that, I'd never even get out of bed. It's my kidneys. They're stuffed. Too much piss: going in and coming out.'

His words linger. We hear a police whistle. In Lente Straat somebody's sprawled half over the pavement. Judging by his wounds, murdered. Two other constables are making a half-hearted attempt to block the body from view while gesturing to the people staring out of the windows and shouting for them to go back inside. One of the policemen shrugs uneasily, as though it's an accident he's unwittingly caused. The other is staring straight ahead as if he'd like to strangle the murderer on the spot with a length of piano wire. Cursing, he comes up to us. He looks wooden, as if walking on stilts, and, despite his fury, his eyes are dead.

'The fucking bastards!'

He shakes Gaston's hand and nods at me.

'Someone you know?' Gaston asks cautiously.

The stilt-walker nods and sniffs, then holds a hankie up to his impressive nose as if we too are cadavers.

'My deepest condolences, Eduard,' Gaston growls.

Eduard shakes his head and goes back to the body.

It's a cold, dark morning, even if the blackbirds are trying to outdo each other in song. I rub my eyelids with my thumb and little finger and look again, hoping my sight has improved. The shock of the new clouds everything. A first dead body feels like a revelation from another world, as if a god or a demon has reduced this man to a bag of blood and guts, bone and flesh, cutting the thread of his life for no reason, without leaving a single clue. As if that god has left his rubbish behind with supercilious indifference to all rules and customs. It feels like something that had to happen. After all, nothing is normal any more; it hasn't been for a long time. The man is lying on his right side. His mouth is half open. One of his eyes is staring dully into the void. His hat is on the street two steps away, an exclamation mark after a long sentence. Look at me lying here. One of his arms is stretched out, palm up, as if there was one last thing he was supposed to receive from the heavens before dying. His straight right leg is under his left and forms, almost playfully, the numeral 4. A red flower has formed around his heart. The back of his head looks like someone has stamped on it, turning it into a gory crater filled with blood clots and the vulnerable pink flesh of his brain. His shoes are worn, but the overcoat and the trousers showing below suggest he had plenty of money. His wallet is lying open beside him. His ID shows that it is Clement Bruynooghe who is lying here, in Lente Straat, close to one of the Jews' ritual slaughterhouses. Someone shot the above-mentioned Bruynooghe, Clement in the back, then put a bullet through his head. The Germans call the representatives of the newly formed Jewish Council to account, apparently threatening reprisals. For some people the occupation is no longer an unpleasant natural disaster, but something that can be resisted. From now on, people will be shooting back. It seems that Bruynooghe made no bones about his sympathy for the occupier.

'A good comrade,' Meanbeard adds.

'Another policeman was there and frothing at the mouth. He's the one who found this Clement fellow.'

'What's his name?'

'Eduard, I think… I don't know him.'

'Oh, that's probably the Finger. Eduard Vingerhoets. Something birdlike about him? Long pointy nose, small head?'

'That's him.'

'I've known the Finger for years. Another true comrade. Before the war we were in a lot of protests together. If you're in the police you always have to be a bit careful with politics, of course. Great admirer of Mussolini—we always made fun of him for that. You have to be honest with each other, even if you're on the same side philosophically, and surely that Italian windbag is comical more than anything else. Compare someone like that to the Führer, not just in terms of character, but also *Weltanschauung*. You feel where the true radicalism lies, don't you? Now, I must say the Finger has never been fond of Jews. Il Duce's prone to beat around the bush on that score, but the Finger, never. He wants them all dead and the sooner the better.'

'Why do they call him the Finger? Just because of his surname?'

'That too, but there was an incident in a bar with some floozy or other... Ah, I'm not in the mood for salacious stories.'

He sighs and shrugs. His spirits are low. Gaspar the parrot died unexpectedly and his mother is not recovering well from an unfortunate fall down the stairs. Meanbeard has to do the shopping all of a sudden, along with the household chores. He says he has to read to her every day too, much to his annoyance.

'You know anyone who'd like to earn a little on the side? Your girl perhaps? What's her name again?'

'Yvette...'

'Even some cooking would help, a little cleaning... That would make life a bit easier for me. I'd like to suggest she keep my mother company with a book now and then, but knowing my mother, she won't accept anyone but me for that.' He sounds a little guilty. Or is that my imagination?

'Yvette knows how to get along with people.'

'That's a good start... Would you do me a favour and...'

'I'll let you know this weekend.'

'Ooph, it's only just Monday. I don't know if... But fine, I'll be patient.'

'So this Clement Bruynooghe was a friend of yours?'

'It's hard to believe... The cowards killed him like a dog. It's provocation. They're trying to intimidate us. But we're ready. We're prepared.'

'Who are "they"?'

Meanbeard lights his pipe. 'Listen to Mr Silver Buttons here. You really are growing in your role as a policeman.' He shakes the match to put it out and rubs his thighs. 'Not the Jews in any case. They're shitting themselves. They're not that mad, everyone knows that.'

'Apparently a few of them have been picked up.'

'Of course. But I'd bet my life it was the work of a Bolshevik. One of those bastards in the resistance. Strange they use that name. In this Europe we're the frigging resistance.'

'But why?'

Meanbeard looks at me in surprise for a moment, then starts laughing. '*Jeune homme…*'

'What?'

'What do you think yourself? You saw with your own eyes how your fellow policeman, the Finger, reacted? Clement was one of us. He worked for the Sicherheitsdienst.'

'I mean, why would anyone risk their life for that? There's no point.'

'A comrade is killed like a dog on the street and you start wondering what the point is? You think everyone always uses their common sense. I'm going to tell you something, my friend. These are challenging times, times in which everyone's inner self is revealed. It's like a striptease, and common sense is an article of clothing like any other. It gets peeled off and dropped on the floor with the rest. That's all there is to it. In this town everyone knows everything about everyone else. They know who's going along with the Germans. Admittedly, it's not that difficult to find out. Only you seem to be lagging behind. You seem to be in the dark about almost everything. But it works the other way round too, doesn't it? I can easily name a few blokes who could have blown Clement's brains out. The Jews they picked up are gone for good, but we know where to find the real culprits. The fools didn't stop to think about that.'

'If you have strong suspicions you can always—'

'What? Surely you're not going to tell me to report it to your piss-in-the-wind police station. You're not all there, are you? Just because you pull on a uniform now and then, you don't have to go along with the boundless self-importance of your paymasters. Reporting something is the very last thing any of us would do. An eye for an eye, dead simple. One phone call and it's done. But that's another thing I'm not altogether in favour of. Not when it's Clement. Shooting a wonderful fellow like that in the back, by God! That's personal. That feels like losing a brother. The only retaliation for cowardice like that is getting your own hands dirty. Hey, why are you sitting there grinning like an idiot?'

'Come on, don't be like that.'

He stands up abruptly. 'You don't know me well enough. Not me and not my comrades. It's time that changed.'

It's May and the sun is shining, but Meanbeard's mother doesn't want anything to do with it. The curtains remain drawn. From her throne, she gestures for Yvette to continue reading. My girlfriend is sitting nice and straight and clears her throat. As usual I have taken a chair behind the old woman. She tolerates my presence but when Yvette is reading I have to keep my distance. 'From the start again, Mrs Verschaffel?'

'No, child. We know it's snowing and our hero doesn't feel like working. There's nothing wrong with my memory.'

Yvette opens the magazine again. The cheap cover shows a drawing of a woman staring out at the reader with her eyes wide and her mouth half open. The story from Volume 9, Number 5 is called 'The Curse of the Count'.

'His eyes caressed the paintings on the wall and lingered on a photograph showing a medieval castle. There was a hint of discouragement in his eyes. That…' Yvette's voice is a little throaty. She coughs, turns back to the page.

'Take a sip from your glass. That's what it's there for.'

Yvette nods, drinks a little and, after glancing past the half-dozing woman at me, resumes reading: 'That was not an unusual feeling for Robert de Tiège. In such moments he even doubted his talent. Life seemed dead and futile, despite art, his work, the honours and accolades. Certainly, he was successful! Beautiful young women called him "maestro" with a seductive glint in their eyes. For whom were their smiles intended: the artist or the bachelor? He did not know. Now, suddenly, he remembered…'

'The blackguard,' Amandine Verschaffel mumbles contentedly. 'No surprise there.'

Yvette looks at her defenceless victim, who is only seconds away from the deep sleep of innocence that only the very old can submit to, and smiles at me before reading on.

'…that he had been invited to Madame Bressoux's for luncheon. What should he do? Ignore the invitation? There would be postprandial dancing. The female guests would be pursuing potential husbands. Robert smirked. Good old Madame Bressoux!'

Grunts are issuing from the easy chair. Like always I have to suppress my laughter. It's strange that Meanbeard doesn't like to read. After all, it never lasts much longer than one or two paragraphs. Then the old woman solidifies into an object which barely has a pulse, miles away from everything, especially her own ailments: the stiff hip, the eye that sometimes lags behind the other, the trembling that makes her left arm so clumsy, her son's blows... All gone to the sounds of the slowly read sentences of a mawkish novel printed on cheap newspaper.

'Yes, good old Madame Bressoux...' I whisper after the grunting has given way to deep sighs.

Nicole is in a tizzy. 'What kind of nonsense is that? Do you really want me to read this to you? You, an educated person?'

I admit it, son: I too have a weakness for trashy novels. I used to buy them at jumble sales: musty magazines from the war years, held together with two rusty staples, dragged out of some cellar to bring shame to my bookshelf with all their tacky plots: lost lovers reunited at the very end, a cursed castle, a devout notary and a malicious coachman, giggling girls and a countess with a hacking cough who wastes away in a box bed while the priest whispers a blessing in her ear. Things like that aren't meant for your own eyes; they have to be read aloud, the way your great-grandmother once read them with pleasure to Mrs Verschaffel for a modest remuneration.

'Come on, Nicole...'

'Are you losing your marbles? I'm not going to accelerate your imminent dementia with this drivel.'

I gaze at her with damp eyes until she sighs and pulls out her reading glasses and studies the shabby pages on the coffee table with her nose turned up.

'Where have you been keeping this?'

'Please, just read it...'

Yes, it's just a story that could almost have been written by a machine with a memory full of index cards that list everything the average person demands from their entertainment. It still grips my heart. I still surrender to it and reproach myself for never having had the talent to write stories like this, ones that are capable, even for just an hour, of transporting people to another world. Do you hear Angelo laughing? I do.

Someone is singing a song in the White Raven, a bar on België Lei. 'When their noses, when their noses, when their noses are so hooked. By hook or crook, by hook or crook, when their noses are so hooked!'

Laughter. 'Where'd you get that from all of a sudden, Sylvain?'

'Come on, lad. Everyone knows that old tune.' Sylvain winks and sips his beer.

'Oh, bloody hell,' shouts the bar's towering owner. 'Now the penny drops. The giant song from the carnival in Aalst.'

'Piss off. Dendermonde!'

'Not at all, Aalst!'

'Dendermonde!'

Close to the table where Meanbeard and I are sitting, someone calls out, 'Aren't you from round that way yourself, Sylvain?'

The barfly coughs discreetly. 'On my mother's side.'

'Not born and bred,' the man next to us laughs. 'I knew it!'

'Fill her up, landlord.'

'Have one on me, Sylvain.'

'Now he's got his nose in the air!'

Sylvain pops up off his stool and cheerfully whacks the bar. 'By hook or crook, by hook or crook, when their noses are so hooked!' He waves his arms like a conductor. A few people watch with amusement and someone joins in hesitantly.

Like all bars in wartime, the White Raven is not well lit. There are a few brownish paintings on the walls, all clearly the work of the same amateur. A view of the Scheldt. The cathedral at dusk. An embarrassing ode to Breughel, with cheerful peasants raising goblets. A few illustrated proverbs, again inspired by the master. If you lie down with dogs, you will get up with fleas. The horse that is next to the mill will carry the grist. No use crying over spilt milk.

'Is it always this lively here?'

'It has been known, yes.' Meanbeard sounds distracted. I see someone coming back from the gents. The dim lamp above the bar shines on his nose. Meanbeard raises a hand to greet him. Eduard 'the Finger' Vingerhoets grins and strides over to our table. He forms a revolver with his thumb and index finger and points it at me.

'I know you. Wilfried Wils.'

'Wilfried's a pal of mine, Eduard.'

'Yeah, of *yours*…' the Finger says scornfully.

'What's the matter? We're both policemen, aren't we? We've seen each other around,' I say.

The Finger snaps back at me, 'You, a policeman? You're a mole. I don't count you as a policeman.' His squinty eyes are close-set. He keeps staring at me as if he can see right through me, like a surgeon who's just opened me up to see which bits are rotten. I don't belong here, maybe not anywhere, and he knows I know it.

'What's got into you, Eduard?' Meanbeard says, trying to rescue what's beyond rescuing. The Finger and I continue to stare at each other.

'What's got into me? Nothing. Everything's fine.'

138

'Leave the lad alone.'

The Finger winks at me. 'Shall I leave you alone? Seeing as your pal's asking so nicely.'

I shrug and sip my beer.

'Come on, Eduard, change the subject.'

'Fine by me… Have you heard the latest? We got him.'

'Who?'

'The bloke who killed Clement like a dog…' Again he looks at me and hisses, 'You were there, weren't you, when we found our Clement?'

I nod. The Finger's nose really is a distraction. It's like you're being studied by an anteater, as if his snout is constantly slapping you in the face. Only now do I notice that he has a moustache as well, more a pencil sketch or something that's been applied with charcoal, a smudge above his little gall-spewing mouth. His lips form new words, revealing stained, rodent incisors: 'We beat the shit out of the murdering bastard. We beat him until all he could do was blow little bubbles of blood.' Again that look at me. 'Off duty, of course. I wouldn't want you thinking I give people beatings when I'm in uniform.' Big grin, yellow teeth.

Meanbeard grins along. 'You handed him over to our friends afterwards, I hope.'

The Finger gave a short shake of his head. 'No, not this time. The Germans don't need to be in on everything. We chucked him in the harbour with everything he had on him, Bonaparte Dock. Blub, blub. He went down like a stone. We won't see him again. By the way, speaking of Germans…'

Meanbeard looked at his watch. 'Yes, he should have been here by now. But he's a busy man. We'll have to be patient. Landlord, another round!'

The giant puts three foaming beers down on the table and wipes his paws off on his apron.

'Lucien, this is my young friend Wilfried.'

'Welcome to my robbers' den.'

The landlord leans on the table with his fists and asks what's keeping 'Red'.

'I was just telling them. He's coming,' Meanbeard replies.

Just then the door swings open and a redhead walks in.

'Speak of the devil and his German appears,' Lucien laughs. The two exchange nods. The German is as big as the landlord.

Meanbeard is up on his feet right away to shake hands. *'Mein Freund Gregor, Wilfried. Gregor, hier ist der junge Freund.'*

I nod and shake his hand.

Without releasing my hand, Meanbeard's friend Gregor looks at him, *'Ist er der Polizist?'*

'Ja, ja,' Meanbeard laughs, 'police.'

Gregor slaps me on the shoulder. *'Krieg macht aus uns allen Polizisten, nicht wahr?'*

'You're exaggerating, Gregor,' the Finger says, again looking at me. 'Even war doesn't turn us *all* into policemen!'

'Schon gut, Eduard. Just joking.'

Gregor nods to Lucien, who goes to pour another round.

It was your father, long ago and before you were born, who ranted to me about the war in Yugoslavia. Everything he knew about it he'd heard on the telly or been spoon-fed by some newspaper or other that made a show of serving up your father's favourite brand of truth in the hope that he and all the other outraged readers would hold out their bowls for another helping of indignation the next day. He was talking about the occupied city of Sarajevo, about the white trucks of the United Nazis (his words) that the furious residents of the city painted all the colours of the rainbow because they considered neutrality such a massive lie, an excuse for complete inaction. I let him rave on because it seemed to do him good and, what's more, he seemed to think that I, his grandfather, was the perfect person to condemn a dirty war from the comfort of an armchair. I could tell that was a factor—that he hoped that I, with my past, would reach out to him, the grandson who had and would experience bugger all his whole life, and lend my blessing to his anger, in other words, tell him it was only normal for him to feel like that, that all war was the work of bastards, and he and I were slurping from the same spoon. He started telling me about the snipers in this current civil war, some place that was apparently called sniper's alley with tall buildings where men with precision rifles lay in wait for a lady trying to do her shopping or a kid that had escaped the attention of its parents. He said everyone had become a target for those murderers and he wanted to know if I could understand that, if I knew how low people could sink and if I'd experienced things like that 'in my day'. And writing this down for you, I think of the same things I thought about back then when I tried to answer him. Of course I've seen people who have been reduced to targets, ready to be destroyed because their time had come—no, actually because there happened to be a demand for it. And now, presumably, I'm supposed to tell you about June 1942, the month that all Jewish men, women and children in this city were ordered to sew a yellow star with a capital J on their coats. In the second week of June I saw a long queue outside the school building in Grote Hond

Straat, the very building where I did my democratic duty for years by lining up every now and then with my ID and my polling card to spin the wheel called 'elections' until I was sick to death of it, until I no longer felt like making a fool of myself in the eyes of the powers that be, who, because of their bureaucratic zeal can never be trusted and have always been occupiers, and always ready to lie flat on their backs as soon as some other power takes over. That same school building was where the Jews had to buy their stars of David (three stars for one franc), get a battery of stamps on their identity cards and sign neatly for receipt. Spit on the grave of Napoleon, who apparently introduced the scourge of bureaucracy to these parts, 'for the greater good' as they say, but in reality for the benefit of a civil service that one and a half centuries later was easily seduced into cannibalism. Our leaders are lackeys, son. That's the tragicomedy: inside every ruler there's an underling trembling in terror. Meanwhile the streets were full of people wearing stars. Some of them seemed ashamed, as if they'd contracted a foul illness for all to see. Others held their noses in the air proudly, prouder than ever of what we may as well call their origins. And we, non-Jewish residents of this city that prides itself on its roll-out-the-barrel and pull-the-other-one sense of humour, thought at first that it was a joke on the part of those ridiculously thorough Germans. But no, the whole city became a vile playground where bullying was encouraged instead of penalized. It was utterly disgraceful and it all happened in broad daylight. Of course, there were also those who casually let slip that only now could we really see how much filth there was out on the streets. Others thought they were being neutral by saying that the badges had the advantage of clarifying things. But once it was obvious that the stars were on people's coats to stay, they were seen as normal and another effect came into play. The Jews' timidity gradually increased because they knew that their stars had turned even more people into assistant tormentors, as nothing invites blows as much as vulnerability. Yes, *mein Freund* Gregor, war turns us all into policemen. Of course, so-called reasonable people never even mentioned this schizophrenia. Those kinds of feelings had to be hidden away. In circumstances like that, people inevitably think: 'It's them or us.' Either become a possible target, or be a possible sniper. The last covering people pull over themselves is the white sheet of their own vulnerability, their being a victim too, no star on their coat of course, but threatened all the same, falling asleep under that sheet in the hope that when they wake up it will all be over. No, it's not right to look down on something like that. A little recognition of that eternal ambiguity would be more honest. Listen to me blathering on, son, cackling like a chicken on its way to the chopping block. Back then, though, I just went along with your father about the filthiness of war, which meant I might just as well have said nothing at all. How do you explain what defencelessness is and what people can be capable of, if the person you're talking to has never felt what it's like to be a potential bastard himself? How do you tell him that to have never felt that way is both a blessing and a curse, and that armchair indignation is nothing more than blind hypocrisy? Sometimes people say you have to stand in someone else's shoes to really understand their situation. But that's hypocritical too, because when they talk about those other shoes, they always mean the victim's. They never say a word about the shoes of those who might have felt stirred to join the persecutors. Before you denounce the bloodthirstiness of someone else, someone you don't even know, who you've only seen on the telly or read about, you should be obliged to experience what it means to have a secret bloodthirst yourself, one that's encouraged by the string-pullers, whose game you're playing whether you want to or not—the bloodthirst, in other words, that is inside everyone. Your world, son, is full of screens, all they've offered your generation, your father's and even your late grandfather's is indignation on command, whimpering along at a safe distance in sympathy with the oppressed and the mangled bodies they describe in such sombre tones. None of you know what it means to be in the midst of violence, to really feel it, and most of the time I think it's a blessing to have never experienced war at first hand. But when I hear yet another epistle from some self-proclaimed expert, I start to doubt that so-called blessing and see myself as a hypocrite, a traitor who has chewed over his heritage until there's nothing left but a bland mush. Denying things, like how they started to say at our station: 'If it's a Jew, what's it to you?' But now I'm sorry. I never told your father all this because I just assumed he wouldn't understand. His sister was burdened by the same questions. But I'm telling you now and now that's all that matters. You.

In this city, Mother's Day is on 15th August, the day the Virgin Mary was taken up to heaven. War or no war, it's a time of celebration and people prepare whatever they can conjure up with their ration coupons. Do you still honour your mother on that day, son? I hope so, even though your parents are long since divorced and you live, so I hear, sometimes with the one and sometimes with the other. To me, that doesn't sound like such a bad arrangement. I found it exhausting having to put up with both my parents in one room at the same time and, if anything, the attempt at staging a family feast on Mother's Day, combined with the icy silence because of Father's latest lapse, made it even worse.

It's with a reasonably full stomach that I find myself standing on the corner of Oosten Straat in a throng of policemen later that evening, not far from the synagogue and only a couple of streets away from home. There are a lot of us, a great many. Fellow officers have been brought in from Deurne, Borgerhout and Hoboken. A few tell us they're from Mortsel or Ekeren. We received the order to gather there on the day itself, or the day before, I can't remember which. Nobody knows what we're there for. The Germans come driving up with masses of equipment. Our inspectors have their mouths clamped shut. Some of us are in a foul mood at having been called in on a holiday. I've already told you that most of my colleagues only speak to me when strictly necessary because of what happened to poor Jean. Suddenly Lode pops up next to me and says he doesn't like the look of it.

'Things are coming to a head, Will.' He'd already been called out earlier that evening to distribute *Arbeitseinsatzbefehlen*, good German for forced labour orders. They'd rounded up dozens of men and handed them over to the Germans. After an hour or two, they'd thought their job was done. Then instructions for them to proceed to Oosten Straat arrived.

They put up barriers on Plantin en Moretus Lei. Looking along the continuation of Oosten Straat towards the station,

I see they've also closed off part of the Kievit district. A few Germans are setting up large spotlights on the corners. Field gendarmes and Sicherheitspolizei jump out of trucks. One requisitioned removals truck after the other comes driving up Van den Nest Lei. 'Requisitioned' is possibly a misleading term here; later I hear that the local removals companies were reimbursed for the use of their vehicles. I have no idea if that's really true. The drivers lean on the bonnets and light cigarettes. We are split up into different groups and instructed to 'accompany' the operation. We cross Plantin en Moretus Lei, enter Provincie Straat and turn right into Bleekhof Straat. Doors are kicked in. Men from the SD drag a father and a mother out onto the street. Followed by crying children and an ancient couple who can hardly walk. The grandfather tears at his hair; his face is an icy mask. His wife is only wearing a nightie and a dressing gown. Her thick eyebrows show under a brightly coloured nightcap. Of course, all of Bleekhof Straat is in an uproar in no time. People yelling and sobbing. Children's screams cutting through it all. Some of them are being dragged down the street by the hair. Meanwhile we're all acting as if we're still just cops. We close off the streets and guard the barriers as if it's a sporting event. The effect is grotesque. I hear myself telling a weeping boy of about sixteen that he needs to calm down and proceed quietly to the vehicle. Other officers help women who have been kicked to the ground by SD men back up onto their feet. 'If you could just come this way...' 'Hold on tight to the little one, ma'am.' And so on, and so forth. Some of them let themselves be carted off like sleepwalkers, vacant and unresisting in their pyjamas, acting out their own nightmare. Nothing is fast enough; everything has to go '*schneller*' and '*schneller*'. The street is now brightly lit; long shadows walk down the pavements. Someone vomits over his shirt front while being dragged along on his heels by two field gendarmes. A woman clasping an extra coat runs after a mother with two sobbing children. The Germans jeer at her and punch her twice in the face when she raises loud objections. When she still refuses to back off they drag her to a truck along with the Jews. Her glance in our direction says enough.

'In whose name are we actually standing here?' I whisper to Lode.

'You're still asking the question. Later you'll hear this never happened.'

He's right. The attorney general, or maybe the mayor, who is now snoring in his bed, will wake up tomorrow morning craving normality, like he does every morning. The late-night operation involved picking up work dodgers, that's how they will probably describe it. But how do you write this down honestly in a police report? 'This evening we provided assistance during an arrest for reasons unknown to us. The number of apprehended individuals, women and children amongst them, is also unknown to us.' The unknown is factored into our pay, along with the feeling of being completely alone here, in this uniform, abandoned to our fate, but you can't possibly entrust that to a police report. Some of us have gone pale or can't bear to watch, but there are plenty who are unmoved. Our task is to make sure none of them escape and we carry out that task. No, you're not allowed past, no matter how desperate you are. You have to get on that truck as the master race demands. But if every one of us is standing here all alone to

147

do a job that doesn't even need to be justified because it will be forgotten again tomorrow, who or what does that make us? It's even more ridiculous because that 'us' no longer exists either. Who am I, surrounded by fellow officers who can no longer stand me? Less than no one, a ghost in a helmet? Mad Meg in that painting, striding through hell with her eyes wide and her sword pointing straight ahead? Has she caused this or is she just a part of it, driven mad by what she's seen? Have we helped to make this possible or are we just witnesses who will never testify about what we are forced to see while on duty?

'If this can happen…' runs through my head like a taunting refrain. 'If all this can happen, if men in uniform can stomp on children, punch women in the face, almost cripple civilians as they beat them into removals trucks marked with one of our names, a Flemish name… If all this can happen… We who are standing here as what?… as relief workers in an inverted world where white is black, during a night that has been lit up as hellish day, like nurses assisting uniformed German-speaking doctors who are combating some kind of human virus with kicks and blows, bellowing and roaring threats at the weeping, the howling and the soiled pants of so many, with blood and puke and shit on the street… If all this can happen, can't anything? Can't anything?'

The Germans are keeping a section of Plantin en Moretus Lei shut off. Lode and I have been ordered to report off duty and go the other way, following Provincie Straat, then turning left behind the zoo to get back to the station.

'What I don't get,' I say, 'is that they are all so…'

'What?'

'Do you remember that time in the snow?'

'Which time?'

'When we had to march that Jewish family to Van Diepenbeek Straat. We just passed their house. It looks like it's still empty.'

Lode looks back and stops abruptly. 'What are you bringing that up for?'

'Because it's so—'

'Give me a cigarette.'

I reach for my pack, shake out two and light them both. We smoke in silence for a while.

'I never told you this, Will, but—'

'You knew that fellow, didn't you?'

Lode shakes his head. 'How did you know that?'

'I saw it on your face.'

'Chaim Lizke is in the diamond trade. A cutter. He's a strange bird, a real fixer. Our dad got to know some of those blokes a couple of years before the war, when a lot of them fled here. He used to go to Pelikaan Straat sometimes for a coffee on his days off, close to the diamond bourse. Everybody there knew Lizke. So did I. He even came to ours sometimes. Understand? This has to stay between us. You know what it's like at a butcher's. Our dad had lots of cash, war was coming... A man like my father always looks ahead. Do you follow me?'

Now I shake my head.

'We bought diamonds. Lizke had contacts. Our dad gave him a percentage.'

'And we helped pick him and his family up...'

'I almost had a heart attack, believe you me.'

*

149

After we've reported off duty at the Vesting Straat station and nodded goodbye to each other, I start walking home. It's getting light. In Oosten Straat I see two constables from the seventh division, which has been keeping a permanent watch over the synagogue since last year's riots to protect it from damage. They undoubtedly recognize me, but give no sign of it. Just to be contrary, I wave. No reaction. The building remains unharmed on the mayor's orders; sleep tight.

The dawning day is a Sunday. Normally I would see Yvette, but I have no desire to bump into Lode, who also has the day off, and I presume he feels the same way. The streets are quiet—too quiet—even for a Sunday. I walk to the Jewish bakery in Provincie Straat. As if a vengeful god is trying to prove a point, it's open and serving a long queue. Across the road and just half a block away, Bleekhof Straat looks like a shut-down flea market, with items of clothing and broken glass everywhere. Some of the front doors are still wide open. In the queue, people hardly speak as they shuffle forward. Someone says he didn't sleep a wink with all the racket, but he's looking at the toes of his shoes. A bony woman thinks someone's pushed in front of her. She raises a finger. 'I'm next!' The baker's wife looks up in fright. What everyone knows remains unspoken, even as a whispered question between the brave. How much longer will these two be baking our bread? Not long, if I remember rightly. A week or two, I think, at most. Someone is gently tugging on my coat. I turn around. It's my Aunty Emma, who works as a maid for a Jewish family on Van den Nest Lei.

'It was quite something...' she whispers.

'And?'

She shakes her head. 'They took them away. The children too. So sad.'

I start to ask how she's coping, but she squeezes my arm. 'Not here, lad, not here.'

Gaston doesn't want to make a fuss about it, but he's heard that I've been seen in the White Raven.

'Whoever saw me was there too.'

'That's another way of looking at it.'

'What's your point?'

'People are saying you're a quisling. But I—'

'Don't want to make a fuss about it.'

'In any shape or form.'

'Who's not a quisling round here!' I shout down the corridor. A couple of fellow officers look around.

'If you want to keep me as your partner, take it easy,' Gaston hisses. Even before I've had time to answer Gus Skew appears out of nowhere, reeking of stout as always, and grabs me by the neck. With one hand he lifts me up against the wall. My feet are dangling just above the ground.

'Gus, let him go...' I see other policemen holding Gaston back. Gus's grip tightens. Helplessly I claw at his face. Gus's knee shoots up between my legs. The intense pain has stars exploding in my head. 'Don't piss yourself,' I think. 'Don't piss yourself.' Just behind Gus, closer to the door, I see the Finger's ant-eater snout. He's laughing, teeth bared, something he probably doesn't do very often. Helpless and furious, I clench my fists. Angelo shows me him begging for mercy with shit in his pants and snot running out of that enormous nose, but the image doesn't calm me.

'So, Wils, you think you can do whatever you like. You think we don't know. But we know enough, matey. You hear me? Every man here knows you reported Jean. Everyone knows you're a bastard, understand? Let that soak in. Think about it for a few seconds. You're a bastard, a dirty scab. I couldn't give a shit whether you think this or that, if you're for the Brits or the Germans. But you need to be more careful. Because if you ever have the gall to pull a stunt like—'

'Gus!' someone shouts.

'Behind you!'

'Gus! Over here, now!'

He lets go and I collapse. The chief doesn't give me a second glance as he shoves the now docile Gus towards his office.

Gus is suspended for two days. Rather than being upbraided for assaulting a fellow policeman, he is censured for breaching a recent provision enacted by the chief superintendent. Talking about politics while on duty is strictly prohibited.

I'm lying on my bed with my trousers and underpants peeled down. Against my better judgement, I've nicked Mum's hand mirror from the bathroom to study my genitals. My scrotum looks terrible: blue and purple and seriously swollen. My penis is flaccid and lifeless, with a bruise shaped like a pig's head at its base. There's a knock on the door. I sit up immediately and call out in agony, 'Occupied!'

My mother's voice informs me that I have a visitor. Hurriedly I pull up my trousers, slide the mirror under the pillow and scramble back to an upright position. Has Yvette dared to show up here unannounced?

'I'm coming downstairs!' I call.

Then I hear Lode's voice. 'I'm at the door.'

I try to adopt a relaxed sitting position, albeit without crossing my legs.

My eyes slide around the room. Is there anything to betray me, showing Lode who I really am or revealing him who is called Angelo? The only thing that occurs to me is to quickly tear down a poem from the wall over my bed. It's called 'Vigilance' and I have written it in my own blood. O, my poet's heart, my grotesque poet's heart.

'Come on in, mate,' I cackle cheerfully.

Lode looks shy.

'Sorry… but I was thinking of you. I heard what happened.'

I offer him the only chair. He sits down.

There are two dusty glasses in the bedside cabinet. I get them out, wipe them clean with the bedspread and offer him a shot of some kind of liqueur Meanbeard recently gave me.

'Cheers!'

We clink glasses and sip. It goes straight to my head. I spread my legs a little wider and tell myself the pain in my balls is fading slightly from the alcohol.

'I feel like I'm to blame, Will. I should have told you they've got it in for you at work.'

'As if I didn't know…'

'I hear that Gus kicked you in the balls.'

'He missed. They don't call him "Gus Skew" for nothing.'

Lode laughs. I do too, but it takes more effort.

Silence falls. I top us up.

'To your health.'

'And yours!'

Lode coughs and looks at the threadbare rug under my bed. 'You can bet your life there are a few real traitors among us. As long as there's money in it… And then sometimes people can't resist picking someone out, someone like you, and loading them with the sins of Israel.'

'Someone has to be the Jew, you mean?'

'Come on, Will. You know what I mean.'

Someone like you: it echoes through my mind. Because as much as I see myself as an outsider, I had hoped it wouldn't be too visible. No, I have to be honest. I didn't want to stand out at all, I just wanted to belong. It was naive to think it was a problem that could be solved by pulling on a uniform. My blue balls make that obvious now once and for all.

'There's one thing I have to ask you, Will…'

'You want some more of this sticky muck?' I laugh and reach for the bottle.

'The White Raven… true or false?'

'True,' I say, pouring the liqueur. 'My old French teacher took me there, the one who helped me get through school.'

'That guy's a rat.'

'Agreed. But sometimes you get to know things by playing dumb.'

Lode whistles quietly. 'Bloody hell…'

'You get me, right?'

'Mate, it's not a game. One false step.'

'Look who's talking.'

Lode starts to laugh. 'I'm not going to tell you everything. Everyone has their secrets. One last thing and then my lips are sealed. The Germans and their little friends like your teacher are in for a surprise if they try to round up another batch of Jews. No, now you should see your face. Not another word.'

The bottle ends up empty.

Hopefully you, my great-grandson, will one day read this, even if we don't know each other and you never requested my memoirs. The aunt you never met, my beautiful granddaughter, who ended up doing away with herself with a rope, did ask about my memories of it all. She wanted to know, she wanted to know everything.

'Keep that old rubbish to yourself,' my wife snapped under her breath while carrying tea and homemade biscuits into my study. She smiled indulgently at Hilde and said, 'Child, leave your *bompa* in peace.'

I looked at her; she was eighteen at the time, with spiky hair and wearing baggy trousers and a ripped vest. Her eyes were made up like a witch's. She looked a fright, I suppose, but it didn't bother me. I saw her as a rebel, with something dark about her too. She'd brought her parents to the edge of a nervous breakdown with her sudden crying fits, slashing her arms, calling out that she sometimes saw visions of beauty and heard voices warning her that she and everyone else needed to better their ways.

I looked at her and held my tongue. I did it so as not to disturb your great-grandmother, because she was scared that my stories might make our granddaughter even crazier. I stayed silent and I have cursed that silence to this day.

*

I've never seen Meanbeard this furious. He's frothing at the mouth. Foambeard.

'You and all those other cops are a pack of scabs! Turncoats, the lot of you!'

'What are you talking about?'

He jumps up off his chaise longue, comes over to stand right in front of my chair, and starts his tirade. 'No, that's not going to work, friend. Don't play dumb with me. I had to calm Gregor down. Do you know what kind of position you've put me in? I presumed you would keep me informed and that's I what I told him, an SD man. "Gregor," I said, "the boy's on our side. You can rely on it. If he knows something, we'll know it too." Now he's rubbing my nose in those words. And I guarantee you that's no laughing matter with a man like him. From one moment to the next, Gregor turned into a hurricane. Roaring. And this, and that! They've had to cancel tonight's operation entirely. And you undoubtedly know why. Your station's crammed with Jew-lovers. No, damn it. That's putting it too nicely, you stupid idiot! Because don't try telling me no money changed hands. The raid's off. Happy now? But you're all going to pay. The lot of you! If not one way, then the other. But it's going to happen!'

'I simply didn't know a thing about it,' I say, as calmly as I can.

'No, that much is fucking clear. It's a good thing Eduard Vingerhoets knew more than you. The Finger warned Gregor straight away. He's someone you can rely on. It's time you got to know your friends a bit better. He knows which side you're on. I told him again.'

'That bastard hates me.'

'Get it into your thick skull: the Finger is one of the few friends you've got on the force. But the question remains, can we really trust you? The question remains, are you one of us? With the Finger there's no doubt, but you? Well, do you have anything to say? Did you or didn't you know your division was so rotten some of the cops are on those hook-nosed bastards' payroll? Yes or no, what's the story?!'

He looks down on me. He's sprayed his outburst all over my face.

I try to control my rage. Does everyone really think they can do whatever they like with me, that I'm at their beck and call, the way my father is so fond of saying? Suddenly an enormous hate rises in me, a hate that sweeps away the smouldering humiliation I've been going through recently. Why on earth am I holding back? Why do people just keep on taking it until they're nothing but soulless dummies? I've finished school, I've done my training, it's enough. I soaked it all up, took what was worth taking, and the rest of my education, that thinly disguised brainwashing that never really took, is over. I wipe the saliva from my face and stand up like a man.

'Did you have to spit in my face like that?'

'Sorry, what? *N'as-tu pas honte?* You're shameless!'

I straighten my back and show him Angelo. I let him see himself being knocked over like a pawn on a chessboard, dragged over the floor by the hair to the stairwell and kicked all the way down. I see Angelo's fists descending on him like hammers and skilfully beating his bearded face to a pulp. I see Angelo's face covered with splatters of blood and how he then unbuttons his fly and pisses on the mush that was once a head. It only happens in my head, but I make sure he realizes. And it works immediately.

'All right, take it easy,' I hear him say. 'I'm a bit on edge.'

'Exactly,' I say.

'I know you're different. But you have to understand… my position.'

'Maybe you should start out by making an effort to understand just who you're dealing with.'

'Goodness.' Meanbeard puts on an uncertain smile. 'Tough talk.'

'Don't ever shout at me again,' I say and leave.

'No,' Lode says, 'not with me. I'm not going to be a part of it. You can scream till you're blue in the face.'

The chief looks at his log. 'I'm going to have to make a note of that, boy.'

'Do whatever you like.'

We're on night duty. It's about three in the morning, 28th August 1942. We're being drummed up for a new operation. There we stand, like little children. And now one of us is talking like a man. Or a fool. There's not much difference.

Gaston tugs on Lode's sleeve. 'Have you lost your mind? Don't make a fuss. You know what it can lead to.'

Someone says, 'It'll be Breendonk for you, pal.'

That's the rumour. Anyone who refuses to cooperate goes straight to the camp of horrors, that's what people are saying. So: here are the names. Go to Terlist Straat. Round them all up.

'If none of us go, nothing will happen.'

'You're making it even worse. This is insubordination, Metdepenningen!'

Gaston leans in towards him. 'Don't exaggerate, chief. Leave it. We'll talk him round.'

Lode looks at the rest of us, shakes his head and leaves without wasting another breath on it. I waver. I don't want it to end like this. I can't see myself being beaten into submission in a camp, surrounded by victims and swine, begging for a scrap of bread and finally realizing that it was my own fault, that I was the one who had stopped the wheel of fate forever.

We're gathered in a deathly quiet Terlist Straat. This time there are no Germans present. This time we really are alone. The names are shared out. There are about twenty of us, maybe more. Two of us are guarding the synagogue in the street. That's where we have to lock them up.

Gaston says again that we shouldn't make a fuss. I sigh.

'We're going to stay calm, Wilfried. Just knock on the door and—'

'Be polite?'

It's Gaston's turn to sigh. We're spread out in front of the doors in groups of two. We all knock at the same time. 'Open up! Police!' It almost echoes in such a quiet street, but that doesn't last long. Pandemonium bursts out almost immediately. Cries and shrieks from the houses. We can't even hear each other speak. Our door opens slightly.

"Teitelboim, Abraham?'

Through the crack we see an elderly man with a beard. He shakes his head. There are tears in his eyes. He's in his nightshirt. '*Nein, nein, nein…*' he whispers.

'Get everyone in your family dressed and pack some food. Please hurry.'

The man tries to slam the door on us, as if we're hawkers with products he doesn't want, but Gaston has his foot in the gap and pushes the door open. Children look out at us from the stairs. Total fear, fear you can never forget. My partner tries again. 'Please stay calm. Get dressed and come with us.' Two women start shouting at once. The waiting takes forever. What can I say? The waiting is getting on my bloody nerves. Finally they're ready. But they start begging, one after the other. One of the women holds some jewellery in front of our noses. '*Bitte, bitte…*'

We push them out the door. On the street the chaos is complete. But as soon as people see that there are no Germans involved, resistance grows. People pull on our sleeves asking for an explanation, '*Was haben wir getan?*' and plead, '*Bitte, bitte…*' But also swear, '*Bastarde! Bastarde!*' and curse us, '*Schande über euch!*' We drag the Teitelboim family to the synagogue. One of the women stumbles while hanging off my arm to beg for mercy. I drag her over the cobbles. Gaston raises his truncheon menacingly. Meanwhile some of our fellow policemen are simply hitting them, in a total frenzy, completely alone in their rage. They're all yelling themselves hoarse. I see one who has to be pulled off a Jew: he was beside himself and wouldn't stop kicking him. For a moment I can't work out who it is who is being so excessive, then suddenly I see the Finger's bony face under his helmet. He sees me looking at him and winks. 'Now the moment's come,' I read in his eyes, 'prove you're not a mole.' It feels like wet shit being rubbed in my face. The Finger tries to catch my eye again, then shrugs, and resumes his kicking.

Blood on the street. People crying, scratching, biting.

'Wilfried, careful! You almost lost one!'

I go after a boy of about seventeen. The street is closed off. He has nowhere to go. Like a child playing a game, he starts zigzagging in the hope of shaking me off. I kick his legs out from under him and try to grab him by the collar. His sudden hatred lashes out. He scores my face with his nails. I punch him. Then again. I drag him over the cobbles. His mother cries out for compassion. She hammers my chest with both hands. I grab her by the neck. We shove them into the synagogue. And so it goes on. At the next house on our list a madman spits in my face. A second later he's on his knees begging for mercy. 'Sir, come on, please…' I say, again as politely as I can. I take him by the shoulder. He lets himself almost fall down the stairs, a sack of rags, suddenly hardly a man at all. Then he just walks along beside me in shame, as if he has let himself be carried away by insanity and now thinks he is acting reasonably again.

Then I see Gus, his face covered with blood. He's standing there weeping, snot running out of his nose. The knee in my balls is immediately forgotten. Seeing someone like him like this is unbearable. I grab him by the elbow.

'Where are you hurt?'

'Hurt? No…' Gus sputters. 'We… I.' He takes a deep breath and tries to wipe the blood off his face. Again he says, 'We… I.' After a few attempts he gets it out, in the middle of the enormous racket. 'This bloke opens the door, sticks his chin out and cuts his own throat with a razor. He spurted fucking blood all over me. And inside… inside…' Gus tries to get a hold of himself while wiping the blood off his face. 'And inside they're dead… All dead at the table. A woman and… five children. Dead as doornails. What is this?…'

Gaston shouts at me. 'Come on, lad, don't stop!' Gus waves his hand as if he has everything under control again. 'I'm fine. Go do your job…'

Gaston is pounding on a front door. 'We'll have to kick it in…' On the third attempt the lock splinters. Someone upstairs shouts down that there aren't any Jews here. Loud swearing follows. 'What have you fuckers done to my door!' We only just evade a full chamber pot that comes smashing down on the floor in front of us and then storm upstairs, knocking a small table over in our rush. A vase topples. We kick in one door after the other on the first floor. 'I'll file a complaint!' shouts a skinny man with not too many teeth. He's standing there in his pyjamas trembling with fury. His wife is quivering in bed with her face in her hands and a pink nightcap on her head. 'Is your name Herschell?' The man hurls his papers in my face. No, evidently not Herschell. And without the word 'Jew' stamped on his card either. 'Our apologies, Mr Vanderwalle.'

'This won't be the last of this, you morons.'

Outside people are crying, gathered around a child who lies quivering spastically on the cobblestones. He's drooling and his eyes have rolled back in his head as he convulses like a freshly slaughtered rabbit. One of us picks him up roughly and carries him off.

It takes hours before we've got them all in the synagogue. Once inside they won't stop pounding on the door and shouting. Then we hear the trucks arrive.

Gaston and I are given a reprimand for having kicked in the wrong door.

'Straight from the mayor, men. He's furious.'

We shrug. The things that happened in Terlist Straat are still eating away at me. Am I the only one? We will forget it together, presumably. Together we will forget it, because all at once I'm one of them again, after what we have been forced to do together.

Lode gets a reprimand too, also straight from the mayor.

'You know why he's not being sent to Breendonk?' Gaston's voice is dripping with venom. 'Because we did what had to be done. We did the dirty work without him. The Germans have got what they wanted. You see that, don't you? That's why he's still home.' He spits on the station floor. 'I need a beer.' He throws down the cigarette he's only just started smoking.

'Keep it respectable, Gaston,' the chief inspector shouts.

Yeah, keep it respectable.

A BUSTED HIP, HALF A MAN

A BUSTED HIP, HALF A MAN. Yes, that's the reason it's taken me months to take up my pen again, dear great-grandson. I feel like I've let you down, as if you've been waiting in vain for the continuation of my story. That's total rubbish, of course, as so far you haven't seen a word of what I've written. I spent late winter and early spring in hospital and it felt like I had jinxed myself. How many times had I refused to worry about slipping and breaking something? I always pictured it out on the street in front of everyone, causing pain and deep humiliation. But it happened inside. I was completely alone and the humiliation went deeper than I could have ever imagined.

As usual I was looking for something. Nicole had long since gone home. I was reading through the last pages of what I had just written and I was stuck. Or rather, I was digressing. That was it. I know what else I have to tell you, it's not that, but suddenly I felt overcome by revulsion. I was sick of myself. I saw my life as a careless pencil line and suddenly longed for some Supreme Being to pick up a rubber and rub me out. I saw that Being blowing on the page. Pfff, and I was gone. It had been a long time since I'd felt like that. Enough. That was the word. And the older you get, the more you feel obliged to fight against that one word and the longing it contains. You know that I survived your grandfather, my son. Emaciated, he lay in bed, locked in a wrestling match with time. Not to live longer, more the reverse. He was counting down the seconds, filling the time that creeps by between the moment you've had enough and death. Watching my own son suffer like that was perverse, a punishment invented by a vile God. Despite their mistrust, they'd let me in to see him, with dirty looks from all sides, his too, but I insisted and he no longer had the strength to show me the door of his hospital room. 'Son,' I said, 'son…' He shook his head, long since a father himself, of course, and stared at me defiantly. 'I've had enough. They can come and get me.' That hit me so deep, as if I alone had subjected him to this life, personally sowing the seeds of his cancer, poisoning him from the very beginning, and his only act of resistance to me was his own complete surrender. I've had enough… 'What about me?' I thought in that instant. He was overtaking his own father with his longing. Some fathers would say, 'I've had my fill, take me instead.' But not me. Only after his death did I too sometimes feel like I'd had enough and I'd pronounce that word as if at a dress rehearsal, without consequences, an echo of the curse my own son had called down on himself, infecting me in the process.

I still knew what to do when I felt that revulsion. I needed to pick myself up again immediately. But melancholy and other sombre feelings are not easy to shake. That was when I remembered a purple envelope filled with family photos. I thought it might console me, although afterwards you always realize that photos are more likely to deepen the gloom. After all, darkness craves more darkness. I searched my whole library, even looking behind the rows of books, shaking some in the hope that the little treasure might be hidden between the pages, but to no avail. Exhausted after several hours of searching, I lowered myself into my recliner, my easy chair, clicked it back and, in that instant, saw at the very top of the bookcase the protruding corner of a purple envelope. How stupid would you have to be to keep something like that in such an impossible spot, exposed, gathering dust and, above all, so high up? Sometimes, often even, people fall victim to their own duplicity. To ask the question was to answer it. I'd put that envelope so high up to stop myself from throwing it away because that was something I couldn't bear the thought of. Now it happens that years ago I had one of those wooden library ladders made to order and... You see where I'm headed, don't you? That's right, this doddery old fool, with, in that instant, nothing but dog food for brains, clambered up like a young buck, didn't dare go any further than the second-last step, reached up ineffectively, ventured a quivering step higher after all, lost his balance and fell down arse and all. Right on my left hip. Crack, said the bone. Unbelievable pain shot through my body from my big toe to the back of my head. It was like a big fat Japanese wrestler had jumped on top of me with his full weight and snapped my bones like so many twigs. For the first time in my adult life I called out for my mother. It came of its own accord and the pain was so immense I wasn't even surprised. I won't spare you the details, as I've resolved to never do that on these pages, and that's why I will now inform you that your poor great-grandfather shat himself completely and lost all control over his bladder. I lay there totally helpless and nowhere near a telephone all evening, all night and through the early morning until Nicole arrived. She walked in with her nose turned up—that's something I'll never forget. The stench must have been unbearable. My throat was too hoarse to cry any more, but I did it anyway.

They patched me up in hospital, St Vincent's, of course, and you're supposed to talk about how dedicated and loving the nursing staff were, but that's not something I can bring myself to say, no matter how true it is according to Nicole. People who empty your bedpan, stick a tube up your dick and wash your body from arse to nostril while constantly trying to strike up a conversation are nothing but a plague. I can't see them any other way. From the first day to the last, almost all I said was, 'I want to get out of here, this is hell.' There was only one solace: morphine. I had never been on a pain pump before and, those first few days in particular, I was very pleased to make its acquaintance. Your generation and your father's are not averse to drugs, I know that, I wasn't born yesterday. But if you ask me, your wacky baccy and the powder some of you snort up your nose don't come close to the fabulous haze called morphine. God, the pleasure of it! It wasn't long before I was insisting that I suffered from a particularly low pain threshold and they just went along with it, probably to be done with my whinging. Morphine dreams pack a punch and it's not even much of a problem when the dream and so-called reality start to bleed into each other as if a gentle rain is merging the colours of a painting left out by an amateur painter who went inside for a hearty dinner with a glass of wine when the sun was blazing down out of a cloudless sky and has only noticed hours later that the weather is no longer particularly summery and his landscape has taken on another form. Suddenly naked women were parading around me inviting me to snuffle up the smells of their bodies, especially between their legs. Feelings I thought I had lost forever rose up inside me. Your great-grandmother was alive again and looking gorgeous under a parasol, sipping a cup of tea, while watching happily and with undisguised pleasure as I abandoned all restraint in a forest of nymphs. My pubic hair was garlanded with a daisy chain, my proud member stood firm, wild boar grunted contentedly in the sun, and two warm mothering mouths were sucking my nipples. I was French kissing like a champion and comparing the saliva of these mythic females like a connoisseur of sweet wine. Love? To be sure, it was an overwhelming love without pain or sorrow, guilt or jealousy. Everything had become one, like those crazy Hindus once wrote in their Kama Sutra. At the same time I experienced the ecstasy Lucretius must have felt while writing his long poem about the building blocks of life, a book I had devoured not that long before with some admiration and even a certain sense of loneliness. All atoms, all one. After a while there was also darkness, I don't mind admitting it, but that didn't stop me from pressing the pain pump again to forget my hip and the bedpan under my bum. The darkness took the form of a work of art under construction, a kind of temple on a piece of waste ground where hippyish youngsters were doing the building work while performing strange rituals to usher in the end of days. A granny took me by the hand and led me deeper into that artwork. Most of the hippies turned out to speak German, but there was also English and I even heard some Dutch. The old lady showed unsuspected vigour and resolution and dragged me deeper into the musty-smelling dark. I heard singing and the sound of someone digging. 'There he is,' the old dear said, and I made out the shape of a young lad, seventeen or thereabouts, just like you, or have you turned eighteen by now, or even nineteen? 'Hello, friend. Everything OK?' I asked. The digging stopped. The boy turned his face towards me and something cold took hold of me. 'My name is Wilfried,' I said, suddenly trembling. The boy gave an impassive smile, as if wearing a mask that had suddenly come to life, and said, 'I know. And you know who I am too…' Behind me I heard the old woman clucking like a spiteful turkey, a bit like the sound Muslim women make at weddings, but joyless and, above all, implacable. 'Yes,' I said, 'I know who you are. You're Angelo.' The mask froze on the boy's face and I felt the woman's nails digging into my bony back. 'You're the only one who knows how filthy it is,' she said, and suddenly I was back in that bed at St Vincent's resolving to keep off the pump until at least midday, no matter how gruesome that prospect seemed at that moment. In the days that followed there were no daisies draped around my paltry manhood and it was mostly family who came to haunt me. One in particular tormented me mercilessly: my granddaughter, your father's sister, your late aunt, who constantly drove me beyond the edge of a terrible rage that took me a long time to shake. 'It's me in those pictures,' she screamed, 'the photos you were looking for, the photos that made you land on your arse…' And then I saw something I had forgotten during the fall: the envelope falling down to the floor alongside me. From then on the morphine didn't give me a moment's peace. Louder and louder I begged them to take me back home with the gnawing pain that remained and yet, eventually, proved manageable without drugs. Finally, I was discharged and delivered up to Nicole and the quiet of my own flat. If thoroughly rested, the hip would come good, they assured me. I'd still be a lively old fellow with a relatively supple body. But I knew better. A busted hip, half a man. Cobbled together.

Although she sadly took her own life before you were born and never even saw you, your Aunty Hilde is inescapable. Her story is tied to us all, including you. Her story is in that purple envelope, visible in the countless photos I have of her, the ones I've looked at so many times with tears in my eyes and then, disgusted with myself, put away again, cursing the envelope without ever being able to bring myself to throw it away. Maybe that's why I'm writing all this down for you, because it's taken me years to accept the idea of that bond. That's something I think I've only realized now, after the fall and all that stupid pain. I'm writing to you to make it clear that everything is bound up together and that was also the cause of the pain that led Hilde to kill herself. When I think back on her (something I've done all too often these last few weeks) she loses her humanity and that makes me furious at her all over again. I try to summon up details of her life. The way she laughed... always with a sharp edge, it seemed to me. If a cat could laugh it would pull a face like Hilde's. Her laughter always sounded like she was ridiculing the world, as if despite her youth she really could see through everything. She'd joke about politicians, about anyone with power and prestige, and the phrase she'd always use was 'poor baby'. That was so killing, the way she said it. My wife couldn't cope with her sarcasm. 'She's got an old soul,' she would say after

173

our granddaughter had come over for afternoon tea and gone home again, 'and that's never good. You shouldn't know that much at her age.'

'She *thinks* she knows things, Mother.'

'You think that's all it is, Father. You're having yourself on.'

What Hilde managed to pierce most effortlessly was pretence. An ability that went back to when she was very little. When St Nicholas appeared at the door with his sack full of presents and her brother, your father, was trembling with fear even though he'd already stopped believing, Hilde greeting the wigged and bearded, fully costumed saint with a terse but fatal, 'Hello, Uncle Lode.' Lode was so bowled over, he used the expression for years afterwards to indicate that he was onto something and people shouldn't try to mess him around. He'd say, 'Bleeding heck. Hello, Uncle Lode.' And every time we'd both burst out laughing and see little Hilde before us, me as a proud grandfather and him as an equally proud great-uncle. That must sound like a pleasant memory, but thinking back on it now I am furious with Lode. If he was anywhere nearby I'd ram his head through a fucking window. Not that anything like that's possible any more. He's been dead and buried at Schoonselhof for quite a while now.

Spring is almost over and I realize I've shut myself off from the world for months. I haven't been reading the papers; I haven't even held a book. Nicole and me, that was it. For months. Even you, dear boy, I've hardly given a second thought. But that's over now. I can walk again without any pain. 'It's a medical miracle,' says the doctor, suddenly relieved that his professional optimism turned out to be a prediction after all. What does someone like that know about being cursed? Even worse, what does someone like that know about freedom? People try to stay out of the clutches of the white coats as long as possible. It's a kind of race against time, but on crutches, with your own body as both stakes and trophy. You mustn't ever submit to those blokes, never let them look you over, unless it's in circumstances beyond your control or because of a fall like mine. As soon as they get their claws into you, your body is theirs. They postpone your death without even taking you into consideration. Before you've realized what's happening, they'll have you on a drip with purgatory seeping into your veins and keep you there for months. One minute you're at death's door and begging admission, and the next thing you know, they've turned you into a kind of earthbound chemical vat. And that's what makes me so furious, that you swallow the illusion of freedom all along and then, right at the end, give yourself over to unfreedom. In the end not even the prospect of death is a comfort, but the whispered hope of recovery is deployed like a little ball bouncing around a roulette table, your body turned into the outcome of a wager against the eternal bank, funded by a less than eternal savings account, betting against an inevitability that all the chemicals in the Port of Antwerp can't prevent. And no matter how long it lasts, you end up going bankrupt at your and everyone else's expense and a few white coats do well out of it, their hands in the till along with the pill peddlers' and the chemical conglomerates'. Meanwhile the blessings of science are praised with delirious sentences like 'It's amazing what they can do these days'. To that end they have you stumbling to death like an exhausted galley slave. Shuffling drowsy-headed through the corridors of their hospitals in your pyjamas, chained to a drip, they praise your courage and fighting spirit, as if the struggle has only just begun. Courage? Is this what they call courage? What bloody good does it do you? You reach the finishing line penniless and completely defeated, unfree after all. That mustn't ever happen. I'd rather die like a dog on the street. *That* is courage.

Nicole, however, watches over me like a German shepherd. Not that I suspect her of collaborating with those who want my old body in their bed and on their drip. No, she's not like that: her mistrust of those legal drug dealers seems almost as great as my own. But when it comes down to it, she will reach for the telephone, call the ambulance and, sighing deeply and whispering that there's no alternative, finally deliver my body up to chemical torment. For the moment she's popped out to do some shopping and freedom beckons, something beckons, something tells me I must go out now. Unaccompanied for the first time, I walk down the street to Quinten Matsijs Lei, catching my breath on Loos Plaats, on one of the cold white blocks that can't decide whether they're art or street furniture and which vaguely resemble a wolf's hook. There is a flame burning in one of my hips that flares up at the slightest exertion, a pilot light fuelled by the fear of falling again and becoming permanently crippled.

Didn't I write somewhere here that I've never known fear in my life? It turns out that's a load of rubbish, and it always was, too. I promise that I will no longer conceal my blindness to my own fear. My untrustworthy body has brought that message home to me. Just like all those other voices in everyone's head, your fear is something you can talk to. You can even bargain with it, just never trust it. Keep your fear at a distance, don't entrust it with your wallet, never lend it to a woman you love and refuse politely when it offers to take you on a trip. Tell fear you know what it is and that's enough for you. Tell it you know it's a teacher. No, people everywhere cry, that's totally wrong: fear is a poor counsellor. Maybe, but it does teach you what it means to live intensely, to value a lie, to play the game, all as long as you're able to keep it at arm's length.

I'm panting, not just because of the effort, but mainly because of my suddenly rewon freedom, which is starting to feel less reckless. Sweat trickles down the inside of my collar. Then I see two army trucks driving up onto the central reservation in front of the police station. Paras with machine guns jump out. Two by two they move east into the city. Four of them give me a friendly nod as they pass on their way to Brialmont Lei. Two take up position in the middle of the street in front of a Jewish school. The other two move on. The two at the school light up cigarettes while a crowd of children come out to race home on their brightly coloured hand-me-down pushbikes. I wait until most of the mob has disappeared and then stand up. I find it less difficult than I expected. After reaching the school I ask if the revolution has broken out. A blonde para of about twenty laughs and tells me they're here for security reasons. 'We're here for you too,' the other adds. I put on an expression that is as innocent as possible and say, 'Thank you.' Has the world gone mad during my quarantine? At the end of Brialmont Lei I see another two standing on the other side of the railway line, close to the synagogue in Oosten Straat.

I turn left into Mercator Straat and head home with a head full of questions.

Unfortunately, Nicole is already back. Of course, she gives me a dressing-down. And this and that. I could have been dead and what would she have done then? I should be relieved it turned out so well! I can count my lucky stars!

'I saw some soldiers,' I say, hoping to calm her down a little.

'They've been here for months!' she snaps from the kitchen.

Months?

'It's all propaganda!' she tells me. 'They're trying to pull the wool over our eyes.'

They're always trying to pull the wool over our eyes, son, and don't you ever forget it. I learnt that long ago, as I told you much earlier. People tell you who they are and what they've come to do in your life and you just have to believe them. Here is your father. Here is your mother. We're here to protect you.

'How long are they here for?' I shout through to the kitchen because it's always amusing to wind up Nicole with her undoubtedly extremist left-wing sympathies.

'Nobody bloody knows!'

'And the police?'

That goes unanswered.

This city is fond of a firm hand now and then. And when someone tells her off, she responds like a whore in a clip joint, or *cabardouche* as they call it here. Talk about law and order and this city starts to coo. She runs a finger over the rim of her champagne glass, looks deep into the eyes of yet another papa who wants it all stricter and then pants, 'Tell me more about discipline and security on the streets?' Order always gets her hot at first, or freedom too for that matter, if that's what's being held up to her. After all, they can offer her anything. The papa who's proposing it just has to come over as self-confident, that's all, and what's he's actually arguing for doesn't really matter. That leads to the kind of misunderstanding that's typical of johns. A papa like that thinks the prize is already his. You'd do the same if a city spread her legs for you like a cheerful slut. But this city gets bored in the end. Sometimes it takes years, but finally she's overcome by her characteristic ennui. The rancour festering in her gall bladder takes charge. Suddenly she views everything with suspicion. The man she put her faith in most of all, the stern father, becomes a figure of fun: she laughs behind his back at first, then more and more openly in his face. Authority is nice, but not always, not when it's unrelenting, not when it's really serious. This city sometimes has a public love for uniforms. She gives short shrift to those who attack the cops. But that doesn't detract from her conviction that every individual cop is probably a loser who needs a uniform to be someone, especially those who lack a sense of humour. Because much is forgiven here if dished up with humour. This city is fickle, with a tendency to hypocrisy, but a thirst for pleasure. She loves hearty, unsparing laughter, but likes to play the victim too and doesn't feel obliged to be fair when calling others to account. A respectable person shits on someone else; this city is shameless enough to shit in her own bed and blame someone else. What's in her heart? That's something I've asked myself far too many times and sold others much too much bull about. But when I feel something, I know it too. Because that's what this old man tells himself: after all these years there's no barrier between his heart and his head, just like the way this city wears her heart on her sleeve and sees her feelings as thoughts or insights. Deep inside this city there is a lack of self-love, she's just not that keen on herself. She has a split personality, it's sometimes claimed, ready to be divided into two diametrically opposed creeds that can't bear the sight of each other. But that's too simple. Mainly she lets herself be divided because she doesn't know what else to do. Put her under a new regime and she will stay calm and submit to discipline, reluctantly or gladly, grumbling quietly or rejoicing as if a new Messiah has arrived. But what really unites her is mistrust and a horror of looking in the mirror. She'd let herself be rebuilt over and over again rather than undergo that. She doesn't love herself, not really, and neither a stern papa nor one who offers more freedom, neither gruff words nor swinging hips, neither a new broom nor a celebration of the arts can fix that. Those who don't love themselves can't love others, that's what the self-help books say. Bollocks. This city can do that, it's just that her love is always a little too sentimental or too provisional, too showy to be genuine or simply too excessive, that's possible too.

'Who's excessive?'

Without any warning Nicole puts a bowl down in front of me.

'Time for your porridge.'

And while I, despite not wanting it at all, obediently shovel down that old-fashioned stodge, I imagine you looking at me and wordlessly asking when I'm finally going to get back to the war again.

Since the night the rest of us rounded up the Jews in Terlist Straat, Lode has been shunned at the station. I'm virtually the only one who still says hello to him in the corridors. To the other policemen he's a coward who has fouled his own nest by refusing to go on the raid. Meanwhile their doubts about me have almost completely faded. With one exception. As far as Eduard Vingerhoets is concerned, I will never belong, never ever, over his dead body, and nobody's going to talk him round.

I'm sitting in the room that serves as our canteen. This male retreat seems completely off limits to the cleaning ladies. The heating's buggered, the ashtrays are invariably overflowing, the tabletops are marked with sticky rings that are flecked with crumbs and ashes, and one of the windows looking out on the rear of a building on Keyser Lei doesn't shut properly. That last bit's not a problem; at least that way we get some fresh air, although the smell of the last shift's cigarettes is still slow to dissipate. I've just started my sandwiches when the Finger comes in. He sits down at my table. It's 2 p.m. There's nobody else there. My physical revulsion for Mr Vingerhoets increases when I see what he's pulled out: a fried herring wrapped in newspaper. Herring again, always herring. This year it's on the menu in every home. A miraculous catch, people laugh scornfully, it's the King of Fishers Himself helping us through these dark days. Although these days His ravaged body on the cross mostly torments people by making them think of a juicy steak. Take this, all of you, and eat of it.

'Friday, fish day,' the Finger grins to no one in particular before starting to pick at the fish. The stench would make you forget any smell of tobacco. I can't taste my sandwiches any more, but I'm not going to give him the satisfaction. I won't leave until I've eaten every last dry crumb, or no, I'll roll a cigarette first and smoke it at my leisure. The bastard can dig into a piece of rotting blubber right next to me for all I care,

I'll never let him intimidate me. If it ever happens, in a brief moment of weakness, I'll be finished. He'll have me in his cage and throw away the key.

'A penny for your thoughts, Wils.'

'Get stuffed.'

'Careful now, I've got an extra stripe on my shoulder.' For the umpteenth time he aims his index finger at me as if it's a pistol. He grins. Blokes like him don't care about rank or position, that's not what counts in their circle. The Fingers of this world exist to fuck things up even more than they were before. Under a previous regime there would have been a better chance of them staying under the radar. Men like him are always pushing the limits of what's allowed and there's always a high risk of their being careless and getting caught. With the current rulers it's different: under them they have the opportunity of a flourishing career because of their reck-lessness, the much too blatant delight they take in it all. Now there's more scope for what used to be unthinkable or, to put it differently, let's say a change of regime always breeds a new variety of scum.

'You're a Jew-lover, Wils, you can't fool me. A stooge of the plutocracy, that's what you are.'

'Think what you like.'

'Very generous of you, punk. Thank you! I know you warned the local Abes in the summer so they had a chance to get away. No doubt they paid you well for it. Others profited too. But you're a special case, Wils. You've got yourself covered. You know what I think when I see you drinking a beer with our goateed friend in the Raven? You know what I think? I think, just wait. That's all. Just wait. Because fellers like you always slip up. Fellers like you get cocky. You should see your mug. The arrogance. Wils, enjoy it while you can… It won't be long. And you, we won't beat up in a cellar somewhere before throwing you off a dock like a crushed walnut. No, we'll gift-wrap you and hand you over to the men in leather coats.'

Not one second does the Finger stop chewing. His rodent teeth keep grinding away with his mouth half open. It's like his words are amplified, trumpeting out of his nose and echoing off the nicotine-stained walls.

'Careful with those bones,' I say in a voice that's thin after all because of the fright he's put into me. 'I wouldn't want to see you choke.'

Words I regret even before they've died away. Unfortunately sentences like that always hang in the air. Time underlines them, drawing them out and making them resonate. The Finger shakes his head and starts to chuckle. 'You're something else, Wils. Fuck me, you're really asking for it. You really don't know who I am.'

I start to roll the cigarette as slowly as possible, despite still having two untouched sandwiches in my lunchbox. I've only just lit it when he starts to sneeze.

'Pardon,' he says immediately, as if he still owes me, the mole, the treacherous bastard, a duty of politeness. But the sneezing doesn't stop and gets even more intense. Hachoo. Again. Hachoo. Bits of fish spray out of his mouth. I lean back as far as I can. His tiny red eyes are suddenly flooded. I stare at that body that no longer knows what to do with itself, abruptly at the mercy of the tickling in that enormous nose and as ineffectual as an overgrown child's. He manages to blurt, 'What the hell's this?' Yes, what's going on with all this sneezing, I think to myself? Eduard Vingerhoets unbuttons his uniform jacket double-quick and sneezes again. Tears roll down his badly shaved cheeks. Another sneeze. His nostrils flare. With his crumpled wet eyes closed, he reaches for his inside pocket. A hankie with light-blue stripes appears. Immediately he presses it to his red and swollen nose. But his brusque fumbling has also caused his wallet to flip out. It's lying on the floor, open and defenceless. In a flash I see a deckle-edge photo of him in a dark suit next to a smiling woman and two children, whose faces have popped up under her hefty bosom, a son and daughter with their mother's sparkling eyes. A dried flower covers the rest of the family portrait. How proud he looks in that photo, how loving too, how… Between two sneezing fits, he snatches the wallet away.

'Don't forget, Wils…' he squeaks, 'don't forget. I know where you live.' He stuffs the wallet back in next to his heart and hurries out of the canteen with the hankie pressed firmly to his nose. I hear him sneeze again on the stairs. Haaa-choo. He's left the half-eaten fish on the table in the greasy paper. I stub my cigarette out on it. My hand is shaking, not Angelo's.

As far as my duty roster allows, I am meant to spend my Sundays with my sweetheart's family. Under no circumstances may I refuse the midday meal. The one time I tried to get out of it, it caused an almighty crisis. 'So, you can't have been so very sick,' I heard the following week, seeing as I'd been spotted strolling through Harmonie Park with a mate who later took me to the Welcome Inn in the German quarter for a beer. Complete twaddle—I'd spent the whole day in bed. Yvette's recriminations were furious, but behind her back Lode was winking at me. The nasty sod had made it all up to ensure that from then on I would feel completely obliged to turn out on parade every Sunday freshly washed and shaven and wearing a neatly ironed white shirt.

Yvette's father recently assigned me a fixed spot at the table, to his left. Directly opposite me sits his son with my girl next to him and Mother sits at the other end of the table. She brings the soup in from the kitchen and dishes it out at the table. She towers over us and follows a strict order. First Father gets his soup, then I, as the guest, get mine, and then the others. We pass our bowls to her one after the other in that order, so she can slowly pour the soup into them. Father tastes his, blowing on it gently first with pursed lips. After he has given a nod of approval, everyone else is allowed to start. On Sundays hardly a word is said during the meal and a certain lethargy takes charge of us all. Wine is served and drunk by the men. One bottle, of course, never more.

After the meal the women do the washing-up; Father disappears behind his newspaper and Lode and I talk a little, sometimes in the living room, sometimes in his attic room, a privilege that occasionally provokes a jealous reaction from Yvette, as it goes without saying that never in a thousand years would it be possible for me to spend even a second alone with her in her bedroom. If we were caught there together, my only way of averting the scandal in the eyes of her father would be to ask him on the spot for her hand in marriage. The only thing we are permitted to do together is go out for a walk, but only after the washing-up has been done and tidied away, and that can sometimes, to our great annoyance, take a very long time.

Lode leads the way up the steep stairs to the attic. Yvette catches my eye for a moment and purses her lips to blow me a kiss. I give her a quick wink.

'Bleeding heck, I stuffed myself and now I feel like a slug...' Lode sighs and kicks his shoes under the bed as he enters the room. It's true. It's still a feast when you eat at a butcher's. Families like his don't need to do without. We're still getting by at home too, especially when my partner and I have managed to nab another black-marketeer, but otherwise it's moans and groans all round. The city and her residents are sick to death of rationing and can hardly bear the sight of yet more herring, as if the whole thing's a game that has gone on too long. There's a lot more begging too. Sometimes you see little children holding out their hands. They rarely get anything.

I sit down on Lode's bed and roll a cigarette. Standing at the washstand with his back to me, he picks up an earthen-ware pitcher and pours water into a bowl, yawning out loud. He takes off his waistcoat and tosses it on the nearest chair, under the skylight. In one movement his braces are off his shoulders and he's pulled off his white shirt and singlet to freshen himself up. Water splashes and drips on the stand's marble top. 'That's better!' he chuckles, flicking back his wet quiff. Droplets run down his back, shining in the autumn sun. He unbuttons his trousers and lowers them together with his underpants. Dancing on one leg and then the other, still without turning, he takes off everything, even his socks. The backs of his thighs are covered with soft, brownish-black hair that runs up to his buttocks. He lets some water run down his belly, goes up on tiptoes, presumably to tip some water over his cock and balls, and carries on washing. His whole body seems to be shouting out to me to enjoy its beauty. But at the same time he acts like nothing's going on, just a routine scrub in the coincidental presence of a friend. Nothing is said, neither of us makes a sound and that makes a mockery of this being somehow routine. I manage to cough or mutter 'Uh-huh', but that's as far as I get. His answer is equally inarticulate while his wet hands run a bar of soap over his buttocks. Again he bends forward to splash more water over his already-clean face, after which he slowly wipes the last suds off his behind with a flannel. The attic walls are closing in on me. My mouth is dry. I feel like the door's been locked. Whatever I do or say in the presence of this naked body, there will be no satisfaction in it, neither for him, nor for me. Meanwhile, deep in my gut, I hear Angelo roaring with laughter. Look at him sitting there on the bed, Wilfried Wils—the great thinker who knows no mercy and longs to lead a stirring life, imposing his will on others—watch him plummeting into embarrassment and banality, as normal as everyone else and therefore doomed to die a surreptitious poser who never managed to escape his predetermined existence. Lode glances over his shoulder at me. The look in his eyes is vulnerable yet proud, a look that evokes both lust and loathing in me, making my head spin.

'Could you pass the towel next to the bed?'

Without standing, I reach for it and chuck the stiff thing in his direction.

Slowly he starts to dry himself. The scent of soap, mixed with the smell of his masculinity, fills the still shrinking room. My brain starts to race like a rat in a maze of doors, corridors and potentially locked rooms. There has to be a way out somewhere. One man's lust is another man's opportunity, Angelo would say.

'I hope you realize,' I say hoarsely, 'who you have to watch out for.'

Still without turning around, still towelling himself off, he asks, 'Who?'

'Eduard Vingerhoets.'

'The Finger? I know what kind of bastard he is. Don't worry.'

'Ever since Terlist Straat he's had his eye on you. He's also the one who snitched to the Jerries about the Jews being warned.'

'How can you be so sure of that?' Lode gives me a sideways glance, slowly running the towel over the leg he's raised up on the chair. I see his balls dangling and think, 'Don't be daft, it's too dark in here, you're imagining things.'

'You know who I drink with. The Finger goes to the White Raven too sometimes.'

Lode turns towards me. He's draped the towel over his shoulders. His eyes are sparkling. I have to keep focused on his face; I mustn't let my gaze drift down.

'Something needs to be done about him. We know that too.'

'Who's we?'

Lode takes a step closer.

'Not you, at this stage.'

Another step closer. One of his fingers goes into his right ear to give it a hearty massage.

'Give us a bit of space…' I say. To avoid saying out loud, 'You're almost swinging your seriously engorged cock in my face as it is.'

It's over. The mood turns, everything deflates like a balloon. No more frog in my throat, no racing heartbeat, no slow movements. Lode turns his back immediately, forces his dick into his underpants and gets dressed.

Is it possible to regret not having done something you didn't want to do? Regretting something that couldn't be, yet somehow makes you feel guilty? Regretting it because you are who you are and the other is who he is? Regretting it because your heart is pounding all the same?

Lode stretches, gives an unconvincing smile. We smoke cigarettes, but can't find any more words for each other.

Yvette calls. I go downstairs.

On De Coninck Plein we walk hand in hand.

Behind the thick, fortress-like walls of the Atheneum I pull her up against me. We kiss. I run my tongue over hers. She sighs, 'Alone at last.'

Aunty Emma has slipped a note in our letterbox inviting us over for coffee at her house in Van den Nest Lei on Sunday: 'I hope everyone's well. You're all invited at four in the afternoon. It has been so long and so much has happened!'

'It's clean here,' my mother says, 'couldn't she come up? A letter of all things. She gets fancier by the minute.' Mother runs her fingers over the paper. 'She does have a beautiful hand. Always has.'

'I hope her German fancy man's not there,' Father growls, though he's unable to hide his curiosity.

'Maybe he prefers to spend his time at the Hulstkamp,' I laugh. Because that detail of her love story won't let go of me: the German stole her heart in Café Hulstkamp on Keyser Lei, once a place where poets and artists bought each other beers and attempted to bend the world to their will over a game of

dominoes. You could find Crazy Paulie there before he succumbed to consumption in some faraway rural village. Crazy
Paulie with his bearskin hat and his bold artistic flair who died
so very young. I never met him but I pick up stories about him
here and there. He went to the same school as me, where he
once, at the start of the previous war, gave a speech that no
one could follow because of his weak, reedy voice. Were his
festering lungs already playing tricks on him even then? As a
poet he was an example to many, but on me, his craziness was
wasted. Or actually, it wasn't, but my love for him is of the
kind that is so typical of this city, where admiration is always
mixed with profound envy. Because nobody who comes after
Crazy Paulie can compete with his playful spirit, his flight to
Berlin and the adventures he had there, his rebelliousness, his
boundless originality, his—yes, I admit it—pioneering, maybe
even the ailment that made him cough and splutter till the
end: he could hardly be more romantic. To think that Paul van
Ostaijen, Crazy Paulie, drank and flirted in the Hulstkamp,
that his spirit might even linger there yet, where Jerries now
buy drinks for local girls in the hope they'll spread their legs…
Why there of all fucking places? It's like gobbing in the face
of the Muse. At the same time, and I'm sorry to say so, but it's
just as likely that if Crazy Paulie's lungs hadn't let him down
and he'd been alive and well, he would have been pleased as
Punch to see the master race marching into his city for the
second time, when they would even demand a place in his own
local. Sorry, but it's just as likely he would have stood there
in a black shirt with his arm up, taking a supercilious delight
in brushing aside his own anti-war poems as juvenilia. You
never know. Who am I to hurl gobs of saliva at the Muse?

Just as likely and sorry to say, but nothing is holy, everything is in motion and nothing at all is true. It's death that makes the artist's life orderly, nestled in his now secure body of work, his immediately legendary preferences and whatever his friends choose to say about him. Death spares you embarrassments, choices that may prove regrettable. And when death fells a young poet, it's showing a hunger for beauty more than anything else. Those who live too long run a serious chance of ending up bunglers or bastards in other people's eyes. Angelo says, 'Lay that lily-white throat of yours on history's chopping block.' Unfortunately, to do that, to even feel the desire to be snuffed out by a premature death, you need the poems that raise your whole being over the threshold of obscurity. And I don't have them yet, and lately my hopes that they will one day find their way onto the page have been few and far between. My diary is a litany of woe and a poem I recently squeezed out of my pen while half-drunk caused me days of embarrassment. It was about 'gulls burning in the inferno' and the 'discipline of senselessness'. Where do I get that kitsch? That's no glorious copulation with the Muse—it's spilling your seed in an already crispy handkerchief. And as an aside, how is it even possible? With all the things I experience every day, the bastards I see, the threats I receive, life on a razor's edge in an occupied city, my poems should read like they've been written in my lifeblood. They should give hardened poetry connoisseurs a coronary. But what I've written up till now would leave even a schoolmistress from the la-di-da Lady's Academy in Lange Nieuw Straat pissing herself laughing before giving me a big wink and telling me I certainly have a lot to learn. 'Give me something lethal God I want to live.' Who wrote that? Not me, damn it, not me! Crazy Paulie, of course. Always that Crazy Paul van Ostaijen.

'Bring your girl to Aunty Emma's,' my mother blurts, as if the day's best thought has suddenly popped into her head.

'Out of the question,' I sigh.

'But you're hiding her from us!'

'What I find a bit rich,' I say, a little louder, 'is her still living there...'

Those who call themselves my parents fall silent.

'Now her Jewish bosses have been carted off...' I add.

'What kind of talk's that?' Father is immediately annoyed. 'That's none of our business.'

'Wear your uniform, Wilfried. She'll like that!'

Aunty Emma is in the hall and shining. She could easily pass for ten years younger, as if she spends her nights on a drip filled with the elixir of youth. There is a nip in the autumn air as she stands there in a summery floral frock with a deep neckline. She has been to the hairdresser's and her lips are painted a vibrant red. Father's eyes almost pop out of his head.

'Careful. You'll catch your death!' Mother hisses, suddenly fifteen years older, suddenly even more grotesquely wigged. Mother did sprinkle herself with lily of the valley an hour ago, something she rarely does and which led my father to decide she was losing her marbles.

'But our Wilfried is wearing his uniform! He looks so handsome! Come in, quick!'

We climb the wide marble stairs with our hands on a wrought-iron bannister decorated with creepers and black hearts. The first-floor doors, more like wooden gates, are wide open. A gramophone is playing. A male voice sings: '*Einmal wirst Du wieder bei mir sein...*' Persian carpets are spread over the floor of a large room. On a side table, encircled by a chaise longue, a burgundy divan and upholstered armchairs, is a beautiful cake, topped with fresh strawberries for fuck's sake.

'Goodness,' my father says, rubbing his trousers.

'Sit down, everyone! Make yourselves at home.'

We each choose a spot and sit down on the edge of our chairs, ready to leap up at any moment if some baroness or other should rebuke us. That's not entirely ridiculous; there are ghosts in this apartment.

'Tea? Coffee? Or would you like to go straight to cognac?' My aunt bares her pearly whites in a smile, as if posing for a pre-war brand of toothpaste.

Mother tries to take on the role of elder sister, she who knows when things are threatening to get out of hand, she who sees things coming while they're still light years away. 'Easy does it, Emmy. Coffee is fine.'

Father nods like a fish out of water.

'*Schatzi! Meine Gäste sind* here.'

Aunty Emma's German doesn't make me want to laugh. You hear attempts like that everywhere these days and who's to say I will ever master the language of Goethe? Through an open door at the rear we hear a hummed reply. I see my father rearrange himself his chair, as if surreptitiously farting. I hear him swallow. Mother straightens her back.

He appears smiling, still doing up the top button of his uniform.

Big. Red hair. *Mein Freund* Gregor.

And yes, the officer clicks his heels, brushes my mother's fingertips with his lips and gives my father and me robust handshakes. A textbook Prussian from head to toe. My heart is racing. I really would appreciate it if he didn't let on that we have seen each other before in a sleazy bar on België Lei. I am also picturing the way he rages and storms in the stories Meanbeard has told me. But now we're here together in the former residence of a wealthy Jewish family. He's in uniform and so am I.

'Very pleasing to meet you.'

'Almost right, darling.' Aunty Emma gives us a wink. 'It's important for him to learn our language, you know.'

'I'm sure it is,' says Father with forced joviality. In that very instant I think I hear him let go a quiet fart, awkwardly strangled, strained and nervous, like a child's at a strict boarding school.

Mother coughs.

Gregor winks at my aunt, clearly infatuated and—in the experienced hands of one of our women—therefore doomed to become a lapdog. Probably with a little missus waiting for him at home. But that doesn't matter, because it's war. What story will he have fed Aunty Emma? Something that came to him easily no doubt. After all, this SS swindler is very plausibly acting like he really has just met me for the first time. Not even his eyes give him away. My armpits are starting to get clammy. The song finishes and the gramophone starts to crackle. He gets up immediately and turns the record over in one flowing movement, like in a film.

'I can't get enough of him!' Aunty Emma laughs.

Revealing something that intimate is unheard of—it's not our way, not the way we do things in this city. Mother almost jumps up she's so shocked. But she suppresses it immediately. A different game is being played here, something foreign, from a different world, and everyone has to adapt.

Aunty Emma fidgets with her hair, suddenly exposed.

'*Warte mal!*' says Gregor, evidently struck by a bright idea. He lifts the stylus from the record and puts it back at the start of the song, walks over to Aunty Emma and holds out a hand.

'Please, Gregor... Not now...'

But her lover insists. Aunty Emma stands up, quickly tidies her hair and starts dancing with him. The two of them sway against each other, somewhat clumsily because of the difference in height. '*Komm zurück,*' gushes the male voice. '*Ich wa-a-a-arte auf dich, du bist für mich... mein Glück.*' They press closer together. Gregor's right hand is resting almost on my aunt's bottom. She has closed her eyes in the meantime, drifting off in a dream from the cinema. We sit there gawping at them. My father pats his trousers a few times uncomfortably, as if trying to tap along to the music. Completely mortified, Mother searches through her handbag, finds her embroidered hankie, buries her face in it and blows her nose. At last the song is over.

'*Soll ich?*' asks the SS officer, nodding at the cake.

'Bitter *sehr!*' his blissful flame answers.

And right away he cuts the cake delicately but without hesitating in equal pieces. Aunty Emma passes round the plates. We eat. No, it's more like unabashed feasting. Biting into whipped cream and staying polite—not easy. To everyone's relief none of us are required to say very much. Aunty Emma carries on with an explanation which soon descends into incomprehensibility, interrupted now and then by Gregor's chortling.

'*Und jetzt Cognac!*'

Gregor gently swirls the generously filled balloon glasses before handing them to us.

Mother refuses politely. Father pretends to hesitate briefly before accepting the glass and taking a sip. 'French, *natürlich!*'

Hearty laughter from Gregor and Aunty Emma. The German slaps his uniform trousers exuberantly as if it's the best joke he's heard in years.

Then he looks at me and says, '*Sie sind Polizist?*'

'*Jawohl*,' I say, '*und stolz darauf.*' Is it me or Angelo who feels compelled to claim to be proud of my job? Or is it the cognac racing through my veins?'

'Goodness!' cries Aunty Emma. 'Listen to him chattering away in German!'

Mother and Father look at me as if they have just realized they have been sheltering a monster all this time.

Gregor raises his glass high and gives me a droll wink as if I'm his ventriloquist's dummy.

'*Auf eine brillante Karriere!*'

'Cheers!' says Father, beating me to it.

The glasses clink against each other.

It's not long before Meanbeard lets me know how much '*mein Freund* Gregor' enjoyed our encounter.

'I knew he had a Mademoiselle tucked away somewhere, but her being a relative of yours… Well, that raises possibilities, possibilities for both of us.'

'Are you mad? Maybe you're not quite right in the head?'

'*Toutes les possibilités harmoniques et architecturales s'émouvront autour de ton siège.* That's a quote. From whom?'

'Rimbaud…' I guess, sick of his guessing games.

Meanbeard looks at me as if he wants to give me a kiss. '*Voilà!* You see for yourself how the forces are gathering round you. It's not like that for everyone. The world belongs to the young. They're the ones who have the opportunities. They're there for the taking along every young person's path. But you have to pay attention! Chances are there to be taken. Otherwise you betray the generosity of the universe and are doomed to live a life like any other. And yes, I know, that's not your intent. You can't fool me... Ah, who do we have here?'

All present in the White Raven look at the lady whose chestnut curls are peeking out from beneath a jaunty yellow cap, and especially at her legs, which are cheerfully braving the cold under a houndstooth coat and end in shoes with heels you would normally only ever see on cinema screens. Jenny's here again, her decline almost hidden under a careful layer of putty.

'You made me a promise,' she says to Meanbeard without greeting him first.

'Sweetness, come now! They have Export here, your favourite beer. Isn't that good news?'

'Save your jokes for someone else! You know I only drink white port.'

'Landlord! A white port.'

'And who's this young fellow?'

She looks like she came within an inch of pinching me on the cheek.

'We have met on a previous occasion, *Ma Dame.*'

'Get an earful of him. At least some people can still act civilified. Yes, go ahead and laugh... It's my own private word. I don't want to be rude, but sometimes I prefer to hear something of my own invention. Our mum had that too. After she found out our hairdresser was the goalie in his pub team she used to call him a nincompkeeper.'

We laugh. Jenny takes a big slug of the port and says she can go on for hours with all her made-up words.

'She's right!' Meanbeard crowed. 'She can go on for hours!'

'But I'm not in the mood for that today. So, friend, what's the story? You make me a promise and then I don't hear a thing. Or are you too embarrassed in front of your cultured pal here?'

'I'll leave you alone then,' I mutter, a little tetchy.

'No, don't,' Meanbeard hurries to say, 'no need. I promised our Jenny a little boutique, here close by, on Charlotta Lei…'

'Boutique is not the right word, eh, lover. The shop in question is a tobacconist's, as it says so grandly on the facade. Or would you like to turn it into a clothes shop? Then you can call it a boutique and you won't hear me complaining. I'd much rather have something like that than a smoky hole in the wall where blokes go for their baccy.' And, *gloop*, with that Jenny's port glass is empty. Meanbeard snaps his fingers at the landlord, but that's something you're not allowed to do in bars like this, not even when the boss is a friend of yours. The finger-snapping is therefore ignored. But Jenny holds her glass up in the air and the landlord soon trots over with the bottle. He tops her up without a word.

'A shop,' I say. 'Big plans.'

A contemptuous sigh escapes Jenny's lips, not so very loud, but enough to keep her paramour, her no-account lover, on his toes.

'It's a question of timing, not money,' Meanbeard continues quickly. '*Mein Freund* Gregor and I have to visit the fellow

198

sometime. It seems he has a Jewish shop assistant who doesn't always wear her star. She has to go, of course. That's easily fixed, probably next week. And then it's up to our Jenny, with her beautiful eyes and fine figure, to go in and ask sweetly if the shopkeeper doesn't happen to have a job for her.'

Jenny raises a gloved hand. 'The idea is still that I'll take over, isn't it? I've had enough of all these blokes telling me what to do. I want to be able to stand on my own two feet. I've really had enough of it. The things I've seen and had to put up with.'

'Not so fast, butterfly,' Meanbeard hushes her with pursed lips. 'One step at a time. Patience.'

I close the door of the White Raven behind me, well sloshed after a few too many beers. At the corner of Charlotta Lei and België Lei, a strong autumn wind lifts a stencilled sheet up from the cobbles, pushes it against my trouser legs, then deposits it next to a puddle full of rotting leaves. I plant my foot on it, read the heading and look round before picking it up and quickly secreting it away, because having this kind of publication in your possession is severely punished, maybe even with death if you're unlucky. Killed for the possession of clandestine words! Angelo grins. Everything counts now and everything is dangerous. I wrote it before, son, this is life on the razor's edge. Sometimes, like during a walk I just described in ever stiller streets with hardly anyone on them as dusk approaches, I see dramatic letters appearing on a screen, accompanied by stirring music, like posters for a film from a Germany that has long since disappeared and is already almost forgotten, although it's only ten years or so since German films like that were screening here too. 'Fear in the Metropolis!' 'Around Every Corner: Danger!' 'Terror on the Streets!' In retrospect they were dress rehearsals, films like drill sergeants shouting that the end is nigh, that the world could expect a criminal mastermind to emerge, that we would soon change into a blood-thirsty mob or a gang of indistinguishable slaves with downturned eyes and hanging heads, undergoing the scourge of a dictatorship propped up by our own leaders. Films like that have now been banned. Now shivers run down my spine when I read the leaflets produced at risk of their makers' lives. For years before the war, films and books depicted fear as if enticing us to one day to create a real occupied city where fear and all the rest of it are completely normal.

I pull the piece of paper out of my pocket and look at it again. The underground press's block letters are messy and smudged: 'First the Jews, now us!' No, it would be better to tear it up immediately instead of holding on to it as a keepsake. The wind carries the pieces of paper off one after the other. Then I see someone waving at me from the far side of the crossroads. It's Meanbeard. He calls my name.

'What did you say?' I shout back and start giggling because I sound so silly, so drunk, so pissed off my face. He keeps waving and gesturing for me to come towards him. He meets me on the corner of Lange Leem Straat.

'I saw you still standing there,' he pants. 'It's a bloody... It's...'

'What?'

'They just found him. The whole bar's in an uproar. It's un—'

'Who?'

'Didn't you hear the shot? Someone must have... How can we have not—'

'Please, calm down.'

Further along people are standing in a circle on the pavement in front of the White Raven. I see Jenny hurrying back into the bar, a gloved hand over her mouth. Meanbeard takes me by the arm. The circle grows a little wider. Eduard Vingerhoets is lying there. Something, probably a bullet, has turned the back of his skull to mush. His right arm is pointing at the door of the bar, his fingers curled as if he could almost reach the handle. It's like the Finger was put down just before the finishing line, just before a cold beer and a whore's warm bosom, put down just before it and therefore just in time. Lying next to him is a sheet of paper with letters stuck to it to form the sentence 'An eye for an eye.'

Meanbeard drops to his knees in the mud and rotting leaves. He bows his head and starts to sob quietly like a little boy who's pooed his pants and has nowhere to hide.

It seems the funeral was only sparsely attended. Meanbeard went, of course. Not me—I had to work. Every day the Finger's widow shows up at our door. The first time she was granted a meeting with the commissioner, who no doubt told her he had every available man on the case and it was only a matter of time before the culprit was caught. Rumour has it that one of the Finger's friends who works as a guard in the prison camp at Breendonk took revenge by clubbing three Communists to death, one after the other, in the middle of the inner courtyard with every prisoner—man, woman and child—forced to watch. But one story was immediately contradicted by another. For instance, that the three misfortunates were slaughtered by a whole gang in a night of fear and terror. Or not—or perhaps they were after all, but there was more to it, because first they cut off their balls. But we are also told that the friend, whose name no one knows, has had to take sick leave because of a nervous breakdown. Meanwhile the Finger's wife perseveres. With photos of her children in one hand and a wet hankie scrunched up in the other as a grieving aid, she has buttonholed every last one of us. Including me.

'He was so honest. Did you know him?'

'A man who always told it like it was, Mrs Vingerhoets. Absolutely.'

'The best father you could imagine. The children come first, that's what he always said.'

'It's so sad.'

'When are you going to pick those bastards up? They're terrorists! Sewer rats! Out on the street, when he was on duty… Have they no shame?'

Evidently nobody has had the heart to tell her that her late husband was discovered one step away from his favourite bar. Everybody knows what goes on in the White Raven, where the ladies let themselves be pleasured between two beers. 'That finger of his,' someone told me just after his death, 'he knew how to use it on those floozies.' Typical that somebody's dirty side only really becomes a topic of conversation when his cold body is lying on a marble slab.

The Finger's widow gives up eventually and stops coming to the station.

Some time later I hear she's on the booze and having it off with a postman. Apparently he's a Communist.

Everyone knows everything. But at the same time bugger all. Normally you'd think that the killing of a policeman would have every unit keyed up and ready to go, that a ruthless man-hunt would ensue until the murderer or murderers had been collared. But that's not how it works in an occupied city. A smokescreen goes up about 'current lines of enquiry' that are being followed closely. Even when he was alive you couldn't find many people who were keen on the Finger. His real friends are in the White Raven and no cops set foot in the place, apart from me. When he dies it's a sigh of relief more than anything that passes through the corridors of the Vesting Straat station. A man like him must have had ambitions. By his age he should have been a good bit further than one stripe more than me on his sleeve. A real promotion never came his way and that says enough. But the debt still has to be settled. A dead policeman demands reprisals, preferably without the intervention of any judges or courts. One's been crossed off on this side, then a few need to be crossed off on the other side, preferably without too much trouble or them having anything remotely to do with the case. The debt is settled by shadowy figures who are not necessarily on the force. Field Command announces 'the deportation of ten Communists as a reprisal for the murder of the police officer E. Vingerhoets'. Maybe that's why we're told those stories about that screw in Breendonk slaughtering Communists, even if most of them contradict each other. True or false, they show that the murder has not gone unavenged. At the end of the day the books must balance, that's what it comes down to. I no longer hear Meanbeard jabbering about vengeance. That tells me enough. It means people have been picked up and carted off, identified by Meanbeard and approved by *mein Freund* Gregor. Lode doesn't approach me about the Finger's death and I'm happy to leave it at that. Who's to say he had anything to do with it? Who's to say I had anything to do with it? A spider doesn't necessarily come rushing out at the slightest trembling of its web. It generally takes more vibrations, more people expressing their will, a larger group demanding a sacrifice or wanting to see some situation or other resolved. That's how things work these days. Maybe that's how they've always worked, but now action and reaction follow that trajectory, deeds and consequences, without any fuss, without any excuses, rough and merciless, unseen and in the dark, but with everyone's full knowledge.

A week later for a change there's something truly interesting to read in the orders of the day, which we are meant to consult every time we go on duty. We have been strictly forbidden with immediate effect—'*en vigueur avec effet immédiat*' as they would write in the statute book—from picking up work dodgers. Orders from the mayor! And the attorney general! Are the bigshots in the town hall starting to feel the heat on the backs of their necks?

'About bloody time,' Gaston says, wiping the beer froth off his lips.

'What difference does it make? How many times haven't we reported back that nobody was home? We never hauled in anyone unless they gave us a mouthful or we didn't like the look of them.'

'Come now, Wilfried! So cynical!'

Gaston laughs.

'And weren't the foreigners so-called work dodgers too?'

Gaston and I have stopped using the word 'Jew' in our conversations. A tacit agreement.

'Watch it, whippersnapper, or I won't buy you a beer.'

'Landlord! Another round!' I call.

'The cat's amongst the pigeons now. He's pulling out his wallet.'

After the beers have been put down on our table, Gaston bends towards me, amusement glinting in his eyes.

'Just between you and me, do you realize what this is going to lead to? I don't know if I've already told you this or not, but our inspector's actually a pal of mine—'

'You could have fooled me—'

Gaston grabs me by the shoulder and starts whispering. 'Don't tell anyone, but he's married to the daughter of, um… Wait. No, that's too difficult to explain. Anyway, someone in my family. And then you soon find out one thing and the other. Turns out this whole palaver about the ban on picking up work dodgers has gone off like a bomb at headquarters. Everyone with an extra stripe on his shoulder's shitting himself, all the way up to the commissioner, apparently. You understand that.'

'No, I don't understand it.'

'Come on, mate. Think it through. We've been picking up people the whole bloody time, foreigners, people from here… And guess what?' Gaston lowers his voice. 'Suddenly the word from town hall is that it's against the constitution. Get it? We've been breaking the law. And we are the law!' Gaston starts to chuckle. 'If anybody ever finds out... that we've been follow-ing orders that were completely illegal... Do you follow me?'

'Like a cyclist in the Tour de France.'

Gaston laughs even louder. 'I'll have to remember that one. Anyway, you can ride at the front of the peloton, as quick and smart as you are. Look, lad, to be honest, I don't want to make a fuss about it, but... this is priceless!'

Priceless indeed. Up to this point our actions have been guided by a tacit agreement: there is no alternative and, what's more, everything's normal. But some people's fear of a day of reckoning has begun to grow. They've started to shift responsibility: from the attorney general to the mayor, from the mayor to the police commissioner, and so on all the way along. In the middle section of the facade of the town hall, where the mayor acts like he's in charge, one can admire two statues that represent the virtues of this city. On the left, fash-ioned after the delusions of ancient Greece, we have Justitia, and on the right, equally classical and therefore harking back to our unquestionably glorious past, Prudentia. In wartime, if not generally, justice is at most a pious afterthought, or something to work on when there happens to be time left over after the real challenges, and that gives more scope for the virtue of prudence. Prudentia is depicted with a mirror in one hand and a snake coiled around the other. The mirror presumably stands for self-knowledge rather than vanity and the snake refers to her ability to maintain control at all times. Prudentia is about making the right decision at the right time. The painter Breughel was working in this city when the town hall was built and his print representing prudence shows food being harvested and salted while Prudentia herself stands on the rungs of a ladder that is lying on the ground with her right arm wrapped around a coffin. At the bottom it says in Latin: 'If you want to be prudent, keep your mind on the future and think of everything that might happen.' Do you see what I'm getting at? Do you understand how much this city was wedded to the virtue of prudence and has, by the way, continued to practise it to this day through a long line of mayors? What the people saw as a new era with new masters and customs had already turned stale in the eyes of the city's administrators. They, dear great-grandson, had undoubtedly caught a whiff of fresher bread to come, yet another new normality with new rulers. As for me, I couldn't smell a thing. I was in the middle of it. I weighed up one side, then the other. I let what one person had told me collide with someone else's confidences. Inside of me Angelo couldn't see any normality; instead they were all opportunities to give life a spin, a mighty spin that would unhinge everything and send the horses on the merry-go-round galloping out into the streets with foam on their lips, all following the big black horse I saw myself astride with my truth hidden behind a sneering mask. That's the truth of the young, who never want to go along with what older people consider normal.

'I need your help.'

Lode's standing at the Vesting Straat exit with a large gunny sack at his feet. It's 6 p.m. and I've just gone off duty.

'Have you been waiting for me?'

'I need your help.'

'Why?'

'You'll see.'

He swings the sack over one shoulder and I follow him. We don't speak. We go up Vesting Straat and cross Keyser Lei in the direction of the Geuzen Gardens, past my old school, the Atheneum, and into Van Maerlant Straat. At one of its imposing homes Lode pulls out a bunch of keys. The building has two front doors: one with a row of doorbells and letterboxes, the other without any. That's the door he opens. We step into a hallway. Lode flicks a switch and a dim bulb starts to glow. There is another door in the semi-darkness at the end of the hall.

'Give me a bit of light…'

Lode passes back his torch and I raise it up above his shoulders and aim it down. The key goes into the lock and the door creaks open. We're in a roofed courtyard that stinks of shit.

'Your father's not fattening up some animal here, is he?'

'Not too loud,' Lode whispers, pointing up. 'There are people living up there and you hear everything. Screen that light.'

On the left of the courtyard there is a green, padlocked door. Lode unlocks it and pushes it open. He gropes around for a light switch and suddenly we're in a high-ceilinged storeroom about ten metres long. Completely empty except for two cages at the end of the room. I hear a pig and some piglets.

'I knew it…'

Lode reaches into his big gunny sack and tosses potato peel and vegetable scraps into the cages. 'That's not what I need you for.'

He takes a broom and sweeps the straw between the cages to one side, revealing a trapdoor. More jingling of keys, more fumbling with a big lock. Lode opens the trapdoor and shines his torch down into the cellar.

'Let me go first.'

With the gunny sack in one hand and the torch in the other he goes down a rickety staircase and turns on a light.

'Come down and close the door behind you.'

Now we're in a dry and fairly lofty cellar, about four metres high by my estimate. Cardboard boxes are stacked left and right almost to the ceiling with a narrow path between them leading to some pallets.

'Can you give me a hand?'

I help him slide the pallets out of the way. They aren't very dusty. Then Lode knocks three times in quick succession on a door and then twice more. Someone on the other side knocks in reply.

Lode pushes the door open and all at once we're in a drawing room, fully furnished, with lamps here and there, a kitchen stove, an armchair and a table with two chairs, a reasonably sized bed and heavy drapes.

'*Haben Sie einen Freund mitgebracht?*'

A smiling Chaim Lizke is standing there to welcome us while drying his hands on a tea towel, a tub of dishwater at his feet.

Lode puts the gunny sack on the table and says he has brought him some bread.

We're in Betty's Tavern in Rotterdam Straat.

Lode looks at me. 'Because you're practically family... That's why.'

So simply because my naive hands have found Lode's sister's? Anyway, wasn't it more the other way round? Didn't she grab mine first? Because her father now greets me with more than a snarl and doesn't take quite so long to offer me a seat? Because their mother now occasionally expresses her concern and offers me the odd maternal rebuke, telling me I'll catch my death, for instance, out and about without a scarf when the leaves are falling? Because he and I now go for a beer together, understand each other wordlessly and seem to have become friends for life? Or because he imagines us sharing other things? Or just because she, the stylish and beautiful Yvette, now has a claim on me for the rest of her life and makes that plain over and over again in her letters? And if it's not that, it's because of her delicious kisses, the breasts she offers me, her promise that I will one day, who knows, perhaps sooner than I think, be able to enjoy much more of that magnificent body, maybe even before I stand before the altar while her mum and dad blubber away because their little girl, the most beautiful, is going to be given away just like that to… Anyway, fine, he's not too bad, but what's his name again?

That's why; all those reasons are why I am now family and have to help Lode take care of the Jew Chaim Lizke, who just now in that cellar looked nothing like the night we drove him and his family through the snow to the bellowing of that pair of field arseholes, some two years ago now, on the way to what seemed like nowhere. He was a miserable creature then, a whimpering lamb on its way to slaughter, but now he seems like a man of the world, a plucky type who entertains us in a sort of bohemian salon, where the hostile universe has been magically banished and he enjoys total immunity in an artistic isolation he has chosen to create his masterpiece.

'You see how much is involved. He needs food. He needs

to be looked after. Because of the butcher's shop, our dad can only go at night. We're keeping Mum and Yvette in the dark. I alternate with Dad but he's getting way too old for this kind of thing. He's going to have problems with his ticker if he doesn't slow down. I talked to him about it. He suggested you himself. Said you're someone you can trust. Of course, I already knew that.'

'So you want me to fill in for you sometimes?'

Lode looks around nervously. Betty's is actually a particularly noisy place. Nobody stands out here. The landlord's wife puts on one gramophone record after the other while he pulls the beers, and the male customers can't keep their hands off the women, continually leading them out onto a dance floor so cramped they're half riding them. People are smoking and arguing, shouting and laughing, and now and then a young lady with a hankie pressed to her tear-stained face runs to the toilets to give free rein to her sorrow about a badly ended conversation with the umpteenth profligate who wouldn't stop pawing her bum. Safe enough.

'Not just that. It's getting too dangerous here. I feel it in my bones. It's going to come undone. He has to go to Brussels. Everyone says there's less checks there. My uncle lives there too. He could get him to Portugal. I've been asking round. A few people have a plan.'

'You've locked that Jew up in there. What if a fire breaks out?'

'Don't worry. There's another exit. He's got the key. But he knows he's only allowed to use it in an absolute emergency. That door gets him more or less out into the courtyard of the house at the back.'

'Where are his wife and children? Not...'

Lode sighs. 'It was a close call… The children are some-where in the Ardennes. His wife is now a so-called nun in a convent in Limburg. It's just more difficult for him.'

'It doesn't look like it.'

'What do you mean?'

'I mean he looks more relaxed than you do.'

'He's an odd fish. I've already told you that, I think. Do you remember you raised the subject yourself and I told you our dad got to know him when he was looking into diamonds? I'm sorry I couldn't tell you more back then. I had to discuss it with our dad first.'

Those last sentences go up a little at the end. They sound a bit too emphatic as well, overly rehearsed. There's something off about his explanation. But is it because he finds it difficult to conceal his true feelings for me and therefore regrets deceiving me even more, or is it something else? Who knows, maybe the father is abusing his son's noble idealism and it's not just about saving a Jew from his fate, but doing well out of it financially while he's at it. Could it be that Chaim Lizke is paying through the nose for my future father-in-law's protection and Lode knows it? But what of it? The risks are enormous. The father is calculating, but maybe the son is too reckless. He's known for his temper, and as I mentioned before, he doesn't have a friend left at the station. Everyone sees him as a scab who let his fellow officers down when it mattered. Nobody will cover for Lode, definitely not just for the sake of one more Jew while so many of his kind have already been put on trains for work camps or worse.

'You understand what happens if they find him? To you, your parents, maybe even Yvette?'

'You're in it now too.'

I freeze. Lode immediately lays a hand on my shoulder. 'I'm rushing things. Sorry.' His hand stays there. I have to look him in the eye and nod before he lets go.

Somebody slurs loudly for the barmaid to put the last record back on again. 'Can't do any bleeding harm can it, twice in a row?' His girl nods furiously to add weight to his words.

The front door swings open so hard the glass shatters. Twenty or so blokes from the Flemish SS come storming in. Screams. They sweep full glasses and ashtrays from the tables with their truncheons. People throng to the door. A drunk who doesn't have a clue what's happening gets punched in the stomach and collapses in a gagging heap. The landlord puts his arm around his sobbing wife. Brats in uniform, hardly a day over eighteen, smash the gramophone records one after the other, with the most enthusiastic unable to stop stamping on the Bakelite shards. Most people have already left the bar. Lode and I stay sitting there. We're not given a second glance. After the entire floor is littered with broken records, the boys hurl a few more bottles against the wall and give the Nazi salute. Then one of them, probably the leader, rummages through the till and takes all the notes. They leave the building, laughing and scoffing.

The landlord looks at Lode in fury. 'Aren't you the son of the butcher here on the square? You're in the police, aren't you? And you stay sitting on your fucking arse while they smash up my business! They're trying to ruin me and you and your mate don't do a thing!'

'Aren't you ashamed of yourself?' his wife sobs at Lode.

'We're not allowed to do anything,' Lode answers as calmly as possible.

'Spineless bastards! We'll find your kind after the war. Get out of my bar! Now, damn it!'

Meanbeard is off on 'an excursion', as he whispered to me himself an hour ago, which means he's gone to see Jenny or some other prostitute, leaving Yvette and me alone with his mother, who only relaxes once her darling son has left the house. She has long since stopped noticing me. Yvette is the one who matters, Yvette with the gentle nurse's voice, who is still, as if it's an almost never-ending story stretched over countless leather-bound tomes, reading 'The Curse of the Count', published in a periodical—Volume 9, Number 5— and consisting of some thirty miserable pages held together by two staples.

'Read on, child. I'm sitting comfortably.'

'But excessive contemplation withers the spirit. Happy are those—so Robert de Tiège told himself—who are lucky enough to awaken in a soft bed without having to ascertain that they have betrayed themselves. The guilty party was none other than he himself! No-one else could be blamed for this betrayal. Forever he would deny himself sleep. His suffocating sense of guilt would not allow it. No, Robert de Tiège himself would forbid it. He would prop his swollen eyelids open with splinters of wood! At dawn they would find him bold upright, as if he...'

A gentle snoring fills the room. The old lady is sound asleep again, like an elderly squirrel that has just consumed an extra-large nut to start its hibernation—her head crooked, a fine thread of saliva connecting her mouth to the shawl wrapped around her shoulders... convinced she's in safe hands.

'That didn't take long,' Yvette whispers cheerfully. Today she has a tic that's driving me crazy. Every now and then, not often, she presses the tip of her tongue firmly against the left corner of her painted mouth. Then the bottom of her tongue is like a little animal, wet and pink, rapidly carrying out some repairs on the gates of lust. She looks at me over her shoulder and gets an inkling.

'I want to kiss you,' I whisper, trying not to pant too much.

She shrugs, but raises one of her eyebrows coquettishly at the same time. A wave of gratitude passes through me. The clips that keep her hair up and reveal her delicate ears; thank you. The lipstick that makes her lips look so passionate; thank you. The way her eyes sparkle through that mascara; thank you very much! That smell of lily of the valley escaping from her fairly decent neckline; a thousand thanks, O universe, for all these things that make my heart consent so gratefully to being ground to dust.

'What say you now, Robert de Tiège, traitor to your own heart?...' she whispers in a mocking voice, still with that raised eyebrow.

Slowly I pull her up from her reading chair and lead her out of the old lady's sitting room. As usual she doesn't notice a thing. I lead Yvette down a few steps to a landing with a vestibule that doesn't go anywhere but is taken up with coats hung neatly on hooks and shoes and hats on shelves on either side. There we stand under the arch of the entrance, lit by a yellow light and surrounded by clothes, worthy of Hollywood, the start of a happily ever after, just before the volume of the music shoots up and the final credits start to roll.

I reach for the light cord. Kiss in the dark?

But her lips have already found mine and we kiss in the light, surrounded by the smells of beeswax, mothballs and shoe polish. I sometimes think of myself as an aroused beast, but her mouth is always there to teach me it's nothing compared to what's going on inside her: a storm of lust, which she resists and lets rage at the same time. A gentle kiss suddenly becomes a devouring and the gasps she lets out now and then move me to a level of excitement I could never reach alone, as if the entire universe is roaring its willingness. At the same time it's all just in my head and I can never fully match her surrender. When my kisses intensify, she calms me down, only to send me soaring once more with a subtle lick of her tongue. I think too much, I suspect, while she simply follows the fire in her belly, sometimes gentle, sometimes overwhelming. What we do with our mouths is a story in itself. Then, and this always happens when my lips are starting to feel raw, she forces me to look deep into her eyes. If I try to compel her to do something like that, she always looks away first. But if her eyes seek mine, she fixes her gaze on me, making me feel much too naked, much too vulnerable, much too alone. In moments like this Angelo will often reveal himself, something she always seems to sense, so that today for the first time she even says, 'There he is again.'

'Who?' I ask, ninny that I am, idiot without qualities, standing there with his eyes lost in hers and otherwise stripped naked.

'The sexy bastard, the dirty traitor,' she replies without batting an eyelid. Try squaring that with the 'sweeties' with which she peppers the letters she is still constantly sending me. My mouth stems the words she wants to add. She turns her head to the left and again her tongue licks a path along mine. Our tongues writhe around each other, sometimes slow and seeking, then fast and joyous, and every change of rhythm makes my head lighter, as if I will never be able to keep up with her, as if in the end I will be no match for her desire, which is so much more inventive than mine, and, who knows, maybe dirtier than I want to find out. I take her hand and put it on my fly, prepared to apologize immediately and for the rest of my life if this offends her. There is, however, nothing to suggest any such inclination. On the contrary, she squeezes me gently with that one hand while pulling the cord and cloaking us in darkness with the other. And yes, she's right, of course, because what I suddenly seem to want so impulsively—was that me or was it someone else?—is best done in the dark. She kneads me through my trousers as if she knows exactly what she's doing and, at the same time, is engaged simply in an innocent exploration, a combination that drives me even crazier. I keep my eyes shut, I can't look now, it all just has to keep happening in pitch darkness. I have to keep kissing her and simply enjoy what she is doing down below. After all, she has just rejected the hesitant hand on her breast and I don't dare reach for anything else. Her fingers have found my zip. She unzips my fly and the excitement with which she does it confuses me, making my head spin. Does she find this just as enjoyable as I do, maybe even more? She's left me behind again. Now she's touching me through the cotton of my underpants and when she discovers the wet spot at the top she squeezes a little harder. Meanwhile her tongue keeps finding new ways to make me gasp for breath. Without hesitating she unhooks the waistband of my trousers. My fly is now wide open. I wonder if she is sneaking glances at me while kissing and stroking my throat, but I still don't dare to open my eyes, as if that would make all this suddenly disappear, never to return. I feel two fingers on either side of the elastic in my underpants. She pulls the elastic towards her first and then pushes the white fabric down. My exposed cock gulps for air and points straight up. I immediately smell my own excitement, my beastlike masculinity, and blush to the roots of my hair. Her mouth finds mine again and her kisses become soothing. 'Come here,' she says, 'come here.' By which she seems to mean: 'Trust me, put yourself in my hands.' My knees almost buckle as she starts to stroke me, and the sounds I make are completely out of my control. When she grips me a little more tightly I tense up for a moment because of the dryness of her hand. But how do you say something like that? What kind of words do you use to convey something so practical? She stops her kisses at once and lets go for a moment. I am still trying to find the words to explain when suddenly I feel her hand again, wet and welcoming. That alone, her wetting her hand without asking, probably spitting silently onto her palm to pleasure me, stops me on the very verge of coming, as close as I am. A chill runs through me. As excited as I am, something dark starts to sing within me, a question starts to take shape to the notes of a melody. 'Why is she doing this? Why is she doing this?' Is it because she knows that we are now 'family', as Lode claims? Does she actually know about the Jew her father and brother are keeping hidden? Does she know I know? Is our union meant to be sealed now, in this way, with me unable to escape, not wanting to escape, and her hand on my twitching cock? Because you're practically family? And why is it Lode I hear whispering that last sentence in my ear? No, that's drivel, stop thinking. Just keep your eyes shut and let it happen. Her mouth hushes me, again she evokes an excitement that is more bestial than passionate. And again I give in, totally hers. She varies the technique with her hand too. Gentle changes to firm; quick tugging becomes calm squeezing. I go from one sensation to the other, no longer knowing where I am, what I'm doing or who I am, nothing beyond the fact that every quiver of pleasure tells me I am hers and hers alone. I am about to explode. And she feels that too. Suddenly she pulls the cord and I am standing there in the harsh light. She tugs even harder. Her mouth leaves mine. She forces me to look into her eyes and says, 'Do it.' Whereupon my semen shoots out and probably ends up between the old lady's winter coats. And then, without letting go of my still twitching cock, she kisses me again, once more with an excitement I don't come close to, not even in the moment of climax.

Suddenly we hear a loud groan. We look at each other.

Yvette soothes me. 'She's dreaming again.'

Silver-buttons never walk alone. That sounds like a bloody song. But it's true: a policeman alone, without a partner, can only look suspicious. Rest assured I've thought about it. What do I wear when it's my turn to feed the Jew? Civvies or uniform? Lode was wearing his while waiting for me. In the end I decide to do the same, hoping I won't bump into any field arseholes along the way who might ask me what I've got in the sack. If you really want to know: two sausages, three potatoes and a bit of horsebread. If you have to go into hiding, you're best off choosing a butcher or a farmer as your protector. Lode left the sack and the keys behind the gate next to the butcher's shop. That makes me nervous too, as it's somewhere I could easily be spotted. We couldn't think of an alternative. While fruitlessly searching for one, whispering in the dark on the way back from Lizke's hiding place, I was overcome by the folly of it all. The set-up wasn't good enough; it needed improving, I just didn't know how. Picture me in the meantime rapping out that code on the door concealing Lizke: a Keystone conspirator, a babe in the woods, a bungler. What's worse: knowing you're an amateur or thinking you can do better but not knowing how? Knock-knock, the door opens and I am welcomed by the enigma Chaim Lizke. He looks at what I've brought for him and asks if he could have some eggs next time. I shrug and mumble something. This time the place smells of brilliantine. Is this man really a diamond cutter, a craftsman? I can't believe it. He sniffs the bread, gently squeezes the sausages, strokes the potatoes, smiles and turns to me.

'*Bitte*, please sit…'

'*Leider keine Zeit*,' I answer.

'*Aber natürlich…*'

Again I think that he might very well be a paying guest, kept here by father and son like some kind of monster from one of the Grimms' dark fairy tales. But who is in whose power? What happens when his reserve of money or diamonds or jewellery is exhausted? Did they agree a daily amount or was it a lump sum? Will Lode's father kick him out if his budget proves insufficient?… But no, that's impossible, the risks are insane. In circumstances like this neither can afford to offend the other. If they told Lizke to piss off because he'd run out of money and he got picked up, it would come as no surprise if he talked them all onto the gallows. Am I the first one to think of this or have father and son considered it too? Can the father still think clearly without being distracted by greed and profit? Because the cards are on the table. If this is just about the money, it's the stowaway who's in charge of the boat.

I ask for the sack, nod politely and already have my hand on the doorknob.

'*Sie scheinen mir ein Intellektueller…*'

I stop for a moment, wondering why he thinks I look like an intellectual and not sure how to reply.

'*Haben Sie Bücher?*'

I ask what kind of books.

He shrugs. Anything, but preferably in German.

I nod and say I might be able to arrange something. There's only one person I know who has German books in large numbers and the thought of borrowing them from him puts a smile on my face for the first time today.

That was how, soon afterwards, I came to appear before the enigma Chaim Lizke with a linen bag full of books, all German. Meanbeard didn't know what to make of my sudden enthusiasm for German literature. Somewhat perplexed, he bundled up a few volumes: some Schiller, Hesse and Jünger. Not all books are attuned to the new national consciousness, he told me. However, as long as his *ex libris* was in the front with his name and some kind of Latin motto, I was welcome to take them all.

Lizke pulls them out of the bag one at a time, arranges them on the slightly rickety dining table and winks. His wide mouth forms a smile. Nodding, as if recognizing old friends, he picks one out after some hesitation and sits down in one of the two worn armchairs. Without giving me as much as another glance, he opens the chosen book and starts to read. Now and then he lets out a sigh of contentment. I am dismissed, it seems. He licks his index finger before turning a page, glances in my direction for a moment, then reads on.

I stay sitting at the table and roll a cigarette. While smoking, I study Lizke. His calm or his capacity to immerse himself in a book from one moment to the next confuses me. It's as if this hiding place no longer exists and any danger he might be in no longer matters. Should I admire his cool-headedness or is this expression of a craving for normality more an affectation? Whatever I may or may not think, it leaves him completely cold. I could sit here blowing smoke rings, yawn ostentatiously or fart, he's not going to look up a second time. Again he licks a finger and turns the page. The silence between us clears the way for other sounds. The ticking of an old clock slows your heartbeat, as if getting you ready to snore loudly in an armchair, like an old cat by a stove. The previously almost inaudible conversations outside now murmur like anxious voices from another world, still too far away to be of any import, too pathetically minute to make any kind of impression. The armchair creaks. Chaim Lizke moves on his seat. He scratches the back of his head and sniffs loudly. He reaches for a hankie and coughs into it. Another page further. A subdued 'Heh-heh…' Is he finding the first pages of *Der Steppenwolf* such a delight or is it more an amused contempt for Herman Hesse's writing talent? I can't tell. 'Careful, first edition!' Meanbeard said. But in the hands of this man, the book is just something to read, not a treasure. Should I impress upon him that he mustn't dog-ear any of the pages, crack the spine or leave too much saliva on the corners? No idea how to say any of that in German.

'*Das sind nicht meine Bücher…*' I try.

Lizke looks up and smiles again. '*Danke schön. Sehr freundlich…*' His chin juts forward a little, his eyes screw up and combine with that frozen smile to form a mask of gratitude and appreciation. 'Very pleased,' he adds, nodding now too, while his eyes return to the printed page.

I sigh and suddenly think it doesn't matter. I have an idea these books will never be going back to their owner. Or maybe they will, but when Meanbeard won't be able to do anything except shrug his shoulders because of other, much more pressing, worries. All at once it strikes me that everything is temporary. I've never thought about it before but now Chaim Lizke's reading in seclusion has driven it home.

But even that realization doesn't make me want to sit in the lotus position under a tree with a gently babbling stream in the background and the teachings of Buddha draped round my bare neck like a comfy silk shawl. Yes, everything is temporary, but the disquiet Lizke evokes in me seems to have broken free of time. It is deep and unpredictable. I can't have him staying here much longer. He's started appearing in my dreams, sometimes wordless, but very present. Yesterday he held the door open for me and whispered like a butler, 'Allow me, sir,' after which he stuck his fingers in his mouth to whistle and a coach appeared out of the fog of Victorian London, in slow motion with two unruly black stallions foaming at the corners of their mouths. Lizke has to go. He's getting under my skin, without me being able to work out why. Lately Lode has been relying more and more on me to provide him with food. It's clear that he's busy doing other things, acts of resistance probably, maybe sabotage. We all notice the increasing tension, as if everything is about to come to a head. Bollocks, of course. Life in this city drags on from incident to incident. One thing leads to another. Occupation or not, that's all it is. Sometimes, when everything seems normal, I suddenly shiver and clutch at my stomach. It never lasts long, a minute at most, as if a robot inside of me has received a communication from a mastermind with a cynical plan to destroy the world.

At our front door in Kruik Straat I'm reaching in my pocket for the key when someone puts a hand on my shoulder and tells me to come with him. Before I realize what's happening, I'm in the back of a car between two men in leather coats. The man who is slowly manoeuvring the car along België Lei has one hand loosely draped over the wheel and is holding his cigarette half out of the open window with the other. Nobody says a word. At Harmonie Park the car turns left into Karel Ooms Straat. The man on my right makes a show of coughing.

'Can't you give us a break from those filthy cigarettes? I haven't got over that bronchitis yet.'

'Kiss my arse,' says the driver.

Nobody says a word to me. I'm cargo that has to be transported from point A to point B. I try to concentrate on my breathing and think of the Jew whose hand I shook in farewell just half an hour ago. I put my hands together on my lap. Here comes the reckoning. Here comes the moment I haven't wanted to picture in detail, but have sometimes imagined on a rare restless night. We reach a residential neighbourhood and the car turns right. What was I thinking? I see Lode warning me, Yvette smiling at me, my mother crying in the kitchen, and I see myself, alone and abandoned, eating sandwiches in Vesting Straat's dirty canteen. I feel my way through possibilities, possible retorts and alternative interpretations, things that have the ring of truth about them, explanations of suspicious behaviour. Here comes your big scene. This is your moment, Wilfried Wils. Don't try to tell yourself otherwise. Start jumping on the spot to warm up in the wings. Make sure you don't shit yourself. Be prepared for anything, especially the pain of truncheons raining down and beating you until you're tender and bloody like an exquisite steak, the kind they used to serve up before the war in Hotel Weber on Keyser Lei, still bleeding and awash in thick brown gravy you could stand a fork up in, bleeding like Christ on the cross. Fear is what keeps you alive, fear is what keeps you alive. This sentence forms a refrain in my head.

We park in Della Faille Laan, headquarters of the Sicherheitsdienst.

There's an enormous commotion on the ground floor with people rushing in and out. I see men in uniform dragging other men between them whose faces are no longer recognizably human. Some mumble something while being carted downstairs. A door opens, letting out a cry of trapped terror before it closes again. Fear is what keeps you alive, fear is what keeps you alive. The men in leather think I'm climbing the stairs a little too slowly and lend a hand so that my feet hardly touch the marble. I struggle not to lose control of my bladder. They plonk me down on a bench in a high-ceilinged corridor like a little child and tell me to wait. A Waffen-SS sentry is posted at a door with a sub-machine gun. One of the men accompanying me knocks and enters. Time for the oral exam, I tell myself. Concentrate and don't lose your self-confidence. I hear Angelo guffawing inside of me, or at least spluttering as he tries to suppress his laughter. Fear is what keeps you alive…

The door opens. The man in the leather coat nods at me and I go in while he leaves and closes the door behind him. Red-headed Gregor is standing there in his black uniform. He gestures at a chair. I sit down.

Gregor tries to tone down his German accent. He doesn't really succeed, but his mastery of our language is greater than I expected when I heard him at my Aunty Emma's.

'Better here than in a bar, Herr Wils.'

I nod. My heart rate starts to come down a little.

'A glass of water?' Without waiting for an answer, he goes over to a side table and picks up a carafe. I empty the glass he offers me in three gulps. Without a comment he refills it.

'You seem a little nervous…'

'My apologies, Oberscharführer.'

Gregor smiles. 'You know my rank.'

'Of course.'

'And you know what I am doing in your city?'

I nod.

'Then surely you have nothing to fear? Unless you are circumcised. Are you circumcised, Herr Wils?' He looks at me for a moment. 'Forgive me, that was not a very respectable *Witz*. Forgive me too for the manner in which you were brought here. I hope that has not made too much of an impression on you. *Na gut*, let us not beat around the bush. As you probably know, the Sicherheitsdienst has reconciled itself to the fact that your police service will no longer provide assistance during the finalization of the Jewish question. *Das ist kein Problem.* After all, this last summer we noticed that your services leak like a... How do you put it here?'

'Like a sieve.'

'*Wie ein Sieb*, almost the same word...'

I nod.

'Our mutual friend has let me know that we can count on you. That would be useful, especially now Herr Vingerhoets has met such an unfortunate end... We know that here and there, there is some, um... subversion present in the police force. Stolen ration books, help for Jews. No doubt a few of your colleagues, perhaps a small minority, are well rewarded for these services. *Nicht wahr?*'

'I don't know anything about that, Oberscharführer.'

'Of course not. Not at once. I understand you. This requires an adjustment. Here.' He taps his forehead with his index finger. 'But you will get there. And there are compensations. Do you understand me? We keep the identities of many of our so-called *Vertrauensmänner* strictly confidential. Of course, we would do the same with you. Some of them receive a remuneration. Unfortunately, I cannot offer such to you. But for everything there is a solution. We will work it out. Your friend knows what I am talking about. There are enough possibilities. What you must do is consider, reflect.'

Gregor lights a cigar, flaps the match to extinguish it and blows out a mouthful of smoke.

'*Gut, dass wir...* I mean, we have your Aunt Emma... We can greet each other there now and then. *Verstehen Sie?*'

'Certainly, Oberscharführer…'

'See it as a possible investment by us in you. And know that your valued friend will always be there to… *sich mit mir kurzschließen*. Do you understand that in German?'

'Yes, as a direct line of contact.'

Gregor blows out a cloud of contented smoke. 'Again, we understand each other perfectly.'

'You know what they say about that dirty German?'

'There are a lot of stories about him, Lode.'

'Open for business, that's what it comes down to. I hear about Gregor and a few of his mates—people from here, right, not Jerries—pulling on their black uniforms of a night-time and dropping in on Jews or people they suspect of hiding Jews. Then they yell a bit and demand money or jewels. And afterwards they head for your favourite bar and knock off one bottle of cognac after the other until closing time. True or false? You'd know.'

'He doesn't seem the type to me.'

'You know what else he likes? Household effects. When those rich Jews are kicked out of their houses, everyone's supposed to keep their hands off the contents. That's the principle anyway. But when you, like our Gregor, have a good relationship with one of the local removal companies, you've got a business opportunity. Who cares about an oak table, an antique bed or a painting on a wall? Out of sight, out of mind. Things get lost so easily. You know where to go if you need an armchair…'

'Still, there are other advantages. The Oberscharführer thinks I'm one of them. That could protect us.'

'Your wording's so careful. You are one of them, aren't you?'

It takes a couple of seconds before Lode starts laughing. 'Come on, things are serious enough as it is.'

I laugh along, as usual. Meanwhile I think about Chaim Lizke and wonder how many jewels or diamonds he's promised Lode and his father. One person recognizes his own small betrayal in the other. I see the harried victims surrendering all their valuables. I see them stripped to their underwear, forced to submit to probing fingers in search of gold and jewels.

'Money…' Lode says, inadvertently answering my thoughts, 'that's what it comes down to. You can't tell me they believe all this stuff about the master race and subhumans, blood and soil, pulling those ridiculous faces with one arm stuck in the air, flogging their supposedly knightly ideals like sideshow hucksters while worshipping their great jabbering tash on the radio like he's some kind of god. All bullshit. It's very simple. The Jews have got the money and that's what it's all about. Organized robbery, that's what it is.'

It all sounds watertight, but I'm in constant doubt, sometimes telling myself I don't have a clue what's going on in this city. Does money really explain everything? Isn't that rather naive? Lode's rant, which seems to have come out of nowhere, sounds like the accusations an adolescent spends a long time rehearsing in his head before levelling them at his father. After all, there are other things smirking in the darkness, monstrous thoughts I have, unfortunately, not yet managed to capture in a poem, energies that spark out like fallen angels, ravings, whispering inside my head, random acts, effects without causes, tragic coincidences, muddled and casual bastardry, sadism too, contrariness and failures of concentration. Why does Lode see clearly when to me it all looks murky? Maybe it's because he's a thief too. No, that's too crude. He sounds disappointed, that's all. He's turned out not to be a hero, but someone who keeps a Jew alive because it all comes down to money. Or not? Have I got it wrong? I can't tell any more; my friend's heart is misted over like a mirror.

'Is that what it's all about, Lode?'

'What?'

'Money.'

'Sometimes, Will, you still sound like a little kid.'

'For you too then?'

'What?'

'So it is the money.'

'Come on, what's got into you all of a sudden?'

Lode looks me in the eyes, searching for something, then shakes his head. Suddenly he's tousling my hair.

'Don't,' I say.

'No,' he says fiercely, 'don't.'

He doesn't.

Cigars for fathers, cigarettes for youngsters, pipe tobacco for grandads huddled over stoves, and chewing or rolling tobacco for gardeners, roadworkers and railwaymen. Welcome to Bruyninckx Tobacconist, behind the counter our winsome Jenny, who, going by her summery neckline with the thermometer at an icy minus two, has not yet adjusted to the prevailing fashions amongst shop girls.

The bell on the door of this robbers' den takes a moment to stop jingling.

'It's handsome Wilfried!'

Her lips form a red O of mock surrender, with her right hand pressed against her forehead as if she's about to swoon. 'It's not easy for a woman like me when you appear. I get butterflies in my tummy.'

'You sound very happy, Jenny.'

Jenny without alcohol is more intense than Jenny on the port. No more drowsy looks, no bafflement in her eyes, no tears threatening to fall at the slightest provocation, a lot less whorish than before.

'Had many customers yet?'

She screws up her eyes. 'Are you making fun of me?'

'How could anyone?'

'Goodness,' she laughs, 'what a charmer. And if you must know, this place is a goldmine. You have no idea how many people can't wait to smoke their ration these days. People have long since forgotten what good tobacco tastes like.'

Jingle-jingle. A customer.

'Your brother-in-arms is in the back room,' Jenny whispers, nodding at the golden-brown curtain behind her.

A narrow hallway stacked with boxes left and right leads to Meanbeard, sitting at a table covered with letters, bills and receipts, lit by a desk lamp of relatively high wattage that makes his head shine and casts menacing shadows in the furrows on his brow. Preoccupied with mental labours or not, he definitely sounds cheerful.

'Welcome to my new shop, *jeune homme*! Pack of tobacco? For you, it's free of charge.'

'Your shop? That's fast.'

'The owner has retired, you could say. I find it regrettable

231

for him, but nonetheless, he did violate a race law. He should have known better. Anyway, I'm now the authorized administrator, or what's it called?'

Meanbeard slides some papers to one side, finally finds his matches and contentedly sucks the flame into his pipe. 'You wouldn't believe the stock Mr Bruyninckx has here… All pre-war. Turkish tobacco, English tobacco… All for his favourite customers. You have to see this!'

He waves a notebook.

I open it. There are all kinds of names in it, followed by crosses, numbers and brands of tobacco.

'Mr Bruyninckx's clientele. Nobody can accuse him of being disorganized. And look at these names…' Meanbeard pulls over other documents. 'Koch, Holz, Rothman, Kubelsky, Gottlieb… All of them Jews on our list who have been evading us. Can you believe it? These fellows are still regulars here. At least two of them popped in this very day. *C'est vraiment stupéfiant!* Don't underestimate them… The inventiveness of the Israelite is beyond description. At the same time their stupid arrogance is so… Can you believe the two today simply announced themselves to Jenny with their own names, holding filched ration books and requesting their favourite brand? Just like that, as if life simply goes on.'

'And what now?'

Meanbeard rubs his temples and yawns. 'We're going to pick up as many as possible in one go. There's no point nabbing just one or two. Word'll get out and we can whistle for the rest.'

'You could announce a sale on tobacco and smoking paraphernalia.'

232

'Bloody hell, that's it. What a brilliant idea. A Jew always wants a discount! It's so simple it's perfect! We'll do it!'

I regret those words so much, as if I've suddenly and through my own fault put myself under a showerhead with ice water, teeth chattering as if I've come down with a fever, cursing my own stupidity, despising the way I sometimes shoot my mouth off, saying things despite knowing better, my arrogance, the bastard inside me, my thoughtless fucking longing to simply join in, to be in on the joke, to be appreciated. Sometimes shame feels like a mosquito bite, sometimes it's a heart attack, sometimes your bones are being crushed in a python's deadly embrace. And nothing anybody ever says will make me forget it. You, dear great-grandson, are the first person I've ever told. Believe me when I say that I only meant that crack about a sale as a joke. It occurred to me and I blurted it out. It was so daft, so bloody cheap and crude. Know too that Angelo, the inner voice that used to hold such sway over me and has now been reduced to a rare whisper, confided in me that night that my shame was a sign of weakness and I believed it and probably fell asleep a little easier as a result. The very same week, after the announcement of a special discount, a dozen keen Jewish smokers were picked up at Bruyninckx Tobacconist.

'When are you going to take me out dancing again, Wilfried?'
Yvette goes over to the gramophone.
'It hasn't been that simple recently…'
'I know that. There's no end to it. For weeks now those blackshirts have been smashing up one brasserie after the other. Right here on the square, too, two nights ago. The

233

Alma, the Lympia, a couple of others. I was in bed and heard the shouting. Those SS idiots can't bear the idea of people wanting a bit of diversion every now and then. That makes you really feel like going out dancing. Is that such a crime?'

'How do you expect me to take you out dancing when one place after another's being wrecked?'

'I'm counting on your ingenuity. You're not going to tell me dancing has been completely prohibited? If you're on the right side, there are still plenty of places to go.' She looks at me like a cat with a mouse.

'And I'm on the right side?'

'You know people on that side.'

She turns her back on me and bends forward.

The stylus comes down on the crackling gramophone record.

'*Plais-i-i-i-i-ir d'amour ne dure qu'u-u-u-u-un instant… Chagrin d'amour dure toute la vie-e-e-e-e…*' The living room is too small for her. She whispers a line from the love song to a standard lamp, moves over to the window with her hands clasped imploringly, as if the moon will hear her, then suddenly leaps back to me with her brows in a playful frown. '*Et pourtant notre tendre roman par ta faute… aujourd'hui vient mourir bêtement…*' Effortlessly she drapes her voice over the nightingale Rina Ketty's, who is doing bouncy revolutions under the gramophone stylus with her tango orchestra. She emphasizes the Italian *chansonnière*'s un-French R even more while placing her hands on her cheeks and adopting a wide-eyed pose in an imaginary circle of light. I can't take my eyes off her and smile. At the end of the song, Yvette does a pirouette in front of her grinning mother, who is leaning on the kitchen doorpost and winks at me. Isn't she talented? Isn't it patently obvious that she has the gift of making other people happy with her voice? Couldn't she move thousands upon thousands of listeners to tears on the great European stages? Her mother and I give her a fervent round of applause. She bows deeply.

'Your father should hear that sometime instead of all those difficult opera things you drive him up the wall with.'

'Oh, Mum, he doesn't like to hear me sing at all.'

'Nothing happens of its own accord. Men need to be trained.'

As if she's said too much, my future mother-in-law looks in my direction. 'Isn't that right, Wilfried?'

'I wouldn't know,' I answer, without meeting her gaze, holding a match up to my cigarette.

Yvette sighs theatrically.

'Fine, I'll get back to the kitchen,' her mother concludes abruptly.

Yvette sits down next to me on the sofa and starts to leaf furiously through a women's magazine she has probably picked up a thousand times before. 'It's all right for you to call our ma "Mum". Or "Mother".'

'Did she say that?' I blow smoke out over the newspaper on the coffee table in front of me. 'No one speaks of the peril of Bolshevism… We want to be recognized as a nation…'

'Would that make you feel uncomfortable?

'I didn't say that.'

'But?'

'Nothing.'

'Look at me. You're more interested in that newspaper than you are in me. What am I to you? A sack of potatoes?'

Suddenly her tongue is very sharp. I look at her.

'You have no idea who I am, Wilfried.'

'Nonsense.'

She squeezes my forearm. 'Who am I? Tell me! What do I want from life? Do you know?'

Like a lover in a bad old-fashioned film where the action's interrupted by title cards with the sighs written out instead of being spoken, I drop to my knees and seize her hand after first stubbing my half-smoked Turkish cigarette out in the ashtray. 'Happiness! Love! You want me!'

'Sit back down. You're making fun of me.'

I sit down again and straighten the creases in my trouser legs.

'Can't we lighten up sometimes?' I sound a little too plaintive. After all, I'm the one who's always too serious—she's told me that dozens of times. Being with me isn't enough fun. I'm too distant and too dark. But that last bit, the darkness, is attractive now and then—she admits that too. More than anything, it's the betwixt and between Wilfried, neither fish nor fowl, who gets on her nerves, who gets her goat, as she puts it.

'Do you think I want you to call our mother "Mum"?'

'Yes.'

She gives me a hard slap on the check. 'No, not at all.'

'Ow.'

'Yes, ow… silly little twerp.'

'You've lost me.'

'What I want is to sing. I want everyone to hear my voice. For them to call me the nightingale of De Coninck Plein, a woman of humble origins whose career has taken her to Milan, Paris and New York. I want…'

'That's what I was just thinking.'

'What I want is to be free. I want the freedom to travel from place to place. I want you to come with me and write your poems. You shouldn't call our mother "Mum". Who knows, maybe we won't get married and live in sin, never settling down. You have to do what you want, just like I want to do what I—'

'Be who you—'

Slap on the cheek again. 'You always interrupt me.'

I grab her tight by the wrist and say in measured tones, 'Being who you want to be is the most difficult bloody thing there is.'

'That's him again. I can see it in your eyes. The bastard's back.'

Aunty Emma waves to us, so full of expectation I regret having arranged to meet her. She's wearing something white with puff sleeves, combined with a double string of pearls hung loosely around her neck. I wave back and lead Yvette over to her, cutting between the other tables at the Hulstkamp. My sweetheart is dressed like a well-bred Bohemian, a Gypsy girl in a wide, high-waisted, black-and-white-striped skirt with a red blouse under an equally red bolero she made herself.

'But what a beautiful girl you are!' my aunt cries, and the women exchange three ostensibly cheerful kisses, executed left and right with twisted mouths to avoid marring the other's cheek with a smudge of deep-red lipstick. Among women, as Yvette recently told me, this kissing technique is an expression of deep respect. In other words, when encountering a woman you would rather drown in a shallow tub full of sulphuric acid, you do exactly the opposite.

After all the kissing, Aunty Emma settles back down cautiously like a goose trying to keep her freshly hatched goslings warm. 'I always come early to get this table. It has the best view.'

'Yvette wants to dance.'

Aunty Emma looks at Yvette with a twinkle in her eyes. 'Oh, that will come, definitely. Don't worry. The moment my Gregor walks in with his all his friends, this place explodes.'

Between the two women's heads, I see a peculiar figure drinking jenever at a table at the back. He has pitch-black eyes, wears his hair as if it's stuck to his head with wallpaper paste, and is clad in a black velvet suit with a red bow tie and waistcoat, over a white shirt with cuffs that come down almost to his fingertips and are trimmed with lace.

'Have you seen that joker there, next to the door to the loos?'

'Oh,' sighs my aunt without looking over her shoulder, 'do you know him? That's Sus. He thinks he's some poet who used to hang around here like a bad smell.'

'Crazy Paulie,' I say, almost boiling over without letting the others notice anything.

'Keep your distance, lad. Sus is seriously gabby and before you know it, he'll have invited himself to our table and our whole evening will be ruined.'

'What's wrong?' Yvette whispers.

'Nothing,' I say hastily with a forced smile, 'nothing.' Sometimes this city and her poets can drive you completely mad. How many fakes, how much verbal diarrhoea? Acting like you're Paul van Ostaijen, how low can a pseudo-bard sink? You can't compel great talent into being by a change of bloody wardrobe. It takes work and living on the edge, not

238

ambition, a pose or clothing you've borrowed from someone else, especially not that. 'So,' I say, 'what would the ladies like to drink?'

Aunty Emma laughs boldly. 'Later it will be champagne, but make mine a cold beer for now.'

Yvette would like some wine. I raise a hand and give my order. 'And for me, a beer with a jenever.'

'Oh my, jenever. Watch out you don't get in trouble.'

'This place is known for its jenever, darling.'

'Make sure you don't get a reputation here too, darling.'

Yvette and I smile at each other, but I can tell from her eyes that she's serious.

Aunty Emma claps her hands together exuberantly. 'What a nice couple you make. You've got spirit, Yvette. Exactly what this one here needs. You wouldn't believe the mouth he had even as a little boy. Do you remember, Wilfried?'

'No,' I say.

'Really?' Yvette teases.

'The lungs on him too. He was hardly taller than this table when he started acting up with his mother and father. "You're not my father!" I can still hear him saying it. And just the same to his mother. We could hardly stop laughing. It was priceless.'

'I'm sure,' I say.

'*Extase sans phrases, adieu la raison…*' sings the gramophone not all that loudly amid the conversations at a dozen tables.

A cheerful Yvette sticks one finger up in the air, '"La java du clair de lune" by Suzy Solidor!'

'Goodness, child. You know your music.'

'She wants to be a singer, Aunty Emma.'

'I can believe it. She's got the figure for it.'

'Suzy Solidor has one of those short blonde hairdos with a fringe just over her eyes. I'd like one like that too.'

'Child, mistreating your hair like that! What an idea. Anyway, that butch look is totally out of fashion.'

'I thought you wanted to sing in the opera, darling.'

'As long as it's on a stage, dear.'

Here are the Germans. Suddenly the place is teeming with uniforms, black and field grey, and my Aunty Emma is in the warm embrace of the city's Oberscharführer and Jewish Affairs Officer. His comrades-in-arms are already three sheets to the wind and hanging off their women out of necessity. They murmur their surnames almost incomprehensibly. Gregor himself is friendliness incarnate, greeting Yvette and me with charm and promptly ordering champagne and a bottle of jenever. Oberscharführer Karl is with a blonde, who has a thick head of curls pinned half up and a dazzling set of teeth. In contrast to Gregor, Karl is a typical SS officer, the kind who only ever deigns to look down on us natives from a great height, but making an exception, of course, for beautiful women like Yvette, who he immediately treats as if she's been waiting demurely for years to be educated by a know-it-all like him. Without her asking for it and even before an ice bucket has been placed on the table, he provides her with an account of the choice champagne houses and which varieties of grape they use to obtain their excellent results. Karl's girlfriend flashes Yvette a smile that would have King Kong blubbering like a sissy. Hauptsturmführer Heinrich refuses to be addressed as befits his lofty rank; after all, he's much too drunk for that, and anyway these officers don't seem to set much store by formalities once the sun has gone down and waiters in livery are surrounding them like nurses with trays full of alcoholic medicine. The Hauptsturmführer has a deep scar on his left cheek and a drowsy eye. He doesn't notice us. Instead he is bestowing his complete attention on the two women he has brought with him, who claim to be sisters. In no time, even more women have gathered around him and he seems to know them all, even if I don't catch him using any first names, preferring to apply '*Schatzi*' and '*Mausi*' by turn as he addresses them.

Ever since the SS settled around us with Wehrmacht officers and hangers-on in their wake, the pseudo-poet has been trying to get my attention by raising his shot glass of jenever with a wink in my direction every time he's about to purse his lips. I ignore him and top myself up. Oberscharführer Karl's ongoing lessons have made Yvette unattainable and, after a few attempts to involve me in the conversation, Aunty Emma has resigned herself to Gregor demanding her full attention while he giggles over stories I can't follow.

Meanwhile the place is filling up. Yvette shoots me a look of silent desperation. Aunty Emma sees it too and whispers something in Gregor's ear.

'*Eine ausgezeichnete Idee!*' he bellows at once.

He snaps his fingers, calls out a few things to the people behind the bar, and immediately chairs and tables are being slid out of the way, the gramophone has been turned up, and he and Aunty Emma are smooching on a square metre. Before I can get up to dance with Yvette, she's accepted an invitation from that cursed Karl. His blonde girlfriend watches them with her with arms crossed.

'Do you want to dance with me?' I ask.

She doesn't even answer. I'm infected with the same disease as Yvette. Her German lover turns out to be blessed with supple hips and other dance skills, so that Yvette visibly relaxes in his arms. The fact that he's finally stopped lecturing her must help too. He keeps staring at her with his mouth half open, as if his dance-floor dexterity might send her into indecent ecstasies from one moment to the next. I knock back two glasses of jenever in quick succession and then messily pour another. The pseudo-poet is onto me. He stands up and grins while closing his eyes and pretending to play a violin, then teases me with a bow in my direction before pushing open the door that leads to the toilets.

'Do you work for these fellows too?' asks a little chap in glasses.

'Do you?'

'*Dolmetscher*,' the pipsqueak pipes up at once. 'Interpreter, in other words.'

'I know what it fucking means.'

'Sorry, pal.'

'You stupid monkey, you stupid little delicate apprentice bastard, you four-eyed cocksucker. You can shove your apologies up your arse, get it?'

'Whoa.'

'Am I a horse or what? Are you a cowboy?'

'I'll leave you to it,' the bespectacled interpreter says calmly.

I have no trouble standing up and moving through the dancing crowd to the toilets. Yvette doesn't even notice me passing by. She's letting herself be led about as if she's in a trance. The poet is standing at the urinal shaking off his undoubtedly tiny cock one drop after the other as if suffering from an enlarged prostate. 'Phew...' he says when he sees me. I grab him by the neck and smash his face into the porcelain in front of him. He's so surprised it's almost effortless and after that he's too stunned to resist a second blow that leaves blood on the white. 'Ho-ho,' he cries at last. Someone else who thinks I'm a bloody horse. For a few seconds I'm not sure what to do with him. I'm even swaying on my feet. But then I drag him into one of the bogs and kick him until he's lying there puking next to the toilet. At least, I think so. I can't be sure, because suddenly I'm back among the dancing couples.

'You all right?' Yvette mimes at me over the shoulder of her still highly diligent partner. I think I nod reassuringly. That too is something I'm not a hundred per cent certain of. I slump down on my chair and pour myself another jenever. The German has his hand on Yvette's bum. I wave and give her the thumbs up. Everything's fine, it's all under control and so are you, apparently? She looks away.

Gregor comes to sit down next to me. Aunty Emma keeps her distance and hugs herself as if she's just witnessed a terrible car accident. Big boss Heinrich is dancing with three women at once, or rather, they're dancing around him as if he's a heathen god standing naked on an altar. I no longer see the waiters, just the trays of drinks going from one end of the brasserie to the other, with no apparent human intervention. I go to refill my glass, but it's still full from the last time. Gregor and I begin a conversation, I think. I say things. He listens. Then he speaks.

Suddenly I'm holding on tight to a lamp post on De Coninck Plein.

Yvette is glaring at me.

My stomach turns. I think I'm going to burp, but immediately start puking over my coat.

I think she's crying. She says, 'You didn't protect me.'

'You wanted to dance, you whore.'

'You're not listening to me. You're not yourself, you drunk. You didn't protect me.'

Another burst of vomiting; this time I'm able to bend over first. Thick green spouts out of my body. I taste bile. I desperately need to shit as well.

'You hear me? You didn't protect me, Wilfried!' She wallops me on the side of the head. My ear starts ringing. I collapse and start to sob. She doesn't look at me and starts searching her handbag for the key.

'Don't tell your brother—'

'Don't you dare. I'll say what I bloody like. Shaming me like that.'

'Don't tell your brother that we... that we... went dancing in the Hulstkamp. It's important... He mustn't know... D'you understand? D'you understand? Sweetie, sweetie...'

Bang. The front door's shut.

Walk home or crawl?

I get a hangover to match. The next day is a Sunday. My mother refuses to say a word to me and my father keeps just as quiet. But no sooner has she turned her back than he starts off about the puke they found in the hall early this morning.

'The toilet was obviously too far away.'

'I don't remember a thing.'

'Well it wasn't me, you pig. You should have heard yourself coming up the stairs. You were as pissed as a whole regiment.'

With the sins of a son following in his father's footsteps after all, I am now paying for all the times it was him stumbling up the stairs. I've been drunk many times, but up till last night I managed to keep it hidden, which probably annoyed the hell out of him. Now revenge is sweet. Given his feeble performance as a patriarch and the open contempt I've shown, he's not going to miss this chance to take it out on me now. You too, Wilfried Wils, have been worsted by male stupidity, the overconfidence that comes with booze, green-eyed jealousy on the dance floor and all the pettiness, the extreme pettiness that normally remains hidden but is enlarged and expanded by the demon alcohol until it becomes a tragicomedy full of sleaze, passed down from father to son for the eternity of a barfly's existence. As if the simple-minded poser I am obliged to call my father has now permanently and to his great relief ascertained that his son shares his bleary liver after all, the only inheritance a weak man considers true and just. Me, weak? Welcome to the club, you little brat.

'I... um.'

'Ooph, you're turning green. Hurry off to the toilet, you idiot.'

I make it just in time. The smell of soap and bleach that always lingers there makes me gag. I vomit, eyes watering the whole time, twisted over the bowl, vomiting again. Slime won't stop dripping out of my mouth. My head explodes. I lie down next to the toilet. Inside of me Angelo is singing a song that makes my underworld peal with pain and regret. Last night's events are full of black holes and the moment I peer into their depths they fill with the stagnant water of humiliating shame. I can't get myself up off the floor and onto my feet. There are only obsessive questions that leave me floundering in murky waters up to my neck. Did I really call Yvette a whore? Is it possible I only felt like smashing that poet in the face but didn't actually do it? Is there a chance of a horrified Aunty Emma launching into a tirade about me to our mother? What was I blathering to Oberscharführer Gregor about? That last question in particular makes me quiver like a rabbit that's been skinned alive and strung up by the heels in the cellar to die. Preposterous image. It makes me puke again. Bile this time, although it feels like it's my gall bladder itself coming up as soft stinking chunks of dog food.

Someone rattles the toilet door.

'I'm busy!' I croak.

'Enjoying yourself?' my mother snaps on the other side of the door. 'It's what you deserve.'

The flower stall at Groen Plaats is still open.

'They're the last ones, sir.'

Orange might not be her colour, and I don't know what her favourite flower is either, but it is what it is, and what's been ruined might be salvageable yet. I need to get to Meanbeard's because I know she'll be reading to his mother again this afternoon. A bunch of flowers isn't enough; I know that too. I need an explanation, something to glue the pieces of her broken heart back together, something to convince her that this really is something that will never happen again. I'll never touch jenever again, my god, that stuff, I've learnt my lesson, really, if I'd known it could turn you into such a mean drunk, I would never... Something like that? Or should I dig into the deep dark recesses of my soul? Something along the lines of her having now, unfortunately, seen what a bastard I can be, that this black-hearted monster is kept under lock and key ninety-nine per cent of the time, but that, unfortunately, she happened to be there on that one exceptional occasion when it burst free, frothing at the mouth and lashing out at everyone, and that too is a part of me, sweetie, forgive me, I am so ashamed of myself, but on the other hand, maybe it's good… I mean, no, not good, but not bad… I mean, not that either… It's only honest, yes that's it, it's only honest that you get to see the other side of me for once, as it's nonetheless part of me, but a very small part, and most of all very well concealed, and that I now feel safe enough to share that too with you, not that I did it on purpose, but you know what I'm trying to say, that we have to get to know each other's bad sides, especially mine, before we can really be sure of each other's love… Something like that?

I'm half an hour too late. She's not there. Meanbeard looks at my flowers and asks if they're for him.

'Smart alec.'

'Your girl left me in the lurch, pal. My mother's strict. It's your Yvette or nobody. So now I'm stuck here. I was going to go do something with Jenny.'

'That's a shame.'

'You've obviously got something to make up for. I can't say I'm surprised. It seems you really played the swine last night at the Hulstkamp.'

'That got round fast.' More than fast. It's an innate quality of probably every city. The tendrils spread far and wide, creeping over everything. Someone relieves himself in one neighbourhood and in no time there are people on the other side of town who know who's caused the stench and which bowel problem explains it. All crammed together in a roofed, windowless playground where rumours, gossip and half-truths try to slowly strangle the breath out of us.

'I bumped into *mein Freund* Gregor yesterday in the Raven. That's where he likes to drink his nightcap, together with his real friends.'

We sit down. We wait. I unbutton my jacket. Now and then the old lady in the next room groans, as if she's just been bitten by a nasty insect. Her son doesn't budge.

'She's really not coming,' I say at last.

'That bloke you beat up in the toilet...'

'Don't bloody start.'

So it's true, seeing as it's already hardened into a story. The proof of the wound of shame that has been afflicting me all day has been delivered and there's nothing I can use to bandage it.

'Sus... such a harmless fellow. Assistant librarian at Conscience Plein. Maybe he's even got a permanent position there because there's not much else he's up to. His poems are even worse than you'd expect from a parvenu like him, a lot worse, but that's no reason to put him in hospital.'

'Ow.'

'I hear he needed a lot of stitches. Gregor had his driver take him to St Elisabeth's. Yes, pal. Go ahead and shit yourself. Sussy-Boy is a friend of the Obersturmführer's...'

'Help, help!' screeches the old lady suddenly from the darkness.

'Just ignore her. She's up to her old tricks again...'

Meanbeard stuffs his pipe and sucks the flame into the tobacco. The old lady calls out again.

This time her son reacts immediately and especially loudly. 'Do I have to bloody well come in there or what?' She lets out a sigh, as if she's a deflating balloon filled with aggravation and mismatched maternal love.

'I'm in deep trouble...'

Meanbeard starts laughing at me. 'Look at him sitting there, the pugilist of the sixth division. Trouble? Let's just say you made up for it, but from the look on your face you've forgotten that bit because you had too much booze in you.'

Gregor looking at me, me saying things, him answering— that's really all I know.

'It's very simple. You're on our side and we help each other. Our Oberscharführer knows that, I know it and you know it too. It's going to get interesting. There's a lot of swindle and theft with the ration books. Omer and I have quite a lot planned for the next few weeks. We'd appreciate your help with that. Help, by the way, that you last night swore a solemn oath to provide, like a choir boy, just pissed off your face and with someone else's blood on your knuckles. Gregor did an impression of you. We fell off our chairs laughing.'

I stand up and button my jacket.

'Oh, you going? Don't forget your flowers.'

'Give them to Jenny.'

'She'll be over the moon. Thank you, Wilfried.'

I must have sent her seven or eight letters, all starting with, 'My dearest darling, still no news from you. It's what I deserve, but still...' She's closed all of her shutters and locked the doors.

After the first couple of letters remain unanswered, I stuff my begging epistles through the butcher's-shop letterbox myself late at night, firmly convinced that the postman is refusing all cooperation, that the universe itself will no longer bend to my ardent longing. Still her silence continues, encouraging me to bang on even more about love and pain, probably getting weepier and more tasteless with every sentence. Angelo is disgusted but holds his tongue. My inner self sounds as hollow as a cathedral after midnight. I lie down on my bed and start crying for no reason. Only the faintest echo gets through to me, nothing more. 'I am not a bad person, I am not a bad person…' I repeat quietly to myself, which makes the crying fits even more intense, so that I walk around the next day with puffy eyes. My so-called mother has come round and forgotten the vomit in the hall. She now looks at me the way she'd look at a suffering cat that's crawled under a wardrobe, and at the dinner table she keeps warning me that it'll be the death of me if I keep it up.

'It's like a festering wound in his head,' she whispers to her husband in my presence.

'He's got to come to his senses,' my so-called father agrees.

With Lode I don't dare broach the subject of Yvette at all. He doesn't give me much chance either. Our paths cross at work, we even go for the odd beer together, but our conversations are about everything except women, love and family. We have a code for Chaim Lizke's food deliveries. 'The potatoes are at the gate,' Lode will say and I, as if hypnotized and still part of the family, proceed to the gate next to the butcher's shop at dusk and deliver the bag I find there to the Jew.

All the while my thoughts are on the letter I've just slipped into their letterbox. Was I being too blunt? Was the end too tearful again, not manly enough, too childish? Wouldn't it be better to simply say goodbye to her and finally behave the way men are supposed to? Does a poet like the one I want to be have any use for a woman who can't keep up with him, who at the first slight setback decides to shun him for the rest of his life? It's true, it really has gone on too long. I'll put an end to it and we'll each go our own way. But why do I suddenly feel so cold or get in such a foul mood when I imagine her being with someone else and doing the things with him that she has already let me do with her? 'Bloody hell,' I think, 'she's turned me into a mewling brat.' And those wheels just keep turning in my head, crushing everything. The flesh and blood of my poethood is drawn through this sighing, worrying grinder and reduced to banal, petit bourgeois mince. After which self-loathing knocks on the door and asks to be let in. And still no Angelo, no nagging voice to tell me to pull myself together. Although he only exists in my mind, I can already see him in bed with her and laughing while he tells her about the minced meat in my head before giving her another... Anyway, I can't go on like this.

Chaim Lizke smiles and nods at me again, takes the food out of the bag and, without deigning to give me another glance, sits down at the kitchen table to pick up his opened book. He really doesn't care whether I stay or not. I sit down on the sagging sofa and compose a better letter in my head, the ultimate letter, a letter that will melt her heart. But as soon as I think about it, I feel like I'm throwing away the last little bit of myself, even though the sentences still only exist in my thoughts.

For about two years I've kept a leather-bound notebook in my inside pocket with the stub of a pencil. In all the times I've pulled it out, I've never got any further than a line that is doomed to instant oblivion, as if the act of pulling the notebook out of that inside pocket is too premeditated and therefore too innocuous, too focused on poethood itself rather than forging poetry that will put the fear of God into everyone. And now that notebook is lying in front of me, with that pencil stub lined up next to it, without me remembering taking it out of my pocket. I open it and cross out the words 'incandescent tale', which I had previously seen as a possible title and now suspect I may have stolen from someone else. Above it I scribble 'Confessions of a Comedian'. Not once does Lizke look up while I fill page after page with filth, with poems that have not yet been thwarted by anyone or anything. At the start of each first line, I hear Angelo holding his breath.

And then, finally, her letter is lying on the tiled floor of our hall. I recognize her handwriting from the top of the stairs. Like my last four letters, hers doesn't have a stamp. She must have posted it through the door herself, as if she too doesn't trust anything or anyone between us. I tear the envelope open. The sheet of writing paper only has a date and a time with a question mark, followed by: 'You can find me on the bridge in City Park.'

She has been giving it a lot of thought. I see that immediately as I approach her on the bridge at the stipulated time. She is standing bolt upright, her feet a little wider than one expects from a lady, almost like a man bracing himself for a row that might end in a fist fight.

'Don't say you're sorry. You've already done that too much.'

Below us ducks are quacking. The winter is almost over.

'I'm so crazy about you,' I say.

'They're just words,' she replies.

'I'll change.'

'Really, why? To make me think it'll get better. I'd rather not. It's a waste of time and I'll only be letting you string me along.'

'Don't you want me any more? Is it over? Say so and I'll accept it.'

'You're in a hurry all of a sudden.'

I shrug like a vaudeville clown, with sad-face make-up and a painted tear under one eye, as well as flat feet. 'It hurts too much. It would be better to have it over and done with right away.'

I look away from her, rest my hands on the railing and look down at a couple on one of the paths below, strolling behind a pram, each staring straight ahead and not saying a word.

'You love playing games so much, Wilfried, you don't even know any more when you're spouting hot air and when you're not.'

'That's possible,' I say. 'It's possible. I don't know.'

'Come here.' She takes hold of me and I feel my body tensing up. 'Just stop it...'

We hug each other and I bite my tongue hard to avoid bursting into tears like a baby.

In that very moment someone wakes up.

In that very moment, Angelo says, 'Comedian.'

And she says, 'That German was touching me. And you did nothing. You didn't protect me.'

She kisses me. I kiss her back.

'It won't happen again…'

'Just forget it,' she says and kisses me again, warm and wet.

And suddenly I no longer have the faintest clue what love is supposed to be.

I'm pushing my writing paper, notes and diaries to one side, dear great-grandson. I've had enough of it for the moment. And there's also a waiting cigar I'd like to savour without Nicole bursting in screeching. I just heard the front door click shut, so I know she's gone out to do her shopping. Maybe I should open a window, maybe not. I'll smoke shamelessly like a factory chimney in a nineteenth-century industrial city on a polluted river. It might make it even more fun later to deny this lung-rotting activity while the smoke is still hanging in the room like a brown mist.

For you I have become the hero of a novel in these pages, one who doesn't know what will happen the moment he goes out the door, and therefore takes one slap in the face after the other, like a fool on a burning mountain who doesn't realize the raging fire was caused by the smouldering cigar he carelessly left in the dry grass. After all, so many things can still happen; what it comes down to is the moment you yourself say or do things that will require you to pay a price—regardless of whether it's exacted a scant few seconds later or after dozens of years. The more I write down for you, the more I let all the things I know be covered over, snowed under, the more I act like this old man is just a ghost, a shadow cast by the young Wilfried, who stares straight into the sun of yet another new day, a youth who understands too little of everything and fools himself that nothing can hurt him. When I thought about the conversation with your great-grandmother that smug dream burst. Just forget it… That's right, just forget it.

I'm enjoying my cigar less with every puff. I'd prefer to just stay Wilfried Wils for a while, an old fellow who's contemplating the things around him. Look at that blackbird outside in the tree, how droll. And there, so cute, that tyke with the oversized woolly hat that's almost covering his sulking face. Look at this and look at that. Keep looking long enough and you'll see a Breughel in contemporary colours with both you and the painter on the outside. Because looking stays looking and in the end it dispels absolutely nothing. I have to think of my doomed granddaughter, Hilde. See us walking together. We stroll down the Meir. Sixteen or thereabouts, she's hooked her arm through mine. The twentieth century has started on its last ten years. We're experiencing the end of history, or so we read in no less than two of our local newspapers, which evidently believe they are announcing something special that has wafted over to us from that eternal foreign elsewhere. Everything is happening in the present, no longer in the past, and from now on nobody will be burdened by the deadweight of yesteryear. Complete bullshit.

'This whole pleasure centre is designed to squeeze money out of you, *Bompa*.'

'Oh, my God. And here I was, just about to treat you to some new clothes.'

'Is there something wrong with these?'

She lets go of my arm and turns on the spot. She's wearing one of my old coats, which she nagged me into handing over. Around her neck she has a long, rainbow-coloured scarf some friend of hers knitted for her. Her feet are in army boots she has decorated with all kinds of symbols in white paint. She is wearing tights with skulls on them. Her lipstick is black and so is her nail varnish. Her hair is sticking straight up. She has countless rings in both ears and one through her nose.

'To be honest, you look a fright,' I laugh.

'Aren't you ashamed to walk down the street with me?'

'Terribly.'

Our arms link up again. How is it possible, I think in that instant, how is it possible that I get to call this glorious degenerate my granddaughter? She has something to say about everything.

'That family man is dressed like a twelve-year-old. The other one hasn't had any for ages. You see that straight away, *Bompa*. Look at those kids! Complete retards! And there! Did you see how those ladies hugged their handbags a little bit tighter when that cool black dude went past? Shit, I've run out of smokes and money too. And I've got a runny nose. Can we go to Groen Plaats? Some friends of mine are hanging out there.'

'You don't mind being seen with this old fogey?'

She goes quiet for a moment. She seems to be taking my question far too seriously and finally smiles as if only she knows my secret and will therefore defy with great contempt any mocking glances she might reap because of the love she feels for her grandfather. It is hard for me to conceal my pride. I'm glad she just babbles on as if nothing has happened.

'This crowd is driving me crazy. If you think about how tourists are always funnelled through this nuthouse before they let them loose on the rest of the city, it tells you everything you need to know. It's so they can squeeze all the money out of them right at the start. And it's no coincidence either that there's a monstrous tower at the end with a bank's logo on it. People are sheep...'

'Does everyone your age think like that?'

'Most of them are losers, so no, not really.'

'I hope you don't inflict talk like this on your grandmother.'

'No,' she says, squeezing my arm, 'only you. You understand.'

Once again pride makes my eyes swim. I clear my throat, I cough, I swallow my tears.

'I'd like to go to Berlin.'

'What do you want to go there for?' I croak.

'At least there's some cool people there. I've already saved the money but they're giving me a hard time about it at home.'

'You're only sixteen.'

'If you could just talk to them...'

'I'm not butting into that.'

'I'm your godchild!'

'That's why. I don't want you ending up in some Berlin gutter surrounded by lowlifes and ruffians.'

'Now you're teasing me.'

'Yes,' I lie, against all my inclinations. Because there's a chance she'll talk me round so that I end up trying to convince her parents to let her go. And that's something I don't want either. I want to protect her.

*

257

'Who do you want to protect, Mr Wils?'

Nicole has a firm grip on my elbow. Suddenly I'm shuffling through the city with her, not my granddaughter. Suddenly I've been dumped back in the present and I don't know how it's happened. Nicole's talking about clothes I need to buy.

'I don't want to protect anyone. I was talking to myself.'

'Sometimes I think you just don't know any more if you're talking to me or it's all just in your head.'

'I've lost my cigar…'

'If that's all you've lost, you're doing all right. You haven't had any cigars in the house for months now. I gave them all away. Don't you remember?'

'Of course I do,' I say as decisively as I can, 'of course… It's a private expression of mine, that's all.'

'You've lost me,' Nicole sighs.

'Me too…' What else is a fellow to say? Grab a bike, then maybe you'll keep up? Nobody laughs at those feeble jokes any more, especially not Nicole.

She leads me through streets filled with mothers and fathers who are convinced that the spring air is good for their offspring even though it's still much too cold. Some families have already fulfilled their duty and are standing irritably at tram stops as if the world has disenchanted them yet again, surrounded by big plastic bags like sandbags trying to form a dam to hold back the melancholy nobody dares mention. My mother, she with the invariably crooked wig on her head, thought of the search for new clothes as something beautiful. I don't think she could have imagined this world, a time to come in which commercialism, whipped up by so much advertising, would turn us all into cheerful babbling brats reaching out with sticky hands to grab something that's been announced as the chance of a lifetime or available on 'special offer'.

I too am led through the shopping streets the same way: like an overgrown child—without a memory, without any past, without any cheerful criticism of this much-praised present. Criticism my granddaughter used to provide nonstop, to my surreptitious pleasure. Today it occurs to me that hers must have been the last intimate voice of resistance in my life, bright and merciless.

Now there's only silence, unless you count Nicole's lively cackle.

When I walk through the city alone, I tell myself I can still manage. With her next to me, the fear of stumbling again and being doomed to a wheelchair starts to rise. At times like this I'm tormented by a dream of being weightless again in the arms of a father who never convinced in that role. Back then the forces that were determined to turn everyone into a docile child instead of an independent adult were omnipresent, just like now.

'Are you short of breath?'

'Why should I be? Because of all the windbags round here?'

'Here we go again,' she says, laughing.

We cross The Boulevard and I see the brightly coloured masses streaming towards me from the Meir.

'Do you really need to subject me to all this?'

She squeezes my hand and for a moment I seem to sense regret at having brought me with her, that she is scared I might fall arse over tit on the spot, inasmuch as I have any kind of arse left.

'It's not much further. And then we'll have everything in one place: there's a shoe shop, and we can find trousers there too, and a there's a shirt specialist for a couple of new shirts like you asked.'

A *shirt specialist*. She's said that to put me at ease. I used to prefer bespoke shirts, but in these banal times I have to make do with a shop that specializes in shirts only. It's been a long time since I was on the Meir. Even when cars were still allowed here, this glittering shopping paradise lay with its legs spread wide. I've never known it any other way. I am one of the last of a generation that weighs everything against war and I can't help but see the boisterousness of the present as a thick scab over the wounds of the past. There is much too much buried in both me and the city. In the sixties the longhairs said there was a beach under the paving stones. Idiots. It's deception buried under those stones. Lever them up and the dead will dance. They're already bloody dancing—there's one over there. I see her standing next to me with an accusatory look. Who failed to protect you, Hilde, my beautiful, foolish, troubled granddaughter? Was it me or someone else? Or did we all make a mess of it together?

'You're sighing as if you've had another difficult night of it, Mr Wils.'

'Wait until you're old, Nicole.'

An open maw of gold and glitter gapes on the left side of the Meir. A well-trodden red carpet extends like a forked tongue lolling out of a fancy mouth full of perfect white teeth. Through a gully flanked by promotional percentages in fluorescent colours ('–50%', '–70%', 'Last-Chance Renovation Sale!') we enter an enormously wide space with people drinking champagne on a platform and tables left and right with even more shops behind them, more lighting, more tinsel. Music and loud conversations creep up to the top of the tall walls, where they are captured in a glass dome before falling back down again.

'I don't think I've ever been here before.'

'This used to be the festival hall, Mr Wils. You remember that, don't you?'

A snake slithers through my guts and into my throat. 'Was that here?…'

Nicole looks worried.

'Let's go over there and sit down for a moment.'

'Bit of heartburn,' I groan, suddenly feeling like a wrung-out dishcloth.

'Sit down. I've got some lozenges somewhere. I'll fetch you a glass of water.'

She only has to rummage in her bag and the lozenge is lying on my wrinkled hand. I suck it and look round. She beckons a waiter who is dressed in black, with a black hole in one ear and the little hair he has left sticking straight up in stiff little wisps. I sip a glass of water while the mint taste of the lozenge makes the sour snake recoil.

Nicole stirs her *café au lait*.

'Are you all right?'

I stare into her candid eyes because I'm in need of some distraction. No, she doesn't have a man. I don't believe she ever has. Does she prefer women? The possibility can't be excluded, but I doubt it very much. How old is that sinewy body of hers, with those frank eyes and that buzz cut with grey gleaming through it? Pushing fifty? Mid-fifties? But she must have known love, or instead of it a deep calm. Maybe she overcame herself or completely reinvented herself, going against everything others ever expected of her.

'You have a scoundrel's eyes, Mr Wils.'

'I'm just looking at you.'

'We're not going to start acting silly, are we?'

'To my eternal shame I have to admit that I don't know a thing about you, that I've never even asked. I suddenly felt a bit embarrassed about it.' I take another sip of my water.

'What would you like to know?'

'Just tell me something.'

She comes from a wealthy family. Her mother has been dead for ages, apparently from the misery of an unhappy marriage. Her father, unfortunately, still only has one foot in the grave, her own words. She visits him now and then, but doesn't really look after him, although that was once her plan. But the old man refuses to go along with all of that and pretends he doesn't recognize her any more. She was a rebel as a child. I believe that at once. She didn't give a stuff about money. Her father's friends were all well-to-do and decadent. The things he put her through. She'll tell me about it some other time, if stories like that amuse me. Holidays in Spain on some mountain somewhere, unbelievable. Madness. But anyway, she chose her own path and emerged the stronger for it. Caring for others has become her life, it's her passion, but… And then she starts off about all kinds of fuss and bother at work, cut-backs, gossip, inspections, superiors who don't know what caring for others is all about, all of the palaver involved, and so on. I nod encouragingly in the hope that her story might take another turn, if necessary the women she's been to bed with who turned out to be no good after all, for instance, but my nods don't help, no amount of self-hypnosis can help me any more.

Her voice keeps getting thinner and her stories impossible to follow.

I give up. I sigh. I lose myself in the festival hall of yesteryear and the events for which this monstrous, golden, consumerism-steeped shithole was once the setting.

On the corner of Brialmont Lei, where it's already hard to imagine that not so long ago Jewish children with yellow stars sewn onto their coats walked past on their way to school, Omer Verschueren is waiting for us. The lawyer I witnessed in all his glory when he was smashing the windows of the Oosten Straat synagogue with an iron bar doesn't recognize me. The puffed-up bastard needs to be crushed one day. It would be a shame if he got to draw his last breath peacefully in bed.

'Call me Omer,' he booms. This time, thank God, Meanbeard skips the song and dance about introducing me as his great literary friend. Instead he asks his mate with a wink if he has 'everything' with him.

'Don't worry about that,' the lawyer answers, patting the left side of his chest.

I turn my collar up against the biting wind, rub my hands to warm them and ask what we're going to do.

'Play detectives!' Meanbeard giggles.

'That's right, young friend,' the bear growls just as cheerfully. 'He's Sherlock Holmes and I'm his Doctor… what's-his-name…'

'Elementary, my dear Watson!'

*

The doors are wide open. A long queue starts out on the Meir and winds into the building, past the wainscoting, under a yellowish light, deep into the broad lobby where it branches out to five neatly lined-up tables, with two civil servants at each with lists of names in front of them, stacks of ration books and an array of stamps next to open inking pads. People used to come here to dance; now it's a distribution centre for ration books. We turn down a side street and go through a door that opens onto a corridor at the back. Meanbeard whispers something to a caretaker, a little fellow with tufts of hair growing out of both ears and little shaving cuts above a greyish collar. Startled, he jumps to his feet and leads us to a small room in the belly of the building. No windows. Nothing on the walls. A bare bulb. Two simple chairs and a steel table. Without a word he leaves us there.

'What time is it, Omer?'

'Dead on ten o'clock.'

Omer stretches and tosses his overcoat at the table. Something heavy falls out of his jacket onto the chair. Omer reaches for it and puts it on the table.

'You acting in a gangster film?'

'You're right,' the lawyer says, putting the pistol back in a deep inside pocket.

'He has a permit,' Meanbeard winks. 'Me too, by the way...' And he flashes his inside pocket with a butt sticking up out of it.

'I'm leaving,' I say.

The two of them look at me. Meanbeard gives a paternal shake of his head.

'What you're going to do is very simple. Go and join the queue. That's all.'

'My mother's already picked up our books.'

'All you have to do is keep your eyes open. There's a big chance all hell's going to break loose. Some people are going to try to slip away. It's very likely there'll be people you know amongst them, people from your station, but in civvies. Just keep your eyes peeled. We'll do the rest.'

'And what if I'm recognized?'

Omer laughs. 'Nobody's going to want to see anything or recognize anyone. You get me?'

Someone knocks discreetly on the door.

'Sir?'

'Come in.'

The caretaker with the tufty ears nods timidly in the doorway.

'I've told the men inside you're here. I had to come and tell you that somebody's presented three books. Two of them with names on the list you provided.'

Meanbeard rubs his hands together theatrically. 'Tell them to take him aside for now.' The caretaker nods timidly again and closes the door behind him.

'What kind of list?' I hear myself asking.

'Our friend Wilfried doesn't quite get it.'

Omer shrugs and scratches one of his armpits. 'Not every-one knows the tricks of the trade...'

'It's actually very simple. First of all we're not rid of the Jews yet. That's because, second, there are still idiots who believe they should help them. And third, we've found out that those idiots are so idiotic they think it's enough simply to queue up with the Yids' ration books and then provide them with food. How crass can you get? And now get out of here, Wilfried. This isn't your place. Go and join the queue.'

I go back out through the corridor and emerge in the narrow side street, where a removals truck is now parked together with an army truck from the Field Gendarmerie and a car in which I recognize the Oberscharführer, dressed in civvies and sitting in the front next to the driver. He gives me a vague smile when he sees me. I hide my red face deep in my collar. It's the first time our paths have crossed since the commotion in the Hulstkamp. I think: 'It's a game, stay calm, this is manageable.' But of course, I don't know anything for sure.

Close together, whispering to each other, I hear the mumbling of the people who are waiting. Nobody looks at me. Some of the women have small children with them. A four- or five-year-old whines that he's tired. His mother tries to hush him with a teddy bear. 'I can't believe they couldn't organize this better,' mutters someone. 'Typical town hall,' says someone else. 'If the Germans arranged it, it'd be a lot better. You can take that from me,' says yet another. The last voice is a little louder, but no one reacts. Other conversations are about the bloody wind that keeps blowing, the falling leaves, or that aunt with phlebitis in her leg who can't get a proper doctor and yes, then you have to lend a hand, of course, even though she's a right bitch, excuse my French, and it would be nice if it wasn't always my side of the family doing the dirty work. Inside the building, people fall silent as if they've entered a cathedral with a dozen priests giving Communion at the front. Many keep their heads bowed, ready to receive some kind of blessing. I see Meanbeard appear at one of the tables. With a short bow he asks a man to come this way. I'm not close, but I can still make out his sarcastic smirk. Without hesitating the man follows him. By now I'm in the long second queue on the left. Time stretches out. I try to make out people I know from the countless backs in front of me, picking out one neighbour effortlessly because of the flamboyant wedge-shaped hat that marks her in my mother's eyes as a woman of questionable morals. Then my attention is drawn by the ear of a man in the queue on the far left, four or five places ahead of me. Something tells me I know him, that I must know him, that it's crucial I identify him. Discreetly I go up on tiptoes but still can't see more than an ear and some black hair under a hat. You'd almost think... But that's impossible. Then the hall stiffens. A sound comes from the room Meanbeard just led someone into. Everything goes quiet, only the imperturbable sound of the stamping of books continues. Something is hurled. A fist smashes down on a table. Now we can hear someone crying. The officials look at each other and promptly resume their name-checking and book-stamping. More crying and a loud 'No!' Now the crowd is getting restless. 'What's going on in there?' People hiss, 'Gestapo, Gestapo...' Somebody curses. The curse moves quietly from line to line. 'Bastards.' 'They're at it again.' 'Is this really necessary?' An official stands up, then sits down again immediately. Meanbeard comes back into the hall. His eye falls on a book that another official has slid to one side. Then he looks at the man at the very front who has just been wordlessly asked to move to one side. Again that sarcastic bow and a hand gesture in the direction of that small room. But this man, a giant of a fellow, an ex-military type with his hair shaved at the back and sides and a bulging bull's neck, stands his ground. Meanbeard hardly comes up to his shoulders. The bull's neck lets his vocal cords rip in the hall where bands played before the war, where the mayor gave his annual ball, where people waltzed and laughed, and men harassed women at the end of a drunken night. 'Who's asking? I'm not taking a step without seeing your papers! The idea of it.' The man crosses his arms. Meanwhile I notice that the man in the hat I can't quite place is unobtrusively letting others go first and taking stealthy steps back that bring him closer and closer to me. Meanbeard pulls his pistol. Everyone recoils. Some people, as far away from the weapon as they are, drop down with their hands over their heads. The people hiss. 'Unbelievable… This is too much.' 'Who is that bastard?' 'Gestapo, Gestapo!' A young chap in knickerbockers and a short leather jacket swears at the top of his voice, says, 'I'm not having this!' and tears back out through the doors to the Meir. By now the queues are swaying backwards and forwards as if on a ship in a storm. The confusion increases when Meanbeard points his pistol at the bull neck's chest. 'Now come with me, damn it!' People crane their necks to see what's happening up the front. The lines, previously neatly separated, are now jumbled together. Someone shouts, 'Coward!' A little old man tries to calm Meanbeard down, holding his hands out in front of him. I see the fist with the pistol go up into the air and come back down again. Cries of horror pass through the hall. Then I finally recognize the shadow on my left as he takes advantage of the confusion to make himself scarce. For less than a second our eyes meet. Chaim Lizke. I don't know if he recognizes me and before I've had a chance to let it sink in, he's gone. It's almost incomprehensible. Then police whistles are blowing and two constables rush, in followed by the youth in knickerbockers, who seems to still believe that in emergencies you're supposed to call in one of our boys in uniform. And as if someone up above is playing cards and laying down their trumps, I see that Lode is one of the constables, his face red with rage. People are shoving and pushing. Children screech. Lode and his partner's whistles are answered by orders in German. As if in a bad melodrama, *mein Freund* Gregor appears from behind the curtains, a mob of field gendarmes in his wake, all with guns raised. Lode is immediately surrounded and carted off. Meanbeard has disappeared. Everyone's shoving their way to the exit. Children fall over, people yell and I, like a bungler who's accidentally stumbled through the gates of hell, fight my way out too.

It's not till early evening that I summon up the courage to go to the butcher's shop. By that time Yvette and her parents are probably worried sick. I've been sitting next to the pond in City Park for hours thinking about it, weighing up the different possibilities as if I, fool that I am, can save myself from the mess I've got myself into with a few masterful brainwaves.

Yvette opens the door. Her eyes are red and the look she gives me is far from welcoming.

'Oh dear, what now?' I hear myself say bravely. 'What's wrong?'

She wipes away tears and leads me upstairs. Her mother glances at me, but doesn't say a word. She too has been crying. As usual her father is in his chair behind a newspaper.

'This is bad for my ticker, people,' I say. 'What's happened?'

'Our hero's barricaded himself in his room,' the father says tartly without lowering his paper. 'Ask him yourself! It's not as if I didn't tell him. Steer clear of that uniform. But the know-it-all wouldn't listen. You see what bloody comes of it!'

'Oh, Father, you've made your point,' his wife whimpers.

I go up a floor and knock on the bedroom door.

'Lode, it's me, Will.'

No answer. I go into the room.

Lode is sitting on the bed with his back turned.

'Downstairs everyone's howling.'

He turns slowly to face me. His right eye has been punched shut.

'I saw everything,' I say.

'What, you?'

'I was in one of the queues.'

'They dragged us off and beat the shit out of us.

'You should have stayed out of it…'

'You going to start now too? If someone comes up to you with a story about some lunatic waving a pistol around in the festival hall, do you have a choice? We're cops, aren't we? Or have you forgotten?'

He opens the door of his bedside cabinet, gets out a bottle of jenever, takes a pull and passes it to me. I knock back a hefty slug and suddenly I'm in the Hulstkamp again, swaying on the spot. Stay off the jenever.

'Sorry. I don't have any glasses.'

I laugh. So does he.

'We didn't even get a chance to see who the bastard with the pistol was. If I ever find out—'

'My old French tutor…' I hear myself saying.

Lode looks at me, rubs his chin. 'I should have known your pal would be there.'

'There was another bloke with him. A lawyer. Omer Verschueren.'

Now Lode is visibly shocked.

'What?'

He takes another swig from the bottle. 'You know what they say about him?'

'Who? And what?'

'That he plays both sides. That shit will do anything if there's money in it. Plus he knows me and my father all too well. Three years or so before the war he was our lawyer.'

'A complete bastard…'

'Not wrong there.'

'Should be put down.'

'Absolutely.'

I rummage for the bottle and take a decent glug of jenever. Everything spins. I shouldn't have done it. Stronger than I am.

'Lode…'

'Don't. Be careful what you say. Better still, don't say anything.'

We sit in silence for a while. I light two cigarettes and pass one to Lode.

'I saw Chaim Lizke there too.'

Lode almost lets the cigarette slip through his fingers. 'Impossible. That's mad. It can't be true.'

There he stands in the semi-darkness of his hiding place, with the kitchen table between us with an open book on it. We stare at him.

'Where did you go?' Lode shouts.

Lizke looks at Lode, then me. His expression doesn't change. Incomprehension.

'You mustn't go out, Herr Lizke. *Nicht nach aus!*'

271

A frown appears on Lizke's face. '*Nach Hause?* No home no more.'

Suddenly there are tears in his eyes, even though he still has an accommodating smile on his face, ready to assist us with whatever variety of folly we might have in mind.

Lode and I sigh simultaneously. Lode throws his arms in the air. I keep staring at Lizke like a child trying to see through a conjuror's tricks.

Lizke sits down without looking at us again.

Tears fall on the table.

'*Alles ist zu einem Alptraum geworden,*' he says to no one in particular.

Lode looks at me questioningly.

'*Alptraum* means nightmare,' I say quietly. 'Everything's turned into a nightmare.'

Lizke blows his nose on a dirty rag.

I see a shudder pass through him before he picks up his book again to carry on reading as if we're the ghosts.

Lode and I are outside a house in Lange Leem Straat. Next to one of the doorbells is a copper plate with 'Flor Goetschalckx Insurance' engraved on it. The name makes me smirk. Lode presses one of the buttons above the insurance agent's. I don't know the young fellow who opens the door. He addresses Lode with a whispered 'Vincent' and I'm introduced as 'Robert'.

There is a smell of wet dog in the hall, an old dog. We climb the creaking stairs as quietly as possible. A gramophone is playing quiet piano music behind one of the doors on the first floor. We are led into a room that looks out over the street, the furthest one from the stairs. It's smoky. A portly, beetle-browed man in his forties is sitting at a kitchen table covered by a crocheted tablecloth. There is a teapot ready, surrounded by empty cups. The man with the questioning eyebrows nods at Lode.

'Who have you brought with you, Vincent?' he asks in a grating voice.

'A colleague of mine, Professor, from the sixth division. He's called Robert. He's been helping me with the Jew I—'

The man admonishes Lode to silence. 'That's fine, my friend. We don't need to know everything.'

I understand why they call him 'professor'. It's easy to picture him at the front of a lecture theatre, the benches packed with fresh young students, smiling while they dedicate themselves to soaking up his wisdom. The fellow who showed us in is clearly a student and the little ginger-headed chap picking his nose across the table from us is obviously another. One of them pours the steaming tea and we sit down.

'Gentlemen,' the professor pronounces, 'the enemy is suffering setback after setback. They can forget about North Africa, they're taking a beating in Russia, and here in our own city not a single Jerry or collaborator feels safe any more. Whatever anyone says, it's clear that after the greatest darkness, the most beautiful light is becoming visible. We mustn't give up now. Every act of sabotage, every spoke in the fascists' wheels is a step forward.'

People gently tap the table in appreciation. The nose-picker lights a cigarette and blows triumphant smoke at the ceiling like a bit player in a gangster film.

The professor looks at me. 'Robert, like your friend Vincent, you can be of great—'

Lode, or 'Vincent', interrupts immediately. 'That's not what he's here for, Professor.'

'Why then?'

'Because of how things are progressing. My Jew has to go.'

The professor looks at the fellow who opened the door to us. 'Guillaume?'

The one who goes by the name of Guillaume tugs one of his earlobes for a second, then starts talking in a thin, almost comical voice. 'The address in Brussels has been arranged. The people there have been informed. The only thing we still need to tell them is when he will be arriving. His papers—'

'I'm working on that,' the professor nods. 'Matter of days. Virtually indistinguishable from real documents. It really is unimaginable, my friends, what people can achieve when they are united. Soon it will be our turn, you'll see. You can feel that people are ready for it. The cruelty of the occupation is helping us win the heart of the nation.'

His eyes are shining. He hits the table, but immediately smiles. 'Sorry. I know we mustn't disturb the peace of mind of Mr Goetschalckx here below.'

Those around him respond with sheepish smiles, Lode too. I'm standing by the curtains and hear a tram passing, slow and squeaking like scrap metal on wheels. The sound of footsteps. Someone calls, 'Stop!' It's like the tram has to sigh before braking. Outside it's ordinary life; in this room the conspiracy of a small band that believes the time is ripe, a revolution with tea and oat biscuits, putting their faith in the professor's beliefs about being in the right and on the winning side, like a little boy striking matches in a storeroom full of gunpowder and seeing every little flame as a sign of shining hope.

'Reassured?' Lode asks cheerfully as we walk towards Van Eyck Lei with our collars turned up.

I don't answer and we keep striding ahead.

'Tell me,' I ask finally with a deadpan expression, 'is this Flor Goetschalckx one of the plotters too?'

Lode frowns.

'He could come in handy, you see. A crew like this could use an insurance agent. For all possible accidents in and around the home.'

Lode sighs. 'What are you, the court jester?'

'Out of the mouths of fools, mate. What are you doing with those amateurs?'

'Shall we not mention some of the places you frequent, *mate*?'

'Such as?'

'All that scum in the Hulstkamp where you dragged our Yvette to? Yeah, I know, you told her not to tell anyone. Are you completely mad?'

'It's safer like that, being in with bastards.'

'Safer for who? My sister? I don't think so. Everyone sees everything in this city. But you think you're invisible. You think it's all a game.'

'Come off it, your professor thinks so too. And so do you. Talk about the pot calling the kettle black.'

'So we're all fools.'

'You're not wrong there.'

'Shall we go for a beer?'

'Ah, sure, why not? Maybe the Hulstkamp's still open...'

'Up yours, "Robert".'

'Same to you, "Vincent".'

A quarter of an hour later we're saying 'cheers' to each other in the Alma.

My uniform has become a comfort. It delineates my days. Going on patrol is a calming ritual amid the daily madness, and in the meantime I've got to know Gaston so well I can complete his sentences as a matter of routine. At the end of our shift we run through the bullshit that's happened to us that day with the deputy superintendent and he writes whatever suits him in the incident log. Generally I hope he'll bless us afterwards. That's what it feels like, an absolution of sins.

'Exactly,' growls Gaston. 'And as long as none of us lot…'

'…makes a fuss…'

'…it will all turn out fine. Blast if you're not making progress, Wilfried. It's a beautiful thing to see a young foal, after wobbling and waggling on its four legs, finally—'

'I get it.'

Gaston laughs his hearty laugh. We're sitting in the canteen and eating our sandwiches before our shift starts.

'Listen to this!' Gaston chortles as he smooths the creases out of his newspaper. 'A pastoral letter from our cardinal. "The inner state of the country grows worse by the day. Acts of violence are being carried out incessantly almost everywhere. It is no longer even possible to keep track of these assaults on life. Where is this river of blood leading us?"'

'Goodness,' I say.

'Things are getting serious when the mitre mob starts squeaking. This line's priceless too. Listen to this: "We ask for an end to bloodshed and a return to patience and calm in the unshakable hope of a just peace." There you have it, all solved. Everyone in the resistance will have read the paper, surely? Now we can go home.'

'And terrorism will be consigned to hell forever…'

'Rest assured.'

Gaston goes to stand up, but starts groaning instead and lowers himself back down again extremely cautiously.

'What's wrong now?'

'Piles, also known as a bloody pain in the arse. Don't laugh. It's caused by drink and that's a weakness we all share. Learn from me before you give yourself over to disgrace and debauchery.'

Gus Skew comes in and says that a bomb has just gone off in Potgieter Straat.

'You should be on your way then,' says Gaston, without batting an eyelid. He winks at me while reopening his lunch bag.

'Don't be daft—it's not on our beat and you know that perfectly well.'

I chime in with, 'It's not our speciality either, to be honest.'

In our neighbourhood full of bars, hotels and jewellers, no bombs get detonated and nobody throws explosives in through windows. Too many Germans out whoring and boozing, I suspect, and bombs aren't exactly subtle, with a good chance of more than one dead body. Here we very occasionally get a dusk shooting in someone's home or on their doorstep, now and then preceded by a warning note along the lines of 'Nazi lackey, you have been sentenced by the people's court.' Sometimes the recipient of one of these threats registers a complaint against person or persons unknown, sometimes not. It doesn't make

277

much difference. Yesterday we happened to have one carted off to hospital, where he soon died. 'I came in to report they were after me,' he muttered before the ambulance arrived, 'and you didn't lift a finger.'

We nod, we establish the facts, we take notes, we draw up a record, we ask for details. When exactly did you find that letter, ma'am? Could you tell us the exact time this took place, sir? Which of the neighbours have been behaving suspiciously, in your opinion? There is a soothing undertone to all our actions; they are designed to induce calm. We are watching over you. That thought, however, calms us more than anyone else.

'That's important too,' Gaston says. 'Nobody has any use for a jittery cop letting on that nothing gets followed up any more and everything's out of our control.'

'It has been for ages.'

'Absolutely. But that's not the point. Your calm and dignity are weapons in times of insanity. Be grateful for your uniform, son—it gives you peace of mind.'

Someone downstairs calls our names at the top of his voice.

The deputy superintendent informs us that we have to go to the Golding in Anneessens Straat.

'A couple of Germans are making trouble.'

'Forget it. Give it to two other idiots.'

'I'm giving it to you two, Gaston. What are you standing here for?'

'I don't want—'

'Gaston,' the deputy super roars, 'if you don't want to make a fuss, don't! Go and do your bloody job for once!'

A couple of our fellow officers can't restrain their laughter, relieved that they're not the ones who have to go to the

Golding. We stride out to loud applause. 'Give 'em what for, lads!' they shout after us.

Brasserie Golding is two doors up from the Metro Cinema in a narrow street full of night spots. There are a lot of people around, but it's only just gone eight and the night hasn't really kicked off yet. For one member of the SS it's already too much. He's leaning on a tree outside the Golding and roaring at the full moon, delirious. Everyone acts like he doesn't exist. Even before we've made it that far a table flies out through the Golding's front window. The drunk soldier ducks, but still gets covered with shards of glass. He looks in, shrugs stupidly as the glass falls off him, waves to his chums and laughs out loud as customers scuttle out of the building like terrified rats. One of them, a fairly sloshed man with a Hitler moustache and an outsized raincoat, stops us on the street. 'They're mad as hatters. It's good you're here because it's really getting out of hand...' Then he pauses, looks us over one after the other and sighs. 'I don't think there's enough of you.'

The interior of the brasserie looks like a battlefield. Chairs and tables scattered left and right. One of the SS men is frothing at the mouth as he smashes a stool to pieces on the bar. Splinters of wood fly everywhere. I see a head pop up and then take shelter again behind the taps. Five other men in SS uniforms are standing in a circle to toast each other, paying no attention to the havoc. A few more are sitting a little further back in the restaurant, surrounded by guffawing women and champagne bottles in buckets. One soldier is sitting by himself at a small table weeping, ignored by all. The frothing soldier is reaching for another bar stool with his bleeding hands when he catches sight of us standing there. With a beaming smile, he calls out to his comrades, '*Hurra, Jungs! Die Feuerwehr ist da!*'

'What's the dick saying?' Gaston asks through clenched teeth.

'He says we're firemen.'

Gaston pulls out his truncheon and hits the blonde Aryan drunk, who has his arms wide and is smiling in welcome, straight in the throat. Coughing and grabbing his neck, he drops to his knees. Everyone is now looking at us. Besides the rattling of the felled SS man, who is having great difficulty breathing, silence now reigns. Everyone has sobered up; everyone is suddenly determined. At the back soldiers are calmly disentangling themselves from their tarts' arms. A champagne glass falls to the floor. Even the one who was just sobbing cracks his knuckles, ready for battle.

'That wasn't the best idea you've ever had, Gaston.'

He ignores me and roars, louder than I've ever heard him before, 'Everyone *zu* house, God damn it! Get out of here now, or you're in for it. *Sie gehen* here *raus* or else. Understood?'

Someone knocks Gaston's helmet off his head. Swearing, he turns and hits the SS man in the stomach. The rest take another step closer, calm and controlled, a killing machine that's ready to devour us, their clown-like prey. One of them picks the white helmet up off the ground, undoes his fly and pisses into it. It takes a few seconds before the soldiers start bellowing with laughter.

'We've got to get out of here,' I say, as calmly as I can.

'My bloody helmet!'

Gaston's sparse black hair is sticking up in sweaty wisps. The SS man shakes off his cock and tosses the helmet back to Gaston. The piss runs down our faces.

Sirens start their loud howling.

Thunder in the distance.

The British. An air raid.

The AA guns start immediately.

Behind the bar we hear a trapdoor slamming shut. The landlord has taken shelter in his beer cellar.

Then we hear a dull bang that makes the walls shake and has everyone running for their lives and suddenly Gaston and I are not comical firemen any more.

'Saved by the Brits,' I shout.

'Get used to it,' Gaston shouts back.

It's a nice day and she wants to go for a ride. Her mother will lend me her bicycle.

'Where shall we go?' she asks.

The things she says, the way she looks at me—they all raise the suspicion that I'm still in limbo as far as her heart is concerned. That feeling makes me shrink, just as I am now, on her mother's rickety bike, a head smaller than her too. We turn into Van Maerlant Straat, past the house where Chaim Lizke is still hidden, which suddenly makes me long to work on my poems, my 'Confessions of a Comedian', which only come to me there, at the table where the Jew reads his books, and don't grow until it's my turn to take him his supplies again. The moment that thought occurs, the poems start swirling around my head. But Yvette is keeping such a close eye on me I can't afford to get carried away. I have to be with her now, nowhere else. We turn left, cross Italië Lei and ride a good distance along Paarden Markt. She follows me without a word, without asking where we're going. Close to the red-light district, I turn right and we cross Anker Rui. There are the boats bobbing on the greenish-black water of Willem Dock, where the seagulls screech louder than anywhere else in the city. We clatter over the lock bridge.

'Where are you taking me?'

'Away from the city,' I say and it sounds like 'away from the dirt and filth'.

We ride past sailors' bars where swaying, hang-head drunks are already leaning on the front walls for support, even though it's still morning. The fishmongers have put their wares out in wooden trays, but there are hardly any sober people around at all. The city hasn't woken up yet.

After London Bridge, where the larger boats are moored, we see the beckoning green of the riverbank, which we follow north.

'Ha,' she laughs. 'Is that where we're going? It's not the season for it yet.'

Although it has already got significantly warmer, summer is still far away. And that's why I want to go to North Castle with its woods, beach and swimming ponds. There won't be a soul there, that's what I'm guessing. I want to be alone with her.

It's quiet.

She stares at the water licking at the abandoned beach. On the poplar-lined opposite bank, not too far away, three fishermen are sitting on their baskets. I take her by the hand and lead her to the bushes and trees.

'What are you up to?'

The look in her eyes suggests she already knows the answer to that question and is now curious about how I intend to go about it. It's a test, that's what she's telling me: do this properly and we have a future; fail and it's over for good.

I spread my raincoat out on an out-of-the-way patch of lawn behind some thick bushes. She sits down elegantly, as if at a picnic with sandwiches and tea, surrounded by gloved butlers.

'Do you have a cigarette for me?'

I ignore her question and kiss her on the throat. I sense her smile. The tip of my tongue traces a path from her collarbone to the back of her ear. The smile grows wider. I run my hands run over her breasts until my thumbs find her nipples through her bra and the cream-coloured fabric of her blouse. I undo two buttons. At the third, her hand seizes my left wrist. My other hand shoots up to her throat and I force her backwards, to the ground. She lets go of my wrist. Her blouse is now open. I slide up her satin camisole while making sure she doesn't slip away. She averts her eyes. When I lick her neck again while holding her down, she can't repress a slight groan. I work her tube skirt up to reveal her suspenders. I nip one of her thighs. And then I bite her everywhere I feel her flesh. That surprises her, but I push her head back down. 'Beast…' she says, but it sounds like a question. And that question only provokes me. I answer with, 'No, it's me.' Me, the bastard, just me. And I push her skirt up until it's under her bum and bite and lick some more. 'I want…' she whispers a few times in a row, 'I want…' Whereupon I answer that it's not up to her to want anything, that she should keep quiet. And miraculously she doesn't smile. I raise her buttocks and pull her lacy knickers down past her stockings. She claps both hands over her crotch. I grab her wrists, push her hands to the ground, stare at her bush and keep staring. 'What are you doing?' she giggles, suddenly nervous. 'I'm going to eat you up whole,' I say, looking her straight in the eyes. She nods very briefly, that's all.

'You filthy swine. Leave that girl alone!'

I turn. A fisherman with a red face and a drooping moustache is staring at me in total fury.

'Shove off,' I say calmly, 'shove off right this minute or you'll be fish feed.'

'Listen to the gob on it.'

I stand up. 'Hello,' I say. 'I'm not joking. Go home. Your mama's got to fry those fish.'

The fisherman looks past my shoulder at Yvette, nods meekly and goes back to the path to the river. I'm still standing with my back to her when she finally whispers, 'Come here.'

'There's something you have to do first,' I say.

I push down my zip. She half rises.

For the first time I feel no hesitation. For the first time I feel greedy. I push my underpants down and am now standing just in front of her. She looks.

'Open your mouth,' I say.

Our love-making lasts until dusk. Now and then a voice comes closer, then moves on again. We pay them almost no attention. I bite her. She rakes me with her nails. From virgin straight to animal.

Afterwards she says, 'What got into you? It was like you'd gone mad…'

And again she's not smiling. This time she's serious.

She wants to wheel the bikes home, even though it really is getting dark by now.

We carry on in silence until she finally says, 'You and that fisherman. He got very scared all of a sudden.'

'Look at this…'

Meanbeard slides two identity cards over to me. One is for a man I don't know, merchant by trade and so on and so forth. The other makes my heart pound. I keep my quivering hands under the table. The photo shows Chaim Lizke. It's fairly recent. Suspicious and proud, he stares up at me. Surname: Goetschalckx. Christian names: Florimond Jozef. Profession: insurer. Below the photo is his height: 1.60 metres. In the box for 'Successive addresses' it says 22 Lange Leem Straat. Signed by 'the Registrar (or his representative)'. In the top right-hand corner a splash of something brown, not yet fully dried.

'Forged, of course,' Meanbeard sneers.

'Really?'

'I'd bet my right arm they're Yids. What do you reckon? Look at those eyes and those thick lower lips.'

We're sitting in a small office on the ground floor of a fancy house on Elisabeth Laan, the new headquarters of the Sicherheitsdienst. The tall windows look out on a somewhat overgrown garden. Blackbirds are singing. One lands on the wrought-iron railing of the terrace, turns its head to look in, turns away again and flies over to one of the chestnuts along the side of the building. To our right is a small bower with arches and columns, ready for a trip back in time, afternoon tea on a scorching day in the nineteenth century, with staff to bring out the cake and pour the tea from a silver pot.

'Still here, Wilfried?'

'Forged, but well made,' I say a little too nervously. 'Or else they just nicked blank cards and filled them in themselves. That's possible too.'

'It does happen. We've known that for quite a while now. It does happen and, most importantly, it happens at your station in Vesting Straat. Do you follow my drift?'

'How did you get these?'

'The same way we get everything, *jeune homme*. A city that is sick, a city that, how shall I put it, tolerated far too many foreign germs for years because the ruling plutocracy of yesteryear constantly protected those alien elements… A city like that takes vengeance. That's unavoidable. It's a law of nature. As soon as the people see an opportunity to really have a say, there's no stopping them. That's how a city purges itself.'

'Snitching, you mean?'

'Come now, what a word. You disappoint me. With your degree of intellectual development I thought you would have at least outgrown the playground.'

'We get those letters too. Half of them seem to have been written by someone who's escaped from the loony bin or wants revenge because the next-door neighbour can't keep his hands off his wife.'

'And the other half are people who want to help their city recover by getting rid of Jews and terrorists who haven't realized their *ancien régime* is over. One of them gave us an address in Lange Leem Straat. "Strange men holding regular meetings at a late hour…" We kept watch for a while. And what did we discover?…'

Keep breathing. My hands are clawing my trouser legs. Here it comes. Here comes the accusation, the spit in my face, the hand on my shoulder, the cell, the end. My mind shoots around this new circuit like a racing car. Will I have to accelerate in a second, denying everything and laughing it off? Or will I need to judge the corner that's coming up and apply the brakes, admitting half of it and twisting the rest?

'Mainly it all came down to one man. We finally picked him up in a building near België Lei. That's where we found these documents, together with the usual flyers and ammunition. Not much, but enough. Concentrating on him was a gamble, but it paid off. Or better put, it's paying off, because the investigation is far from complete.'

'What's it got to do with me?'

Meanbeard looks out of the window at the garden. It has started drizzling. 'Did you know the Germans are so disciplined that not only does a volunteer like me have to put in an official application for a special interrogation, but that almost every employee has to too, regardless of rank or position?'

'No, I didn't know that.'

'Gregor is not fond of all this bureaucracy. And I admit, it's tedious, even ridiculous, but on the other hand you can only admire their having so much self-control in times of war. We're no animals. But sometimes it's a beast you need. And yet that self-control, the paperwork… Strange. Anyway, our request was approved fairly quickly. We have good news. Our suspect has confessed that someone from the police is involved in his group. Someone from your station.'

'Who?'

Meanbeard rubs his hands. 'That's why I had you come here, Wilfried. This is a moment you don't want to miss. Omer's working on him. If you ask me, we'll know everything there is to know in less than an hour.'

The door swings open and we hear a man screaming as we go down the stairs. The cellar is divided into cells where shadows sit behind bars in total silence. I only hear one woman mumbling the Our Father. Meanbeard opens a metal door. Fear and filth waft out to meet me. The professor is hanging by the wrists, manacled and chained to an iron bar, naked and bleeding. Someone in glasses is leaning against a table to roll a cigarette. It looks like that little arsehole from the Hulstkamp who came over to tell me he's a translator for the SD. Now he looks at me contemptuously, licks the paper and lights his cigarette.

'Perhaps you know Joris…'

'We've met,' I nod.

Omer turns towards me. He's rolled up his sleeves and wipes his bloody hands clean. He's wearing a butcher's apron over his clothes. There are rods and sticks on the table next to him, along with glasses and a bottle of cognac.

'And?' Meanbeard asks while he too removes his coat and rolls up his sleeves.

'It's taking too long for my taste,' Omer whispers.

The professor starts sobbing and swears quietly, 'Bastards, dirty bastards…' The words come bubbling out. Snot is running from his nose. His face is completely swollen. One of his arms looks broken. His hands are curled like talons. Some of his fingers no longer have nails. The rest of his body is a patchwork quilt of bruises, deep wounds, clotted blood and splashes of brown.

Omer pours himself another and looks at us questioningly. No, I don't feel like a cognac. Neither does Meanbeard. Omer shrugs and knocks his back in one go. Four-eyed Joris takes a sip of his too.

The professor's sobbing grows louder. 'It's enough!' he shouts suddenly. 'It's enough, you fucking bastards!'

'Now he's getting a big mouth,' Omer grins. 'Listen to him bleat…'

Meanbeard goes up close to the professor. 'You'll have to excuse me, you piece of shit, I wasn't able to persevere with my studies like you. So I'm a bit slow on the uptake when an intellectual like yourself chooses to communicate that he's sick to death of something. I don't get what he's saying, you see. Then I try to work out what exactly "it's enough" might mean.'

Omer goes over to Meanbeard's side, though not without giving Joris and me a wink first, as if we're in for a treat, the biggest joke ever. 'We're actually the ones who get to decide what's enough and what's not. I know this is difficult for an elite chap like you, one who's spent his entire life looking down on people like us. Yes, spit it out, feel free. Aren't we traitors in your eyes, you Jew-lover? People you're allowed to shoot in the back and leave to bleed to death on their own doorstep? Am I lying, maybe? But now, unfortunately, you with all your so-called intellectual disdain are a complete nothing.' Omer gives the professor a tremendous punch in the stomach. The sobbing stops for a moment. Everything stops for a moment. For a moment I think, when will it be him? When will the lawyer get his?

'Joris! Water!'

Four-eyes reaches for a bucket.

'Out of the way…' he mutters. Omer and Meanbeard both take a step to one side. Joris throws the water over the professor as hard as he can. He comes to with a start, raises his head and looks at me; I'm standing back a little but still in plain view. The professor keeps staring at me, opens his mouth, vomits blood and suddenly seems to smile. It's a mad sight that makes my heart beat so loud I'm afraid everyone will hear it.

'Robert,' the professor exclaims. 'Robert and Vincent, those two together, those two from the p… from the p… from the police…' He shakes his head and vomits up more blood.

I try to stand straight, but the sound of the stupid false names Lode gave almost makes me faint. Immediately the professor's head droops again.

'Robert who?! Vincent who?!' Omer and Meanbeard shout at the same time, pounding him with their fists. The professor has stopped groaning and sobbing, and is nothing but a lifeless punching bag.

'Joris!'

Four-eyes holds the bucket under the tap, fills it with water and says again, as calmly as last time, 'Out of the way.'

Again the bucket of water splashes over the professor. Again he comes to with a start. Again his gaze seeks me out where I'm standing nailed to the spot.

He splutters out bubbles of blood first, then nods, half in my direction, 'He's jus—'

I see myself charging towards him in a complete panic, shoving Omer and Meanbeard out of the way. 'Who is Robert?! Who is Vincent?!' I hear myself bellow while kneeing him in the balls. The professor blacks out, deflating like a balloon.

'Idiot…' Meanbeard sneers.

'Joris!'

Another bucket of water in that battered face.

Nothing.

He hangs there without a peep.

Omer sighs. 'I think we need to fetch the doctor. Joris?'

'I'm on my way...' Joris sighs, and snaps at me that I'm an 'amateur'.

It's now 2 p.m. and pouring with rain.

'Fuck...' says Lode for the third time. 'How do you know?'

'You know how I know.'

'Is that swine with the goatee involved?'

I nod.

'So we're in deep shit.'

'If I'm not mistaken that bungler you call a professor doesn't know our names, or does he?'

Lode shakes his head vacantly. Meanwhile I see him thinking about a dozen other things. 'He doesn't know any names, but... we did once have a meeting where we've stashed Lizke. God that was stupid of me. That's where we took the photo for his identity card.'

'And now?'

'The Jew has to go. Today.'

Lizke is shocked and flinches away from us while raising his arms protectively in front of his face. The chair he's sitting on falls back; the lamp over the table starts to swing. Immediately he grabs a hammer that he probably found lying around here and has kept close as his only weapon ever since. We can no longer help him and he's sensed it at once.

The hammer in his hand states clearly that we're now like all the rest.

'*Keine* panic!' Lode says with all the calm he can muster.

Lizke wavers before sitting down again and apologizing while he wipes the sweat from his forehead. He puts the hammer down and listens to what we expect of him.

'*Nein. Nein!*'

I look at Lode and sigh. After all, what are we asking of him? We're proposing that he set out without any papers to make his way to an address in a city he hardly knows. We're trying to fob him off with a lottery ticket instead of a feasible escape plan. And he knows it.

'*Ich gehe nicht.* I stay here.'

'*Hier bleiben, kaputt.* We *kaputt* too. *Alles* fucked, *Herr Lizke! Keine chance.*'

I have to look away from Lode, otherwise I'm likely to burst out in nervous giggles.

'Say something, Will! Tell him it's the only way.'

'*Alles oder nichts, Herr Lizke. Es gibt keine andere Möglichkeit. Verstehen Sie? Wir sind verraten.*'

During Lode's explanation, Lizke didn't look at him once. Me, he stares at, as if a mystery is hidden in my eyes. Then he meekly takes his coat off the rack.

Lode raises his eyebrows. 'Blimey, he's scared of you.'

'A good thing too,' I say.

It was Lode's idea to escort the Jew to the railway station in uniform, but now we're walking past the Geuzen Gardens on our way to Keyser Lei, my discomfort with the plan increases, as if we're about to be unmasked at a costume ball. It's

Saturday and the sun is shining. There's a serious amount of people out on the streets. Trams jingle past and there are masses of people sitting at the café tables and staring out at passers-by, and therefore at us. In Van Maerlant Straat the crowd isn't too bad, but now we're getting closer to the station, Lizke has started mumbling anxiously, and when he sees two German officers on the other side of the zebra crossing he stops abruptly.

'*Nicht stehen*, walk…' Lode snaps, but Lizke is transfixed. Without a word to each other and almost synchronized, we grab him by the elbows and cross the road with him between us. The officers are satisfied with nods and vague salutes in their direction.

'Bloody hell,' I sigh. 'What we going to do at the station?'

'Just buy a ticket and put him on the train to Brussels,' Lode whispers back, as if talking about a reluctant child.

'*Entschuldigung?*' Lizke squeaks.

'Everything's fine,' Lode says with a contrived wink.

But we're amateurs. We're bunglers. We're clowns. Our pigeon breasts are decorated with a row of silver buttons and our heads are crowned with white pisspots. We're the start of a joke: 'Two fools in fancy dress were walking down Keyser Lei with a Jew when…' We're done for, our uniforms are in danger of becoming transparent and the Jew seems to be marked with a star sewn onto the front of his coat and a target painted on the back.

At the corner of Van Ertborn Straat and Keyser Lei, close to the Rex Cinema, we stop. We can't cross because of a demonstration. Dozens of men in the uniform of the Black Brigade are marching towards the railway station. Flags everywhere, banners everywhere. 'One Leader, one Movement, one People' we read on one and 'Victory to National Socialism' on another. They're beating out a rhythm on drums and tambourines, singing and keeping step. But the crowd on the street aren't cheering like they were a few years ago. Almost nobody raises their hat in the air or calls out 'Flanders forever'. Hardly anyone even stops to watch, unless it's the odd bumpkin in from the country, plodding around the big city for the first time and taking off his cap while staring at the ground, as if to show respect for a funeral procession. A few SS soldiers salute, that's all. Between us we feel Lizke shudder. We're holding him tightly but discreetly by the wrists. Finally the procession is past and we can cross over.

The Jew keeps mumbling, '*Wir folgen den Toten.*'

Following the dead, as if ghosts can dance in daylight.

We've almost reached the station.

It's crawling with uniforms: SS, Wehrmacht, Field Gendarmerie, here and there one of ours. We keep saluting and stubbornly walking on at the same time. The Black Brigade turns left towards the zoo, probably for a recruitment speech full of hot air and blather, after which they'll all salute the flag with their paws stuck up in the air. As the last of them go round the corner, I peer through the confusion—people rushing to catch a train, travellers standing at hotel entrances with their baggage, women kissing each other hello or goodbye and men patting each other on the shoulder—and see Omer and Meanbeard at an outdoor café. Like two vaudeville characters, they're sitting there to soak up the sun. Omer raises a hand to order another. I pick up the pace, manoeuvring us away from the road and closer to the buildings, and immediately doubts rise. Did I see them sitting there or not? But I'm too scared to look back to check. I feel tainted, trapped, observed.

'What is it?'

'Let's take the Pelikaan Straat entrance.'

'*Was ist los?*'

'*Kein Problem,*' I bark at Lizke. 'Calm *bleiben.*'

We cross the road. Lizke tries to wriggle loose.

'Stop it...' Lode snaps.

Trying to keep someone under control like that while hauling him to the side entrance with his feet dragging is a complete spectacle but no one in the crowd looks up. People have got used to it. They don't want to know. Hardly anything even registers any more. Everything stays normal and will stay normal forever. I look back over my shoulder, half expecting to see Omer or Meanbeard trailing along behind, ready to collar us at the last moment.

'Fuck!' shouts Lode.

Lizke has taken advantage of that one movement of mine, that brief instant of inattention, to break free and is now running away from us like a madman, zigzagging between the travellers with his hat in one hand and a modest suitcase in the other. It takes a moment before Lode and I, totally stunned, have set off in pursuit. We follow him into the station and see him striding to the central hall. We push people out of the way. I reach for my whistle, but Lode shakes his head just in time and rushes to the Astrid Plein exit. I run up the wide staircase to get a better view. Sweat is trickling down my forehead. Nothing. No Lizke. Then I see Lode coming back by himself.

We've lost him.

*

'Just tell us what it is…'

Mother can't bear another second of her sister's hand wringing. Father has taken cover behind a newspaper. I'm sitting numbly at the kitchen table, weighed down by deep sadness and not even capable of standing up and going to my room, too tired to withdraw like a sick cat under a wardrobe. How much longer must I be the son of these two?

Aunty Emma sighs. 'I don't want to bother you with it.'

'Then go away again,' Mother answers firmly. 'You can't come bursting in here with tears in your eyes and then start talking nonsense. I took our dinner off the gas just for you because I could see something was wrong.'

'In other words, you've already bothered us,' sounds from behind the newspaper. Father is hungry. He winks at me. I sigh in reply.

'No, Father. That's not true either. And you're always welcome to stay for dinner. There's not a lot though.'

'Not like at yours, Emma,' my father tries again. Over the last few months he's developed an obsession with other people's food, which in his fantasies grows more and more abundant compared to what we get at home. He mostly blames his wife for the consequences of the increasing shortages and my diminishing ability to find a way around them. She's starving him.

'Ah, shut up for once. I've bloody well had it up to here with your idiotic jabbering!'

Silence. Mother's sudden outburst has stunned everyone. My father, who's suddenly turned as white as a sheet, lets his newspaper sag. Aunty Emma's mouth is hanging open. My mother has lowered her eyes, but she means it, that's clear, she's not taking a single word back. Father stands up, clears his throat and says he's going out to get some fresh air. We hear the front door closing.

'Good riddance with all his nagging,' Mother says, still just as determined, without her voice trembling or catching. She nods in my direction and asks Aunty Emma if she should chase me off too. Then the two women burst out laughing. I stand up.

'Not at all,' Aunty Emma says, 'just stay there.'

'Has your German left you?' Mother asks.

Aunty Emma shakes her head. 'No, it's because of what he just came to tell me. He's completely distraught. I had to calm him down. I've never seen him like this before.'

'Stop beating round the bush, Emma.'

Something I can't quite place has slipped into Mother's tone, as if her shouting just now has released something she has kept hidden from us all. Aunty Emma doesn't notice; not that noticing things about other people is her strong suit anyway.

'A month ago they got a new colleague from the Eastern Front, Hauptsturmführer Schmidt or something like that. Gregor and the others didn't get along with him that well. I met him once. Very quiet, no drinker. He always looked like he was in a complete rage. Gregor said he refused to understand how they do things here, that Russia had hit him hard, he'd seen too much and been through too much, it more or less drove him mad and... It makes me sick to think of it... That fellow picked fights with everyone, especially Heinrich...' Aunty Emma looks at me. 'You know him. He was in the Hulstkamp once when you and your girl were there... Remember?' Aunty Emma sees me turning pale and tells me with a stabbing glance that she won't be digressing into how drunk I got or what happened in the toilets. 'The Hauptsturmführer with the scar on his face, quite a jolly chap. Heinrich…'

'I remember him vaguely.'

'Well, this bloke from the Eastern Front shot him. Can you believe it? Germans shooting each other? This Schmidt fellow drew his pistol and shot him dead as if it was nothing. Shouting that they were all profiteers. Incredible. My Gregor works day and night.'

'So did they lock the madman up?'

'No,' Aunty Emma says quietly. 'Gregor was lucky, because that fellow started shooting at everyone in sight. In the end it was Gregor who got him. He could have been killed…' She starts to sob.

'Child, come now…' My mother gently squeezes her sister's shoulders.

'Some… times…' Aunty Emma has started bawling and can hardly speak. 'Sometimes… I think… it's all going to pot… You're in love, you love each other so much, and you make plans… but so many things can go wrong… Sometimes I think: it's over, it's finished… and where does that leave me? Do you understand?'

She rubs her stomach. It's playing up again. Back to where she started.

'Oh, come now. Things won't come to that,' my mother says while looking at me, sharper than ever, perhaps seeing me sharply for the very first time.

Aunty Emma says goodbye. I hear her sobbing quietly at the front door for a moment and then she's gone.

'Your father's probably found a safe haven somewhere by now, don't you think?'

298

I shrug.

'Dear, oh dear...' After putting dinner back on, she sits down opposite me again. 'So now they're at each other's throats. What kind of circus is this turning into? They come here stealing like magpies, sticking everything they can find in their own pockets, getting pissed off their faces, messing around with women like our Emma, who's actually a complete ninny, no matter how much I love her, and what happens in the end? They start killing each other... All because of the money from the foreigners who settled here. You see where it leads. Those Jews have driven that whole nation mad with greed. They deserve each other.'

'Yes,' I say, 'it's always someone else's fault.'

'Don't you ever get tired of your own drivel, Wilfried?'

Shadows can talk. No clotted blood on the floor of this room, and none of the dried meat or vegetables I delivered either. Meanbeard's German books are still here, together with a coat, some forgotten underwear and a worn sock. The rest has disappeared together with Chaim Lizke. I'm finished. Or not? It's hard to say. Lizke's place of hiding has become my refuge. I fill page after page here with my poems, my 'Confessions of a Comedian', as if there's no end to it, as if the end itself has been abolished and everything just carries on unceasingly towards the mouth of hell, a goal that can never be reached. The only thing we've heard, what Lode has picked up around the place, is that the professor was locked up for a while in Begijnen Straat, then carted off to a camp. That's all anyone knows. Everything drags on and nobody comes here to kick in the door. Nobody arrests me and drags me off, hauling me off stage like a failed actor. So I just keep listening to the shadows and writing away at what is supposed to become my first collection of poetry. The outside world has become an excuse, an intermezzo for the hours I spend here. I can still smell Lizke. I pick up the hammer he found here. Now and then I think I see him, in a dark corner with an apologetic grin on his face, or I feel him sitting next to me at the table while the ink leaks from my pen to form letters on the page. I write about treacherous bastards and not knowing the truth, about blood on the ground and blows to the face, about children who will be born with a caul, about misleading delays and ambiguous friendship. In a brightly lit room, I have two sworn enemies smile while they speak, each with a glass in his hand and a knife under the table. I have soldiers march behind protesting mothers with their flies unbuttoned. I give newspapers wheedling mouths. I make people with hunger in their eyes join long queues to shuffle past mounds of slaughtered dolls. I rub tortured bodies with honey and decorate them with sprigs of thyme while gramophones blare, 'Another hero has been born!' Whereupon everyone in the room sings in reply: 'Ta-ra-ra Boom-de-ay, you are so still today!' I dedicate a poem to Lode, but tear it up at once. Then I see Lode and Yvette together in an incestuous dream and the poems present themselves like street-corner sluts, obscene and clacking their tongues. I'm King Midas in reverse. My words transforming everything into shit and filth instead of gold. Sometimes I lay down my pen and reread a few poems. Is it all too monotonous? But the manic urge to write is only discouraged for a few seconds. Whenever it's time for me to head home I hear Angelo sighing with satisfaction. Finally,

finally. A son is arising here whose verse will pile scorn upon his clapped out, sentimental poetic fathers, casually annihilating their stubborn conceit.

It's these words, O great-grandson, that abruptly catapult me back into my own study and this century, temporarily cutting me off from my story. I think they're accurate enough, but at the same time this burgeoning poetic soul has become so strange to me, so disassociated from everything that has happened in my later life, that I feel like laughing in his face. You idiot! You arrogant piece of scum! You ignoramus! For the life of me I cannot recall the state of mind that gave rise to those words. What I do remember is that the collection was published after the war. Was there rejoicing? Probably not much. Was there scorn? Perhaps, but that's something people forget just as quickly. Was this the rebellion of the son in the house of poetry? People need a bit of nonsense now and then—propped up by will, ambition and a vision of the future, true, but no less ridiculous for all of that. You keep a lot of your nonsense to yourself. Occasionally you bother someone close to you with it. It's seldom ennobling. If I saw you reading all this, I'd avert my eyes and leave the room with a gracious smile. But even while closing the door behind me, I would feel my heart trembling with impatience. If you later informed me that you'd finished reading it, I would look at you with an expectant gaze like a dog that's tried to please its master with a new trick, even if the novelty consists of a fresh turd squeezed out on the bath mat for the very first time. Vanity is what makes you share. And that vanity is ridiculous and the ridiculous makes you vulnerable.

I never let Yvette read anything. I kept her away from my poetry. Outside the poems, normality ruled; in the poems, everything else. That's how the young Wilfried would have put it.

Looking back I would have liked to give my granddaughter all kinds of things to read because I felt she understood me, that she knew what I was talking about even if she herself had hardly experienced anything. But when she was about nineteen, Hilde started closing herself off from me. From one day to the next I had to ascertain that the apple of my eye, my ally, the rebellious family member I saw as part of my tiny conspiracy against everything and everybody, no longer wanted anything to do with me. I lost sight of her, she let us know through her parents that even our rare family get-togethers bored her and, when I had put my pride to one side and finally dared to ring her up to ask 'how things were going', it was made clear to me that she was too busy with her studies to come to the phone. I heard that she was taking medicine to banish her dark dreams. In my imagination, those pills were slowly hollowing out her skull, dissolving everything that linked her to me first, before then, after reducing the rest to mush as well—banality with neither highs nor lows—what next, what next… I wept bitter tears for her. But that too brought no release, no more than the rage and resentment that came to torment me. Nothing gets you down more than fury about something you can't understand. It wouldn't pass, it kept smouldering away, pointless and irrational, until every memory had been scorched and charred and I was certain that it was those pills that had alienated her from me and, even worse, that that was also why she was taking them, to get away from the dark monster she recognized in me and knew as her own. How haughty, how pretentious. But the bloody thing is… I sometimes think it still.

Nicole knocks on the door.

'Go away…' I say.

'I've run your bath,' she answers, opening the door. 'Oh dear, your eyes are all red.'

'From the cigars,' I say.

'You haven't had any for months, Mr Wils. I gave them all away. Have you forgotten?'

With a firm grip on my arm, she leads me to the bathroom.

She undresses me, ordering me to stick this arm in the air and then that one, lift my foot while leaning on her shoulder, in other words, not to make it too difficult for her. With every manoeuvre she says, 'So… that's right' or, 'There you go… excellent.' Her little encouragements comfort me, I'll admit that honestly. I lift my arms up high, hold on to her shoulder, catch a whiff of that peculiar, neutral-smelling skin lotion nurses are so crazy about, and whisper urgently, 'Careful, careful' when she helps me into the bath a little too fast for my liking.

'Let me do that…' I say as she reaches for the soap.

'I need to do your back,' she sighs.

'What's been happening, Nicole? What do the newspapers say?'

She washes my back and rattles off her overview: 'The soldiers are still in the streets, the refugees keep coming, stocks are about to crash as per usual and the European Union is a lie.'

'Spare me your cynicism, Nicole.'

'I wouldn't dare, Mr Wils. And just give me a second. You can't get out of that bath alone.'

'As if I don't know that,' I say, almost relaxed in the water whose temperature she has decided, almost back in the delusion of the beginning, with me as a baby and her as my mother.

'No more pocket money for me,' Yvette says laconically.

She hands me the letter with the black border in the middle of one of my panic attacks. I'm picturing myself stripped naked on a parade ground with club-wielding executioners approaching from all sides. 'You're disgracing yourself in front of everyone!' an SS officer roars while the shit runs out of me and I quiver and weep in the presence of those who call themselves my parents and are now staring at me with their noses turned up. 'Haven't you learnt anything from us at all?' That could be the finale for that one poem I'm—

'Sweetheart… The letter. You're not even looking at it.'

Meanbeard's mother has apparently kicked the bucket. Verschaffel, Amandine, née Leyers: born in the days when people rode in coaches and the streets stank of horseshit, died with aeroplanes flying overhead, their bellies full of bombs, like dragon mothers about to give birth. Did she suffer? No, it says she was called to God in her sleep, undoubtedly with a linen bonnet stretched over her head and swathed in several layers of nightwear, dreaming perhaps of an adulterous count, a willing kitchen maid and an artist with a wounded heart, a world full of rakes and whores, without a son in sight.

'He's finally finished her off.'

'You're exaggerating, my love…' I sound like a poet with a tooth abscess.

Yvette raises her eyebrows while holding a burning match to her cigarette. Her parents are under no illusions as to where she picked up her new habit. 'In his bed, of course,' I heard her father whisper recently behind the kitchen door, which happened to be ajar. 'That's obvious.' Whereupon her mother hissed a furious 'Shhhhhh' as if throwing a bowl of water on the fire of his paternal possessiveness. Of course, there's no fooling her father. One look at her tells him everything. Sometimes we race to North Castle on the bikes to undress each other behind a bush. But the weather keeps getting better and there are more and more people out walking or fishing, even the odd person who's brave enough to paddle in the water. Sometimes it's just very brief moments at her house, which require me to slip unnoticed past the butcher's shop. At mine it's virtually impossible and the cellar where I write my poems and where we kept Lizke hidden is simply unthinkable for me. She's always saying we have to hurry, there's not much time. Sometimes I feel like she lets me inside her because otherwise I'll get too out of control, too mad with lust. Sometimes it's about her, and our love play is an answer to her own pitch-black restlessness, which it briefly soothes, like a piece of tender meat tossed to a vicious dog. Perhaps it's the restlessness her father recognizes and blames me for stoking. But he hasn't got strict with his daughter. On the contrary. After all, her father is convinced that he is now embroiled in the ultimate struggle for her heart, that things have got serious, because slow and steady Wilfried Wils is not going anywhere. He's all smiles now, although his eyes are as hard as ever. Not once does he mention his beautiful daughter to me, let alone the fact that his son and I have let his Jewish milch cow escape. 'I made up a story that explained it,' Lode told me when I asked about it. Bollocks, of course. A butcher like him doesn't fool that easily. And meanwhile—

'Sweetheart! What cloud are you on?'

'Excuse me. I just said you shouldn't exaggerate.'

'And I'm telling you your pal finally wore his mother down. The number of times he yelled at her... It was incredible. Sometimes he didn't give her anything to eat all day long. Or he'd give her such a terrible fright the poor woman would clutch at her heart and start to cry. Do you think that's normal? And he didn't care two hoots if I knew or not. In the end I couldn't bear the sight of him.'

'Uh-huh,' I say.

'He hit her...'

I nod. Why did Yvette get a death notice when I didn't?

They're burying the old lady in St Andrew's, her old parish. Late Gothic on the outside, baroque on the inside, a church for sinners with style, in sharp contrast to the down-and-outs gathered on the side entrance steps. Children, old people with trembling hands, a woman with a baby. I hurry past, running late. Yvette didn't want to come. 'I don't want to see that mother-murderer's face again!' But I do. I want to see Meanbeard. I want him to see me, so I can read his face and judge where I stand.

The church is much too big for the modest turnout. I stand at the back, recognizing the landlord of the White Raven, flanked by two men who could be a couple of his regulars.

At most there are some twenty mourners, spread out over the pews. Not a single German is present, nor anyone from the Flemish SS. I can't see any bosom friends like Omer

306

either. A few old people and some of his sentimental drinking buddies, that's all. Two wreaths near the coffin. I'm too far away to read who sent them. I slink a bit further to the right to get an angled view of the people at the front. Jenny is sitting next to Meanbeard, as if the funeral is suddenly doing double service as their wedding too, albeit in a minor key. Every time he rubs his eyes or lets his head hang, she routinely rests a gloved hand on his back, like someone calmly assisting a retching friend. She herself has paid attention to every last detail of her clothing, a bride in black. It's a shame she couldn't resist that crimson lipstick, but that's Jenny for you. Meanbeard, still bending forwards, lets out loud, echoing sobs in response to the priest's whispered words. It sounds so grotesque it's easy to imagine this grieving son, this newly minted orphan in his late forties, grinning like a fiend behind his turned-up collar. I wait until the time has come to pay your last respects by the coffin and join the end of the queue. We shuffle forward. It's Jenny who sees me first. She squeezes Meanbeard's arm. I make the sign of the cross next to the coffin, bow deeply and accept a holy card from the sexton. Before turning at one of the pillars to return to the back, I see the look on his face as he stares at me. Is that fury in his eyes or fear?

A few days later he mumbles 'Christ almighty...' when I appear at his front door with, tucked under my arm, various books in German that I borrowed from him for the entertainment of a certain Chaim Lizke. He scans the street in both directions before letting me in. It's more pulling me in, hurried and embarrassed.

'Who's that, sweetness?' Jenny calls, a little bored and clearly in the bedroom.

'Were you already in bed? Sorry…'

Meanbeard looks at me and shakes his head.

'Come up to my study with me.' He calls out to Jenny that it's nothing, just me.

We climb the stairs quietly. He closes the door carefully behind us, then snaps at me, 'You've got some gall.'

I put the books on one of the side tables. 'I know. I should have brought them back long ago.'

He looks at me in astonishment, his jaw literally dropping. 'Who do you think you are? How did you become so bloody full of yourself?'

'My innocence makes me weep…'

'What?'

'*Mon innocence me ferait pleurer. La vie est la farce à mener…*'

'…*par tous.* Yes, boy, I know it too, you show-off. Are you really coming up with Rimbaud now? Not everything's a farce. What gave you that idea? You're not him, you're no Rimbaud! You're a fucking traitor or a fool who doesn't know what kind of game he's playing. Don't you understand that? You should see your face! What kind of mask is that… What is it with you? How is it possible that I let myself be… Me, of all people, by you!'

He's trying to talk as quietly as he can, but at the word 'you' his anger comes rushing out loud and clear.

'Sweetheart?' sounds immediately two doors along.

'It's nothing, Jenny. I just sneezed!'

With a quivering hand, he pours himself a liqueur and knocks it back straight away. He pours himself another. Nothing for me. I sigh and sit down in one of his reading chairs.

'I have no idea what you're bloody—'

'No!' Meanbeard stretches an arm out towards me. His eyes flame. He reminds me of a picture of the Grand Duke of Alba, the Iron Duke, Governor of the Netherlands, who burned the rebels here at the stake, an illustration in the bright colours that thrilled me as a schoolboy without my knowing why. The broken limbs of tortured bodies left out for the crows to pick, black silhouettes on gibbets, banners high in the sky, the duke's horse lifting one of its front legs as if hesitating at the edge of an abyss its rider doesn't even suspect, the feverish rings around Alba's bulging eyes as he looks at the peasant scum who are so recklessly defying him with their raised pitchforks. 'Crush this lunacy! Take them to the gallows!'

'You seem to be enjoying this. Are you retarded or what?'

'Not at all,' I say, 'but if you could tell me what—'

'Come off it, you're doing it again! You're treating me like an imbecile. Stop the act! I know—does that make it clearer? I know about you. You're the bastard, you're the traitor! That silly bugger of a naive half-baked professor said so in so many words. Did you really think kicking him in the balls would shut him up? I could tell something was fishy right away. We got it out of him before the day was over, Omer and me... Do you have any idea?...'

Meanbeard turned back to the drinks cabinet and poured himself another, which he knocked back as quickly as the others. 'Do you have any idea what kind of position you put me in?' He looked at me for a moment, shaking his head. 'Obviously not, because otherwise you would have shown your face around here much sooner. Gutless bastard or moron, I can't quite work out what you are, maybe both rolled into one.'

Once I was accused of theft at secondary school. I'd stolen somebody's pencil case, felt seriously guilty about it and then completely repressed all memory of it afterwards. When the headmaster confronted me with my deeds, I felt the injustice of a false accusation rising, but at the same time that feeling struggled with the realization of a lie that was hidden so deep it assumed a life of its own, taking charge of my memory in the moment of confrontation.

Back then, tears came. Not now. Now I smile. I don't know why either.

'No!' Meanbeard shouts at the sight of my grin.

'Sweetheart, what's going on there!'

Meanbeard opens the door for a moment and makes placatory noises in the direction of the bedroom.

'Leave it to us. I'll be there soon. Promise!'

He closes the door and raises his hand to me. I stand up. He pushes me back into the armchair.

'I vouched for you,' he whispers, 'personally... If they figure out what you were up to at their headquarters... they'll come for me too. Do you understand? Then the leather coats will be at both our houses and they'll put us up against the wall without mercy, whether your aunty's fucking Gregor or not.'

He grabs me by my lapels and pulls me half up out of the chair.

'Do you have any idea what I had to do to get Omer to keep his trap shut?'

'Let go of me.'

Meanbeard freezes. Suddenly he looks old and shabby, a hermit in a threadbare dressing gown, surrounded by vermin. 'Omer got the keys to all the Jew houses I had left. That was

my nest egg. Those furnishings were the crème de la crème...'
He lets go of me. 'It's just a game to you, you bastard. But it's
people like me who pay the price. We've brought the Jews in
this city to their knees. The parasites who tormented us for so
long are almost all gone. That was a promise we kept. That
was partly my achievement, despite the hypocrisy of people
like you, despite the never-ending opposition you expect from
truly everyone, but not from the people you see as allies. When
you start thinking you're being cynical about every last thing,
that's when you walk into a trap and let people take you for a
ride. You're living on borrowed time, you bastard, and I'm the
one who's taken out the loan on behalf of both of us. Do you
understand? No, you don't get it. I can see it in your face...'
Another glass. Now he's stuttering while drunken tears run down
his cheeks. 'But not even that will stop me... Rest assured... Not
even that will ruin things... All I want... a tobacconist's together
with Jenny... where we can take it easy... without a Yid in sight,
in a city that can breathe again and is grateful to people like me
for the sacrifices I've borne, the deceit I've had to endure, the
betrayal by bastards, the betrayal by you. Now get—'

The door swings open. There's Jenny in a lime-green negligee.
'That's enough boozing now, you hear me?'
Her breasts dance under the flimsy fabric.

The zoo's grand reception hall is packed. Lode got the tickets
and now he's predicting that Stan Brenders and his big band
are going to 'tear the place down'.
'This place is full of *zazous*!' Yvette whispers excitedly.
'Bleeding heck, all that Brylcreem,' Lode mocks, although
he uses pomade too. But these *zazou* upstarts go a lot further

with their hair than Lode and I would even consider. The grease really is dripping out of the locks hanging down in long threads over their high shirt collars. They're wearing trousers that are just that little too short and their scrawny chests are wrapped in outsized double-breasted coats with lots of extra pockets that most of them refuse to take off in the hall. Because in times of scarcity you have to live big, you have to act like textile coupons are easy to get, even if you can tell from the majority's hollow-eyed faces that they only just get enough to eat. They all have umbrellas with them because that's what they do: use umbrellas as walking sticks and refuse to open them even when it's pouring. They're sitting spread throughout the hall. The *zazou* girls lay their heads on their boyfriends' narrow shoulders or wrap a dominant arm around the narrow span of their bony backs as if those young swingers are in danger of falling apart at any moment. The women are mostly in pleated skirts that come down to just above the knee and they have a clear preference for curling their hair. They are all made up to look pale, with here and there a little mauve under their cheekbones. Yvette loves their square shoulders and the fact that a lot of them keep their round, black sunglasses on inside, as if the hall is lit with the blazing sun of the Côte d'Azur.

'Get an eyeful of that,' says Lode. 'What a bunch of posers.'

'Yes,' I nod. I see him staring at all those peacocks like a bird of prey, all those skeletons wrapped in cheerful colours. Faced with all this fresh energy, only five or so years younger than the two of us, I feel Father Time pushing me along the road to nowhere. None of these dandies is anywhere near as cold-blooded as Lode and me. It's almost unbelievable that neither of us has had a nervous breakdown and we haven't said a word to each other about the sword hanging over our heads. Lode doesn't need to tell me he's still cooperating with his friends in the resistance. One glance at him is enough. He seems to have a constant smirk on his face, as if he could detonate a hidden bomb at any moment. It's like he's defying the whole world with that expression, more and more recklessly. But so far the world seems insufficiently interested. And I have my nightmares, my periods of swaggering confidence followed by panic attacks, my this and my that. What really does my head in is that the *zazous* seem completely indifferent. They really don't give a shit. Music is all that counts. They want to dance and do as they please. Sitting there slumped on those seats like babies with their eyes half shut and their lips puckered, waiting for their girl's maternal teat. No, I feel it. It's over. I'm already too old. And nothing's even started yet.

'At least there's hardly any Jerries here...' Yvette laughs and her teeth gleam too white for words.

'It's true. Finally no Hunnish in our ears.'

'Hun-what?' Yvette laughs.

'They've been here for years and you've never heard that? The Hun doesn't speak German, he speaks Hunnish.'

It's something my father says. He's had enough. No decent food, having to queue much too long for coupons and not a decent summer coat or pair of new shoes to be found in the whole city. According to him the clothes left in his wardrobe aren't fit to go out in.

We hear some rustling up the front—musicians taking position behind the curtain—and the buzz stops almost immediately. The curtain rises.

There's Stan Brenders, bowing to the audience, together with some fifteen musicians, greeted by whistling and furious applause. Stan Brenders is god. He bows again and gives us a little wave. The musicians sit down. Stan turns to face them and it's like the sky comes blaring down on top of us. His baton conjures up one ecstatic dance fiend after the other. Right from the first melody you see the women moving on their seats and the men clicking their fingers.

'Go, Stan, go!' a few shout after yet another number, when the applause dies down for a moment. Brenders looks over his shoulders and winks shyly.

'What a nice man!' Yvette sighs.

'Boom, head over heels,' Lode laughs and looks at me. In his eyes I don't see any real happiness, only darkness.

Meanwhile the horns are all standing up and it's as if we're taking off with them. A lot of people have got up on their feet too to cheer them on. 'Go! Go!' The ushers are having trouble getting them to sit back down again. Some of the *zazous* are not so easily tamed. A tenor sax starts a high-speed solo while the other horns sit down again. His notes swerve around countless curves at a million miles an hour. When he is finally playing the refrain together with the rest, he too gives us a little nod while we clap until our hands are almost shredded. Lode is going wild. He whistles loudly with his fingers in his mouth and shouts at the top of his lungs, almost impossible to understand. Then the trombonist stands up while fanning ever longer notes out over us with his damper.

'Drink?' Lode asks, holding a hip flask up in front of my face.

I nod and take a slug. The jenever burns. Unable to keep her eyes off the stage, Yvette hasn't noticed our little tête-a-tête.

After I've passed the flask back, she turns her head and tells me urgently that we have to keep our eyes on the drummer. The drummer, the drummer!

'Jos,' Lode explains, 'a local lad.'

The rest of the band backs off while the drummer starts a solo. He looks out through his round specs and nods encouragingly and we all start tapping out the beat, louder and louder. People keep jumping up and the ushers are having an even harder time of it. Jos gives a roll on his snare drum, makes his cymbals sing, sends thunder into the hall with the pedal on his bass drum. Suddenly he stands up and starts dancing around his drum kit without losing the beat. People cheer. Again he looks at us and nods to the rhythm of the clapping. Then he abandons his drum kit altogether and starts playing on the boards of the stage, on the bannister leading down to the auditorium. We're still clapping along, but softer so we can hear the drumsticks, now tapping his horn rims. He keeps it up, drumming his way deeper and deeper into the hall, following the armrests of the seats until he reaches a young woman, who jumps up in front of him. From the armrest his drumsticks go to her enormous belt. Now we're all holding our breath and clapping along almost inaudibly. The tips of the drumsticks keep tapping out the beat in perfect time on the metal buckle, as if under it, in the young woman's belly, a new accelerated time is about to be born while she proudly plants her fists on her waist and lets the drummer have his way.

'Oh, oh, oh,' Lode pants, covering his eyes as if watching any longer will plunge him into even deeper trouble or drive him to more desperate deeds. Then the drumsticks leave the belt and Jos makes his way back over armrests, floor and bannister to the wooden stage and finally the drum kit, like a character in a film that's being run backwards before our eyes. The rest of the band come together again for the finale, louder than ever, then it's very still for the briefest of moments before everyone is on their feet clapping, whooping and whistling. The drummer looks at us a little sheepishly, as if he has already forgotten what kind of god he was just a minute ago. Stan Brenders, on the other hand, stays god, even if he too looks a little shy.

'The war is almost over! I can feel it! We're almost rid of all this misery!' Yvette cries with tears in her eyes and one fist in the air. The whole city can feel it. They can all bugger off and leave us alone! Up yours, it's over!

Lode and I nod at each other but neither of us feels that joy.

People keep shouting and applauding. Then the house lights go on. I urgently need the gents. Yvette nods. I walk down the marble stairs. My full bladder is just an excuse. I need to be alone for a moment. There are already quite a few elated men standing at the urinals with one palm planted on the wall and their feet back a little to give their cocks free play and keep their shoes and trousers dry. I retreat to one of the cubicles and unbutton my fly. I hear Lode call my name.

'Here!' I answer.

'Open up!' He hammers on the door a couple of times. 'Come on!'

'I'm busy, you idiot!'

'Come on!'

I slide the latch open and Lode immediately squeezes in. His hand goes to my throat and he pushes my head back against the wall while closing the door behind him.

'Tell me why…' he whispers several times. His breath smells sour. I can't get a word out. He's squeezing my throat shut. 'Tell me why…'—now sounding furious—'we haven't been picked up yet? You're the mole. You're the bastard. It's you. You're the traitor.'

Then he tries to kiss me.

GROPING THROUGH THE DUST,
GASPING IN THE ICY
WINTER AIR

G ROPING THROUGH THE DUST, gasping in the icy winter air, that is how your great-grandfather sees the first survivors emerge from the rubble of the Rex Cinema, people like walking corpses, with dazed expressions and blood trickling out of their ears, not knowing which hell they have left behind or what underworld they have now ended up in. The rocket, the V-2, the Germans' second weapon of retribution, drilled deep into the packed cinema like a bolt of lightning hurled by an Aryan deity, a deity who no longer gives a shit about hitting targets, as long as he strikes terror into his enemies. Terror? You can rest assured of that. The city has been liberated but her inhabitants are quivering in cellars, desperate and famished. My parents have been camped in ours for about three months now, but although she who calls herself my mother has made up a bed for me there too, with a sad piece of material hung up between their sleeping place and what they hope will become mine, I refuse to bow to her unbearable pleading and continue to insist that I'm not cut out for cellars and would rather die if that's what it comes down to. If the bombers and bolt-throwers have written my name on their weapons like the merciless, murderous and, above all, vindictive supreme beings they are, nothing's going to help; lying in your own stench between your so-called parents in a cellar won't make any difference, you're doomed anyway, and besides, you still die, you do it every day.

Just two days after what is now two hundred and fifty dead and countless wounded, all of whom only wanted to watch Buffalo Bill on the silver screen one cold afternoon—so many dead that the Americans have decided to store the crushed and ripped bodies temporarily in the zoo as the morgues are so full they can't even get the doors shut any more—my beautiful Yvette tells me she is pregnant, that my sperm was too fast for both of us and soon there will be a new life in a city where death is still staggering around like a stuffed but never sated, totally pissed, reckless whoremonger.

'*Hello, this is Joe.*'
That's my Aunty Emma speaking in her best English and the way she says hello sounds very '*now*'.

Standing in our best room is a great big fellow, a Canadian Indian, one of our liberators, a sergeant no less, not just a soldier without stripes or medals. Mother has finally consented to have him over. It wasn't so much his character or race that bothered her, it was more having to leave the cellar to put the best room in order again. Temporarily leaving her fear behind and surrendering to the randomness of fate. But she's not alone. The whole city has finally accepted that these days death can do for you between a fart and a burp, between the soup and the potatoes—both figurative at the moment seeing as there's almost nothing left to eat, and that's another thing my mother's not happy about, having someone over from another continent without the requisite feast on the table. 'When does the war start?' goes a bitter joke. 'When they turn off the sirens...' It's the truth too. There are so many winged bombs falling every day now, so many V-1s, and so many rockets, V-2s, that there's no longer any point in even turning on the sirens, because over the last few weeks they've been wailing constantly. So, starting this week we don't hear anything any more, and whatever falls from the sky falls from the sky. 'Have another drink, José!' 'Gladly, André, except we're all out. There was another bottle, but your wife just dropped it!' I've never heard as many jokes as I have these last few weeks. The grimmer everything around us gets, the more people laugh. But their laughter is not what you'd call hearty, more something that's midway between coughing and puking.

'*Hello, hello,*' my father says, trying out his English and sounding like a radio operator battling poor reception.

Joe doesn't say much. He stands among us like a totem pole, but his eyes are gleaming. My hand disappears in his, though at least he doesn't squeeze.

'*Emma tells me you're a policeman.*'

'*Oh, yes…*' I say and realize I sound like a vain French actor who's pretending to have mastered the language of Shakespeare and John Wayne. What am I supposed to say? Yvette has gone to work with needle and thread to patch up the worst bits of my uniform so many times there's almost nothing left of it. The English, the Americans and the Canadians, like this heathen idol in our own home, couldn't care less about the dignity of our uniform, let alone what it's supposed to represent now the occupier has left the city and is taking a beating in his own country. We're the butt of jokes, good-natured ones, but jokes all the same. In their eyes we don't seem entirely real, with our white helmets and worn black capes and the holes in our boots. They tell us to stay back when another bomb has hit, looking at us as if we're children who are getting in the way. They burst out in unabashed laughter when I blow my whistle after seeing yet another dead body. They tolerate us, that's all, and even that only within strict limits. As far as they're concerned it would be better if we just stayed home for a while. That's not something they'd ever say out loud, these jovial, relaxed liberators of ours, but you see them thinking it. We're the clowns, they're the heroes. And what's more, they're never sure where our sympathies lie. Don't a lot of us still secretly stand in front of a portrait of the Führer with our right hand stuck up in the air when no one's looking?

Sergeant Joe sits down to drink some weak tea.

Aunty Emma's beaming. During the chaos of liberation she moved as fast as she could to the other side of town: a small flat near Schilder Straat, behind the Museum of Fine Arts. We didn't hear a peep out of her after that, not even when the first V-1s wiped out lots of her new neighbours and silenced the wild joy of liberation forever. Mother was at her wits' end, even though Aunty Emma wasn't on any of the lists of dead and wounded. A few weeks later we heard from her after all. But it wasn't until winter that we saw her again, after Christmas and New Year, and immediately in the company of Sergeant Joe.

'We met at the Hulstkamp.'

'Don't you need to speak English?' Mother asks. 'You can't, can you? Even our Wilfried, the genius of the family, can hardly manage that. Or am I wrong?'

'I'm a fast learner...' I say and slurp my tea.

'*Hey, Joe*,' my father chuckles. '*Everything wonderful?*'

'*The best is yet to come*,' the Indian nods.

My so-called sire has had to sweat it for a while, but now everything really is '*wonderful*'. Despite his membership of the 'movement' he has been able simply to continue working at the town hall. 'They're going to track me down,' was his frightened comment when the Allied tanks were rolling through the streets. But they didn't track him anywhere. Typical of my father, happy as a sandboy to have never meant anything, to have remained so insignificant that nobody bothered to look into him. He gives Joe the thumbs-up. Joe replies in kind and suddenly he laughs, baring his gleaming white teeth for the first time, like a coconut that's been cracked opened to expose its insides.

Mother recoils. 'They can't conceal their savage origins.'

'Excuse me!' says Aunty Emma.

'I'm smiling too,' my mother replies, and it's true.

Sergeant Joe isn't like most of the Canadians, who seduce the women of this city with stories about the enormous ranches they own back home or drive them wild with voluptuous tales of wealth. All those supposed landowners go back home, sometimes with a woman they've knocked up, mostly like thieves in the night. Joe stays and opens a bar with his Emma. After a while they rechristen it the Cheyenne, because Joe has figured out that people here like being served by 'a real Indian'. A feather headdress hangs on the wall behind the bar and there's a tomahawk above the glasses. A real one, according to Joe, once used to scalp whites. The bar is a success, Emma's marriage to Joe less so. But 'married is married' as my mother says after each of her sister's crying fits. Twenty years later Aunty Emma goes mad, shouting and seeing ghosts. Dementia, they say. In the end, just before they cart her off to some institution or other, she roars that 'that nigger' in her bed isn't her real man, then lisps the name of her German lover ('*Ach Gregor, mein Liebchen!*'), who she hasn't seen since the summer of '44 and who, in that wartime autumn, ordered some fifty men machine-gunned in the Netherlands and either ended up in a ditch with a bullet in his own head as a result, or has been relaxing beside a swimming pool in South America ever since, but has remained, in her glaucomatous eyes, her one and only. She dies and Joe looks down on her coffin with tearless eyes. A year later, the war catches up with him after all and he too dies, silent and far from all other Indians.

'I SAVED YOUR LIFE,' Omer says. 'Yours and your mate's, Lode Metdepenningen.' He sighs and growls like a declawed circus bear. 'I even knew where you were keeping that Jew. I fucking knew it all. Why do you think I'm here now? I've been keeping my eye on you. What are you doing here? I know about the storeroom they've got in here. Didn't your mate tell you I was his father's lawyer? I'm a patriot and they're after my blood. They call me a collaborator! Can you believe it? Ungrateful bastards. Hunted like an animal.'

We're in Van Maerlant Straat, where I was just about to open the front door. Omer steps out of the shadows and grabs me by the lapels of my overcoat. He stares deep into my eyes. It's been days since he's had a shave. You can smell the desperation on his breath.

'I knew Lode's old man had Jews tucked away. Of course he did. He was in it for the money. They were his best friends, those diamond traders. He saw it as an "opportunity". He said that before the war even started. I knew all about it, but I kept my mouth shut. More to the point, and I repeat, without me, you and your mate, the good-looking butcher's boy, would be rotting away in a camp now, more dead than alive, or already in a hole in the ground. You get me?'

'Let go of my coat, Omer.'

'Let me in. That's all I ask. Or are you too ashamed? Has the butcher still got a dirty Jew hidden in here paying with sparklers, one who doesn't know it's all over?'

'It's all over for you. You're wanted.'

'And you? What have you done? What's on your conscience? You're a two-faced bastard and you know it!'

I push the door open and lead him to the former hiding place of Chaim Lizke, the Jew who got away. He looks around and asks what all the papers are.

'Poems,' I answer. 'I come here to write.'

Omer forgets his own fear and despair for a moment and roars with laughter. 'You write poems? Who do you think you are? Everything's fucked, there's hardly a wall left standing, it's raining bombs, everyone's living like rats in a hole, and his lordship writes poetry. He sits down here with a peacock quill and an inkpot and worships his Muse like a born pen-pusher. Is that what you have to do to keep from going mad?'

'Sit down,' I say calmly, but I'm already picturing him hanging from a hook by his tethered feet, bleeding into a pan like a slaughtered pig, like Mussolini and his lover, like useless meat.

Omer slumps down on a chair. He's already forgotten his laughter, it's all melancholy and self-pity again. 'My mother's house got hit last week. I'd been hiding there for months. It took our mum too. Blew her head right off… Do you know what seeing something like that does to you? Your own mother?' Snot is running out of his nose. He's not even a caged bear any more, a St Bernard in the snow with a broken leg, unable to do anything beyond softly whimpering.

'I've got gold… If you help me it's yours. I have to get away from here. I have to go to Spain. I've got friends there.

You and your mate can arrange documents. Your station is as corrupt as anything, isn't it? What you did for all those Yids. Can't you do it for me too? I was born and raised here and I protected you, I protected you… Without me you were…'

'There's a blanket over there,' I say. 'It gets awfully cold in here.'

Lode laughs, 'You're mad.'

I pull out the key.

'You say you come here to write poems?'

When we enter the hiding place, Omer is nowhere to be seen. I look around, then hear a vague snoring in the dark.

'Shit,' Lode whispers. 'Who's that?'

Completely exhausted, the lawyer is lying under a blanket and a bunch of old newspapers, like a tramp sleeping rough.

'Mr Verschueren?'

Omer shoots up as if waking from a bad dream.

'Leave me in peace! Bunch of bastards!' he shouts automatically.

Lode looks at me. 'I don't get it.'

'Hold him down,' I say.

'But why…'

Omer lashes out, but when he threatens to scramble up, Lode shoves him back down again. I go over to the table with my poems on it and find what I'm looking for in the cutlery drawer.

'Hold him down on the ground!'

Omer roars, trying to scratch Lode in the face.

I use the hammer Chaim Lizke pulled out that last time to defend himself against us to cave in the lawyer's skull:

bringing it down three or four times in quick succession. Once narrowly missing Lode's ear, but effortlessly avoiding Omer's flailing arms. He keeps shuddering; I keep hitting the side of his bald head, now more a bowl of red porridge than a skull.

'Stop…' Lode says. His face is covered in blood. Mine too probably.

The hammer is sticky in my hand.

'You know he needed killing,' I pant. 'He couldn't just die in bed, not him. You agreed with me.'

Lode stares into space.

I search Omer Verschueren's pockets.

I find a gold lady's watch.

'THEY DIDN'T SPIT IN YOUR FACE, did they, *jeune homme?*'
'No.'

'They do that sometimes when you queue at the gate here. I heard about a lady who had a shit bucket tipped out over her, out on the street, just like that, from one storey up. She had to go back home. She couldn't let her husband see her like that.'

'My,' I say, 'it never stops.'

'But you probably saw enough in the beginning.'

'You can rest assured of that.'

In the beginning means at the end, when the Germans had withdrawn and the Brits and Canadians were all celebrating. In the beginning means not being able to be a cop because everyone seems to be walking around with guns. In the beginning means joining in with all the others in the hope that people might calm down a little. In the beginning the fury was so intense it became a festival, with people locked up in cages in the zoo, and us watching and telling bystanders, 'Keep it a bit respectable.' In the beginning there was chaos, dark and dangerous. In the beginning there was nothing left, not a mayor anyway because he'd seized on a conflict with the Flemish SS to change his stripes and clear out before it was too late. For a little while there was nothing and we were all subject to the whims of the street, totally sozzled heroes linked arms with stone-cold-sober thugs. In the beginning there was revenge and everyone said rightly so, because it's only normal after so many years of misery. Everyone? No, not those who were now on the other end of the whip, because they immediately cried that it was a great injustice they would never forget, let alone forgive. And the others yelled, 'Shut your trap, blackshirt!' The new beginning began with a drawn knife, followed by a procession, zigzagging at first and out of step, but gradually growing more and more disciplined, with normality as the camouflage net under which the bastardry continues: eternal discord with the powerful few rising above it, the permanent winners, who never get their trouser legs smeared with filth or their shoes scuffed, who know the meaning of 'prudence' and can judge situations in advance and arrange them to their own advantage. For them there is no beginning or end. For them everything just keeps going.

Behind the bars of the visiting room, Meanbeard coughs.

Everything smells of carbolic acid, the disinfectant they use in hospitals and morgues, but also of piss and shit, despair and unshakeable belief, rotting away like a lump of meat teeming with the maggots of misunderstanding.

'No one comes to see me,' he says.

'Thanks,' I say.

He looks up, laughs on the wrong side of his face. 'Yes, you...'

'Better than nothing.'

'Have you heard about Omer? A couple of bastards smashed his head in. They found him on The Boulevard. Apparently it took a while before they could identify him. You hardly hear anything here, but news like that gets through. The jackals come and whisper it in your ear first chance they get. I thought he'd managed to get away. Spain, I hoped… But no, just beaten to death. Such a beautiful human being, so cultured, so much class. He knew Ancient Greek. Long bits of the *Iliad* off by heart. And then, for no reason… like…'

Meanbeard starts to sob. His bulging eyes give birth to big tears. He looks away, wipes his cheeks, blows his nose into a rag he immediately puts back in his pocket.

'But they're not going to get me. *Non! Non, à present je me révolte contre la mort! Le travail paraît trop léger à mon orgueil: ma trahison au monde serait un supplice trop court.* Do you understand? They can't take away my pride. I didn't betray my principles. I will continue to resist death. Like…'

'Like Rimbaud.'

'*C'est ça…* Although that big-mouthed genius poet might have looked down on me for still being alive, for not having been put up against a wall and shot. That would have been honourable, that—'

'Come on.'

Meanbeard sniffs. 'Why are you here?'

'To see you, of course.'

'Maybe it's so you can laugh at me. Have a good look. Feast your eyes. Were you there when I was sentenced?'

'No,' I say.

'I looked them all straight in the eye. I didn't bow my head or deny anything I'd done. "I did it for everyone"—that's what I said. They almost exploded with indignation! The gall of the man! I should be ashamed! My comrades sitting next to me in the dock all looked away. A few hid their faces. They were ashamed of me, of the things they'd all done. One of them hissed that I'd lost my mind and had to shut up. But then I cried even louder, "I'm no lackey of the plutocracy and I will never become one! I have always served my country, my people and my king by fighting the Jews!" And then it went quiet. The prosecutor clutched his heart. He was so furious he couldn't speak. The judge looked at me and said, almost with respect, "I believe you, Mr Verschaffel, but the facts are still the facts. You broke the law." And then I shouted, "Which law?!" I got life.'

'A few years inside and, who knows, maybe they'll let you off.'

Meanbeard brushes my sentence aside as irrelevant. Suddenly he's almost cheerful, as if he's found a subject that will perk him up again. 'How's the tobacconist's? How's our Jenny doing?'

I don't know what to say to that. When the city was liberated Meanbeard was one of the first they picked up. A furious mob dragged 'our Jenny' out of the tobacconist's, shaved her head and painted a swastika on her forehead before taking a photo of her together with a few other women, surrounded by an elated throng. Meanbeard must know that, or he must have heard rumours at least. Yeah, what's a Jenny going to do after something like that? Where can she go? Back on the game, I suppose.

'She doesn't even write to me. Well, she doesn't really have a gift for words.'

'I've lost touch with her.'

He looks at me and I can tell he doesn't believe me.

'And the shop?'

'Someone else is running it...'

'But what the... That shop's mine. Signed and all! I have the papers!'

'Just let it go.'

Meanbeard suffered a major heart attack five years later. The story goes that they left him to die like a dog, that it took a whole hour for a doctor to get there. That's what someone told me, anyway. I've long forgotten who.

I DUG OUT THE POETRY collection again, great-grandson. I searched and finally found it. What was once a promise on the page, as fresh as that morning's bread, now looks as old and forgotten as the person who wrote it, locked up in the past. The coarse, rationed paper has turned brown and feels almost like cardboard. The sad little picture of a woodcut under the name 'Angelo' on the cover and the greasy letters that form my poems on the inside pages can't even be called old-fashioned any more; instead they seem to come from a world as lost as Atlantis. *Confessions of a Comedian*—even then, the ironic intent of the title was overshadowed by the grim design, universally accepted as the norm in a period that was still suffering the aftershocks of a grim era. MCMXLVI, it says, printed in 1946 in other words, by Advance Publishing, which was run by a magazine publisher who was always a little scared of me after I paid a visit to his home on Paarden Markt to let him know how presumptuous it was of him to assume that a policeman couldn't be a poet.

It's sometime in November 1946. We're in Betty's Tavern in Rotterdam Straat and the publisher is busy demonstrating how shy he is. Not that long ago gramophone records were being smashed on the floor in here. We're still drinking pathetic, watery beer because the shortages aren't over yet. With just a few other people, I'm celebrating my collection finally seeing the light of day. I'm glowing because I'm kidding myself that I'll soon be a full-time writer, one who'll never have to wear a uniform again. My wife Yvette is not by my side. She preferred to stay at home with our son, your future grandfather, who is almost two and coughs himself silly at night in his cot. I know she's long stopped kidding herself about anything. She knows she'll never become a singer, never be a nightingale of the international stage, but simply a mother and a housewife like so many others, though at least one who makes her own clothes and draws jealous glances all over the neighbourhood for her style and class. It's cold comfort when pushing a pram or boiling nappies, I know that too, but at least it's something. We don't talk about it. She's grateful and even looks like she's in love when I pull back in time and don't run the risk of making her pregnant again. That's our unspoken agreement. One child is more than enough, but neither of us would say so to anyone else, or even each other. The moment we did, it would become a scandal.

Standing there in Betty's, waiting for more friends to arrive, I'm not thinking about any of that. On the contrary, I'm luxuriating in the thrill of it all. I hear a loud 'Ding! Ding! Ding!' in my head, the sound of a hammer beating an anvil to shape the glowing metal of my will into something useful, four horseshoes, for instance, to nail steaming hot to hooves so I can ride the Muse. Yes, that's what I'm telling myself in that instant. I can't imagine that in the next few years the Muse will hardly emerge from the stable, at most to graze a little in a paddock, but never to gallop away with me on her back and that I will stay a policeman for the rest of my life and never become the poet I dreamt of being. Yes, I will continue to write and I will be published, by publishers increasingly more prestigious than that poor joker from Advance Publishing. In the end I'll even be included in the *Overview of Dutch and Flemish Literature*, where they will describe me as 'idiosyncratic' and 'recalcitrant', as I wrote at the start of this story, but that's as far as it will ever go.

The door opens and I think, 'Not him, surely?' No, it's not Chaim Lizke. Just some wanker who looks like him. He's been swallowed whole by history and then discreetly puked up in a corner as a ghost. He sometimes appears here in this bar, on other occasions, somewhere else. Sometimes his spirit demands atonement, sometimes he's melancholy. Sometimes he seems to belong, mostly not at all. That's no way to find peace, anyone could tell him that. But having a wandering ghost that terrifies everyone now and then is preferable to being forced to admit that he was ever real.

Around me they're not talking about ghosts. Gaston, who's still on the force, is talking about politics because it's almost that time again: elections are coming up.

'I don't want to make a fuss, but it's just like before,' Gaston spits. He pulls a newspaper out of his inside pocket and unfolds it at a cartoon showing the pre-war mayor—who is running for election again in this post-war era—as a whore on a chaise longue above a caption saying, 'Whose mistress?', because he is surrounded by coarsely drawn, hook-nosed, cigar-smoking Jews waving wads of cash.

'What do you mean like before?' someone asks.

'The Jews pulling the strings again, of course.'

'What do you expect?' asks another. 'This city runs on diamonds.'

'I meant that as a joke,' Gaston says. 'Look up the word sarcasm sometime.'

'Gaston, the Jew-lover… That we'd live to see the day.'

'Come on, lads…' says Gaston.

'Let's not make a fuss,' I say. 'Who wants another beer?'

The landlord has overheard and shakes his head furiously.

'I've got something much better! I've still got two crates of stout in my cellar from before the war. What if I donate them? On the house, of course! For the city's finest who always helped us in such difficult circumstances!'

He descends to his cellar to the sound of cheers.

'If Lode heard that…' I say, almost out loud.

Just then he comes in with an older man, one whose neck is too scrawny for any collar size at all.

'Your timing couldn't have been better!' I call.

Lode nods, but doesn't join in the laughter. Here and there along the way, he pats one of the others on the shoulder. I get a measured 'Congratulations on your book'.

The professor shakes my hand and looks into my eyes. That makes me realize that I once kneed this man in the balls as hard as I could in the Sicherheitsdienst torture cellar.

He shrugs when he sees me turning pale. 'We all have to carry on. Life just keeps going.'

I swallow, curse under my breath and think, how are you supposed to do that? How do you explain? Where do you start? Or do you just say, sorry, it was by accident, or not entirely, but anyway, you know what I'm trying to say?

The professor accepts the glass of stout I offer him and calmly leafs through my *Confessions of a Comedian*, looking up now and then with a friendly smile and glugging down beer. 'To the start of a literary career!' he asserts firmly in the end, promptly holding out his empty glass.

'Landlord, another stout for the professor!' I shout in relief.

Lode looks at me. It's a studied gaze. He wants me to see how much disgust he can express for me without moving a muscle, without puking his guts up all over me. I simply order another glass of stout for him too. There's no other way when it's family. If someone can't stand you, you stand them a beer.

WHEN YOU CONSIDER someone a soulmate and give her all your love, you think you understand things about her that dumbfound others, drive them to despair or wrack them with anxiety. My granddaughter slashes her arms and my sin is that I think I know why. I quietly believe I understand what she's doing or subjecting herself to. I think I know what's burdening her. More than that, I am convinced she's weighed down partly with the baggage I've given her, that she's the recipient of a bill of reckoning I unwittingly passed down with my genes.

'What can we do with her?' Yvette laments when she's had yet another phone call from our son about him having tracked Hilde down to some drug den or other, completely out of it and talking gibberish.

'Nothing at all,' I answer. 'Let the girl be. She's just a kid playing silly buggers.'

But to me she's not a kid and she's not playing silly buggers. In my eyes they're acts of resistance, signs of great inner anguish. I am convinced she's being urged on by the voices that force people to finally discover themselves, to become who they have to be, who they really are, and that, as I've already said, is the most difficult thing of all, because the world doesn't grant that privilege easily and other people always want you to be like everyone else.

*

You understand everything. You put everything in perspective. You lull yourself to sleep.

After yet another round of therapy or a forced admission to hospital, she reappears at our front door, radiant as ever. She's got a pink balloon with 'Hello, I Love You' printed on it and is all sweetness and light to her grandmother while giving me a wink that betrays the truth. I wink back and whisper that she shouldn't let them manipulate her. She gives no sign of having heard. She's wearing black lipstick and a black long-sleeved top decorated with scythe-carrying skeletons. A ladybird is walking over her shoulder and then suddenly it's gone. She is no longer my granddaughter. They've pumped her full of medication that burns away the insides of her skull, making her normal, something she won't be able to bear, something that will lead her to the abyss.

She says, 'Dad said I have to come and tell you not to worry. I'm going to straighten out and go back to uni. My enrolment's all ready. Good, huh? And which one of you is most pleased?'

'As long as you're happy,' my wife says, as pleased as she could possibly be.

'What are you going to study?' I ask.

'History!' Hilde beams.

You know why. You think it's the way it has to be. You try to fool yourself into thinking you should be proud. But she no longer rings you up, you don't hear from her at all.

'She's on the up and up,' Yvette says. 'She's probably got a boyfriend. She's studying hard. She's finding her way.'

'Yes,' I say.

But inside I'm fuming because in the meantime I've heard from Lode that *he* does see her, regularly even. That's what he tells me during our weekly chess game.

'She's got all kinds of questions.'

'About what?'

'The old days. Does she do that with you too?'

'Sometimes,' I say curtly and dangle my bishop in front of Lode's queen as bait. Of course the bastard doesn't fall for it.

You hope. You grit your teeth. You try to be patient.

She has disappeared.

Nobody's seen her for three whole days.

Yvette goes into our bedroom, locks the door and starts crying on the bedspread.

I say to the door, 'It'll be OK.'

She keeps crying. She won't let me into the room. I lash out at the cat.

An icy steel fist takes hold of an artery and won't let go.

You don't think anything any more. You listen to your breathing. You feel your heartbeat.

Then the phone call comes.

They have found her, strung up on a rope, hanging in an old wartime bunker that's normally completely closed off, hanging *there* for a reason, I feel it.

Sobbing I scratch on the bedroom door.

'Open up, for Christ's sake… It's bad news. Open the door, sweetheart. Please.'

But the door won't open. The crying just gets louder and louder so that she's practically screeching, until hours later when she can't keep it up any longer and finally appears, suddenly aged so much there's nothing left of her. 'You didn't protect me,' she sighs and that's all. And maybe even that's not entirely true. Maybe she doesn't say anything at all.

You don't know. You did know. You kid yourself about all kinds of things.

But that's what everyone does every fucking day, damn it, everyone does it and mostly without consequences. Everyone does it and it doesn't cost them their grandchild. Most of them plod undisturbed to their grave. Not you.

She's left a note behind.

Bompa is a bastard.

That's all it says.

But those four words are enough.

Yvette drinks two bottles of port every day and I don't get another word out of her.

Every morning she goes out for a new supply of booze, then locks herself in.

I sleep in my study. Now and then I still hear her sobbing, that's all.

Bompa is a bastard.

My son, my daughter-in-law and my grandson stare at me. They ask why.

Because of the pills, I say, because of the antidepressants you all made her take. In the end they drove her completely mad.

They don't want to ever see me again.

My son says, 'I hope you die a slow death.'

They are the last words I ever hear from him.

I see him six months later at my wife's funeral.

'She drank herself to death,' I hear Lode saying behind me in church, just like that, as if it really doesn't matter whether I hear it or not.

'WHAT YOU STILL DON'T REALIZE is that I'm the only person in your life who's not scared of you. Is the penny dropping? Our Yvette, your son, your so-called friends... everyone. Did anybody from work ever show up when you said you wanted to buy them a round? Nobody. You and me, that's all. You and me and we both know why. Because you dragged me down into your filth. You murderer... And no, what I told your granddaughter wasn't bloody revenge. I just told her the truth because I had no choice. And what happened afterwards... It's bloody killing me. I can't sleep at night. But if it's my fault, it's yours too. If I'm paying for it, you have to too... Why do you think my sister drank herself silly? Fear. Everyone's frightened of you the way you can never trust a mean dog, the way you can never trust someone who's blind to himself, to what's inside him, and always acts like it's everyone else who's faking it, as if nobody knows what he's up to, as if nobody else knows how to cope with the filthiness, while you yourself haven't got a clue how you reek of the filthy dirty bastard you are, you, the great poet, with nothing but black spots on his heart, nothing but betrayal—'

'It *was* revenge, Lode. Don't try to tell me otherwise.'

'Ah, lad.'

*

Lode dies and is buried at Schoonselhof. Survived by his wife. Yes, he got married. Just after the war, like me. With a man like him that woman won't have got much enjoyment out of the state of matrimony. On the other hand, you never know. She cries her eyes out in the church. She doesn't give me a hug or even shake my hand. These few lines are all she deserves.

So many times I've wanted to piss on the grave of Metdepenningen, Lode. Never have. I'm haunted enough as it is.

I'M ALMOST FINISHED.

 I'm done.

Nicole moistens my lips.

Nicole says you don't exist.

She doesn't put it that bluntly. 'It's like the cigars you don't smoke any more, Mr Wils. You gave them up so long ago.'

She looks at me again and I think she's doing it out of love. Or pity, that's also possible; at my age you don't need to keep up the facade of differentiating between the two. 'Your grandson doesn't have any children...' she sighs quietly.

I laugh and can't stop.

'Oh, Mr Wils, easy now, watch out you don't choke yourself.'

She's right, son.

Because fucking hell, what kind of bastard trick is that, bursting out laughing at a moment like that?

But it is a joke, thought up by Angelo or some other monster that feeds on what happens inside your head.

Because if you, my listener, do not exist...

Who's to say someone like me exists?

Who's to say we exist?

Not you.

I WOULD LIKE TO THANK
Herman van Goethem for his light in my darkness
Koen Aerts for his encouragement and comments
Stef Franck for his brotherliness, hospitality
and the right books at the right time
Luc Coorevits for his Behoud de Begeerte
Katrijn van Hauwermeiren and Charles Derre
for every email and every conversation.

I THANK
my mother, my brother, my family, my friends
and also the Nymph,
who heard it all day after day
and gave me so much love the whole time
and keeps giving it to me.